SECRETS OF THE FEARLESS

Also by Elizabeth Laird

Paradise End

A Little Piece of Ground

The Garbage King

Jake's Tower

Red Sky in the Morning

Kiss the Dust

Secret Friends

Hiding Out

Jay

Forbidden Ground

When the World Began: Stories Collected in Ethiopia

The Wild Things *series*

Elizabeth Laird

SECRETS OF THE FEARLESS

MACMILLAN CHILDREN'S BOOKS

For Jenny and David

First published 2005 by Macmillan Children's Books
a division of Macmillan Publishers Limited
20 New Wharf Road, London N1 9RR
Basingstoke and Oxford
Associated companies throughout the world
www.panmacmillan.com

ISBN 1 405 04890 5

Typeset by Intype Libra Ltd
Printed and bound in Great Britain by Mackays of Chatham plc, Kent

Acknowledgements

Many people have helped me write this book. In particular, I would like to thank:

Kevin Connor, of the Corps of Guides on HMS *Victory* (for information on life in Nelson's navy)
William McDowall (ships and sailing)
David McDowall (historical and military detail)
Angela Mouscadet (the Napoleonic period in France)
Bernard Mouscadet (details of French names)
The staff of the London Library, the National Maritime Museum, the City Museum of Edinburgh, the Musée National des Douanes in Bordeaux and the crew of HM Frigate *Unicorn* in Dundee.
And, most important as always, Jane Fior, for her constant advice, support and encouragement.

My great-great-great grandfather John Allen was snatched by the press gang when he was still a boy, and sent to sea. He found himself serving as a third-class boy on the famous frigate HMS *Imperieuse*. His captain, Lord Cochrane, was the most daredevil sailor of his time. (Patrick O'Brian's character Jack Aubrey is based on him.) John must have taken part in many hair-raising escapades, both at sea and on land. Another member of the crew was a young midshipman, Frederick Marryat, who was one year older than John. He grew up to become a famous captain, and the writer of *Mr Midshipman Easy*, one of the most popular books of the nineteenth century.

John was taken prisoner at the storming of an Italian fort in 1813, but he escaped, according to family legend, 'with the help of a kind French lady'.

He was discharged from the navy in 1815, at the age of twenty-two, when Napoleon was defeated at the Battle of Waterloo and the war with France came to an end.

Introduction

It's 1807 and Europe is at war. Thirteen years ago, France was being turned upside down in a violent revolution, and many rich and noble French people were dragged to the guillotine, where their heads were cut off.

A strong man has risen from the ranks of the army to become the leader of France. His name is Napoleon Bonaparte. Many people admire him. He's a brilliant organizer, with modern ideas on how a country should be run. But he is, above all else, a soldier. A conqueror. One by one, he has invaded the countries around him. Italy, the German states, Austria, the Netherlands, Spain, Poland – they have all fallen into the power of France. Britain, protected by the waters of the English Channel, remains independent, but not for long, if Napoleon can help it.

While his armies march on land, sweeping resistance aside, the picture at sea is very different. Britain's great admiral, Lord Nelson, has outsmarted the French navy at every turn. Great battles have been fought, which the British have won. The last huge conflict was two years ago, in 1805, at Trafalgar on the coast of Spain. There Nelson's fleet won the greatest battle of them all, while he lay dying of his wounds.

Now, the task of the British navy is to keep the French ships penned into their ports and harbours. The British navy patrols the English Channel and the Atlantic, capturing French ships whenever it can and stopping any others from putting out to sea. Meanwhile, a British army has landed in Spain and is helping the Spanish to resist the French invaders.

This huge national effort means that hundreds of thousands of soldiers and sailors are needed. Some men have volunteered, but not nearly enough. To make up the numbers, press gangs scour the countryside, snatching men from their homes and workplaces and sending them off to man the ships. And it's not only men who work the great ships of war. Young boys are living, fighting and dying alongside them, as if they were men themselves.

PART ONE

OCTOBER 1807
OUT OF EDINBURGH

Chapter One

It was a wild night, raw, with rain in the air. The bitter wind picked up a fallen pigeon's feather by the castle at the top of the hill and whirled it all the way down Edinburgh's long High Street to the palace at the bottom. It howled round the crazy jumble of chimney pots on the tops of the towering narrow houses, making the pigeons stagger on their ledges. Far down below, in the tight little wynds and closes, cats crept for shelter into doorways and under steps, fluffing out their fur.

A man and a boy, their shoulders hunched against the cold, were walking down the hill, ignoring the bursts of song and laughter erupting from the taverns. Neither of them spoke until the man cleared his throat, put a hand on the boy's shoulder and said, 'The question is, John my boy, what do we do now?'

'How should I know?' said John, shrugging off his father's hand. He moved on a step. He was cold, tired and very hungry, and wanted only to get back to their lodging.

His father stayed still, shaking his head mournfully.

'Johnny, I can see that you haven't understood what's happened to us, and I can hardly bear to break it to you.

They've done it at last, the villains. They've destroyed me completely.'

John shifted from one cold foot to the other.

'Father, I don't understand what you're saying. Who's destroyed us?'

'Who? Why, Herriott Nasmyth, and that scoundrel of a lawyer. They've done what they set out to do long ago – cheated us out of everything, the house, our little bit of land, our few cows . . .'

Cold fingers pinched at John's heart.

'The house? You don't mean Luckstone?'

Luckstone was home. It always had been.

'Luckstone, yes.' Patrick Barr had to clear his throat as he spoke.

'They've taken Luckstone from us?'

Patrick nodded. John stared at him, dazed. He'd been born at Luckstone, twelve years ago, in the old stone tower house with its thick walls and massive oak door, with the tiny turret on the roof and the arrow slits for windows.

'I don't understand. How could we ever lose Luckstone? Barrs have always lived at Luckstone. It belongs to us.'

Patrick Barr sighed.

'Were you not listening this afternoon, Johnny? Well, I don't blame you if you weren't. Four hours is an awfully long time to be stuck in a stuffy lawyer's office, going over and round and getting nowhere. But the plain truth is that Herriott Nasmyth has done for us.' He laughed bitterly. 'He made up his mind to take Luckstone from me a year ago, and he's set about it so cunningly – he's ruined me. If we try to fight on, it'll need money, the very substance we are so woefully without.'

John swallowed hard. He could hardly take in the enormity of what had happened. Luckstone, where the old grey walls stood in a flower-studded meadow that ran down to the edge of the small sheltered bay, where he'd fished in every pool, jumped from every rock and fought every boy for miles around, and where his mother and his unnamed baby sister were buried in the kirkyard. Why hadn't he listened more carefully this afternoon as the lawyer droned on? He wouldn't have allowed this to happen. He wouldn't have *let* it happen. He would have fought back, hard, with his fists if necessary.

Another thought struck him.

'If we don't have Luckstone any more,' he said, 'where are we to live? What are we going to do?'

'That's just what I was asking you,' his father said, with solemn satisfaction at the coincidence.

Not for the first time, John felt a rush of exasperation with his father.

'How could you ever have let them do it?' he said, trying to keep the quiver out of his voice.

Patrick Barr spread his hands helplessly.

'I wish I knew myself. Mortgages, bond notes, credits, debits, interest, deeds, covenants . . . who can understand it all anyway?'

The wind, even stronger now, was penetrating through John's woollen coat, but it wasn't the cold that was making him shiver.

'I'm going back to the lodging house,' he mumbled, turning away so that his father wouldn't see the tears in his eyes, and he walked off fast down the narrow wynd that plunged down the steep hill off the High Street.

It would have been utterly dark if light from a dozen candles hadn't been streaming out from a first-floor window overhead. Sounds were floating down as well, the music of a fiddle and a harpsichord, men's voices, a woman's cry, laughter and the clink of bottles. John stopped and looked back, waiting for his father.

'That's him, up there,' Patrick said, an unusual note of bitterness in his voice. 'Nasmyth himself. This is his lodging. Listen to the man. Laughing like the demon he is. Drinking his way through my money – *our* money. You know what, Johnny, if he was to come down and stand before me right now, I do believe I might – well, I could punch him. *Punch* him.'

John looked up, startled. His father's normally mild face was suffused with red, and the blood vessels were standing out on his temples. John had been feeling almost blind with anger too, but the sight of his father's expression alarmed him. He caught hold of Patrick's arm.

'Come on, Father. Let's go.'

Before they could move, a low door burst open, and Herriott Nasmyth himself, unmistakable in his dandified, long-tailed, tailored coat and polished silver shoe buckles, lurched out into the narrow wynd. Although John and his father were no more than six or seven steps away, Nasmyth didn't see them. He was looking back over his shoulder, roughly tugging on the arm of a young woman, dragging her out into the wynd, ignoring her struggles to release herself.

With a last vicious jerk, he pulled her free of the doorway. She was young and pretty, but John barely glanced at her. He was staring at Herriott Nasmyth himself, the man who had cheated him of his birthright. John's fists were balled and his heart was pounding. He didn't have time to say anything. Two other men had appeared now. One stayed in the shadows, and John saw only a glint of dark red hair and a long lean nose. The other was young and slender, with fair locks straggling down over the bright blue cloth of his coat collar, his blue eyes watery with drink.

'Take your vile hands off me!' the girl was panting, twisting her arm as she tried to wrench herself away from Nasmyth's powerful grip.

'It was a jest, Herriott,' the young man said nervously. 'I didn't mean to – look, let's play on. I'll bet my horse against my sister. What could be fairer than that?'

'You lost her, Sweeney. I won her. It was all in the cards. She's mine now.'

'I am *not!*' the young woman shouted. 'How *dare* you set me as a stake! Put me down! Let me *go!*'

The fury in her voice seemed to goad young Sweeney. He set his weak mouth and plunged forward, trying to knock Nasmyth down. His blow was feeble, but lucky. It sent Nasmyth rocking on his heels, and the girl managed to shake herself free.

'You wicked creature,' she shouted at her brother. 'My uncle will hear about this,' and wrapping her cloak round her shoulders, she pushed past John and his father and darted up the wynd towards the High Street.

Nasmyth, looking after her, caught sight of Patrick Barr. He stared at him through bleary eyes, and a slow smile spread across his flushed face.

'A very good evening to you,' he said mockingly, wobbling as he tried to make a low bow. 'Allow me to present myself. The new master of Luckstone, at your service.'

'You . . . you,' choked Patrick, starting forward, but before he could reach Nasmyth, young Sweeney, whose temper was now at last aroused, came in to deliver another blow. He caught Nasmyth off balance and sent him reeling against the wall.

Nasmyth shook himself, as if he was throwing off the alcoholic fumes in his brain, and fixed his narrowed eyes on Sweeney.

'You'll be sorry for that,' he growled, groping in the pocket of his coat.

The red-haired man had been barely visible, drawn back in

the shadow behind the doorway, but now he ducked his head and stepped out under the low stone lintel into the wynd.

'For heaven's sake, Herriott,' he said urgently. 'Stop this foolery. Now's not the time to make yourself conspicuous.'

But he spoke too late. John saw the light glint on something in Nasmyth's hand. A second later, Nasmyth's arm had lunged forwards. Sweeney gave a little cry, then doubled over and slowly crumpled to the ground.

'Come away, Johnny,' Patrick whispered in John's ear, pulling him.

The red-haired man had been leaning over Sweeney's body but now he straightened up.

'You're a fool, Herriott,' he said scornfully.

'He was the fool, Creech. He insulted me. He tried to cheat me, too,' Nasmyth said.

John, backing up the wynd behind his father, looked over his shoulder and saw that Herriott's face had gone a sickened white. Then his eyes were drawn to Creech, the red-haired man, who was staring intently at Patrick's departing back.

'Murder!' Creech shouted suddenly at the top of his voice. 'Help! A man's been stabbed! The villains are getting away!'

John felt his father start with shocked surprise and his hand close convulsively on his arm.

'Run, Johnny! Quick! Run!' he whispered.

The panic in his voice infected John. He obeyed instinctively, hurtling out of the wynd in the wake of his father, who was already pounding down the High Street on winged feet. Behind him, he could hear windows being flung open, voices shouting and footsteps running on the cobble stones.

'A man with a boy! Yes, an unprovoked attack!' he heard Creech's penetrating voice say. 'Up that way, towards the High Street. If you're fast you'll still catch them!'

Chapter Two

J ohn was half doubled over with a stitch in his side, and his breath was coming in painful gasps when he and his father reached their room at last. It was a small place at the very top of one of Edinburgh's tall, tower-like houses, and they had taken the six flights of steep stone steps in flying leaps.

As Patrick fumblingly tried to fit the heavy key into the door's lock, a woman's head, topped with a lace-trimmed cap, poked out from the room alongside. It was Mrs Armstrong, the landlady.

'Mrs Armstrong, good evening,' panted Patrick, trying to make a polite little bow while his trembling fingers worked at the key.

The landlady stepped out on to the small landing with a swish of her long skirts. She cocked her head flirtatiously to one side, making her grey ringlets bob against her cheeks.

'Why, Mr Barr, whatever's the matter?' she said, her eyes sparkling with curiosity. 'I heard your feet on the stair pounding away like hammers. I thought the devil himself must be after you.'

'In a manner of speaking, he is,' said Patrick, trying to

laugh. 'I'm sorry, Mrs Armstrong, but Johnny and I must go. At once, in fact.'

'Go? But you can't! It's late! And I'm sure you haven't even had any supper. If there's something wrong with the room, dear Mr Barr, you only have to say . . .'

John dived between them, wrestled with the key and managed to turn it at last. He darted inside and stood for a moment looking round helplessly, unsure of what to do. He knew without being told that there wasn't a moment to lose. The hue and cry was up all along the High Street. The whole city was buzzing with people. With the murdered man lying in his blood for all to see, and their rage stirred up by the sinister Mr Creech, they would be searching everywhere for a man and a boy. In these closely packed wynds, where everyone knew the business of everyone else, it would be only a matter of minutes before someone remembered Mrs Armstrong's lodgers, father and son, strangers from Fife. The mob would burst in down below and race up the narrow spiral stair, and John and his father would be caught like rats in a trap. John's eyes darted round the little panelled room. He and his father had brought few possessions with them to Edinburgh, expecting to spend only a day or two sorting out the troublesome business with the lawyers before returning in triumph to Luckstone. They had just one small chest, a bundle of clothing and a satchel containing papers and the little money that Patrick had been able to scrape together for the journey.

John began to gather everything together. He crammed his father's spare clothes into the chest, tied his own into a bundle, then began to collect the scattered papers and put them in the satchel.

'. . . a cold pork pie and half a ham . . .' he heard Mrs Armstrong say.

'Well now, that's very good of you, ma'am. But you must allow me to . . .'

'No, no, my dear sir! I wouldn't—'

Her voice was cut off by a crash as, far down below, the heavy street door was thrust open.

'Up there! Aye! At the top!' came the excited voice of Maggie the old washerwoman who lived in a cubbyhole right by the door. 'I heard them go up ten minutes ago! Shifty eyed, the pair of them. I knew they were up to no good. They didn't fool me!'

She was drowned out by the sound of footsteps beginning to run up the first stone steps of the long flight of stairs.

Mrs Armstrong burst into the room where John was standing frozen in panic. Her normal leisurely manner had dropped away.

'Give me the chest, John. Good lad. Look, there's one more paper, there, under the bed. Now bring the bundle and the satchel. Quick. Into my room.'

Before he knew what was happening, John had been swept out on to the landing and in through the door of Mrs Armstrong's own tiny apartment. He was just in time to see one of his father's long legs disappear into a cupboard in the wall before Mrs Armstrong lifted the heavy plush cloth that covered the table in the middle of her parlour and pushed him underneath. A moment later, the cloth was raised again and the chest was hurled in after him.

'Not a word,' she hissed at him. 'Whatever you hear, stay silent until I tell you to come out.'

The next sound was so surprising that it made John breathe in sharply. With a rustle of her heavy petticoats, Mrs Armstrong had settled herself at her little spinet by the chimney piece, and had begun to rattle out a tune on the small ivory keys. The rhythm was ragged and there were more

wrong notes than right ones, but it was a brave sound never-
theless.

She had started on a second air when there was a hammering at the door. John jumped in fright, buried his face in
the rough cloth of his bundle of clothes and hugged it to his
chest as tightly as if he was a drowning man clutching a spar.

The music stopped. He heard the scrape of Mrs
Armstrong's chair on the wooden floor, and then the creak of
the hinge as she opened the door. The clamour of voices and
tramping of feet on the landing pierced him with terror. He
squeezed his eyes tight shut.

'Well, goodness me,' he heard Mrs Armstrong say lightly.
'Whatever's the matter? Is there a fire? Have the French
invaded at last?'

A confused jumble of voices answered her.

'Mr Barr?' Mrs Armstrong answered calmly. 'Yes, he was
here – but he's left. He set off on the Glasgow road an hour
since. He murdered a man, did you say? I'd never have
believed it.'

The raucous, cracked voice of the washerwoman came out
from over the heads in front.

'You're hiding him in there, Janet Armstrong! I know you
are! I heard them roaring up the stairs a quarter of an hour
ago. We're coming in to search!'

Mrs Armstrong managed a trill of laughter.

'Is that you, Maggie? What's the good of being a washerwoman if you don't scrub your ears out? You're as deaf as a
post, you know you are, and if you heard anyone running
anywhere it'll be the first time in ten years!'

'What? What's that she said?' came Maggie's voice again,
and everyone round her laughed.

A man's voice said, 'We're sorry to disturb you, Mrs
Armstrong. We didn't want you to be bothered by any murdering villains, that was all. Goodnight to you, now.'

'And to you,' Mrs Armstrong answered politely, and John's grip on his bundle began to loosen as the door closed with a click.

The music tailed away to nothing. For a long moment, Mrs Armstrong didn't move, then he heard her skirt sweep across the floor, and the cloth was suddenly raised.

'Come out now, John,' she said unsteadily.

Patrick had already burst out of the narrow cupboard in which he'd been wedged among the neatly folded clothes of the landlady's late husband.

'Mrs Armstrong,' he was saying, 'you have saved both our lives, and we owe you everything. Everything! If there's anything Johnny or I can do for you . . .'

'You can leave at once and get as far away as you can from my house,' Mrs Armstrong said frankly. 'They'll be back, and I'll not be able to divert them a second time. Take your things. Here's the pie and the ham. I'll tie them in this cloth. Creep down the stairs now while everyone's away.'

'Mrs Armstrong, dear ma'am . . .' Patrick began again.

'Oh come *on*, Father,' said John, tugging at his arm.

'Go on with you.' Mrs Armstrong was hustling them towards the door. 'And don't tell me where you're going. It's better for me not to know.'

Patrick smiled wryly.

'I couldn't tell you anyway, because I don't know myself, but if you keep insisting that we've taken the Glasgow road, you'll put them off our track.' He looped the strap of the satchel over one shoulder and hoisted the little chest on to the other. John picked up his bundle of clothes in his left hand, and Mrs Armstrong placed the cloth filled with food in the right.

'Thank you, Mrs Armstrong,' John stammered. 'I don't know what to say. Just *thank you*!'

Chapter Three

Flitting like black shadows, one tall spindly one and a shorter, stockier one, John and his father stole down the wynd. They ran, stumbling over loose stones, splashing through mud and puddles, the still stormy wind plucking at their clothes, and came up at last into the new part of the city, where wide streets and squares marched away north towards the sea.

'Wait, Father!' panted John. 'Stop a minute. Where are we going, anyway?'

Patrick had been plunging on down the road, the wooden chest bumping against his back, but he came back, set it down on the ground and straightened himself, flexing his cramped shoulders.

'Leith. The port of Leith. By sea to London. On the Leith smack.'

'*London?*' John's mouth fell open. He had never imagined he would ever, in his whole life, go anywhere so far away. 'Why, Father? Why London?'

'You . . . we . . . have an aunt in London,' panted Patrick, his chest heaving. 'Only surviving relative. Difficult woman, but who knows – probably has a heart of gold. A house in

Shoreditch. Blood thicker than water. She'll see what trouble we're in. Bound to take us in.'

'London,' repeated John, turning the idea over in his mind. The awful, blind panic in his head was subsiding. It was good to have a plan, however wild it sounded.

'How far is it to Leith?' he said, trying not to sound complaining. 'Only my feet are sore and I'm awfully hungry.'

'The pork pie!' exclaimed Patrick cheerfully, though he looked nervously over his shoulder as he spoke. 'Brace up, Johnny. It's only a mile and a half to Leith, no more, and with the pie inside us we'll fly.'

They ate fast, cramming the succulent pie into their mouths.

'We'll keep the ham for later,' Patrick said indistinctly, licking his fingers and picking up the chest again. 'We must hurry on now. Creech is a clever man. He'll be sending men out in all directions.'

They set off again at a fast pace, filled with new energy.

'Why does Mr Nasmyth hate us so much?' asked John, trotting to keep up. 'Why has he treated us so badly?'

'I've thought and thought about it,' replied Patrick. 'It puzzles me, John, more than I can say.'

They paused for a moment to look back up the long straight road. It was reassuringly empty. 'It can't be only for the house itself. I know we love Luckstone, but it's small – only a few rooms piled on top of each other up the old tower. It's strong, of course. Fortified. You know how thick the walls are – six feet at least – and the door's so massive it's a struggle even to open. It could withstand anyone coming upon it to cause trouble. And then there's the wee bay sheltered from the sea. A boat can come up there and be well hidden. At the same time there's a great view from Luckstone. A man can stand on the headland and count all the ships coming and going, in and out of the port of Leith. I can only imagine that there's some strange business the man's engaged in, something murderous and secret, but what it is I just don't know.'

The road to Leith, which was crowded with carriages, carts and pedestrians during the day, was deserted at this late hour, but John's ears caught the unwelcome sound of a horse's hoofs approaching from behind them. Patrick had heard it too. He grasped John's arm and pulled him down behind a flight of steps that led up to the front door of one of the houses fronting the road. They crouched, motionless, in the shadow.

As the rider passed, they could make out in the dark only a rough shape, a figure wrapped in a heavy coat with a hat pulled down over his eyes. They waited until the faint outline had been swallowed up by the night before they dared to come out of their hiding place, and then they set off again at their former rapid pace.

John had been thinking furiously as he'd huddled against his father behind the steps.

'Surely it would be better, Father, if we just went back and told everyone it wasn't you who killed that man. That it was Mr Nasmyth?'

'It would, Johnny, but unfortunately they might not believe us. Mr Creech would swear that I was the murderer, and Herriott has the money to pay for the most expensive lawyers.'

'The girl, though. She'd speak up for us.'

'Maybe, but it would be her word against Creech's, and he's a man of influence.'

'It's wicked! It's wrong! It's so *unfair*!' John burst out.

'Don't waste your energy on anger,' Patrick said, his voice unusually harsh. 'I've spent night after night consumed with it. We're in a pickle, Johnny. We need to concentrate now on how we can get out of it.'

John swallowed hard.

'What'll happen if they catch us, Father?' He resisted the temptation to move closer into his father's long shadow. 'What'll they do to us?'

'Oh, it'll be the Tolbooth prison, no less,' Patrick's voice had suddenly lightened. His spirits, always mercurial, seemed to have risen again. 'For me, mind, not for you.'

'And then what, Father?'

'I'll escape, of course.'

'You won't. You won't be able to.' He thought, but he didn't say, 'And I'll be alone.'

They had passed the forbidding old prison that loured over Edinburgh's High Street only yesterday. No one, John knew, could ever get out of it once they were locked away inside its heavy stone towers, behind its iron-bound doors and high, barred windows.

'No, it'll be easy, Johnny, you'll see, with a little help from yourself, but there's no need to worry about the Tolbooth. No one will catch us. We'll get safe down to London and live the life of princes in Shoreditch, with your Auntie Sarah, who'll take one look at us and love us, like the long-lost relations we are.'

Chapter Four

Half an hour later, John and his father were trudging down the quay in the port of Leith. The wind, which had fallen now, had whipped the clouds away, and a half-moon shone. It lit up the ripples on the water in the harbour and glanced off the wet cobblestones.

A couple of men, no more than dark shapes against the indigo sky, were lounging against a bollard. They murmured a polite 'Good evening to you', but John was aware of their eyes on his back as he hurried after his father.

'No one could be looking for us here yet, could they?' he whispered to Patrick. He was thinking uneasily of the horseman who had passed them on the road.

Patrick didn't answer. He was scanning the ships moored alongside the quay.

'Is it that one, the boat to London?' asked John.

'I don't know, son. No, it's surely too small.'

Someone cleared his throat behind John, making him jump. He turned to see that the two men had come right up to his father and were standing uncomfortably close to him.

'The smack to London?' one of them said. 'It's been gone a day now, sir. Went out on last night's tide. The next one could be docking here tomorrow morning, if the wind doesn't veer round to the north.'

John had been so sure that the boat would be there, tied up at the quay, ready and waiting to carry him and his father out of this nightmare towards a new adventure in London, that the disappointment made him rock on his feet.

'What are we going to do now, Father?' he cried out sharply.

In the dim night he could see that Patrick was biting his lower lip.

'Well now, well,' Patrick said, setting the chest down on the cobbles. 'So there's no chance of leaving until tomorrow, at the earliest, eh?'

'None at all,' the shorter man said, with strange eagerness.

'And it's a bed you're needing, and a drink inside you,' the other said.

His heartiness sounded a little forced, but his words made so much sense that Patrick couldn't help nodding.

'The King's Wark tavern,' the larger man went on. He pointed towards a set of windows in the row of houses behind the quay from which a warm yellow light was streaming.

Patrick picked up his chest.

'We can't go there, Father,' John whispered, tugging at his sleeve. 'It's the first place anyone would look if they came after us.'

The two men were already walking ahead of them, towards the lighted windows.

'Don't you see, Johnny,' said Patrick in a low voice, 'it'll look a lot more suspicious if we don't take a bed in an inn. Lurking in the street all night like criminals – we'd be as noticeable as flies on butter. If anyone comes looking for us we'll offer them false names and put them off the scent.'

They had reached the inn, and Patrick was already following the two men into the smoke-filled warmth inside.

It was so delightful to be indoors, in the warm and out of the cutting wind, that John stumbled gratefully to a bench by the fire and sank down on it, letting his tiredness overwhelm him.

He was dimly aware of Patrick talking to someone – the landlord, he assumed – on the far side of the room, but his eyes were on the blaze, on the red glowing coals, and he stretched out his hands towards it to warm them.

Patrick came back a moment later with a bowl of hot soup for him.

'Get this down inside you, Johnny,' he said merrily, and John saw that his father's spirits had bubbled up again. He was cheered, but a little alarmed at the same time. If Patrick had a drink or two, and an expansive mood came over him, he might start to entertain the company, forget the danger they were in, and let down his guard.

The two men had followed Patrick and settled themselves beside him on the bench, mugs of ale in their hands. John could see them clearly now. The older man was heavily built, with a red bull-neck, and the buttons on his yellow waistcoat strained across his stomach. The younger was thin and nervous looking. He sat with only the ball of his right foot touching the floor and set his knee to jerk up and down. The movement sent a quiver along the whole bench.

'So,' the older man said jovially, 'what brings you two travellers to Leith on a wild night like this?'

Patrick took a deep drink from the mug the man had given him.

'We're on our way to London.' Patrick took another gulp. 'I have . . . matters of business to attend to. Matters of business – in Shoreditch. That's a district of London, you know.'

'I did know,' the man said drily.

'What sort of interests?' asked the other. 'In the shipping line, are you? Merchandise?'

'Shipping . . . no.' Patrick stared into his drink. 'More like . . . business.'

John had become aware of a quietness that had fallen over the other drinkers in the room. He looked at the landlord, who shook his head slightly as if conveying some mysterious warning. John swivelled round, and caught the eye of a broad-shouldered young man in fishermen's boots, whose face was flushed with ale.

'Hey, you over there! Take care!' the man called out loudly to John, making every head turn towards him. 'Those two villains are from the press gang! They'll trick you. You'll take the king's bounty afore you know it and end up going out to sea, pressed into the navy.'

The two men on the bench were smiling uneasily.

'Hold your tongue, you drunken troublemaker,' the older man said. 'We're no press gang. I'm His Majesty's recruiting officer, and if an honest man wants to do his duty and go to sea, if he wants to fight the French for king and country, and safeguard his wife and children, then we're here to help him fulfil a noble ambition.'

'Help anyone? Noble ambitions? You?' jeered the fisherman. 'I tell you –' he jabbed a scarred forefinger towards Patrick – 'if you don't mind yourself, next thing you know you'll be dancing a hornpipe on a man-o'-war, and having your head blown clean off by a French cannonball!'

Patrick seemed unimpressed. He laughed and took another sip.

'Recruiting officers, is it?' He eyed the two men with interest. 'I wondered why you were so kind as to buy me a drink. But you've found the wrong man in me. Gentlemen are exempt from being pressed into the service, as I'm sure you know.'

'Is that so, sir?' The recruiting officer smiled thinly. 'But how is it that if you are a gentleman, which I don't doubt, you come to be travelling so very light, with nothing for the long voyage to London but a small chest and a bundle tied up in a cloth?'

'That,' said Patrick, draining his mug, 'is none of your business, my dear sir. I'm a gentleman, and a property owner . . .'

As he said the word 'owner' he faltered, and shook his head as if trying to clear it of unpleasant thoughts.

'A property owner, eh?' John could tell that the officer was only pretending to be impressed, and his uneasiness grew. 'And where might this property of yours be situated?'

'Dundee,' said Patrick, plucking the name at random out of the air. 'My estate . . .'

But John's gasp of horror silenced him. Patrick looked down at John's whitened face and followed his eyes across to the door.

A tall thin man, followed by two others, was standing in the doorway, removing his hat to reveal a head of dark red hair.

'It's Mr Nasmyth's friend, Father! It's Mr Creech!' John whispered faintly.

Mr Creech had spotted Patrick at once.

'Over there,' he called out commandingly, drawing the attention of everyone in the room. 'The man by the fire! Arrest him! He's wanted for murder. He stabbed a man up in Edinburgh in cold blood, this very evening, and then he ran for it!'

Patrick had started to his feet. He looked round wildly, but seeing no escape route put his arm round John's shoulders and drew him close.

'The man's lying,' he said, in a trembling voice. 'The

22

murderer's his friend, Herriott Nasmyth. I witnessed the deed myself.'

There was a long silence.

'If you witnessed it yourself, why did you run away?' someone shouted from the far end of the room.

'Take him,' Creech said to the men behind him, who surged forward.

They found their way blocked by the bulky form of the recruiting officer.

'He's mine,' he said shortly. 'You can't have him. He's volunteered to serve his king and country. He's taken the king's shilling.'

'The king's shilling? Joined the navy? I have not!' shouted Patrick.

'What's this, then?' said the younger man triumphantly. He had taken Patrick's mug, and now he turned it upside down so that the coin which he had slipped into the bottom of it fell into his hand.

Patrick tried to pull himself free from the officer's hand, which was now gripping his shoulder.

'This is outrageous! You planted that coin there yourself. You can't! I . . .'

The officer shook him in a manner that was not unfriendly.

'Take my advice, my lad. A career in His Majesty's navy, even for a gentleman like yourself, is better for your health than a dungeon in the Tolbooth. Take him out, Daniel!'

Before John could understand what was happening, his father was being bundled out through the door of the inn, with the officer, who had picked up his chest, hurrying after him.

'Father!' screamed John.

He scrabbled on the floor for the bundle and satchel, and darted after them, but before he could reach the door he felt a hand tugging at the satchel. Mr Creech was trying to wrench it off his shoulder.

'The documents,' Mr Creech was saying. 'Your cheat of a father hasn't handed over all the documents. Give them to me!'

'Get away from me!' yelled John at the top of his voice.

He lashed out with his foot. The tip of his boot caught Mr Creech's shin with a satisfying crack, and the man yelped and let go of the satchel strap. A second later, John was out of the inn, running after his father and the recruiting officer, who were already halfway down the harbour stair, about to step into a small boat moored to a ring in the dank slippery wall.

'Let me go!' Patrick was shouting. 'I can't leave my son! Get your hands off me!'

But the rope had already been untied, it had splashed down into the water, and the gap between the boat and the harbour wall was widening as the younger man vigorously worked the oars.

'Johnny! Go to London!' Patrick was calling out. 'There's enough money in the satchel. Your cousin's name is Sarah Dawes. Mrs Dawes in Shoreditch. Find her!'

Behind him, John could hear feet on the cobblestones.

'Bring my father back!' he shrieked out across the water. 'I'll go into the navy with him! I'm volunteering! Take me too!'

He heard a laugh from the boat, and the splashing stopped. The oarsman was turning it now, coming back towards the steps.

It hadn't quite reached them when John heard voices at the top.

'He's down there! Get the satchel off him!' he heard Mr Creech call out.

With a flying leap, John jumped across the expanse of

water into his father's arms, almost knocking him over the side and making the boat rock violently.

'Careful, lad. You'll have us over,' growled the officer. Then he laughed. 'Two for the price of one, eh? Nice work tonight, Daniel. Row for the receiving ship as fast as you can, before old copperlocks up there comes after us.'

Chapter Five

John had been out in a small boat many times before. He'd even had a little craft of his own at home, a shallow, leaking tub. Summer and winter, it had been pulled up on the sandy shore of the tiny bay on the coast of Fife, just below the hillock on which the tower of Luckstone stood. He and his friend William had pottered about in it countless times, fishing for crabs and playing at smugglers. But he had never rowed far out of the bay into the open sea. He had never before felt the powerful swell of the dark deep water under the thin boards. He had never been out at night, either, watching the lights of the shore flicker more and more dimly as they were left behind.

Now he could see more lights in front. Three yellow pinpricks were bobbing about some way ahead of them. He could make out the bars of lanterns, black stripes across a fiery glow, and the rigging from which they must be hanging. The moon had been hidden behind clouds again but it came out suddenly, and John saw the looming shape of a ship, quite close and coming closer, as the two recruiting officers pulled at the oars.

No one had said a word since they'd set out from Leith

harbour. Patrick seemed to be stunned, motionless, not even responding to John's tentative tugs at his arm, while the recruiting officers only grunted occasionally with the effort of rowing. But as the little boat bobbed alongside the huge dark wall of the ship, which was now towering above them out of the sea, Patrick started, and struggled to his feet.

'No, no, this is impossible. You cannot . . . I refuse to . . . I absolutely insist . . . we must be returned at once to . . . I shall pay you, of course. There is no question . . .'

A head had already appeared over the side of the ship, and the recruiting officer was calling up to it, 'Two more for you – a man and a boy.'

'Send 'em up,' said the head, in a London accent. 'I don't want no trouble, mind. This musket of mine's loaded, and it don't like deserters.'

The recruiting officer had caught hold of the rope which edged the cleats, the rung-like steps hammered into the side of the ship, making a kind of ladder.

'Get on with you now, get up there,' he growled. 'Hey! None of that! Catch hold of him!'

Patrick had begun to peel off his coat, and John could tell that in his desperation he was about to dive into the water.

'Father! No! You'll drown!'

The young recruiting officer lunged across and caught Patrick in a bear hug.

'Knock him out,' the older one said brutally.

'Anyone trying to swim for it, I'll shoot him!' called out the voice from above, and, looking up, John saw white moonlight glinting on the long metal barrel of the musket.

The boat stopped rocking as the fight went out of Patrick.

'Don't shoot!' he shouted anxiously. 'You might hurt the boy.'

Then John's arm was roughly grabbed, the rope was

pushed into his hand and someone was shoving him from behind, up the first few steps.

'Climb, can't you? Are you going to take all night?' the man above shouted down. 'You want a musket ball in your head? I'm ready to oblige!'

His feet slipping on the wet narrow cleats, his hand clutching at the rope, John climbed. A moment later, rough hands hooked under his shoulders and hauled him on to the deck, and a minute after that, Patrick followed him. There were confused shouts and bumps from below, coarse laughter, then the regular creak and splash of oars as the recruiting officers began to row back towards the shore.

John had no time to look round. Three or four big men, their faces invisible under the brims of their high-crowned hats, had surrounded him and his father.

'I must protest. There has been a terrible . . .' Patrick was trying to say, but there was no time for more. A grating in the deck had been lifted, revealing a gaping black hole. John was pushed down into it. His feet only just managed to find the steep steps, or he would have fallen hard on to the wooden floor below. A moment later, the grating had clanged shut overhead, and he and his father were in almost total darkness.

The first thing to hit John was a smell so foul it made him retch. He put his hand over his nose to try to block it out, but there was no escaping it. It crept in round his fingers, seeping in everywhere. He tried to breathe through his mouth, but could still sense its revolting pungency.

And then he heard the noises. All around him, in the dark, things were shifting, breathing, scratching, snoring. His skin crept. Were there people down here? Or animals? Or . . . ?

A voice close by made him jump. It was sharp and complaining.

'How many more are coming down here tonight? There's no room for a baby, never mind grown men.'

'No other poor souls, as far as I know,' said Patrick. 'Good God, what a stench! Is there no window that can be opened to let in some air?'

The other laughed mirthlessly.

'Window? Air? Where do you think this is, my bonny lad? The king's palace?'

'No, but the foulness! Surely for the sake of health . . .'

'You're new to the navy. That I can tell.' The man sounded friendlier. 'Never been at sea before, I'll be bound. Taken today, were you?'

'This evening! In a tavern! In a most outrageous act of . . . of piracy!'

'Aye, the shock. You'll be suffering still from the shock. I'm feeling it myself. It was yesterday they took me. I was sailing into Leith on a merchant ship out of Newcastle. We'd been at sea, me and my shipmates, two whole years. We thought we'd slipped past the navy, God rot them, but they caught us. We'll be out of this hulk in the morning, sent on board some man-o'-war and then blown to bits, most likely, by a French cannon before the end of the year.'

'Can't you be quiet over there?' came a voice from further away.

'Yes, some folks is trying to sleep,' someone called out from the other side.

'There's a little space here by me,' the man said more quietly. 'You can sit against the bulkhead. Is that a boy you have with you? What age are you, lad?'

'Twelve,' said John, and in a sudden rush of self-pity his throat tightened with tears.

The man gave a melancholy chuckle.

'Twelve! I was ten when I . . .'

'If you don't hold your tongue, I'll come over there and cut it out of you,' another furious voice called out.

John felt a guiding hand lead him along. He followed it, groping through the pitch dark, and stumbled at last to a halt, then felt himself pulled down to the wooden floor. Behind him he heard a crack and a cry of pain as Patrick hit his head on a low beam, and then his father was sinking down beside him. John snuggled up to him, trying to block out the stench by pressing his nose against Patrick's coat, which still held the faint, sweet, familiar tang of soap and heather and fresh air.

Their new friend had fallen silent in the darkness. John could hear him moving about, stretching out on the floor, and then a few moments later came heavy snores as the man fell asleep.

Patrick made no attempt to lie down. He had slumped forwards, his head drooping between his knees. His shoulders were moving convulsively, and John knew, with a lurch of his own stomach, that his father was crying.

'We're still together, Father,' he whispered in Patrick's ear.

Patrick didn't answer.

'We still have our things. I have the bundle and the satchel. You have your chest, haven't you?'

It was all he could think to say.

There was a long silence, then at last Patrick raised his head.

'Yesterday I was Patrick Barr of Luckstone,' he said in a hoarse whisper, 'a gentleman, if a poor one, a man who could hold his head high. Tonight I'm a pauper, a man on the run, pressed into the navy, the lowest of the low. I've failed you, Johnny. You deserve a better father than me.'

'No!' John spoke more loudly than he intended, provoking an irritated grunt from nearby. He lowered his voice to a whisper again. 'We'll tell them tomorrow. We'll explain that it's all a mistake, how we were tricked, and that we don't know anything about the navy, and we were just on our way to London. We'll make them listen to us.'

Patrick only groaned.

'We've got friends who'll speak out for us,' John went on, trying to sound more certain than he felt. 'Our neighbours at Luckstone. You could write a letter to them. Or to Aunt Sarah. Even Mrs Armstrong would take our part, if she knew what had happened.'

The thought of Mrs Armstrong brought to mind the ham she'd packed for them, so many long hours ago. He realized suddenly that he was hungry again. He reached for his bundle, and pulled out the greasy package.

'Here, Father,' he said, pushing a piece of ham into Patrick's limp hand.

Patrick shuddered.

'I couldn't eat anything at all. The foul stench here is making me so sick I fear I shall shortly lose whatever remains of the pie.'

'Try some,' John said, through a full mouth. 'It's awfully good. It makes the smell go away – a bit, anyway.'

Patrick obediently put a piece into his mouth.

'You're right, Johnny. It is indeed excellent.' He sounded momentarily stronger. 'We may as well enjoy it. It's the last decent food we'll be tasting for a very long time, since we're to be fed from now on at the expense of His Majesty.'

Chapter Six

John lay on the hard boards of the ship's lower deck, tossing and turning as the long hours of night slowly passed. Confused and terrifying images chased through his mind. Once he managed, for a few blessed minutes, to imagine himself back at Luckstone, but then a rat ran over his foot, making him start up in horror. He tried without succeeding to banish the face of the dying Mr Sweeney, the murdered man, which seemed to stare up at him from the blood-stained cobbles of the Edinburgh close.

'There's one comfort,' he whispered, in a vain attempt to cheer his father up, 'Mr Sweeney'll certainly haunt Mr Nasmyth forever and ever and drive him mad.'

'Oh there's no doubt of it, no doubt at all,' Patrick answered, in a hollow voice.

Mr Creech's pale, malignant face kept appearing: a nightmarish vision, his eyes staring intensely, his long spidery arms reaching out to snatch his satchel. He's a common thief, as well as a trickster, John thought bitterly, remembering the tug at his shoulder as Mr Creech had tried to pull the satchel away from him at the inn. He was a fool if he thought it was full of money. There's only a guinea or two left, and a pile of old papers.

He could see the lawyer's office in his mind's eye now. He hadn't wanted to go in with Patrick at all. He'd wanted to stay on the High Street where a juggler had been performing.

Once inside, he'd been too bored and irritated to notice what was going on between the men. Now he tried to remember. Something odd had happened at the very beginning. When he and Patrick had entered the stuffy little office, Mr Creech, Herriott Nasmyth and Mr Halkett the lawyer had been huddled together at the table, peering down at a small booklet lying open on the table. As soon as the Barrs had appeared in the doorway, Mr Nasmyth had reached out to pick up the booklet, but the lawyer had snatched it away before he could touch it and quickly hidden it under a pile of deeds.

Everyone had sat down then, and the long hours of wrangling had begun. John had shifted about resentfully in his chair, staring out of the window for the most part, wanting to be outside, listening to the minutes tick past on the long-case clock which stood in the corner of the room

How could I have been so stupid? John kept asking himself. Why wasn't I *listening*?

There'd only been one break in the endless dull afternoon. Someone had called up from the street below. Herriott Nasmyth and Mr Creech had gone downstairs to see whoever it was and Mr Halkett had thrown up the sash window and leaned out to talk to them from above. A gust of wind had set all the papers fluttering on the desk, and some had blown on to the floor. John and his father had gathered them up and put them back on the desk.

The meeting hadn't gone on for very long after that. Herriott Nasmyth, prompted by the enigmatic Mr Creech, had become more and more aggressive and demanding, while Patrick had seemed increasingly bewildered and defeated. At last he'd stood up.

'You have ruined me, Mr Nasmyth,' he'd said with simple dignity. 'You have cheated me out of everything.'

With trembling fingers, he'd gathered up the papers on the table in front of him and bundled them into the satchel. Then at last John had been able to leave the horrid, stifling room and get out into the street again. He'd been sharply disappointed to discover that the juggler had gone.

The night was over at last. For the first time, in the few gleams of daylight that penetrated the hold, it was possible to see the dozens of men huddled together in this dank, stinking hole. They had moved out of the dark corners and were crowded together under the grating, trying to breathe in the fresher air. Their hair was matted, their clothes dirty and their eyes wild with anger. Some were cursing, others shouting, and several were brawling, flailing their arms about as they tried to punch each other. They struck fresh terror into John's heart.

One tall young man took the bars of the grating in both hands and shook it, sending thuds echoing through the hold of the ship.

'Let me out of here! You have to let me go!' he shouted, his voice cracking. 'My wife's dying at home. Who's to look after the bairns?'

A man appeared above. John caught a glimpse of white breeches, a scarlet jacket criss-crossed with dazzling white bands and a tall black hat with a red and white cockade.

'There are soldiers up there, Father,' he whispered to Patrick.

A snort came from the man who had befriended them the night before.

'Soldiers? They're no soldiers. They're marines, curse their eyes. You'll see more than enough of them before you're through.'

The man grasping the bars of the grating screamed as the marine stamped on his fingers.

'Shut up all that noise!' the marine barked out. 'You ain't going nowhere, boys. You're in the navy now. Make your minds up to it, or we'll have the lot of you in irons. Lift the grating, sergeant. No, easy, you dogs. Come up nice and slow, one at a time. And no monkey business. Anyone tries anything, it counts as mutiny, and that means you'll hang from the yard arm.'

John, clutching his bundle and with the satchel over his shoulder, clambered up the steep companionway after Patrick. He blinked in the brightness and shivered in the cold morning air. The other pressed men were crowded so close in the small space on the deck that he couldn't see much. More scarlet-coated marines surrounded the miserable bunch of unwilling new recruits. Sharp bayonets glinted on the ends of their muskets. They stood to military attention, formidable and threatening.

'Move along there, boy. Report to the surgeon.'

John felt a prod in his back and stumbled forward. He found himself standing in front of a table behind which the surgeon was seated. The man wore a pair of spectacles on the end of his nose, and he was writing in a ledger.

'Age?' the surgeon said, without looking up.

'Twelve.'

'Twelve, *sir*,' rapped out the marine, standing to attention behind him.

'Yes, sergeant, that will do,' the surgeon said wearily. He turned back to John. 'Open your mouth.'

Nervously, John obeyed.

The surgeon looked into it quickly, then away again.

'Any fevers? Fluxes? Ulcers?'

'No.' He caught the marine sergeant's eye and added hastily, 'Sir.'

'Good. He's seaworthy.' The surgeon wrote something in his ledger. 'Next one.'

John moved aside while Patrick took his place. He was now standing by the netting that ran round the sides of the deck, and he could see through the holes to the shore beyond. The little port of Leith, lying snugly by the sea, was temptingly close. 'Don't even think about it,' said a gruff voice behind him.

John turned. Another marine, an older man, stood behind him. He pointed upwards. Halfway up the ship's mast was a platform, and John could see another scarlet coat up there, and the outline of another musket.

'Anyone who tries jumping gets a bullet in the back,' the marine said with relish.

He saw John shudder and went on, in a kindlier voice, 'Look over there, lad.'

John followed his pointing finger. A magnificent three-masted man-o'-war, with all sails billowing, was racing towards Leith harbour. Its bows sliced the green water, turning a creamy foam along its sides. Pennants flew from the tops of the masts, and bright signal flags fluttered from the rigging. The ship was no more than a quarter of a mile from the shore, and the gap was closing fast.

'It'll crash into the harbour wall!' said John.

'HMS *Fearless*? Not she,' scoffed the marine. 'Watch this, if you want to see seamanship.'

A flash followed by a puff of smoke rose from the side of the ship, and a second later a loud boom made John start back.

'It's the French! An enemy ship! They're firing on Leith!'
The marine laughed.

'Don't be daft, boy. That's just a gun salute. To let every-one know she's arrived. Now watch.'

John could see that the ship was swarming with men. Sailors were everywhere, crowding the decks, clinging to the ladder-like rigging, balancing along the wooden yards from which the sails hung. Deftly, listing over towards the water, the great ship rounded into the wind, and John could see the splash as the anchor plunged down into the sea. At the same time the sailors aloft, working like one man, hauled up the sails, tying them neatly to the yards. A moment later, HMS *Fearless* was lying still and quiet on the water, her flags and pennants drooping.

In spite of himself, John could not suppress a gasp of admiration. He might soon be on board a ship like that, working like those men. The thought terrified him, but almost excited him too.

He looked round for his father. Patrick was still standing by the surgeon's table and, to John's surprise, he was smiling. A wild hope surged up in his breast. Had his father achieved the impossible? Were they to be released? Ducking under ropes and skipping over spars, he darted across to the table.

'What's happened, Father? Are they letting us go?'

The smile faded from Patrick's face.

'No, Johnny. No chance of that. But this excellent doctor has discovered that I am not precisely cut out for a seaman's work. There is, by an extreme stroke of good fortune, a vacancy as a clerk to the captain on board the . . . what was the name of the ship, my dear sir?'

The surgeon had gone back to his ledger, and didn't look up as he answered.

'HMS *Splendid*,' he said.

'HMS *Splendid*!' Patrick said admiringly. 'How very fine. My worst nightmare, after all, is not to be fulfilled. The captain's clerk! I shall have a cabin to myself, which you will share, Johnny, of course . . .'

The surgeon looked up sharply.

'Share your cabin? With this boy?'

'He's my son,' Patrick beamed. 'Perhaps you didn't realize. The most unfortunate circumstances have driven us to take this desperate step, but . . .'

'It's out of the question.' The surgeon, who had momentarily fallen victim to Patrick's charm, was losing interest in him. 'There's a full complement of boys on board the *Splendid*. Your son is to join the *Fearless*. I heard her cannon firing just now. She'll be sending a cutter shortly to take the new crew members off.'

John felt the blood drain from his face, and saw that Patrick, too, had gone a ghastly white.

'Separated!' Patrick cried. 'No, no, my dear sir! It's impossible! My only child, just twelve years old!'

The surgeon shook his head.

'Resign yourself, Mr Barr. I've done my best for you. You are a fortunate man. The chances of a pressed man becoming a captain's clerk are very slim. But I can't perform miracles.' He looked at John and smiled as if seeing him for the first time. 'You're a strong-looking boy. You'll do well on the *Fearless*. She's an excellent ship with a popular captain, good discipline, a contented crew. They'll make a man of you, young John. You'll have reason to thank me one day. Now step aside, please. I have a great deal of work to do today.'

Chapter Seven

The next hour passed in a daze of shock and confusion. Patrick seemed so stunned by the blow that was about to fall that he was barely able to say a word. He followed his son mutely as John was led away to be issued with his new sailor's clothes, and only found his voice when John had changed into the ill-fitting white trousers, full-sleeved shirt, waistcoat and short blue jacket he had been given.

'My word, Johnny,' he said, his voice cracking as he tied the red scarf round his son's robust neck and balanced the straw hat on his thick thatch of blond hair. 'You're a proper sailor now. A real Jack tar. If only your mother was alive to see . . .'

He turned aside and blew his nose loudly into his handkerchief.

John looked down at himself. The new clothes seemed to have turned him into a different person, someone years older. In spite of the dread of parting from his father, he couldn't help feeling a small shiver of excitement too. He flexed his shoulders. He had grown quickly recently, and his old coat had been uncomfortably tight. There was room to spare in this new jacket.

They moved to a quieter corner of the deck, away from the shouts and whistles, as streams of small boats arrived at the ship's side, bringing on goods and men and taking off groups of pressed sailors. A dreadful, hollow feeling was lodging itself in the pit of John's stomach, but he could see that Patrick was feeling even worse.

'You mustn't worry about me, Father,' he said anxiously. 'I'll be fine. We'll find a way to get back to each other somehow. They can't keep us apart for long.'

Patrick only groaned.

'Here, boy. Take this. It's yours.'

A sailor who had been helping to give out the clothing was holding out John's freshly tied bundle to him. It was much bigger now that it contained the clothes he had been wearing before as well as his new naval spares.

'Thank you,' John said absently, taking it from him and turning back to Patrick.

A shrill blast from a whistle had heralded the arrival of another small boat alongside, and several more men were clambering up the side of the receiving ship on to the deck.

'All hands for HMS *Fearless*!' came the order, repeated down the ship. 'Into the boats! Look lively, boys!'

'Already! No! Not yet!' cried Patrick, catching John in a crushing hug. But John was struggling to break free. Beyond his father he had seen a pair of deep dark eyes and a long pale face that had sent his pulses hammering with fear.

'Father, let me go! There's Mr Creech!'

Mr Creech had seen them and was forcing his way through the milling crowd of men on the deck. Behind him were a couple of marines.

'That's the man, the thief!' Mr Creech was saying, his voice high and sharp. 'I accept that he cannot be released to face the justice he deserves, but I insist that my property, which he has stolen, be handed back to me.'

Patrick was staring at him, anger and bewilderment chasing each other across his face.

'A thief? First I'm supposed to be a murderer, and now you say I'm a thief? How dare you, sir! How *dare* you!'

'A leather satchel,' Mr Creech said to the two marines who had accompanied him. 'The papers inside it belong to me. I demand that he return them immediately!'

Patrick's anger had turned to contempt. He squared his shoulders, gathering his dignity.

'You, sir, are a liar and a cheat. The satchel you refer to contains papers of personal significance, a few letters, some mementos of my dear wife, documents relating to my property . . . ah, my *former* property. Open the satchel, Johnny. Show the gentlemen the few poor things it contains.'

John looked down at the table where he'd laid the satchel before he'd put on his new clothes. It wasn't there. He looked under the table, on the deck beside it, behind a stack of casks nearby. The satchel was nowhere to be seen.

'But it was here just now! Father, it's gone. Someone's stolen it! That man who made up my bundle, he must have taken it!'

Mr Creech's hand shot out and his fingers bit deep into John's arm.

'Don't play off your tricks on me. Give me the satchel. Now.'

John tried to shake himself free. Mr Creech's painful grip only tightened.

'I haven't got it! Can't you see? It's not here! Tell him, Father!'

With a lunge of surprising strength and deftness, Patrick plucked Mr Creech's hand off John's arm. He seemed to be taking the loss of the satchel philosophically.

'You should be ashamed of yourself, sir,' he said witheringly, 'to attack a mere boy in this way. Why are you trying to plunder us still further? You have already taken from me my home, my reputation and my son. The loss of my last few possessions is nothing to me. I am even relieved that fate has intervened to spirit the satchel away before you can put your wicked hands upon it.'

'Search the ship!' Mr Creech called out, a note of desperation in his voice. He turned to the marine nearest him. 'I insist that you search the ship. I'll pay you double.'

The marine looked round uneasily.

'Don't speak so loud, sir, please. We can't do no more for you. As it is we've taken a risk. If our captain knew what we was doing, he wouldn't like it at all. Best come with us. There's nothing more to be had here.'

They each seized Mr Creech by an arm and forced him away.

Through the gap in the crowd which they had made, John could see a group of men being herded towards the side of the ship.

'I have to go, Father,' he said, his voice trembling.

He couldn't bear to prolong the pain of parting any further. He flung his arms briefly round Patrick's neck, then picked up his bundle and darted across the deck towards the huddle of men who were being hustled by impatient marines over the side of the ship, down into the small cutter bobbing on the water below.

He was about to follow them when a man caught hold of his ear, tweaking it painfully.

'You, boy, what's your name?'

'John Barr. Sir.'

The man was consulting a list in his hand.

'You're for HMS *Fearless*?'

'Yes, sir.'

The man had found his name. He looked down at John. His eyes were a cold piercing blue and were set too close together. The words HMS *Fearless* were blazoned across the front of his black hat.

'Then you'll be feeling the end of my rattan before you're much older.'

John stared back at him, surprised. What had he done? It sounded as if he'd already been caught breaking a dozen rules.

His frank gaze seemed to infuriate the man, who flushed a dull red.

'You've an insolent eye on you, John Barr. I'll be watching out for you. I'll break you if I have to. John . . . Barr.'

He let go of John's ear and thrust him towards the opening. John tumbled down the side of the ship so fast he nearly lost his footing on the cleats, and he jumped down clumsily into the boat, sending it rocking from side to side.

Already sitting in the boat were a dozen of the other captive men who had been pressed into service. There were also six marines, their muskets trained on the pressed men, and eight sailors, each holding an oar. Their forearms were strongly muscled, and all of them had long hair tied in a pigtail down their back.

'Watch out, landlubber!' one of them called out cheerfully to John. 'You'll send us all to Davy Jones! Come and sit by me, and don't fidget.'

He seemed to notice the misery in John's face. 'Here, there's no need to look like that. You're joining the *Fearless*! The pride of Nelson himself, God rest his soul. Fought at Trafalgar, we did, alongside the *Victory* herself. The *Fearless* is the finest ship in the fleet, ain't she, boys?'

'She would be, if you weren't on board!' another sailor called out. The rest laughed.

John, nursing his bundle, looked up at the great hulk of

the receiving ship towering above him, hoping to see Patrick looking down. Instead he saw something that made his heart miss a beat.

Mr Creech was still on board. He was talking to the man who had so painfully pinched his ear. Their heads were together, as if they were sharing secrets. As if they knew each other well.

'Who's that man up there?' he asked the sailor sitting next to him, 'the one with the staring blue eyes?'

The sailor sent a stream of tobacco juice spewing into the water.

'That's Mr 'Iggins, that is. And if you want my advice, steer clear of 'im. 'E's the bosun's mate. Nasty bit of work, if 'e takes against you.'

Mr Higgins was climbing down into the boat himself now. The sailors waited respectfully until he had settled himself in the bows, from where he could look back down the length of the boat at the sullen, unwilling new members of HMS *Fearless's* crew. Then they pushed off from the ship's great side with powerful thrusts of their oars.

John had forgotten the men all around him. He was looking up at the deck of the ship, where Patrick's face had at last appeared.

Goodbye, Father, he was saying silently to himself. Goodbye. Goodbye.

The strip of water between the boat and the ship was widening with frightening speed as the sailors pulled on the oars. John kept his eyes on his father's face for as long as he could distinguish it from the mass of others looking out over the side, and when he could make it out no more he turned aside and looked out to sea, so that no one would notice the tears sparkling in his eyes.

Chapter Eight

I t was all John could do, as the boat neared the great war-ship ahead, to prevent his silent tears from turning to outright sobs. He was half crazed with panic and grief. The rocking sea beneath him and the vast bulk of the ship louring over him seemed to have surged up out of a night-mare. He knew, though, that they were real. He knew they had claimed him, in one terrifying snatch, and that every-thing familiar, everything he knew, had been torn away from him.

The kindly sailor beside him gave him a nudge as the boat bumped against HMS *Fearless*'s great wooden side.

'Brace up, young shipmate. You'd best stem the tide and swab your cheeks. Don't want all them up there to see that long face of yours, do you? First impressions, as they do say, goes a long way. Scramble aloft sharpish, that's my advice, before Mr Sourface Higgins gets out his rattan.'

John took in only half this speech but the gist of it was clear enough, and the sailor's friendly smile gave him a glim-mer of comfort. He steadied himself, swallowed hard, dashed his sleeve across his face and fixed his mouth in a wavering smile. The man was right. To go on board crying like a baby would be disastrous.

He took a deep breath, slung his bundle over his shoulder, grabbed at the guiding rope and shot up the cleats as fast as he could. Before he knew it, he was standing on a low-ceilinged covered deck, looking in bewilderment at the scenes of wild confusion all around.

It was the noise that struck him first. Shouts, shrieks of laughter, the rumbling of casks rolled along the wooden boards, a hammering from somewhere below his feet, the squawking of a large, brilliantly coloured bird, even the moo-ing of a cow made up a deafening racket. On top of it all came the sudden clang of a bell, a blast from a whistle and shouts of 'Away aloft! Unfurl sails to dry!' passed down in relay from man to man.

Only a little daylight penetrated through the opened lids of the gun ports that ran down each side of the gun deck. What meagre light came through was half blocked by the massive barrels of the great guns themselves, long black cannon, each one resting on its wheeled cradle. But it wasn't the guns that sent John's mouth falling open and made his eyes start out with shocked surprise. It was the sight of the women. There were dozens of them, some stout, some skin-ny, some pretty, some plain, but all of them dressed in bright cheap clothes, so low cut that their bosoms were almost completely exposed. It was their shrieks that he could hear, their high heels drumming on the deck, as they danced and cavorted with the sailors, many of whom were reeling about, already half drunk. In all his anxious fears of the night before, he had never imagined an orgy such as this. He watched in horror as a woman sank back against a gun, lifting her skirts. A hot blush rushed up into his cheeks and he hastily looked away.

'What's the matter with you, boy? Make way, or you'll be

rammed amidships,' came a hoarse voice behind him, and he turned to see a giant of a sailor, who was bent half double under the weight of an enormous trunk strapped to his back. John stepped back smartly, crushing himself against a stout wooden bulkhead, to let the man pass.

'Make way, make way!' the man shouted as he tried to force his way through the swaying mass of women and sailors. 'Captain's luggage coming aboard! Make way!'

The other pressed men and their guard of marines had come aboard now. The marines snapped to attention as their sergeant appeared. In their long-tailed scarlet coats and smart high-crowned black hats, they stood out from the mayhem surrounding them like red-hot pokers in a bramble patch.

'You – John Barr,' came the voice that John was already starting to dread. He looked round to see Mr Higgins standing uncomfortably close behind him. 'Who gave you the order to come first aboard? Who told you to put yourself forward? Impudence! I'll teach you.'

He was holding in his hand a short thick rattan cane, and he cut John a vicious blow with it across the shoulders. John bit his lip, trying not to flinch.

'Mr Higgins! Mr Higgins!' A boy not much bigger than John, with crinkly fair hair and a freckled nose, had wormed his way through the crowd towards them. 'Mr Erskine's compliments, and will you bring the pressed men up to be rated.' He had been eyeing the bosun's mate nervously as he spoke, and added a hasty, 'Sir.' He turned to John, stared at him curiously for a moment, then gave him a broad wink. John managed to flash him an answering smile before the marines, who had come smartly to attention, began to carve a way through the mass of people, with the pressed men sullenly following.

The boy stayed alongside John as together they scrambled

over coiled ropes and racks of cannonballs, climbed up companionways and dodged past men bowed down under baskets and sacks.

'I'm Tom Todd,' he said.

'I'm John. John Barr.'

'You're Scots, then, like me?'

'Of course I'm Scots. What else would I be?'

John's answer came out more indignantly than he had intended, but Tom Todd only laughed.

'Och, on this ship you could be anything, anything at all. They're English, most of them, and Irish, some, and Portuguese and American. There are some Africans too.'

'Africans? You mean Negroes? I've never seen one. Are they really black?'

'Aye. You'll see.'

'You've been to Africa, then?'

Tom adopted a slight swagger.

'No, but I've been to America. And to Spain, and Italy. You will too mebbe.'

They stood back to allow two other boys to pass. These were no more than two or three years older than John, but they were dressed in spotless white breeches, long-tailed blue coats with gold braid on their high collars and black glazed hats.

'Officers. Midshipmen,' Tom murmured, pulling respectfully at the tuft of hair above his forehead.

John bit his lip. If, when he'd been master of Luckstone, Patrick had seen fit to send his son to sea, John would have been a midshipman himself, all decked out in a smart uniform, with silver buckles on his shoes.

One of the midshipmen caught John's eye, and a faint frown creased his forehead. Reluctantly, John copied Tom, pulling his forelock too. The midshipman nodded imperceptibly and walked on.

They had arrived now at a less crowded section of the ship. A group of officers was sitting around a table.

'Yon's Mr Erskine, the first lieutenant,' Tom whispered, pointing to the man on the left, whose uniform, even more magnificent than the young midshipmen's, gleamed with brass buttons and gold braid. The man's head was half turned as he talked to a grizzled old sailor standing behind him, and John could see only his profile. His face seemed to be handsome, strong around the mouth, with laughter lines running out from his eyes. But then Mr Erskine turned. John gasped and stepped back. A hideous scar ran up the man's left cheek, puckering his eye, dragging at his nostril and pulling one side of his mouth up into a wolfish grin. John's heart missed a beat.

'I know, I know, he scares the babbies in their cradles,' Tom whispered. 'But Mr Erskine's a great gun. He got his wound in the Battle of Trafalgar, fighting alongside Nelson himself! Killed two Frenchies with one sword thrust. Spitted a . . .'

He broke off abruptly as Mr Higgins's hand shot out and grabbed his arm, then darted nimbly out of reach to dodge the swinging rattan.

'Get back to your quarters, boy,' growled Mr Higgins, 'or I'll . . .'

But Tom, not waiting to hear the rest of the threat, had already disappeared down the nearest hatchway.

The disturbance attracted the attention of the men at the table, and they turned to watch as the marines marshalled the pressed men in front of them. One by one, the unhappy new crew members mumbled their names, told their trades and were assigned their duties, until only the small group standing near John was left.

He thought for a moment, as the officers pushed back

their chairs and began to stand up, that he'd been forgotten, but Mr Higgins pushed him roughly forward.

'A boy, sir,' he said, addressing the first lieutenant with an obsequious smile. 'Volunteered yesterday. Needs some sense knocking into him. I've a mind to have him as my servant. The brat I had before deserted at Yarmouth.'

John's stomach kicked with fright.

The lieutenant's one undamaged eye surveyed John coolly.

'Your name?'

'John Barr.' John was looking desperately along the line of men behind the table, looking for a sign, a sympathetic face, for anything that might hold out the hope of a reprieve.

'And can you read and write, John Barr?'

'Yes, sir.'

'Well, well. And you have never, so far in your young life, been employed as a servant?'

'No, never, sir.'

The man beside Mr Erskine, whose small round face was as wizened as a monkey's, butted in.

'Studied mathematics, have you?'

'Yes, sir. For five years at school.'

The man shot Mr Higgins a sharp look full of hostile triumph.

'Smart lads in gunnery is hard to come by, Mr Erskine. I could do with him to apprentice. We're likely to be short, the way things are looking.'

'Then he shall be yours, Mr Tawse,' Mr Erskine said lightly. 'A career as a gunner awaits him. Did you hear that, John? You will join Mr Tawse, the master gunner, and obey him in all things.'

Before he had finished speaking, shouts and the smart stamps of marines snapping to attention swept towards them along the deck, and a moment later the figure of a short, stout man appeared, amid whispers of 'It's the Captain. Here comes Captain Bannerman.'

It was hard to see, at first glance, how such a comical little man could command the respect that John could read in the faces of all those around him. Although Captain Bannerman was clean shaven, springy tufts of hair sprouted from his ears and nostrils, while his black eyebrows bristled like an angry hedgehog's prickles. But everyone present, except for the pressed men, straightened themselves smartly and touched the brims of their hats.

The captain's eyes swept over the miserable huddle in front of him and John saw his jaw work, as if he disapproved of what he saw. His eyes, though, didn't show contempt. It was almost, thought John, trying to read their expression, as if he pitied them.

Captain Bannerman stood still for a moment, gathering everyone's attention. Then he stepped up on to the first rung of the companionway behind him and cleared his throat.

'Most of you men, I know,' he began, 'have recently been pressed into His Majesty's service and have not volunteered to serve of your own free will. You will be feeling sad today.' His voice was forceful and carried powerfully. Some of the pressed men groaned and nodded their heads. 'But you are here, lads, for a noble cause. The French are at the door of our nation. Bonaparte has swept through Europe. If he is not checked, his soldiers will soon be rampaging through the streets of our own dear towns and villages, killing, raping and setting fire.'

The captain's voice was rich and strong, and as his words rang out, his eyes settled on John. In them, John saw a fierce enthusiasm, which sent an answering shiver of excitement racing through him.

'Though today, boys, you may curse the fate that has brought you here, tomorrow you will bless it, for you are

51

now, each one of you, a man-o'-war's man, you are joining the crew of HMS *Fearless*, the finest ship in the finest navy in the world, veteran of Trafalgar, praised by the great Nelson himself. You will be treated honourably. You will learn to be good seamen and brave in battle, and when at last this war is over, and you are at liberty to leave this ship and return to your families, you will know that you have saved them from a cruel fate, and served your country as her true and faithful sons. Mr Erskine, proceed to rate these men.'

Chapter Nine

The racket on the lower deck had grown even louder by the time John followed Mr Tawse, the master gunner, down to his new berth. Mr Tawse was small and moved neatly, like a cat, turning once or twice to check that John was following, and giving him each time an encouraging grin, which wrinkled his wizened face even more.

Stepping over drunken sailors, avoiding dancing women and ducking under low beams, Mr Tawse reached at last a canvas awning that separated the lower gun deck from the cramped space at the stern of the ship. He lifted this, and John followed him inside.

Only a little light penetrated through the gun ports cut in the stern of the ship. Two great guns stood at these, their barrels pointing out to sea. The rest of the small space was crowded with casks and crates, boxes and chests. A lantern hung from a low beam and, in the light it cast, John saw the faces of four boys turned towards him and four pairs of eyes looking him up and down.

'John!' said Tom Todd, jumping up from the chest where he'd been sitting. 'Are you going to mess with us?'

'Mess? What mess?' John said, bewildered.

A short, skinny boy, whose close-set eyes were watching John with no sign of friendliness, said, with sneering wonderment, 'A little gentleman! And a regular landlubber! Stupid too. I'm not about to give the time of day to the likes of 'im!'

'Hold your adder's tongue, Nat Claypole,' said Mr Tawse, cuffing him sharply round the head. 'John Barr's to be your messmate. That means –' he turned to John and emphasized each point with a stab of his forefinger – 'you eats here and you sleeps here and you works here and you learns here. You're one of my lads now, and that means you'll do just what I say.' He paused, and added with a ferocious frown, 'Even if I command you to put on a lady's dress and dance a hornpipe.'

John's eyes opened in alarm, but the other boys grinned.

'Or climb the mainmast upside down and sing "Come loyal Britons all rejoice"?' sang out Tom.

'Most certainly,' nodded Mr Tawse gravely.

'Or jump overboard and drown hisself,' muttered Nat sourly, too low for anyone but John to hear.

'Or . . .' began the third boy, a heavily built young giant, whose brow was creased with the effort of thinking of something clever. 'Or . . .' He stopped and shook his head, looking confused.

'Whatever you say, Davey,' said Mr Tawse with a pat on the boy's shoulder. 'Now, my young men, it's dinner time, and if I'm not mistaken, Mr Jabez Barton is approaching with viands to delight you all.'

As he spoke, the canvas screen lifted and the big-boned, fair-headed gunner's mate came in. He was carrying a wooden pail in one hand and a pile of loaves in the other, but what caught John's eye and made him stare was the brilliantly coloured parrot that was perched on the man's shoulder, lovingly nibbling his ear. And then the smell of hot salt beef stew hit his nose, and he realized that he was hungry. Desperately, ravenously hungry.

The boys had scrambled to take their places on the sea chests which served as benches at the table. It was already set for a meal, with plates, mugs and spoons. John moved forward shyly and saw properly, for the first time, the fourth boy. He was slight, smaller than the others, with dark hair tied back in a pigtail. His dark watchful eyes were wary, but as they met John's blue ones the boy's face relaxed into a friendly smile.

'I'm Kit,' he said, 'Mr Tawse's servant.'

There was a space beside Nat Claypole. John made to sit down, but Nat stuck out a sharp elbow and turned ostentatiously away.

Kit frowned at Nat and shifted up to make room for John. Gratefully, John slid into the place beside him.

'One more boy, do I zee?' the man with the parrot said, in a slow, west-country voice. 'Bless me, there's boys a-coming up through the floor and out the gun barrels. There's more of 'em every time I look.'

As he bent to set an extra plate, mug and spoon in front of John, the parrot squawked and flapped its wings, revealing a gorgeous flash of scarlet feathers, and a stream of green goo shot out from under its tail and landed on the table.

'That's not nice, 'Orace. Not nice at all,' said the gunner's mate reprovingly, taking off his greasy neck cloth and wiping up the mess.

'Is that his name? Horace?' John dared to ask.

'Aye. 'Tweren't me that give him such a fancy name. 'Twas Mr Erskine. "That's a fine bird you have there, Jabez," he sez to me. "What's his name?" So I sez, "Parrot, sir." "Parrot?" sez he. "What kind of a name is Parrot? Call 'im 'Orace." "Aye aye, sir," I sez, so 'Orace 'e be, and 'Orace 'e'll stay.'

He had already ladled out a generous portion of stew on to John's platter. John picked up his spoon, desperate to begin, but before he could take his first mouthful, Nat Claypole leaned across the table and pretended to slip, giving John's plate a hard shove. It would have shot down into his lap, spilling all its contents, if Kit hadn't quickly caught it.

'Oh dear, oh dear, oh my, what an accident,' said Nat, looking around at the others as if hoping for their approval, but none of them looked back at him. He flushed and began to eat quickly, his left hand holding tightly on to his hunk of bread, as if he was afraid that someone might snatch it from him.

Mr Tawse and Jabez Barton with several other members of the master gunner's crew had settled themselves at another suspended table beside the second gun, leaving the boys to themselves. No one spoke as they ate their meal. Although the stew was too salty, the meat tough and the loaf hard, John devoured his helping, and ran the last crust of bread round his platter again and again to soak up any remaining smear of gravy.

He looked up when he'd finished and saw that the other boys' eyes were on him.

'Have you never been before to sea?' said Kit. There was a slight foreign lilt to his voice.

'No,' said John, 'and I never wanted to either. But my father was taken by the press gang, yesterday, and I didn't have anywhere else to go, so I volunteered.'

'So where's your pa now, then?' said Tom.

'He was sent to another ship. He's on the *Splendid.*' John answered gruffly.

'Oh aye, the *Splendid.* Not a bad sea-boat. Only sixty-four guns though. We're a seventy-four.' Tom smirked with pride.

'They told my father he was to be the captain's clerk.'

'The captain's clerk!' Nat said, nastily mimicking John's

voice. 'An officer! Mind your ps and qs boys. *Mister* John's daddy's an officer.'

Tom turned on him.

'Stow it, Ratface. You're a spiteful toad.'

Nat took out a piece of cord and a pocket knife, turned his back on the others and began to fiddle with them.

'Is that your bundle, John?' said Kit. 'Do you not have a chest to put your things in?'

'You can share mine,' said Tom.

'Ain't no room in yours, Tom,' said Davey. 'No room to hide a cockle shell in there.'

'Have you been in my chest again, Davey Gow?' demanded Tom angrily. 'You made me a promise. No more rummaging. You said, after last time . . .'

'I never rummaged, Tom,' Davey interrupted anxiously. 'I just looked. I never took nothing. I just . . .'

'What have you hidden in it, then?' said Tom, exasperated.

'Only a little dead mousey,' said Davey. 'It had to go somewhere nice and warm.'

'You put a dead mouse in my chest? You great looby. Don't you know it'll rot and stink and infect all my gear?'

'It smelt good yesterday,' said Davey, hurt. 'I found it while I was mucking out the hen cages. I thought you'd like it, Tom.'

Tom gave an exclamation of disgust, jumped up, manhandled Davey off the chest he was sitting on, and opened it. Holding his nose with one thumb and forefinger, he pulled out a dead mouse with his other hand and hurled it out through the gun port.

'Don't you ever – ever! – go putting things in my chest again, mind now, Davey.'

Nat looked round and snorted.

'You're wasting your breath. There's no telling that

beef-witted bonehead anything. They ought to have dropped him overboard months ago.'

Kit leaned over to whisper in John's ear.

'Davey fell from the rigging last year. He hit his head so bad. He was training to be a topman – one that works up with the highest sails. He didn't speak for a long time, and now his wits are all confused. He just looks after the hens and cows. Mr Tawse says he's getting better, though.' He shook his head, as if in disbelief, and then spoke more loudly. 'But it's true what Davey says, that Tom's chest is full. Mine's half empty. You can put your things in mine, John, if you like.'

He got up from the table and went across to a stack of long wooden cases that were lashed to the wall. John followed him.

'What's in all of these?' he asked curiously.

'Muskets, pistols, cutlasses,' Kit said casually, 'for when we go to battle stations.'

The word 'battle' sent a shiver down John's spine.

'Have you ever been in one – in a battle?'

'No, but if we're heading south towards France, we're sure to see action. It's two years since Trafalgar. We slammed the French navy then, but Napoleon's still riding high in France *and* Spain. There's bound to be another battle soon.'

'Is that where we're going? To France? Or Spain?'

Kit shrugged.

'They tell us last of everyone. I don't know. Thundering Sam's waiting on his orders.'

'Who's Thundering Sam?'

'The captain. Captain Samuel Bannerman. Everyone calls him Thundering Sam. Because of his loud voice, I think.'

He thrust out his chin, opened his eyes wide, deepened his high-pitched voice as low as it would go and growled, 'For king and country, lads, and the last man up the ratlines'll be clapped into irons!'

John laughed. Kit's mimicry was so excellent that for a moment the captain had stood before him.

'He's good, though, isn't he? A good captain, I mean?'

John remembered the rush of enthusiasm the captain's speech had sent coursing through him. He held his breath, willing Kit to say yes.

'He's the best,' Kit said simply.

He had opened his chest now. There were a few spare clothes in it, a book half hidden under a cloth, and a bulging linen bag.

'The bag,' Kit said awkwardly, shuffling it aside. 'Just something of my mother's.'

'I won't touch it,' John said quickly.

He picked up his bundle and untied it. The purser's assistant had tidily folded his clothes before wrapping them up. He picked up his new shirt and trousers, ready to place them in the chest, but then stopped, startled. Lying between the layers of clothing, its straps folded neatly, was the satchel.

'What is it? What's that?' asked Kit.

'Oh, nothing. Just something of my father's,' said John, putting the satchel quickly down into the chest. Following some obscure instinct, without knowing why, he hid it under a layer of clothes.

Chapter Ten

John had little time during the rest of the short winter afternoon to think about the reappearance of the satchel. It must have been by pure chance that the man on the receiving ship had bundled it up with his clothes before Mr Creech had come looking for it. But why had Mr Creech gone to so much trouble to get hold of a shabby old leather satchel? There was nothing in it, after all, but a sorry muddle of dog-eared papers.

There must be some deed or other in there, thought John, that Father overlooked. Maybe it . . . no, it couldn't be – but what if it was something that showed what a cheat Mr Nasmyth is? What if it proves that Luckstone really is ours after all? I'll look through it as soon as I get the chance.

His heart lifted at the thought, but he told himself he was being foolish, and a moment later Mr Tawse called out to him.

Mr Tawse was looking through the contents of a gun case, making Jabez squint down the barrel of each musket and check the workings of the flintlocks.

'We'd best get you kitted out with your hammock, John,

before the day's much older,' he said. 'Get Kit to take you down to see the purser.'

'Yes, sir.'

'Did ye ever want to be a drummer boy, young John? In the army like?' said Jabez.

'No,' said John, puzzled.

''Cause that's what you'd be zaying in the army. It would be "Yes, zir" this, and "Yes, zir" that. It's "Aye aye, zir," in the navy.'

'Aye aye, sir,' echoed the parrot.

''E knows.' Jabez cocked a loving eye up towards the bird, who was sidling backwards and forwards along the lid of a cutlass case. 'You listen to 'Orace. You does what 'Orace tells you, you won't go far wrong.'

'Yes— aye aye, sir,' said John.

The purser's den was on the orlop deck, in the deep dark bowels of the ship. To reach it, John and Kit had to fight their way through the swaying throng of carousing women and sailors on the lower gun decks, scramble down a companionway and grope their way forward in the semi-darkness of the orlop deck. Short as they both were, even they had to bend down, as the beams overhead were so low.

It was quiet down here, apart from the creaking of ship's timbers as she moved up and down on the water, and the thuds and shouts from the gun deck overhead. The air was thick, and there was a rotten smell of foul water which made John wrinkle up his nose.

He was so busy peering forward into the gloom, trying not to bang his head on the beams, that he didn't notice that Kit had stopped and he nearly bumped into him.

Kit put out a warning hand. Peering over his shoulder, John saw two dim figures standing by a stack of full sacks.

'You didn't see anything, then, when he stowed his gear away?'

With a sinking heart, John recognized Mr Higgins's voice.

'No, sir.' It was Nat, speaking eagerly, as if anxious to please. 'He kept his back turned, all sneaky. Him and Mr Tawse's servant, that boy Kit, they was whispering together. Like they was hiding something.'

'Whispering? Hiding something? They don't even know each other.'

'Well, but maybe they do, sir. Very thick together, they was, and him and Tom Todd too, like they'd all known each other before.'

The watching boys saw Mr Higgins's arm go out as he cuffed Nat's head.

'Don't be foolish. And don't try to be clever with me. You'll get some pennies if you do as I say, but you can keep your ideas to yourself. And if you open that loose mouth of yours . . . What was that?'

His head jerked up, as if he had heard something. He swivelled round, peering into the darkness. Kit and John, in the deep shadows, held their breath.

There was a moment's silence, then the two dim figures moved away behind a partition.

'This is what I want you to do,' came Mr Higgins's voice, but the boys could hear no more.

It was me they were talking about. I'm sure of it, thought John. It's something to do with the satchel again. If only I could find a corner where I could hide away and look.

Kit had gone on ahead, and John had to hurry to keep up with him before the darkness swallowed him up.

Half an hour later, John had been issued with his hammock and the boys had climbed up through the layers of the ship to the deck above.

'In the daytime, you stow your hammock here, see?' said Kit.

He untied the canvas that covered the nets running round

the edge of the deck to reveal a wall of tightly packed hammocks. John hardly saw what he was doing. After the stuffy darkness of the lower decks, the fresh air up here was wonderful to breathe. He looked round, almost surprised to see the familiar profile of Edinburgh still there on the horizon and the huddle of houses round the port of Leith. He'd been transported into another world since he'd come on board the *Fearless*. It was hard to believe that the old world was still there, unchanged.

He noticed for the first time a line of ships, some big warships, like the *Fearless*, others smaller frigates and cutters, which lay with their sails furled at anchor out in the Firth of Forth. Was one of them the *Splendid*? Had his father been taken out to her yet? It was horrible to think that he was probably a mere mile or so away, yet far, far out of reach.

He looked down over the side of the ship. Small boats were crowding alongside, the people in them shouting up to those on the decks above. Men and women were climbing on and off the ship, and barges full of supplies were being lifted on board with ropes and winches.

If I could get down there without being seen, and hide in one of those boats, I could get ashore, thought John.

He was almost ready to try it, his feet itching for the feel of solid ground under them, but almost at once the urge passed. Where would he go, once he was on land again? Where would his next meal come from?

He was aware that Kit was watching him curiously.

'We'd best go below again,' Kit said. 'Mr Tawse, he doesn't like us going round the ship when we're in port. He doesn't like us seeing all the . . . you know, the women and everything.'

Reluctantly, John followed him down the nearest hatchway.

'Do you like him? Mr Tawse?'

Kit shrugged.

'Yes. He's good. Only when he drinks too much grog – then you'll see.'

'He gets angry?'

'Angry? Wild! You'll see.'

The now familiar space behind the canvas screen appeared to be empty when Kit and John went inside, except for Nat Claypole, who was kneeling on the floor with Kit's chest open in front of him, his hands reaching inside it.

'Hey! What are you doing, Ratface? Get out of my chest!' shouted Kit, darting forwards.

Nat jumped up. His eyes shifted guiltily, but he stabbed an accusing forefinger at John.

'Ask him. He's a thief, he is. Stole my pocket knife when we was having our dinner. I seen him. Picked it up off the table when no one else was looking. Found it just now, didn't I, where'd he'd hidden it in your chest.'

'You liar! He's lying!' John could hardly see for the red mist clouding his eyes. He leaped forwards, fists bunched, but Nat had dodged out of the way, and John had to catch hold of a low beam to prevent himself from crashing down on to the deck.

'Your knife was in your pocket all the time, Ratface,' said Kit with disgust. 'I saw you put it there yourself.'

Tom and Davey had appeared now.

'What is it? A fight? Did John punch Nat?' said Tom hopefully.

'No, but Nat deserves it,' Kit said scornfully. 'We caught him looking in my chest.'

Davey made a distressed noise.

'It weren't me. I never did. I never looked in your chest, nor in nobody's chest, Kit,' he said.

The others ignored him.

'Nat said I'd stolen his pocket knife. He called me a thief.' John was panting with indignation.

Kit pushed Nat out of the way, slammed down the lid of his chest, picked it up and took it behind the nearest gun, tucking it away under the barrel.

'What's this? What's the noise and fuss?'

Mr Higgins's unwelcome face appeared through the gap in the canvas screen.

'It's that boy, John Barr,' said Nat, his voice high pitched. 'He's a thief, he is. Stole my pocket knife. I found it in Kit's chest where John stowed his baggage.'

Mr Higgins stepped further in.

'Thieving is a very serious matter,' he said, with grave satisfaction. 'Thieves get a flogging, and it's no more than what they deserve. Where's the proof?'

'Here! Here!' said Nat excitedly, holding up his knife.

'Proof of what?' said Mr Tawse, appearing suddenly. 'Why, Mr 'Iggins, to what do we owe this pleasure?' His small frame was stiff with dislike.

'A matter of discipline, Mr Tawse. This boy here, John Barr, has been accused of stealing.'

The master gunner's eyes narrowed.

'Who by?'

'Nat Claypole.'

'Stealing what?'

'My pocket knife. From the table. At dinner time,' said Nat smugly.

'Witnesses?' rapped out Mr Tawse.

'Yes, I saw him, sir,' said Kit, poking his head out from behind the gun where he was still crouching. 'I saw Ratface – Nat, I mean. He put the knife away in his own pocket, then he just pretended to find it in my chest. It was all spite, sir. Just plain spite.'

'Thanking you kindly, Mr 'Iggins, for your interest in my

boys' morals,' said Mr Tawse icily. 'Now, if you would be so kind as to leave . . .'

He indicated the canvas screen with a dismissive gesture.

'Wait a minute.' Mr Higgins had hooked his thumbs into the buttonholes of his jacket and was standing firm, his feet apart. 'The father of this boy was accused of theft this very morning by a respectable citizen of Edinburgh, within my hearing. It's my belief that John Barr is the son of a notorious criminal, and that he himself is harbouring stolen goods. I demand that his belongings be searched.'

The master gunner drew himself up to his full height, so that his eyes were on a level with Mr Higgins's chin.

'May I remind you, Mr 'Iggins, that you are on my premises?'

'And may I remind *you*, Mr Tawse, that matters of discipline in this ship come under the bosun's jurisdiction, and that as I am the bosun's mate, they fall to me. Do I make myself quite clear?'

They stood in silence, glaring at each other.

'Please, sir,' said Kit, breaking into the silence, 'I don't mind if you search my chest. John doesn't mind either, do you, John?'

He dragged the chest out from under the gun, picked it up and carried it over to the two men. Mr Higgins bent down and flung it open.

John stared into it, his heart in his mouth. What was all this mystery? What was there among his belongings that everyone seemed so eager to possess? And if, by some awful chance, there was something incriminating in the satchel, and he was branded a thief – the thought of the shame and the punishment that would follow made his blood run cold.

Mr Higgins had knelt down and was eagerly throwing John's and Kit's few clothes out on to the deck.

'One pair of canvas trousers. One spare jacket and neckerchief. One pair of torn breeches,' itemized Mr Tawse with awful sarcasm, picking up the garments one by one as Mr Higgins threw them down.

John's mouth had fallen open. There was no sign, anywhere, of the satchel. He looked up and caught Kit's eye. A mischievous grin had crossed Kit's face, but he covered it at once with an air of wondering innocence.

'Well,' said Mr Higgins at last, rising awkwardly to his feet, 'everything seems to be in order.'

'So it does,' agreed the master gunner with mock surprise.

'I'll be off, then.' Mr Higgins was already backing uncomfortably towards the canvas screen.

'There's one more little matter that perhaps I can oblige you with,' said Mr Tawse with painful politeness. 'I believe I heard you explain this morning to Mr Erskine as how you were short of a servant. Nat Claypole here was assigned to me, but I find after all that he don't suit. I believe he would do for you very well.'

'No! Mr Tawse! Please! I never meant – it was all a mistake!' said Nat, whose face had gone a sickly green.

Mr Higgins nodded curtly.

'Thank you, Mr Tawse. You, Nat, get your belongings and come with me.'

Chapter Eleven

Silence fell when Mr Higgins, with the unhappy Nat following him, had gone. John moved first, making for where Kit still stood beside the gun, only to find his way blocked by Jabez Barton's massive chest.

Mr Tawse elbowed Jabez out of the way.

'Sit down,' he said curtly to John. 'All of you, sit down.'

Without a word, the gunner, his mate and the boys took their places at the table.

'Now then.' Mr Tawse's small round face, normally so cheerful, had lengthened with severity. 'I want the truth, John Barr. All of it. Accusations has been made against you. Thieves on a ship is what none of us wants. Shipmates must sleep easy in their 'ammocks knowing that their few possessions are safe and sound. What have you to say for yourself?'

John took a deep breath. The injustice of the accusation had stung him to fury and he was afraid that he would violently lose his temper.

'I never even touched Nat's penknife,' he began, trying to control the rage in his voice. 'He took against me as soon as I came on board. I didn't do anything to him. First he tried to upset my dinner, and then . . .'

Mr Tawse held up his hand.

'Kit here has spoken for you as regards the penknife. Was what you said correct, Kit? You're on your honour to tell the truth.'

Kit nodded, his face reflecting the seriousness of the occasion.

'Yes, Mr Tawse. I did see Nat put his knife in his pocket. John couldn't have taken it. Nat did try to spill John's dinner. He's a nasty boy, Mr Tawse. He was nasty to all of us. He—'

'We are not concerning ourselves with Nat,' said Mr Tawse, 'but with John. John, we accept Kit's evidence. You did not steal Nat's knife.'

John shuddered with relief.

'Thank you, Mr Tawse,' he managed to say.

'But –' Mr Tawse's forefinger tapped the table – 'other things was said. Mr 'Iggins expressed the belief that you have about you stolen property. Is this true?'

His brown eyes, clear and stern, stared into John's.

John hesitated, unsure whom he could trust. He looked sideways at Kit, taking courage at his reassuringly trusting smile, then back at Mr Tawse and down at the table. At last he came to a decision.

'No,' he said, 'but there's something I don't understand. Please can I tell you what's happened? I'd like to tell you all of it.'

It took nearly half an hour to recount the whole story, starting with the loss of Luckstone in Mr Halkett's office, the murder of Mr Sweeney in the close, the furious mob, the press gang in Leith, the unexpected appearance of Mr Creech on board the receiving ship and his strangely desperate attempts to acquire the satchel.

'So where is this satchel now?' The dent between Mr Tawse's eyebrows had been getting deeper as he tried to follow the complicated tale.

'Well,' said John reluctantly, 'it was there when I untied my bundle. I put it away with my other things in Kit's chest.'

'You mean it's disappeared since you boarded this ship?'

Mr Tawse's eyebrows had risen now, wrinkling the leathery skin of his tanned forehead into deep lines.

John looked at Kit, whose eyes had opened in a question. John nodded. Kit stood up from the table and dived under the gun. He wriggled out again and held the satchel up for everyone to see.

''Ow in 'eaven's name did it git down there?' said Jabez Barton, who had been following John's story open-mouthed, but with increasing bewilderment.

'I hid it,' said Kit, looking anxiously at Mr Tawse. 'I reckoned there was some trouble in store for John. We heard Nat and Mr Higgins talking in secret when we went down to the purser's for John's hammock. Something to do with John's gear being stowed, and something that was supposed to be in it. I saw how surprised John was when he saw the satchel. I suppose I just guessed, I don't know why, I . . . well . . . I thought it was best to hide it.'

He faltered to a stop.

Mr Tawse held out his hand for the satchel, undid the clasp, pulled out the contents and laid them on the table.

'Now then. What do we have here?'

Everyone bent curiously to look. John picked up the dog-eared papers and leafed through them.

'This is . . . I don't know . . . oh yes, it says Bill of Sale. It's for our cows at Luckstone. And this is . . .'

'A lease on a field.' Mr Tawse took it from him and laid it aside.

'Here's a letter,' said Tom, who had been trying to spell out the first line.

'Put that down, Tom Todd,' barked Mr Tawse.

'Sorry, sir,' mumbled Tom, blushing.

'It's from my mother, the last one before she died,' said John, hastily taking it and folding it up.

'Nothing. There's nothing here of note.' Mr Tawse was placing the papers in a pile as he scrutinized each in turn. 'A contract for a bushel of wheat. A deed of covenant, but out of date. The last will and testament of one Joseph Barr. A marriage settlement. A warrant – Hello! What's this?'

He held up to the lantern a little booklet and riffled through the pages. It was made up of a few thin pages of India paper, on which were written, in a tiny, spidery hand, small columns of numbers facing corresponding columns of words.

'I . . . I don't think I've ever seen that before,' John said, wrinkling his brow as a memory knocked faintly in the back of his mind. 'I don't know what that could be. Some kind of accounts, perhaps? It's not my father's hand.'

Mr Tawse held the paper up to the lantern and peered at it closely.

'Could be accounts, I suppose,' he said doubtfully. 'Plenty of numbers, anyway. I can't make head nor tail of it at all.'

He put the paper down on the table. Jabez picked it up and squinted at it. Horace ducked his head down and tried to take a peck at it. Jabez jerked it out of the parrot's way, accidentally hitting the lantern, which began to swing wildly. Jabez put the paper down, steadied the lantern and tapped Horace smartly on the beak.

'You mind your manners, 'Orace. Don't you go nibbling at what don't belong to you.'

'Put them papers away, lad,' Mr Tawse said to John. 'There's a bit of a mystery here. It's my belief that this Mr Creech of yours . . .'

'Please, sir, he's not *mine*,' objected John, revolted.

'You know what I mean. It's my belief he's taken hold of a mistaken idea about the contents of this satchel. There's nothing there of value that I can see. It's what young Nat Claypole was doing that I don't understand.'

'Mr Higgins knows Mr Creech,' said John. 'I saw them talking together on the receiving ship. And Mr Higgins and Nat were talking secrets together down below.'

'Accusations against an officer on board this ship is what I won't tolerate. Not for any reason.' Mr Tawse fixed John with an awful frown. 'The ways of bosun's mates is wondrous strange and passing all knowledge, and it's not for jumped-up boys to question them. Keep this satchel tucked away and out of sight, that's my advice. We don't want no more poking and prying and mysteries here. And now we'll close this whole sorry business. I hereby state, young John, that you are free of all suspicion. I believe you have told us the whole truth. No one could make such a story up, anyways. I ain't never heard a thing to match it, though most men in the navy have a tale to tell that would curl the hair of a mermaid.'

'Nothing exciting ever happened to me,' Tom said regretfully. 'My father sent me to sea. I'm to work for him on his brig trading out of Ayr when I've learned to be a seaman. He says the training's finer in the navy.'

'I ran away from my master,' said Davey with simple pride. 'Laid him out with a good blow to the jaw first, flat as a flounder, even though he was the biggest blacksmith in Rye. Couldn't have done it if he hadn't been drunk. He won't bully me ever again, will he, Mr Barton?'

'He will not, Davey, zo long as you behaves yourself, and becomes a good seaman, and looks after them animals, zame as you're told,' said Jabez comfortably.

John turned expectantly towards Kit, hoping to hear his story, but Kit was inspecting the sole of his foot, trying to pull out a splinter with his fingernails.

'Don't think too hard of Nat, boys,' Mr Tawse said into the silence. 'Beaten and starved he was, all his life, like a puppy no one wanted. It's no surprise his character turned as sour as milk that's left to curdle. I was sorry for the lad. But there was no making a gunner of him. What's the first rule of gunnery, Tom?'

'To maintain the discipline of the gun crew and obey the gun captain at all times,' rapped out Tom.

'And the second, Kit?'

'To remain steady under fire,' said Kit, without lifting his eyes from his foot. 'Even if the head's shot away from your shoulders.'

'That's enough of your sauce. What's the third, Davey?'

'To . . . to be . . . um . . . speed. Quick,' Davey brought out triumphantly.

'Good lad. Now then, boys, keep yourselves quiet and out of mischief till it's time to pipe down the hammocks. I have business with Mr Erskine.'

By the time the short supper of ship's biscuit, cheese and cocoa had been taken, and the hammocks had been fetched down from the decks above, John was so tired that he would have fallen asleep anywhere, standing, sitting or lying down, if he'd been left alone for a moment. He was still just awake when Tom showed him how to untie his hammock, hook it between two beams and shake out the pillow and blanket it contained. He was yawning so hard his jaw felt it would crack right open as he bent to take off his shoes, barely noticing that he was the only one to do so as the others were all bare-footed.

It was harder than he'd expected, climbing into his hammock. It rolled away from under him, tipping him out. He summoned up a sleepy smile at the others who were laughing at his clumsy efforts, and at last, with a desperate thrust of his feet, he managed to get in and stay in. He had barely pulled the blanket over himself before he fell into a deep, exhausted sleep.

The pipe of a bosun's whistle, shouts of 'Larboard watch ahoy!', curses, groans and the scuffle of men's feet coming from the far side of the canvas jerked him awake. He lay with his eyes wide open in the dark, wondering for a long moment what kind of dream he'd fallen into. The events of yesterday churned through his mind. He turned over and cried out with fright as he nearly tipped himself out of his hammock.

'Go back to sleep,' came Tom's sleepy voice from the hammock only a hand's breath away to his left. 'It's only the watches changing. We don't have to go. It's still just the wee small hours.'

John grunted in reply. Although it was cold, the air, heavy with the smells of tarry ropes, stale breath and unwashed men, was almost too close to breathe. There were strange sounds all around – Jabez Barton's deep growling snores; lighter ones, ending in a whistle, from behind the partition marking off Mr Tawse's tiny cabin; a kind of whimpering from where Davey slept; bumps and cries; the clang of a bell, and the endless straining creak of the ship's wooden beams.

Where are you, Father? he thought. Are you awake? Are you thinking of me?

A feeling of dreadful sadness swept across him. He sniffed, rubbing the end of the blanket savagely across his nose. Then he felt a hand from the right, coming from where Kit slept. It took hold of the edge of his hammock and gave it a shove, so that it swung gently a little from side to side. The sensation was wonderfully comforting, as if he was a baby being rocked in his cradle.

Quite suddenly, he was asleep again.

Chapter Twelve

The ship's bell ringing at half past six brought the crew springing to life, but John was so dead asleep that he heard nothing. Shouted commands of 'All hands ahoy! Up hammocks ahoy!' and the shrill blasts of the bosun's whistle barely penetrated his dreams.

He came to with a start as a painful tap from someone's rattan cane landed with a thwack on his back.

'Show a leg! Out or down! Jump to it!'

He rolled over, trying to sit up at the same time. The hammock twisted out from under him and he landed painfully on the hard wooden floor of the deck. Kit, Tom and Davey were already fully dressed. Their blankets were stowed neatly in their hammocks, which had been unhooked from the beams, and they were folding them up, lacing them into tight neat rolls.

John hastily tried to copy them, made a mess of it, and started again.

'Like this,' Tom said, pushing him out of the way and rolling John's hammock himself.

Kit and Davey had already disappeared, their rolled hammocks under their arms.

'Come on, quick!' Tom said. 'We've to put them away before Mr Tawse inspects us. You'll not want to be there when he finds it's not all to his satisfaction.'

The last wisps of sleepiness cleared from John's head as he dashed away in Tom's wake. A moment later he was on deck. The shock of cold fresh air was like a douche of water. He gasped as it hit him and drew deep sweet breaths into his lungs.

The deck was crowded with barefooted men, bleary eyed, red nosed, many barely recovered from the drunkenness of yesterday. They were yawning and scratching, bad tempered and mostly silent. Between them stalked the officers, blue coated, gold braided and commanding, rope ends in their hands.

Another whistle howled through the morning air.

'All hands make sail! Man the rigging!'

A shudder seemed to run through the ship from bows to stern as hundreds of men swarmed up the rigging to unloose the sails from the great yards from which they were suspended. It was clear that the women and traders, the visitors and hangers-on had left the *Fearless* during the night, shaken out of her like fleas from a blanket. One last small boat-load of women was being rowed hastily ashore. They were waving with cheerful desperation to the ship, but the men on board, transforming themselves rapidly from a drunken rabble to a disciplined, efficient force, seemed to have forgotten them already.

All around John, men were hauling on ropes or letting them out, covers were being lashed down, tackle and gear were being lifted and moved. From below came the sound of fifty men's voices singing as they laboured to turn the vast spokes of the great winch that pulled up the anchor.

'Bosun! Start that man!' came a booming cry from above. Looking up, John saw Captain Bannerman standing, legs apart, arms crossed, behind the rail of the quarterdeck. He shrank against the netted hammocks as the bosun, a terrifying figure in a black-brimmed leather hat, bore down on him with his cane raised. He put up his arm to fend off the expected blow, but the bosun surged past him and brought his cane down with a crack on the back of the man who had been leaning woozily against the mainmast.

John looked round for Tom, but he had disappeared. A shout from above of 'Away aloft!' made him glance up, and his heart lurched with fright as he saw Tom far, far above his head, climbing like a monkey up the ladder-like rungs of the rigging.

'Here, boy, get up there and pass the brace through the bullseye,' said a gruff voice behind him.

John spun round. The instruction had come from a heavy-set sailor, whose sleeves were rolled up to reveal a mermaid tattooed on each massive forearm, and who was hauling on a rope nearby.

'A . . . a brace?' stammered John. 'I don't know – I'm new.'

'Damn your eyes! Get below, and stay out of the way!' the man said with a scowl.

Hastily, John obeyed.

On the covered gun deck below, the wild scenes of yesterday were impossible to imagine now. Men were on their hands and knees, scrubbing the boards with big flat stones. Others were washing the tables and stowing away chests.

Mr Tawse, looking taller somehow, stern, almost alarming, in his cocked hat and full gold braid, was inspecting the guns down the length of the ship, Jabez Barton following gravely in his wake, his head permanently bowed beneath the low ceiling.

John hovered uncertainly, not knowing how to employ himself. He didn't wish to seem idle, but he didn't know where to go or what to do. Fortunately, Mr Tawse, who was now far down the gun deck, looked round and saw him. He beckoned and John ran up to him.

'You'll start your new duties with me this afternoon.' Mr Tawse was brisk and impatient this morning. 'In the meantime, you must begin to acquaint yourself with the workings of the ship.' He pointed to the nearest companionway. 'Get yourself up there. Now. Mr Higgins is ready to show you the ropes.'

'Mr Higgins, sir?' John's heart had skipped a beat, but Mr Tawse was staring at him, his brows raised, as he waited disapprovingly for John's obedient response.

'Aye aye, sir,' John said, taking a deep breath. Mr Tawse had already turned back to the gun he was inspecting, pointing out a fault to its crew, who were listening and nodding respectfully.

John was now used to the ladder-like companionways that connected the decks, and he was already learning to run up and down them with ease, but his palms were clammy with dread and his feet nearly slipped on the rungs as he emerged on to the deck of the fo'c'sle above.

In spite of his fear, he couldn't help giving a gasp of surprise. During the few minutes that he'd been below, the vast white sails of the *Fearless* had all been set and the ship was fully underway, the wind catching at the canvas, thrusting the bows forwards through the cold green water. He looked up. Men were still up there, working above the sails along the yards, right to the very tips. They stood on nothing more solid than ropes, and seemed to be dancing on the wind, creatures of air, miraculously keeping their balance as the ship rose and fell beneath them. The sight of them made John dizzy.

I couldn't. Never. I couldn't ever go up there, John thought with a shiver of dread.

'You. John Barr.'

He spun round. Mr Higgins was standing behind him, holding his rattan in one hand and bringing it down with smart, threatening taps into the palm of the other.

'You're going to learn the ropes from me, boy.' He spoke with malicious satisfaction. 'And once I've finished with you, you ain't never going to forget them again.'

John swallowed hard.

'No, sir. I mean, yes, sir.'

Mr Higgins's hand shot out and he took hold of John's ear in a painful grip.

'There is nothing, *nothing* you can hide from me,' he hissed. 'I'll discover all your secrets. In the end you'll be glad to give me what you know is not yours.'

Mr Erskine appeared on the quarterdeck at the far end of the ship and seemed about to approach the fo'c'sle along the linking gangway. Mr Higgins released John's ear and stepped back.

'The forestaysail halyard,' he barked, tapping his finger against a rope. 'Say it.'

'The fore . . . forestay . . .' stammered John.

'Forestaysail halyard.' The prompt came with a vicious cut from the rattan.

'F-forestaysail halyard,' John managed to say.

The next hour was the most painful that John had ever spent in his life. He danced at the end of Mr Higgins's cane while the names of the ropes – strange words he had never heard before – were barked in his ear. With each hesitation came a painful swipe of the rattan. The sailors working at different tasks on the deck nearby smiled as he passed, remembering their own first lessons in seamanship. While one of them was watching, the flicks from the rattan were bearable. But as soon as the sailors' attention was elsewhere, Mr Higgins sent the cuts raining down hard on John's head, across his back and arms, wherever they would inflict the most pain.

'You will report to me here tomorrow at the same time,' he said at last, releasing John with a final crack across the shoulders, 'and if so be as you can't tell me the names of every rope, faultless, as I points to it . . .'

He left the threat unfinished, to let John's imagination do its worst.

As John stumbled down towards his berth again, he caught sight of Nat Claypole. A smirk of triumph lifted Nat's mouth at the sight of John's face. John turned away, biting his lip till it almost bled.

The long morning had ended at last, and whistles blew as the men were piped to dinner. From one end of the gun decks to the other, legless tables, which had been pegged to the beams, came rattling down between the guns, and a few minutes later almost the entire ship's crew was sitting down around them, waiting while one man from each table went to the galley to fetch the food.

A sigh of relaxation seemed to run along the length of the ship. The boys felt it too. The dinner of oatmeal porridge, bread, cheese and ale was not very inviting, but they fell upon it with sharp appetites.

'Learning the ropes, was you, John?' said Davey, wiping his mouth with the back of his hand. 'I seen Mr Higgins after you with his cane.'

'I have to recite all of them to him tomorrow, and I can't remember one of them.' John put down his spoon. He had eaten enough of the mess on his plate to stop his hunger, but he couldn't force down any more. 'Halyards, sheets, braces, stays – they're all in a muddle in my head.'

'It's not so hard,' Kit said quietly in his ear. 'There's some on this ship with wooden pegs for heads. If they can learn them, you can. I'll show you later if you like.'

'Did Mr Higgins send you up aloft, John?' Tom called down the table.

John shook his head.

'That's a shame. It's good and calm here in the Forth. Tomorrow we'll be out in the open sea and there'll be a fine old swell on her with this wind that's blowing. I wouldn't like to go up my first time when she's bucking about like a—'

'You 'old your tongue, Tom Todd,' growled Jabez, who had approached the boys' table unseen from the other side, where Mr Tawse and his crew were eating at another table. 'Eat your vittles and bide quiet.'

Tom subsided, but when Jabez had returned to his dinner he looked at John with shining eyes.

'You don't need to be scared, John. There's no need at all. It's grand up there. They'll only let you go half the way up anyway, until you're strong enough to pull in the sail. I'm to be one of the topmen. You've seen them, haven't you? They're the only ones who may wear the scarlet waistcoats on the ship. They work right up high in the topgallant sails. The topmen are the best. Everyone respects them. They . . .'

His enthusiastic voice ran on, but John was no longer listening. The rise and fall of the ship, the stuffiness and stench overlaid with the smell of the food were combining to horrible effect. He stood up from the table, holding his hand to his mouth and just made it to the nearest gun port, from where he vomited his dinner down into the sea.

Chapter Thirteen

John's first short bout of sea-sickness was over almost as soon as it had started. By the time the ship's bell had announced the end of the break, and the hundreds of men aboard the *Fearless* had hoisted their tables up to the beams again and begun their afternoon duties, he was feeling less nauseous, though he was still battered and bruised all over from the blows of Mr Higgins's rattan cane.

'Boys,' said Jabez, ''Tis cutlass inspection this afternoon. Cleaning and sharpening is what they do need. Kit, when you've finished a-cleaning Mr Tawse's shoes, fetch out the long cases by the bulkhead there, so Mr Tawse can cast his eyes across them. No, John, not you. You're to come with me. Take your shoes off and leave them here. They'll be naught but a hindrance where you're going. Now, lads –' he jerked his thumb towards the low bar that ran across the room, on which his parrot was perched – 'keep an eye on 'Orace. Out of zorts 'e is today. Tweaked my nose sharp this morning, and now he's sulking.'

John followed Jabez up to the deck above. The ship was sailing fast. The coast of Midlothian was slipping past, and Edinburgh was already far behind. Soon they would have left the sheltered waters of the Firth of Forth and be heading out to sea.

'Zee over there?' said Jabez, leaning on the hammock nets and pointing towards a huge black rock that reared up out of the sea nearby. 'I seen a great whale there once. Monsters there are, in Scottish waters. Things unearthly that no mortal should know of. Now lay aloft. Get up them ratlines.'

The command came with no change of tone or expression and for a moment John didn't understand. Jabez jerked his chin upwards. Beside him the ratlines, rope ladders with rope rungs, ran upwards to a horrible height, ending at a platform halfway up the dizzyingly high mast.

John felt the blood drain from his face.

'Only one way to learn 'ow to get aloft,' Jabez said calmly, 'and that's to get on and do it. 'Ere, your face is the colour of old pea soup. You ain't going to be sick again? I seen you cast your dinner overboard.'

'No, I'm not sick now. It's just that I'm . . .'

'Fearful. 'Orrible fearful. As is only sensible, seeing as 'ow you ain't never been up no rigging in your young life before. Climbed trees, did you, back 'ome?'

'Yes. All the time. But . . .'

''Tis the same, only excepting that trees has a nice 'abit of staying still, while a ship, she 'overs and she bu and she skips and she dances like a demented 'orse. But you get used to it. Up you go. The wind's against your back her on the larboard side, pressing you into the ratlines. You couldn't fall if you tried. Get going, John. Growl you may, but go you must.'

John looked up at the rigging and back at the gunner's mate. Jabez's eyes were kind, but his mouth was set in a firm line. There was no help for it, John could see that. And it would be a hundred times better to go aloft for the first time with Jabez Barton than to be bullied and beaten up at the end of Mr Higgins's cane.

He took a deep breath, squeezed his eyes shut for a moment, then made a grab at the ratlines. The tarry ropes felt reasonably strong and solid. He stood for a moment on the hammock netting, learning the shape of the rungs under his hands and feeling the rise and fall of the ship on the swell, then he began to climb.

It's only a ladder. I'm only climbing a ladder, he told himself. I mustn't look down. Don't look down. Look at the ratlines. Look at my hands.

He was a long way up, and his breath was beginning to shorten with the effort, when he felt a tugging on the ropes beneath his hands and feet as the wind veered round to the south and the masts and sails took the strain. The ratlines seemed to lurch and shiver in his grasp. Whistles and muffled shouted commands came from below. Sailors were running about on the deck, working the ropes, loosening and tightening, manoeuvring the sails to catch the best of the wind. They seemed miles below, horribly far down. The wind had freshened and was plucking at his clothes, tearing the tails of his shirt out of the waistband of his trousers. He was hit by a blast of air that turned his knees to water and made his head spin. He clung tightly to the ratlines, unable to move.

Then, from just beneath him, came Jabez's rich, Devon voice, raised in song.

'Oh, a sailor's life is a merry life
They rob young girls of their heart's delight . . .'

He broke off.

'Ain't the moment for star-gazing, young John. The zun's still got a ways to go before 'e goes to bed. 'Twon't be till then that the stars pop out.'

'I . . . I can't go on,' whispered John.

But Jabez had started singing again.

'Leaving them behind to sigh and mourn,
They never know when we will return.'

Jabez had climbed a little closer. His voice was now coming from directly below John's feet. Its calmness steadied him, and he felt his courage creeping back. Almost without realizing, he began to climb again.

He was out of breath when at last he reached the platform. This was large enough to hold several men, and there was one standing on it already.

'Oof!' panted Jabez, stepping up on to the platform behind him.

The other man, who looked no more than eighteen or nineteen years old, and who was wearing a bright scarlet waistcoat, laughed.

'We don't often see you up here in these lofty parts, Mr Barton.'

'I should think not,' said Jabez, recovering his breath. 'Used to climb about like a monkey I did, when first I came to sea, but now I'm a gunner's mate, which is a fine respectable thing to be, and I leave the monkey business to the likes of you. This young lad John is what brings me up aloft. I'm showing him the way. Now, John, this gentleman is the captain of the maintop, and since we've been on the subject of monkeys, I would venture to state that there's not an animal in Africa as could run about the rigging more handily than him.'

As if someone aloft had heard, a shout came from above, and a moment later the young seaman was racing up the next set of ratlines. He was lost to view for a while behind the sail's billowing canvas, but then John saw a flash of red from almost the highest point of the mast. Men were still working right up there, spread along the yard of the topmost sail. To his horror, John saw the young maintop captain take off along the yard from which the highest sail hung. He was balancing on the swaying spar of wood as the ship lurched beneath him, with nothing for his hands to hold on to. When he reached the very tip he dropped down to straddle the yard and began to work at some invisible arrangement of ropes.

The sight of him had made John shudder, but it had done him good, too. The platform where he was standing, which a minute ago had seemed so horribly high and exposed, now seemed quite low down and safe.

'Mr Barton, sir,' said a familiar voice. Kit had appeared, swinging himself up round the outside of the platform with all the agility of a squirrel. 'Mr Tawse's compliments, and would you oblige him by returning immediately. Two of the cutlass cases have shipped water, and the cutlasses are in a shocking condition, Mr Tawse says.' He put his head one side. '"Done all to blazes,"' he said, in imitation of Mr Tawse's voice, '"and the devil's to pay."'

'Oh, here's trouble.' Jabez's broad forehead was creased now with a worried frown. He appeared not to have noticed Kit's play-acting. 'Rusting cutlasses!' He had already taken hold of the ratlines and was starting to go down. 'Get down below, you two lads, as quick as you can. 'Twill be all hands to cleaning and polishing. Rusting cutlasses! Very nasty.'

Kit had started to follow Jabez, but he looked up and saw John's face. At the thought of climbing down, paralysing fear had gripped John again. The ratlines looked horribly loose and insubstantial seen from above. The distance down to the deck seemed immense. The swell was rising and the ship was moving unpredictably, rolling as she came further round into the ever strengthening wind.

Kit scrambled back up again and stood beside John on the platform. He took hold of John's arm and shook it.

'I know how you are feeling,' he said. 'I felt it too, the first time, and many times after. Now I can go up and down like a monkey. You have to be like a monkey too.'

He pushed his tongue into his lower lip to make a monkey face, and looked so funny that John couldn't help smiling. 'I'll manage it,' he managed to say. 'It's just this bit, the first bit. Stepping out into . . . nothing – to get on to the ratlines.'

'Yes.' Kit nodded. 'I will guide you, hand by hand, foot by foot. Look. You do like this – your right hand here, right foot so, left hand takes hold of this one.'

John, watching carefully, noticed for the first time how small and delicate Kit's hands were, and how slim his wrists and ankles.

'Like that you will be fine,' Kit went on. 'There. You have done the worst bit. Now you just go down. Step by step. It's easy now.'

It was easy. John felt the safety of the deck come nearer and nearer and he jumped down the last few steps, bouncing triumphantly on the balls of his feet.

'I never thought I could do that. I never thought I'd get up there, or get down again,' he said, following Kit along the deck. 'You helped me. You really did.'

'It was nothing. You will be good at climbing, I'm sure of it. You only need to practise. The aptitude is there.'

John looked at him curiously. Kit had dropped his joking tone and sounded for a moment almost like an adult, a teacher talking to a pupil.

'How old are you, Kit?' he asked curiously.

To his surprise a vivid blush spread over Kit's cheeks.

'Thirteen,' he said. 'Come, John, we must hurry. Mr Tawse is in a temper already. He will be angry if we delay.'

PART TWO

APRIL 1808
THE BORDEAUX BLOCKADE

Chapter Fourteen

Anyone who had known John as the miserable, scrawny, twelve-year-old boy who had so unwillingly joined the crew of the *Fearless* would have hardly recognized him six months later. The thatch of straw-coloured hair that had stuck out in such an unruly way all over his head had grown long and thick and was now tied at the nape of his neck in a neat sailor's pigtail. He had passed his thirteenth birthday before Christmas and had grown hugely, both in inches and in weight. Hard work had developed the beginnings of fine muscles on his shoulders, arms and chest. His hands, as well as his feet, which were always bare, were knotted with calluses, and stained black with the tarry ropes he constantly handled. Without knowing it, he walked the decks with a sailor's roll and spoke in a sailor's jargon.

The *Fearless*, whose task it was to keep close guard on the mouth of the river Gironde, to prevent any French ships from entering or leaving, had spent the long months crisscrossing the river mouth, buffeted by the violent winds and sudden storms that blew across the Bay of Biscay. John had been vilely seasick at first, but that had soon passed.

He had learned quickly. With Kit's help he had soon

mastered the ropes (even to Mr Higgins's grudging satisfaction). A few weeks later, he could tie all the knots and splice a rope. By the end of the next month he could sew his own clothes and had proved himself a quick learner in the complex skills of gunnery.

The iron routine was soon drummed into him. Like the rest of the ship's company, he sprang to obey each order, knowing the harsh discipline that would fall upon him if he delayed by an instant. He scrubbed and washed, blacked the guns with tar and water and polished brass with brick dust. He was constantly bruised and buffeted, sometimes falling with an unexpected roll of the ship, sometimes receiving an irritated blow from Mr Tawse, or a much harsher thwack from Mr Higgins's rattan cane. He was used to the pain and discomfort, inured to the bitter cold and constant damp, and even relished the plain, often unpalatable food.

He was well acquainted now with those working closest to him. Mr Tawse, the master gunner, was strict, but fair. He watched over the great ship's weapons like an anxious groom over his thoroughbred horses, and any careless damage that came to them put him in a towering rage. He demanded obedience and respect, but he listened to both sides of an argument, and the boys had learned exactly how far they could go in tickling his sense of humour. John had learned to trust Mr Tawse and wanted his good opinion. He was afraid of him only when the grog took hold. The fumes of rum and water seemed to inflame the master gunner's temper, and he'd lash out over every small annoyance.

Mr Tawse was a man to respect, but John had learned to love Jabez Barton, with his kindliness and slow Devon speech. He learned far more from one hour of Jabez's quiet, patient teaching than from a day under the lash of Mr Higgins.

There were moments each day when he was almost happy.

These usually came after supper, when the ship's work was done, and from the tables nestling between the guns came the sounds of men at ease, sitting over their grog, telling stories, whittling at sticks, singing songs and reliving old battles, while the boys invented games and teased each other and wrestled.

But there were many more times when he was miserably sad. The sight of a seagull flying free towards the land, or a Scottish seaman's voice ringing out from among the great variety of English ones, would set off an aching homesickness. Then, every bit of him would long for Luckstone and his father. An empty, hollow feeling would settle inside him, a terrible loneliness, and not even Tom's banter, Davey's clumsy friendliness or Kit's quiet sympathy could reach him. The damp, crowded ship seemed like a cruel, floating prison. The permanent stench and complete lack of privacy made him seethe with disgust and frustration.

Often he was afraid. He had become used to going up aloft, faster than he would have thought possible. Shinning up the ratlines was nothing to him now, although sidling out on the ropes along the yards still made his stomach lurch in alarm, especially in the storms of winter, when the wind blew hard and the ship rolled and pitched on the swell. His first gale, when the ship was well out in the Bay of Biscay, had tested the nerves of every man on board. For two days the hatches had been battened down, huge waves had washed over the sides, soaking the hammocks, the decks had been fouled as every man had been sick, and as the ship had plunged down and reared up again John had thought time and again that his last hour had come.

The storm had been bad enough, but a jolt of even sharper fear shot through him every time he caught sight of the round, shiny, black hat of Mr Higgins, and saw the malice in the man's cold eyes.

Gradually, alongside all the other feelings that crowded in upon him, a sense of pride had found its place too. The *Fearless* might be engaged only in the unglamorous, routine work of patrolling backwards and forwards along the coast of France, but she was a great ship, a famous ship. She had fought under Nelson at the Nile and Trafalgar. She was a ship of the line. A man-o'-war. And he was a man-o'-war's boy now. He belonged to the *Fearless*. She was his ship.

But always, in the back of John's mind, especially after gun drill, was the knowledge that one day the *Fearless* would go into battle. One day a French ship would attempt to break the blockade and slip out from the mouth of the river, or would try to approach from the sea and batter her way past the *Fearless* to reach Bordeaux. Then her great guns would not boom out across an empty ocean, but would blast their deadly load of hot metal into the sides of an enemy ship, ripping away her masts and rigging, and the enemy would respond in kind. When that moment came, many would die. More would be injured. Limbs would be shot away, faces scarred for life . . .

I'm not sure I'm brave enough, he would whisper to himself, a sick feeling in his stomach. I'll want to run down and hide in the hold. But I mustn't. I mustn't even think of it.

'I can't wait, I just can't, to get another pop at the Frenchies,' Tom Todd said one day, as they all sat down to dinner. He was pointing an imaginary musket at an invisible target, making the others duck as he swung it round the table. 'When we took the *St Colombe* a year ago it was the best fun. Oh, John, you ought to have been there. You'd have loved it right enough, I know you would.'

'You've told him all about it before, Tom,' murmured Kit.

Tom ignored him, and swept his invisible musket round again.

'We closed in on her off Brest, passed her to windward,

shortened sails and hove to. Then – crash! – our guns gave
her a broadside, and a broadside from the *Fearless* is something no one will ever forget! She came back with answering
fire, of course, and – phew! But it was awful close! A cannon-
ball came *that* near to taking my head right off my shoulders!
And then we boarded her, and . . .'

'*You* didn't,' interrupted Kit. 'Mr Tawse sent you below
when the firing ceased. "Get below, you imp of Satan," he
said, copying Mr Tawse's voice so well that all the others
laughed. '"Dancin' about like a sandfly on a rottin' jellyfish."
I heard him. When you came back up it was all finished.
Anyway, it was not a proper fight at all, Mr Barton says,
because the French sailors were half dead with scurvy. Mr
Barton said he'd never seen such a sorry lot of poor fellows.'

'Poor fellows? They were *French*!' Tom's eyes sparkled
with scorn. 'Every one of them a Johnny Crapaud! Snails for
their dinner and the stink of garlic on them all! One
Scotsman's a match for ten of them, my daddy always says.'

Kit frowned and seemed about to say something, but
changed his mind.

'What do they do with the . . . if someone's killed?' said
John, as casually as he could.

'It's over the side and into the deep,' said Tom cheerfully,
tipping his arms in a graphic demonstration.

'But first they sew you nice and tight into your hammock,'
said Davey, coming suddenly to life. 'And down you go to the
bottom, and all the little fishies have a nice dinner. And
the crabs. 'Twon't happen to me, though. A fortune-teller
told me so. I'm to live till I'm seventy and marry a beautiful
dark-haired lady and travel to foreign parts and see signs and
wonders.'

'And you believed all that?' scoffed Tom.

'Yes. She said,' replied Davey simply.

'I'd rather be eaten by fish than maggoty old worms

anyway,' said John, who had been giving the matter some thought. 'Though not crabs. I don't like the idea of crabs.'

Kit, who had been mending the cuffs of Mr Tawse's best blue uniform coat, held it out to Tom so that he could cut through the thread with his pocket knife.

'You make me shiver with all this talk of fishes and maggots,' he said disdainfully.

The canvas screen moved aside and Nat Claypole's sharp, ferrety face appeared.

'Come to make trouble have you, Ratface?' Tom said rudely. 'Who are you calling thief this time?'

Davey looked anxious.

'Not me. I never took nothing. Been muckin' out the pigs all day.'

A nervous smile crossed Nat's face.

'I just . . . I came to see you.' He was eyeing the table of boys warily as he approached. 'Never said sorry to you, John, like I ought to. I know it was a long time ago. I was 'opin' you'd forgotten all about it. 'Twas Mr 'Iggins made me set you up. I knowed you wasn't no thief. I've wanted to tell you all this time.'

'What did he pay you, you wee swindler?' jeered Tom.

'Nothin'.' Nat slid on to the chest beside Kit. ''E's that mean, you don't know the 'alf of it. Give anything I would to be back in 'ere, messin' with all of you.'

'You should have thought of that before you went a-sneaking off to him,' said Tom severely.

'I know. I know, but I've paid for it. Look.'

He lifted his shirt to show his thin bony back. The other four took in their breath sharply as they saw the mass of welts and bruises that covered it.

'Beats me up for nothing, 'e does, all the time,' sniffed Nat, wiping a sleeve across his nose. 'His last lad, 'e couldn't take it no more. Jumped over the side one night, off

Yarmouth. Drowned dead before 'e ever reached the shore, I reckon.'

'The little fishies will be happy, then,' said Davey, looking almost pleased at the thought.

John had been watching Nat closely, saying nothing, as he tried to work out if the boy was sincere, or whether he had come on an underhand errand for the bosun's mate. But Nat's misery was unmistakable, and there was something like pleading in his close-set eyes as he turned his face towards John.

'Is there something you want, Nat?' John said, puzzled. He was unable to help himself feeling sorry for him.

'Yes.' Nat looked grateful. ''E's on about that satchel of yours again. The one 'e swears you brought on board.'

'My satchel?' John stared in surprise. 'But why? There's nothing in it. Only old stuff of my father's. And why has he remembered it now? I thought he'd given all that up months and months ago.'

'There ain't no satchel in Kit's chest now,' said Davey. 'Weren't one in there yesterday, anyways.'

The others turned on him accusingly.

'Davey!' exploded Tom. 'I'm warning you, I'm *telling* you. Next time you poke your fat fingers into someone else's chest I'll have you taken up for a thief. You'll be hanged from the yardarm.'

'But I haven't got a chest of my own, Tom,' Davey said reasonably. 'And I didn't *take* anything. I just stowed my little bit of mirror away. 'Orace likes my little bit of mirror. He likes to tap 'is beak on it. And it's like I said, there weren't no satchel in there. Where did you hide it, Kit?'

Nat stood up.

'I don't want to know nothin' about no satchel,' he said quickly. 'I don't want to know if there ever was one, or where it is if it's there. Mr 'Iggins would beat it out of me quick as a wink if he got a sniff of it.'

'Yes, but *why*?' said John.

'No point in asking *me*, is there?' complained Nat. ''E's a deep one, Mr 'Iggins. Very restless 'e's been lately. When that frigate brought letters a week ago, 'e received one that sent him into the vilest temper I ever seed. Beat me black and blue, 'e did, just because I dropped 'is second-best 'at and dented it. These last few days I seen 'im up on deck at night, with his dark lantern. More than once I seen 'im flashin' the light out into the dark, as if there was someone out there.'

'Calling up the mermaids, that's what he's doing,' Davey said knowledgeably. 'Beautiful girls mermaids are, with long golden hair. I'd like to see a mermaid.'

'Pah!' Tom elbowed him aside with disgust. 'Sounds like he was sending signals. Out to where?'

Nat shrugged.

''Ow should I know?'

'Towards the coast of France, or out to sea?' Kit had put his sewing down and was watching Nat intently.

'Not a bleedin' navigator, am I?' Nat said, aggrieved. 'In the dark it was, an' all.'

'Did anyone answer? Was there a signal back?' asked John.

'Not that I saw. 'Ere, there's the bell. I'd best be off to polish his shoes or 'e'll break my arm like he said 'e would.'

A moment later, he was gone.

Davey stood up and went across to the tiller beam where Horace was sitting, his head tucked under his wing. He began crooning to the bird and stroking his head. John, Tom and Kit sat and looked at each other in silence.

'I'll look through the satchel again,' John said at last, getting up to retrieve it from where it had been stowed, half forgotten, behind a bulkhead. 'There must be some answer to this mystery. There has to be!'

Chapter Fifteen

John frowned over the little notebook, turning its pages slowly. He had forgotten its very existence during the long months at sea. He held it up to his eyes, trying to decipher the crabbed handwriting and make some sense of the strange words and irregular columns of figures. He could see nothing in them at all. He put it down on the table and pushed it away from him.

'Here, John, can I take a look?' said Tom. 'Not private, is it?'

'I don't even know if it's private or not,' John said irritably, handing it to him.

Tom flicked through the few small pages.

'Och, it's all nonsense,' he said, losing interest. 'It's not even English as far as I can see. "Pont . . . fleuve . . . navire" – there's no making anything of it.'

Kit looked up sharply.

'You permit me to look, John?'

'Of course.'

Kit took the book in his slender fingers.

'But the words are in French! *Rivière, côte, ville*,' he said.

'And the names, they're of French towns. Look here, Verdun, Fontainebleau . . .'

He stopped and bit his lip, then looked up to see the others staring at him.

'I didna ken you could speak French, Kit,' Tom said, his normally open face suddenly closed with suspicion. 'I knew you were a foreigner, of course, but you made us believe you were Italian, or Spanish, or some such thing. Always wondered why you never spoke of your folks and your home. Secrets to hide, are there, Kit?'

The blood rushed to Kit's face.

'I never told you, or anyone, anything about myself, Tom,' he said. 'You believed what you chose. But my mother was as English as you are.'

'Was? She's dead, then?'

Tom was leaning forward, his nose sharp, like a hound on the chase. John, equally curious, was watching closely. In spite of Kit's humour and brilliant mimicry, John had always sensed an aloofness in him, an intense desire for privacy, which had repelled curiosity. Now, though, that a breach had been made in Kit's defences, the truth would surely come tumbling out.

The boy stared at them, his face defiant.

'If you want to know so much, I will tell you. My father was French. You don't need to look at me like that, Tom. I don't have any reason to love the government of France. My father was . . . he died in the Red Terror, after the revolution.'

'Oh ho!' crowed Tom. 'A duke or a marquis was he? An aristocrat? Did they slice off his head – whoosh! – with the guillotine?'

Kit's eyes squeezed shut for a moment, as if he had received a blow, and John gave Tom such a powerful nudge that Tom almost fell off the chest he was sitting on.

'You're an orphan, then, Kit?' he said, longing to know more, but put off by the blank, closed look that had settled on Kit's face.

Kit nodded briefly, then picked up the notebook. He held it close up to the swinging lantern.

'Words, numbers, letters, numbers – what *is* this?' He read on, muttering to himself, then suddenly turned and was about to say something when the ship's bell rang and the bosun's whistle sounded.

'All hands to gun drill!' came the command, bawled along the decks and down the companionways.

Instantly the boys leaped to their feet, the book was stowed in the satchel, which was poked back into its hiding place, the table was raised to the beam above and all four of them, along with the other six hundred men of the *Fearless*'s crew, had scattered to their separate gun stations, as cries of 'Cast loose the gun!' and 'Roll out the gun!' roared out from the throats of seventy-four gun captains.

There was never a moment to think during gun drill. The seamen, stripped to the waist, were working at top speed, every man in each of the seventy-four gun crews knowing to a split second of timing exactly what he had to do. While they worked, the ship's boys and the youngest marines transformed themselves into agile powder monkeys. It was their job to fetch up the gunpowder from the powder store, deep in the bowels of the ship. The task had terrified John at first. A false step on a companionway, a spark from a clash of metals – anything could set the gunpowder off to explode. The danger was so great that only one cartridge at a time could be carried up to the gun, and another had to be fetched from below for every firing.

On his first few gun drills, John had raced empty-handed down to the powder store fast enough, but once the gunner there had thrust a full cartridge through the wet canvas curtain into John's hand, he'd felt his stomach lurch with fright. On the return journey to the gun deck he'd held the cartridge out at arm's length, almost tiptoeing along, scared that it might at any moment blow up in his face. He'd soon learned. His slowness had made Mr Stannard, the captain of the gun to which he'd been assigned, snarl and call him all kinds of horrible names. John had become as agile as the other boys, tucking the deadly cartridge inside his jacket just as they did, and swarming up the companionways as fast as the best of them.

He'd even begun to enjoy the gun drill and take pride in his speed and nimbleness. He was used to praise now, instead of curses.

Today, though, there would be no friendly slap of congratulation on the back from Mr Stannard. John couldn't concentrate. He felt clumsy and kept stumbling. Once, he slipped on the orlop deck companionway, badly bruising his shins, and the crew had to wait ten precious seconds for his load of gunpowder, making them late to fire. Mr Stannard gave him a hard clout on the head for that, and the seamen let out a string of curses, but it didn't help. He couldn't stop his mind from going over and over again the words and letters in the booklet. He was heartily glad when gun drill was over at last and he could sneak back to the gun room.

Mr Tawse and Jabez were settling down to their daily round of grog.

'Ninety seconds between firings,' Mr Tawse was saying with satisfaction. 'It's a deal sight more than old Frenchy can do. We'll be ready for any of 'em as soon as they shows themselves out at sea. Give it to 'em for real, we will then.'

'When's that likely to be, Mr Tawse?' said John, his stomach tightening at the thought.

'How should I know, lad? Lookouts up aloft spied one of our frigates this morning. She signalled that a French warship had been seen approachin'. Wants to slip through our blockade and get upriver to Bordeaux, I shouldn't wonder. She'll come our way, if we're lucky, and we'll take her. Nice prize money handed out all round.'

'She'll be coming out of the West Indies, more'n likely,' said Jabez, cocking his head sideways away from Horace, who was lovingly tugging at the lock of heavy blond hair behind his ear. 'Could be gold on board. Time we saw a bit of action. Dreadful dull it is, lurkin' around 'ere, on and on, with nothin' to show for it.'

Mr Tawse set his glass down on the table.

'Information, that's our problem,' he said, wiping his mouth. 'Or lack of it. Bonaparte, 'e always seems to know what we're about to do. Gets everywhere, passin' on all our secrets with his havey-cavey spyin' ways. But our side, we never seems to know what . . . 'Ere, John, what's the matter with you? Swallowed a fly?'

An inarticulate cry had burst out of John. As if a candle had been lit inside his head, illuminating the dark places, he had suddenly seen what the meaning of the notebook in his satchel might be.

'Mr Tawse! I think I know . . .'

At that moment, Kit burst through the canvas screen.

'John, your book! It's . . .'

'A code!' they both said together.

'What is all this?' said Mr Tawse irritably, draining his glass. 'Sit down, you two. Hoppin' about like fleas on a dog's back. You make my head spin.'

John fetched out the satchel from its hiding place, took out the booklet and laid it open in front of Mr Tawse.

'We discovered – Kit did – that these words are in French, sir,' he said. 'And each one pairs up with a number. It was when you said just now about the frigate signalling us. They did it with flags, didn't they? You showed me the signal book, with a flag against each word. What if these numbers are like the flags? What if they stand in for words, French ones, so that spies could send messages in code?'

'You could write a long message if you replaced the letters with these numbers,' added Kit. 'I was thinking about it all through gun drill. If this really is a French code book, our side could read any secret messages of theirs that we find.'

For a long moment, Mr Tawse stared down at the crabbed markings in the booklet. Then he looked up, his brown eyes alert and serious.

'If you're correct . . .' he began. Then he slapped his hands down on the table. 'By God! If you're right – I'm taking this direct to Mr Erskine. No, I'm taking *you* to Mr Erskine. Hasty does it now, lads. Clean shirts and trousers. Wash your hands. You're going nowhere near no quarterdeck in a state to cause me disgrace. Jump to it! Come on!'

John was already pulling his clean clothes out of Kit's chest. A moment later, he was dressed and was washing his hands in the bucket by the table. Kit, who had turned modestly away, as he always did when changing his clothes, was ready a moment later.

Mr Tawse looked them over them critically.

'You'll do,' he said. 'Now follow me. And mind your manners up there, do you hear? No talking till you're spoken to. Respectful behaviour. No staring about like a couple of landlubbers.'

'Aye aye, sir,' John and Kit snapped out together, but as they followed Mr Tawse up the nearest companionway, John nearly laughed out loud at the way Kit was waggling his eyebrows and pushing out his lips, in exact imitation of the captain.

In his six months on board the *Fearless*, John had never once been on the quarterdeck. Though it covered nearly half the stern end of the ship, it was reserved for the officers. He had looked across at it often enough, from the fo'c'sle in the bows, and had looked down on it when he had climbed the rigging above. He had often seen Mr Erskine's neat, well-groomed figure, surrounded by young blue-coated midshipmen, and the shorter, rounder shape of Captain Bannerman himself, striding the quarterdeck in lonely, almost regal splendour, sweeping the horizon with his telescope.

John turned to Kit with a grin of excitement as they trod up the steps in Mr Tawse's wake, but to his surprise Kit didn't respond. He was clearly in no mood for acting now. His face was pale and tense.

A pair of marines was standing guard at the door at the far end of the quarterdeck, their muskets by their sides. They jumped to attention as Mr Tawse and the boys approached.

'What is your business here?' barked one.

'A matter of urgency for Mr Erskine, my lad. And don't tell me he ain't with the captain, for I know full well 'e is.'

The marine pursed his lips, but turned and tapped lightly on the highly polished door. A servant opened it.

'Master gunner to see the first officer,' he said disapprovingly. 'On "a matter of urgency", 'e says.'

The door closed, but it opened a moment later, and Mr Erskine came out. His one good eye opened wide when he saw the two barefoot boys standing awkwardly beside the master gunner.

'I hope it's important, Mr Tawse. The captain and I have matters to attend to.'

'I believe it is, Mr Erskine. John, show Mr Erskine the book.'

John fetched the booklet out from the inner pocket of his jacket.

'It's like this, sir,' he said, 'I've had this since I came on board, though I didn't know it, and it's already caused me some trouble, and I didn't know what it was, but I think I do now, sir. I think it's a code. It's partly in French, Kit says.'

The first lieutenant had been frowning as he tried to follow this muddled speech, but when he'd looked through the booklet he raised his eyebrows in amazement.

'How did you get hold of this?' he said.

'I . . . It's a long story, sir.'

Mr Erskine carefully shut the booklet and gave it back to John.

'The captain needs to hear about this immediately. You'd better come in and tell him about it yourself.'

Brilliant light from the setting sun flooded into the captain's cabin through the long rows of windows which stretched across the entire end of the room. It sparkled on the crystal glasses, the silver spoons and the polished surface of the great mahogany table, dazzling John and Kit and making them blink.

Captain Bannerman was standing at the table staring down at a chart.

'What is this?' he snapped, his ferocious jaw working.

'Sorry to disturb you, sir,' said Mr Tawse, a note of humility in his voice which the boys had never heard before. 'The lads 'ere 'as something to show you.'

'To show me? What?'

John felt a prod in his back as Mr Tawse pushed him forwards.

'It's this, sir,' he said, putting the booklet into the captain's hands.

Captain Bannerman flicked through it impatiently, then, his attention caught, he held it closer and his brows snapped together.

'A cipher, by God. It's a damned French cipher. How, in heaven's name, did this come to be in the possession of a pair

106

of scrubby ship's boys, and why haven't I been informed before?'

'Tell the captain, John,' Mr Tawse said, looking a little anxious himself, 'and mind you tell 'im proper.'

Hesitant at first, but growing in confidence as he spoke, John told his story again. Silence lay on the great cabin as he related the scene in the lawyer's office, and the captain's eyes under their mighty brows never left his face.

'And it's my belief,' John finished off, 'that my father gathered up this book when he picked up the papers from the floor where the wind had blown them, and accidentally put it with his own in the satchel.'

'Quite possible. Very possible,' rumbled the captain. 'Halkett's the fellow's name, eh? Scurvy Edinburgh lawyers. Trick an honest seaman out of the coat on his back if they could.'

John's voice faltered as he recounted Mr Higgins's attempts to get the satchel, and he dropped his eyes in the face of the gathering wrath in the captain's expression.

'What's this? My own bosun's mate? In some secret business with a French spy book? Mind what you're saying, boy. Is this the truth? Mr Tawse, is the boy telling the truth?'

'Aye, sir. I believe he is.'

The captain seemed about to explode into speech, but he drew a deep breath, tightened his lips and said, 'Mr Tawse, take these two boys out on to the quarterdeck while I confer with Mr Erskine. Not a word of this business is to pass to anyone else on board this ship, do you understand? Not a word, lads, or I'll have you in irons on bread and water for a week.'

A moment later, Mr Tawse and the two boys were out once more on the deck, the curious eyes of the marine guards boring into their backs.

'Mr Higgins isn't really a French spy, is he, Mr Tawse?' asked John. 'I don't see how he can be.'

The idea seemed incredible to him. French spies, he'd always supposed, wore masks and long black cloaks, carried daggers in their hands and looked like Spanish bandits.

''Ow should I know,' answered Mr Tawse. 'Besides, it ain't your business to think ill of your betters until the captain 'isself gives you leave.' But he spoilt the effect of this crushing speech by adding, 'I never did like the man. Never trust a fellow who ill-treats 'is servants, that's my motto. I'm right sorry that I gave Nat Claypole over to 'im whenever I see the misery in that poor boy's face.'

The sun had set by the time they were summoned back into the great cabin and the lantern had been lit above the table. John looked around the room, marvelling at its spaciousness, the portraits on the walls, the elegant tables and chairs and the colourful rug on the floor. The cramped, noisy quarters of the seamen on the gun deck just below the floorboards seemed to belong to another world.

'Mr Tawse, and you boys, John – is it? – and Kit.' The captain was addressing them from the chair at the head of the table. 'This is a delicate matter of high importance to the war, the safety of Britain, her king, her soldiers and her seamen.'

The solemnity in his voice brought goose pimples out on John's arms. He was listening with every nerve.

'You have done well so far,' the captain went on. 'You will be called upon to do even more in future. You understand, I take it, the importance of this little book?'

'We thought it might be a French code for writing in secret, sir,' said Kit, speaking for the first time.

Captain Bannerman's eyes rested on him.

'Good. You are the boy, are you not, who recognized that

this book was written in French? How do you come to know that language?'

Beside him, John felt Kit stiffen.

'My . . . my father was French, sir,' he said.

'Then your name is not, in fact, Smith, as Mr Erskine informed me?'

'No, sir.' Kit's hands were clenched tightly by his sides. 'I was obliged, for certain reasons, to assume a name that . . .'

'Your real name?' rapped out the captain.

Kit lifted his chin.

'Christophe de Jalignac. My father was the Marquis de Vaumas. He was guillotined by the revolutionaries before I was born. But my mother was English. She was the daughter of Mr Stapleton of Farnhurst Park in Surrey.'

John shot a sideways look at Kit, amazed at this revelation. Mr Tawse's mouth had fallen open with surprise, but Mr Erskine was looking at Kit with a puzzled expression, as if he was struggling to recall a memory.

'And how is it,' the captain said, 'that such a well-born young gentleman is a common ship's servant, not acting with the officers as a midshipman?'

Kit was looking more and more uncomfortable.

'My relatives are all dead, sir. I have no money, and no one to take an interest in me. I am content, sir, to be where I am. There are reasons – I don't wish any notice to be taken of me, sir!'

The captain shot him one more curious glance, then nodded his head and turned to John.

'You have realized, John, that a certain member of the ship's crew, Mr Higgins, the bosun's mate, in fact, has behaved in a manner to arouse our suspicions. It is highly improper for a boy to be privy to doubts about his superior, but in this case it is unavoidable. Lads, you are going to set a trap for our bosun's mate.'

'A trap, sir?' John's voice came out as a squeak.

'Mr Erskine, explain,' the captain said, with a wave of his hand.

Mr Erskine leaned forward, a smile lighting up the good side of his face.

'I believe you will enjoy this, boys. You will leave the booklet with me tonight, and I will make a copy of it. When I have returned it to you, you will remove from the satchel any papers you wish to keep and put the booklet back in it. You are to let Mr Higgins's young servant – what was his name? Ah yes, Nat – find it and steal it.'

'Steal it? But surely . . .' John blurted out.

Mr Erskine held up his hand.

'Listen, John. If the French believe that their code has fallen into our hands, they will change it, and issue new code books to all their people. Our advantage will be lost. They must believe that they have recovered the code book, and that its identity remains unknown. They'll go on writing messages in this code, and if any fall into the hands of the British, our secret service will be able to read them. Think what this means – the movement of the French armies, the secret orders of Napoleon, the positions of their ships at sea – what a gift that will be to our country! Now do you understand?'

John was grinning with excitement.

'Yes, sir, but how will Mr Higgins be able to return the book to the French, once he has it in his possession?'

'The boy Nat has told you already that Mr Higgins has some kind of signalling system in operation,' growled the captain. 'We must wait and see. If the rascal is working for the French, as we suspect, he'll make a move. And once he shows his hand . . .'

The scowl on his face was terrifying.

'Precisely,' nodded Mr Erskine. 'And in the meantime,

we'll send the copy off on the next British frigate that comes this way, so that our secret service can make use of it at once.'

The scowl had suddenly vanished from the captain's brow and a rumble of laughter was shaking the front of his white silk waistcoat.

'An adventure, boys, eh? But secrecy is vital. Mr Tawse, how many of your people know of this matter?'

Mr Tawse frowned.

'My mate, Jabez Barton, but 'e's a good man. Keeps 'is mouth corked up tight as a bottle when 'e 'as a mind to it. Tom Todd, he's a rattle but 'e weren't there when this came out. Davey, though . . .'

'Davey doesn't know,' said Kit. 'He was busy with Horace while we were talking. He can't have heard what we were saying.'

'Horace? Who the devil is Horace?' said the captain.

'Mr Barton's parrot, sir,' answered the master gunner tartly, 'and a plaguy bird 'e is too. Beak on him like a black-smith's pincers.'

The captain threw his head back and let out a roar of laughter.

'A parrot! I think we must trust the parrot. I will leave it to you, Mr Erskine, to ensure the silence of the marines at my door who will have seen and heard more than is good for them. Now, Mr Tawse, there will be speculation as to why you have made this visit to the quarterdeck, which will arouse Mr Higgins's suspicions when he hears of it. You must give the reason that . . . um, ah . . . Mr Erskine! A good reason, if you please.'

'The boys found a jewelled cravat pin that you have been missing, sir. It had fallen into the scuppers, and Mr Tawse brought them to return it to you in person,' Mr Erskine said smoothly.

'It will do. I suppose it will do,' said the captain, nodding.

'Now, Mr Tawse, that is all. I wish to know as soon as the booklet is in Mr Higgins's possession. Take these boys down. Oh, and, Mr Tawse, instruct the cook to make a sugared plum duff for them, and tell him to be lavish with the raisins.'

Chapter Sixteen

Ｉt was Mr Erskine's custom to visit and inspect every part of the ship on alternate days, so it was no surprise to anyone when he arrived the following evening. The boys were eating their supper at one table and Mr Tawse and his team of seamen were at the other.

Everyone scrambled to their feet and pulled their forelocks respectfully as the first lieutenant entered.

'Captain's compliments, Mr Tawse, and would you report to him after supper. He has some instructions concerning tomorrow's gun drill.'

'Aye aye, sir,' said Mr Tawse, his face blank.

John suppressed the desire to dig Kit in the ribs.

'What are you gapin' at, you perchful of gannets?' Mr Tawse barked across at the boys. 'Sit down and finish your porridge before I tips it overboard for the sharks.'

He disappeared soon after. When he came back, supper was over. Tom and John, tired out after their day's work, were yawning over a game of draughts. Kit was reading in a corner and Davey, with clumsy fingers, was trying to mend a rent in his jacket.

Mr Tawse paused by the table.

'Tom,' he said, 'have you worked out those calculations I set you yesterday?'

Tom jumped to his feet.

'No, sir. I'm sorry. I . . . I forgot, sir.'

'You *forgot*?'

'Aye, I did, sir.'

Mr Tawse swept the draughts pieces off the board.

'If,' he said, with an awful frown, 'you show yourself unfit to learn the noble arts pertainin' to good seamanship, I shall be obliged to set you as a servant to an officer, as I did to Nat Claypole. Nat would happily give up 'is position to you, I make no doubt of it at all.'

Tom's face paled under his freckles. He darted across to his chest and began to fumble about in it. John watched him, but turned as he felt a slight pressure on his shoulder. Mr Tawse was already moving back away from the table, but the booklet could now be seen half hidden under the draughts board. Casually, John picked it up and tucked it inside his jacket. He put the draughts pieces away in the box and took them across to Tom.

'Best put these away now, then,' he said.

Tom was anxiously scanning the pages he had withdrawn from his chest.

'Mathematics! It's all Greek to me,' he said with disgust. 'How's a body supposed to fathom the likes of this?'

He held out a blotched and crumpled scrawl.

'It's not so difficult,' said John. 'I'll help you with it, if you like.'

He went across to the stack of cutlass cases and retrieved the satchel from its hiding place behind them. Then he returned to Kit's chest from which he took out his own neat mathematical workings. He slid his mother's letter out of the satchel, stowed it safely in Kit's chest and slipped the sheets of calculations and the booklet into the satchel, which he carried across and laid openly on the table. Tom's head was already bent anxiously over his work.

'It's like this,' John said, leaning over to look at Tom's page. 'You have to calculate the angle of the gun's elevation and the distance to the target. Do you see?'

'No, I don't,' Tom said.

Patiently, John explained again, but his inner voice was saying, Come on, Nat. Come now.

Nearly an hour had passed. Soon the bell would sound and the order to fetch down the hammocks would be piped round the ship. John had almost given up hope of Nat, when Tom, whose mind had been flagging, looked up and crowed, 'Why, it's Ratty! What are you after this time, Ratface?'

Nat slid in through the canvas screen.

'Just came down for a bit, didn't I, to get away from 'im,' he began. Then he saw the satchel lying on the table. A flash of excitement, quickly suppressed, sparked in his eyes.

John stood up, deliberately turned his back on the table and went over to the bulkhead where Kit was still reading. Tom scooped up his workings with relief and took them across to his chest.

From the corner of his eye, John saw Nat hesitate. Desire and fear chased across his face.

Go on, John urged him silently. Take it.

But Nat didn't. He stood wringing his hands, then he coughed nervously.

'That's the satchel, ain't it, John? – the one Mr 'Iggins is lookin' for,' he said at last.

His openness took John by surprise.

'Yes. What about it?'

'John, I'm askin' you, I'm beggin' you, let me 'ave it.' Nat's words came tumbling out in a rush. 'Mr 'Iggins, 'e's on at me day and night. Won't give me no peace, 'e's that set on it. I could 'ave stole it from you, but I ain't no thief, whatever some people says. If you knew what 'e was like, if you could see what 'e does to me . . .'

He stopped, his voice thick with tears.

John pretended to hesitate.

'Why don't you just let him have it, John?' came Kit's voice from the shadows. 'You said yourself, there's nothing in it.'

'I'll make it up to you. I don't know how, but I will. I promise.'

John shrugged.

'I don't want that old thing, anyway,' he said, trying to sound reluctant. 'I just wish I understood what it was all about. What can Mr Higgins possibly want it for?'

''E thinks there's something in it,' Nat said, his narrow face relaxing into a rare smile. 'Something as is going to make 'im rich.'

John laughed.

'He must be crazy. If there were riches in it, what would I be doing on board this ship?'

''E *is* crazy! That's what I keep telling you,' insisted Nat. He sidled up to the table, grabbed the satchel and clutched it to his chest. 'You don't know 'ow much this means to me, John. I won't forget. Saved my life, you 'ave.'

A moment later, he had gone.

As John turned to hide his smile of triumph, he saw that Mr Tawse was watching him. The master gunner dropped one eyelid in a solemn wink, then got up and left.

The bell sounded, the shrill whistle of command blew and the crew hurried above to fetch down their hammocks.

'That was masterly, John,' whispered Kit, his face alive with a mischievous grin as they hooked up their hammocks to the beams. 'I never knew you could act.'

'You're not the only one,' began John. He wanted to say more, but found that something odd had happened to his voice, which had come out with a deep grating sound it had never had before.

'It's broken,' he thought, with a mixture of pride and embarrassment. 'My voice has broken.'

After the long weary winter months of blockade duty, as the *Fearless* tacked backwards and forwards across the mouth of the Gironde in all the filthy weather that the Bay of Biscay could throw at her, only the relentless discipline of the ship and the rigid timetable of watches, maintenance and gun drills had kept the huge body of men from growing mutinous with boredom.

News from home, letters from families and accounts of the progress of the war, came only seldom, when a British frigate appeared with news and renewed orders from the admiral. John and Kit had never taken much notice of the comings and goings of other ships, but they now began to scan the horizon for signs of a mast.

They were rewarded less than a week after Nat had taken the satchel. The wind being fair and the day fine, the crew had been ordered to the upper decks to wash their clothes. Soon every available space was full of tubs of water, with men working over them, and the rigging was a-flutter with drying shirts and trousers. John, looking up from the tarry stains he was trying to scrub from his jacket, saw that the frigate, which had seemed to be sailing past, was in fact fast approaching, her bows slicing through the creamy foam. He slowed down, spinning out the job for as long as he could, while the frigate hove to alongside the *Fearless* and a launch was hoisted out to fetch her captain on board.

He watched surreptitiously as the frigate's captain, resplendent in gold braid and a fine cocked hat, was piped on to the quarterdeck, and saw him disappear into Captain Bannerman's cabin. He emerged shortly after, a bundle of letters and papers under his arm, and was soon being rowed back to his own ship.

A few moments later, as he bent over the tub, John became aware of a pair of black buckled shoes and two legs clad in white stockings and breeches. He looked up into the face of Mr Erskine.

'Well done, boy. Keep scrubbing. Cleanliness for health and good seamanship, eh?'

'Yes, sir.'

Mr Erskine seemed about to move on, but stopped, and said, 'Do you take an interest in natural history, John?'

'I – not much, sir.'

'You should. The habits of birds, for example, are instructive to us all. You may have been aware that a rare . . . ah . . . an unusual foreign bird has been resting on this ship for some time.'

'No, I – oh *yes*, sir. I know what you mean.'

'This morning I observed that it left us and took up a new roost on the frigate that visited us just now. It will no doubt arouse great interest among the scientists when it reaches London.'

John was trying not to laugh.

'Will it, sir? How . . . how remarkable.'

His voice had embarrassingly plunged again, and he said no more.

'As you say, remarkable,' said Mr Erskine, smiling pleasantly. 'Carry on, John. Keep scrubbing.'

The wind from the south was balmy, although it was only April, and the clothes dried quickly in the spring sunshine. Putting his clean trousers on, John noticed for the first time how short they had become.

'They've shrunk,' he said disgustedly to Tom, who was tying his still damp red neckerchief round his neck.

'It's not the trousers. It's you. You've grown. Taller than me you are now. Only by a whisker, mind.'

It was true, thought John, as he shinned up the ratlines to help take in a reef at the command of the bosun's whistle.

The ship had needed more careful handling these last few days. The long, straight, flat coast of south-west France, with its endless silvery beaches and low sand dunes, had been a mile or more away, as the *Fearless* had stood well out to sea. Now, though, Captain Bannerman was risking her in the treacherous shoals and sandbanks nearer into shore. Skilful navigating and constant vigilance were needed, and the sails had to be adjusted all the time.

'What does old Sam think he's doing?' John heard a member of his gun crew grumble. 'He'll get us stuck fast in the shallows, if he don't mind out, so Frenchy can come and take a pop at us.'

'You shut your trap,' Mr Stannard snapped at him. 'Captain knows what he's about. Tides, winds, sandbanks – they ain't no mystery to him. He can see a lot further than the bottom of a glass of grog, which is more than can be said for you, my lad.'

He was more irritable than usual, but then, thought John, everyone seemed on edge these days. The long boring task of patrolling was wearing down both officers and men. Discontent swirled about the ship. The fine weather, which should have cheered everyone up, seemed to make them more frustrated at being pent up on their crowded, floating prison, while they dreamed of long summer evenings with lightly clad girls at home.

A crisis came a few days later when a sailor, ordered to clean up the lavatories, swore at a midshipman and refused to obey. All the ship's hands were piped on deck. The marines, bayonets fixed, lined the upper decks and gangways, and their drummer rolled out a solemn rat-tat. The sailor was stripped to the waist and tied to a grating. Then, under the eyes of the whole crew, Mr Higgins flogged him till his back was flayed with cruel, bleeding stripes. Though this was not the first flogging John had witnessed, he flinched at every stroke, and thought he would be sick. He wanted to turn away, but the officers were moving about among the crew, listening out for rebellious murmurs and forcing everyone to watch. He shot a look at Kit, who was standing beside him. Kit's face was so white that John was afraid he would faint.

Everyone was subdued after the flogging. There was no laughter or cheery talk on the decks that night, but no more open complaints were heard.

When John turned into his hammock, he found that he couldn't sleep. He couldn't get out of his mind the savage pleasure he'd seen on Mr Higgins's face, or the limp body of the sailor, who'd fainted dead away when at last they'd cut him down. He felt overcome by sadness and thought, for the first time for weeks, of his father. Where was the *Splendid* now? Was Patrick still on board her and, if so, was he safe? When would they ever see each other again?

He tossed and turned for a long time, then felt his stomach gurgle and knew he had to go to the lavatory. These were in the bows, at the very opposite end of the ship. He stumbled up the steps of the nearest companionway into the open air.

The moon was up. Clouds moving slowly across the sky parted for a moment, and moonlight, cold and white, flooded the sea and the empty sands of the French coast nearby. The *Fearless*, riding quietly to anchor, her sails hanging loose, was a lonely thing in a quiet world, where the waves, crawling lazily towards the beach, were all that moved. The only sounds were the gentle whistle of the breeze in the rigging and the water slapping softly against the ship's hull.

John shivered. There was something eerie in the scene,

some hidden menace that he didn't understand. He walked quietly to the bows and relieved himself. He would be glad to get back to his hammock.

Then, nearby, he heard soft music. Someone had started playing a fiddle. Looking round one of the ship's boats that sat on the deck, he saw a group of sailors, the men of the night watch, sitting together, singing and talking to keep themselves awake.

The moon had gone in now, the light had left the sea and the ship was in darkness, except for the lanterns that swung from the rigging. John was feeling his way back to his berth when something odd caught his eye. On the shore nearby, a light was flashing.

John frowned. There were no villages along this part of the coast, no harbours and no ports. Who could be out there, on the empty sand dunes, at this time of night?

On, off. On, off. On, off.

The flashes were regular.

It's a signal, thought John, his pulses quickening. Someone's signalling the *Fearless*. Who are they trying to alert?

He looked along the side of the ship. There was a denser patch of shadow where the edge of the quarterdeck rose above the waist of the ship where he was standing. He peered into it. Was someone standing there? He couldn't be sure. But then the dark mass in the shadow moved and John saw an answering flash as the shutter of a dark lantern was opened and closed, opened and closed.

He gasped with excitement.

'It must be Mr Higgins,' he breathed. 'He's signalling to the French again!'

He was about to creep forwards to try to see more clearly, when a hand came down heavily on his shoulder and another was clamped across his mouth.

'Quiet,' came a whisper in his ear. 'He mustn't see you.'

He recognized Mr Erskine's voice and his heart stopped jumping in his chest.

'Go back to bed,' the man said softly in his ear, 'and not a word to anyone about what you've seen tonight.'

Chapter Seventeen

The *Fearless* had slipped further south than usual from the mouth of the Gironde, the broad river on whose banks lay the great city of Bordeaux, thirty-five miles to the south, but early next morning she was hastening back, beating northwards on a freshening wind to resume the blockade.

John had been sent up to the fo'c'sle to help the sail-maker, who was sitting cross-legged on the deck, patching holes in the *Fearless*'s spare sails. The ship was rolling awkwardly, her sails half reefed, buffeted by the tricky currents that were even more treacherous at low water. John was just stretching out his hand for more thread, enjoying the warmth of the sun on his arm, when he heard the lookout at the masthead above call out, 'Sail ho!'

Captain Bannerman's huge voice bellowed out at once from the quarterdeck.

'You up there! At the masthead! What does she look like?'

'A square-rigged vessel, sir,' the reply came floating down.

'Where's she sailing to?'

'Out from the river mouth. Out to sea, sir!'

'A breakout!' exclaimed the sail-maker. 'A French ship

making a run for it! So that's why we've been lurking so far away. Making the enemy feel safe, luring him out, where we can nab him. That's what Thundering Sam's been at, you mark my words. He's a canny one. We'll see some action now, I don't doubt.'

He dropped the canvas he was holding and went across to the ship's side to take a look. John followed, but however hard he screwed up his eyes, he could see nothing but the shining expanse of tide-ripped water sparkling innocently in the morning sun.

'It's too far away still,' said the sail-maker, returning to his work. 'Only visible from up aloft. We'll see him all in good time. Here, boy, what are you doing with that needle?'

News of the French ship's break for freedom had spread like fire through the *Fearless*. Men from every part came crowding up on deck and stood staring out to sea, talking loudly.

'Silence, fore and aft!' Captain Bannerman roared.

John looked across from the fo'c'sle, and saw the captain standing, four-square and stocky, his hands on his hips, gazing up at the lookout on the masthead high above, while a group of officers trained their bristling telescopes on the horizon.

'Masthead! What do you see?'

'A large man-o'-war, sir. Bearing away to the west.'

The next command sent a shiver through John, and his heart started hammering in his chest.

'All hands clear the decks for action, ahoy!' bawled Captain Bannerman. 'Beat to quarters!'

The marines' drums rolled. Whistles sounded.

This can't be happening, thought John. We can't be going into a real battle. It must just be a practice, like every other time. But his sweating palms and tingling scalp told him otherwise.

The ship, which had been relaxing a few moments earlier in the easy-going routine of a sunny morning, had leaped to life. Every one of the six hundred men on board raced to their tasks with well-practised, silent efficiency. Within seconds, the spare sails John had been working on were rolled up and they, along with the sail-maker and his mates, had disappeared below.

John, darting below, found that already, in the last few seconds, the tables had been lashed up and everyone's chests had been taken down into the hold. Davey was collecting the pewter plates from the rack on the wall and stowing them into a packing case. Kit was looping up the canvas screen so that the whole gun deck was one long space, from the bows to the stern of the ship. Tom, who was almost beside himself with excitement, was helping Jabez lift down the musket cases.

'You stop that skitterin' about now, Tom,' Jabez said severely. 'No use you'll be to your king and country if you tires yourself out afore things hots up and the dashing about begins.'

But his was almost the only voice to be heard, as the crew, with no need of spoken commands, made the ship ready for the action to come. The gun decks were miraculously empty. Nothing, no tables or benches, no personal possessions or pets, no boots or jackets or hats, cluttered the bare boards now. At the far end of the gun deck, where the small cabins for the officers were ranged on each side, the flimsy partitions were being knocked out and their clothing, books, washstands and instruments were all being swept away.

John took all this in with a glance and leaped to his own task, which was to take down the canvas screens that surrounded Mr Tawse's tiny cabin and carry them below.

'What shall you do about 'Orace, Mr Barton?' Davey was

asking Jabez when came back. 'What if the battle should frighten 'im out of 'is senses?'

His voice wobbled anxiously.

Jabez shot him a measuring glance.

'You don't want to go worrying about 'Orace,' he said kindly. 'The Lord giveth and the Lord taketh away. If so be that it's time for 'Orace to give up 'is feathers as decorations in some fine lady's 'at, ain't nothing we can do to save 'im. You leave 'im be, Davey boy. 'Orace 'as been in more battles than you or I be ever likely to see, and 'e'll live through many more.'

'Fortune-teller told me I'd live till I was seventy and marry a beautiful dark-haired lady, Mr Barton. Do you think she was right about that?'

'Zed that, did she? Then it stands to reason there ain't no need for you to worry. Now you get over there and give Mr Tawse a hand with unpacking the cutlasses. And mind you don't cut yourself in half. Mortal sharp, they be, every last one of them.'

'John!' Mr Tawse called out. 'What are you thinking of, idlin' about there? Get up on deck, find the bosun and inform 'im with my compliments that the cutlasses and muskets is all in order to be issued to the men.'

'Aye aye, sir,' said John, glad of something to do.

The eerie emptiness of the gun deck below was in sharp contrast to the busy, crowded action on the open decks above. The *Fearless*, skilfully navigated through the sand-banks near the coast, was out at sea now, leaning into the wind, surging through the water. Dozens of sailors were still working aloft, crowding on every inch of sail, as the *Fearless* went in pursuit of the enemy.

John, darting about in search of the bosun, stopped in his tracks as he caught his first sight of the ship ahead. She was still only a small thing on the horizon, but even from this distance he could see that she was a great ship, a powerful, fighting man-o'-war, an opponent to be reckoned with.

'How long before we catch her up?' he asked the sailor nearest to him.

The man shrugged.

'Three or four hours, maybe. Captain, he'll outrun her easy. First time in action for you, is it?'

John nodded.

'You'll get through all right and tight. No time to think in a battle. You just have to do your best to be a hero and make your mother proud.'

John nodded. There was no point in explaining that his mother was dead.

Father would be proud, anyway, if he could see me doing well, or even if I just come out alive, he told himself.

The idea of Patrick witnessing a battle almost made him smile. He'd drop his musket, fall over, or get excited and start quoting from ancient tales of old. He pushed aside the idea that the *Splendid* might have been in action too. There was too much to think about just now to start worrying about his father.

The formidable figure of the bosun appeared through the crowd of men. John hurried up to him.

'The master gunner's compliments, sir, and the small arms are ready for issuing.'

He was rewarded with a grunt and hurried back to report to Mr Tawse.

It took only a short time to distribute the weapons to the men. The drill had been practised a hundred times before.

'What now, Mr Tawse?' John said, anxious for another task. Jabez answered instead.

'You shift along to join your gun crews, boys. Be brave lads now, and do your best.'

Before the boys had time to disperse, the bosun's whistle

twittered and the command 'All hands on deck!' echoed through the ship, shouted from man to man.

John and Kit hurried up together.

'John, listen,' Kit said, his dark eyes fixed on John's with painful seriousness. 'If anything should happen to me, if . . . Take my chest and what's in it. And don't be surprised at what you find. You might not . . . You'll think . . .'

He was struggling to find the right words, but before he could continue, Nat appeared beside them.

'Are you ill, Nat?' said John, noticing the sickly white colour of Nat's face.

'I'm scared. Real fearful,' Nat said frankly.

His small frame was shaking with shivers.

'I'm scared too,' said John, relieved to be able to confess it. He turned back to Kit. 'And if I don't make it, will you somehow get news to my father, on board the *Splendid*? Will you tell him . . . I don't know what – that I was thinking of him now, and all the time since we parted. Something like that.'

Nat beside him gave a mirthless laugh.

'Ain't no one to care if I lives or dies. Ain't no one I can leave no message for.'

They had reached the open space below the quarterdeck, where the whole crew was mustered. As the *Fearless* rose and fell on the long Atlantic swell, her expert crew using every trick to catch the wind and speed her on her way, John glimpsed the French warship ahead. She was a fearsome sight. Though still a mile or so away, the gap was slowly closing.

Captain Bannerman appeared at the quarterdeck rail and silence fell, as everyone looked up at him expectantly.

'Men,' he began, his great voice pitched at a rich low tone, 'we are about to go into battle. You have proved yourselves patient and diligent during these long months of blockade, and now you will be tested to the limits of your courage. Some of you are hardened warriors. Some of you have never fought before. But all of you must remember what we are doing here. The ship we are pursuing is our enemy. Those who sent her out to sea, and those whom you will fight, wish to conquer and subdue our great nation. Could we bear to see King George chased off his throne and Napoleon crowned at Westminster? No! Do we want our wives and children to be at the mercy of Napoleon's rabble army? No! Then we will fight, and fight like tigers! You are the finest body of men that I have ever commanded, and I know that you will nobly do your duty.'

A cheer that was more like a roar broke from the crew, and there was a rattle of muskets as the marines, massed in ranks on the quarterdeck, presented arms. Then came the sound of fifes and drums behind them. Everyone recognized the tune, and the words of 'God Save the King' rose from six hundred throats.

As the music died away, a strange elation seized the men. John felt it too.

'If Johnny Crapaud takes my head off with one of his cannonballs, I'll bequeath to you my Nancy,' the sailor beside John was saying to the friend beside him.

'I'll be too busy for women and all that malarkey,' the other laughed back. 'I'll be drinking down the money we'll get when we've captured this plum prize.'

The minutes ticked by. Slowly, steadily, the *Fearless* was closing in. The innocent morning sun lit up the French man-o'-war, glittering on the barrels of the many guns bristling from the sides of her massive black hulk. As John watched, her sails dropped and he could see her sailors climb into the rigging to furl them.

'Knows she can't escape old Thundering Sam,' said a voice in the crowd. 'Look at her. Making ready to stand and fight.'

The bosun's whistle sent the *Fearless*'s men racing aloft to take in her own lower sails, but then he saw no more, for the next command sent everyone down below to join their gun crews.

'If I don't see you again before it starts, good luck,' John said to Kit. His throat was tight. He wanted to say more. He had suddenly realized how much he liked Kit and relied on his friendship, but he couldn't find the words to tell him.

'Good luck to you too,' said Kit, shaking the hair back from his face. 'And you, Nat. You were wrong just now. I'll care if you die. So mind you don't.'

A smile broke over Nat's thin face.

'Oh, Johnny Frenchman can't kill *me*,' he said, with an attempt at a swagger, and then he was gone.

A strange feeling of unreality had come over John, but he was more aware than ever before of everything around him. He noticed as if for the first time the shifting patterns of sunlight reflecting off the sea on to the low ceiling of the gun deck. He took in the acrid smell of sweat from the six men in his gun crew, who were already standing beside their gun.

Mr Stannard was making a final check of the hand spikes, ramrods and shot of the gun. The men were in their usual positions, each one precisely placed, as if they were rehearsing yet again. The familiarity of it was steadying.

'All you have to do, lads, is remember your drill, listen out for the commands and hold steady under fire,' Mr Stannard said to the circle of grim faces. 'If I should fall, number two will take my place.'

A strange calm had descended upon HMS *Fearless*. No one talked much. The creaking of the ship's timbers as she floated to her destiny was all that could be heard.

Someone handed out cotton to stuff into the seamen's ears, to deaden the deafening crash of the guns. John saw the lips of several men move, and he guessed they were praying.

The young seaman next him was rubbing his hands, over and over, round and round, as if he was washing them.

'Powder monkey!' Mr Stannard called out suddenly. 'Go below for the first cartridge!'

John took off like lightning. From every gun a boy or a young marine was doing likewise, streaming down the companionways towards the powder magazine. John received the deadly package of gunpowder from a hand thrust through a hole in a woollen curtain, and stowed it with even more care than usual inside his jacket. A moment later, he had sprinted back to his gun and was putting it carefully in the salt box.

He could feel from the sideways rocking of the ship that she was drifting now.

We must be almost upon her, he thought, his heart skipping. It's going to start now.

Mr Stannard leaned over the muzzle of the gun to peer out through the gun port.

'Is she close, Mr Stannard?' one of the young gunners asked, nervously licking his lips.

'Aye. I can see her name too. She's the *Courageux*. That's the *Courageous*, I reckon, to the likes of you and me.'

Someone aloft had begun to sing, and one by one the gun crews joined in.

'You Frenchmen don't boast of your fighting,
Nor talk of your deeds on the main . . .'

But the words petered out as the gun captains up and down the gun decks began to call out their orders.

'Cast loose the gun! Run out the gun! Elevate! Load with cartridge! Shot your gun! Prime! Point! Make ready!'

The men jumped to obey in perfect unison, then waited, silent, their muscles tensed. John's ears were pricked. Every one of his senses was alert.

Boom! Crash!

The eerie stillness was shattered with terrifying suddenness. Then came a sound like iron hail rattling against the walls of the ship. From further down the gun deck a terrible scream rang out, as the first round of French shot, pouring through a gun port, took its first two victims.

'Hold steady, boys,' Mr Stannard said, his young face grim. 'Wait . . .'

'*Fire! Fire! Fire!*'

The command, shouted from one hoarse voice to another, ripped through the ship. The *Fearless* trembled from stem to stern as her guns roared out flashes of orange flame. Smoke drifted back through the gun ports, but John didn't wait to see it clear. He was dashing away already to fetch the next cartridge of powder.

From then on, he had no time to think or feel. Time after time the *Fearless*'s guns roared out, and time after time the *Courageux* sent back her deadly fire. The men at their guns had torn off their jackets and shirts and were working stripped to the waist, their bare feet slipping in the blood that was soon staining red the sanded floorboards. They worked like demons, cheering each round as it was fired off, ignoring the terrible damage inflicted by the French cannonballs, which were smashing holes in the sides of the *Fearless*, each one taking off a head or a limb and sending in its wake deadly flying splinters, as sharp as spears.

'Well done, my brave boy! Well done!' shouted Mr Stannard every time John raced back to him with another round of gunpowder.

John didn't feel brave. He felt nothing except for the need to keep running, to keep his gun supplied. He saw without taking in the terrible sights around him, the wounded men, the severed limbs, the blood running in the scuppers, and he barely heard the cheers, screams and groans. He was aware only of the regular pounding roar of the guns and the deadly answering hail of fire. He realized suddenly that he was speaking out loud, and found he was repeating, over and over again, the words of the Lord's Prayer.

'Our Father, which art in heaven . . . Our Father, which art in heaven . . .'

He stopped only once, when he bumped into Tom, who was running to supply his own gun at the far end of the ship.

'Nat's down,' Tom panted. 'I'm supplying his gun too.'

'What, Nat? He's not dead?'

'I don't know, but Kit is.'

The air seemed to spin round John's head.

'Kit? Dead? It's not true. It can't be true!'

But Tom had already dashed away.

'Move on, can't you? Are you hit, or what?' Another powder monkey was pushing him aside.

John nearly stumbled as he hurried back to the gun deck, and the terror that his cartridge would fall and explode drove everything else from his mind. But when he reached his gun he saw that it wouldn't be needed after all. A French cannon-ball had hit the gun's muzzle, rendering it useless, and its deadly ricochet had hit two of the crew, killing one outright and taking the left arm clean off the other. The remaining sailors were now helping to carry the injured man down to the surgeon in the cockpit below.

Mr Stannard was standing alone, wiping his forehead with a bloody hand.

'A horrid business, eh? Too many brave fellows dead. But grieving's a folly, eh, John? Grieving's nothing but a folly.'

John saw that his hands were trembling.

Kit, he thought. No, it can't be true.

He wiped his arm savagely across his nose.

'Listen,' said Mr Stannard, gripping his arm. 'Can you hear it?'

'Hear what, sir?' sniffed John.

Mr Stannard didn't answer, but a slow smile spread across his face.

'The silence, lad. The silence. The firing's stopped. It's over!'

John turned his head to listen. The gun captain was right. There was hardly silence, as the groans of the wounded rose from right and left, but the terrible rattle and crash of the guns and muskets had ceased. And now, from above, he could hear a ragged cheer go up, an English cheer.

'We've done the job,' Mr Stannard said, sliding down till he was sitting with his back against the wooden carriage of the gun. 'We've taken her.'

'Please, Mr Stannard,' said John, 'can I go below and look for my friends?'

The gun captain's eyes were closing with exhaustion. John didn't wait for an answer, but darted off as fast as he could.

Chapter Eighteen

John hardly knew where to begin in his search for news of Kit. The whole ship was in such a state of chaos that he felt almost lost even in the most familiar quarters. There were gaping holes in the sides where French cannonballs had smashed right through the *Fearless*'s timbers. Above, on deck, the sails were in tatters, torn to rags by grapeshot. Splinters and spars lay everywhere, and the decks were red and slippery with blood.

He was in too much of a hurry to look closely at the French ship, which now lay quietly alongside, but a quick glance showed him that her masts had been shot away and her rigging and sails lay half submerged in the sea. The French sailors, sullen and defeated, were being mustered on deck by gleeful British midshipmen.

Hurrying through the debris, stepping over exhausted men, John hunted for Tom. Tom had been the one who'd known about Kit. He'd know what had happened.

Instead of Tom, he found Jabez Barton. The gunner's mate, with a ruffled Horace clinging to his shoulder, was gathering up bloodstained cutlasses, which had been assembled in a pile on the deck. Though his face was blackened with gunpowder, his eyes brightened at the sight of John.

'Eh, lad, but you did well. I seen you in the battle. Up and down, dodging in and out, more like an imp of Satan than one of God's own creatures. You'll be the speediest powder monkey in the fleet, I'll be bound.'

'Mr Barton, Tom told me about Kit.'

Jabez shook his head sorrowfully.

'Aye, poor boy. A nasty wound in the shoulder. I zee him fall myself.'

'Where is the . . . What did they do with the body?'

'With the . . .' Jabez looked puzzled. 'Oh, you mean – no doubt they cast him overboard, John, down into the deep, like all the other poor brave fellows. 'Tis a dismal thing to think on, the end of a boy's life, for all 'e weren't naught but a skinny, sour, unhappy bit of a lad, but even zo—'

'Sour? He was never sour!' John said hotly. 'He was my friend. The best I ever had.'

Jabez looked surprised.

'Nat Claypole? Your friend?'

It was John's turn to look bemused.

'Why Nat, Mr Barton? Why did you say Nat?'

Jabez shook his head.

'I thought you knew. Didn't Tom tell you? How Kit and Nat was up on the deck where their guns was positioned? Well, Nat saw a Frenchy up in the tops aiming 'is musket, and 'e jumped right in front of Kit. Took the ball into 'is own 'eart, like the proper little 'ero we never knowed 'e was. Knocked Kit flying, but 'e saved 'is life. The next ball caught Kit, but only in the shoulder. Down in the operating room 'e'll be, I don't doubt. 'Ere, John, where are you going? You don't want to go down there. 'Orrible it is, the sights to behold down there.'

But John hadn't waited to hear end of this speech. He'd

taken off like a leaping dolphin and was hurtling down the nearest companionway towards the surgeon's lantern-lit domain in the dark bowels of the ship.

Even if he hadn't known where to find it, the cries and groans of the injured men would have shown him the way. He hesitated as he neared, dreading what he might see.

Mr Catskill, the *Fearless*'s surgeon, had set up his operating table at the far end of the cockpit. His broad back half hid the man who lay stretched out in front of him, but in the light of the lantern swaying overhead John could see that Mr Catskill had a saw in his hand, and that he was using it with all his strength on a man's arm. A whistling scream emerged from his patient's throat, in spite of the gag he was biting on, and there was a thud as the severed arm fell to the floor.

John turned away, his stomach rising.

One of the surgeon's mates, whose clothes were smeared with blood, pushed past him, a basket of rolled bandages in his hands.

'Out of the way, boy. What are you doing, humbugging around here, getting in the way?'

'I'm looking for a boy. Kit. Kit Smith,' said John. 'Is he here? He has a musket ball in his shoulder.'

A strange look, almost a smile of amusement, crossed the man's face.

'Oh, you want *Master* Kit, do you? Over there. In the corner. Nasty wound, but he'll do.'

Kit was lying in the quietest part of the cockpit, at the end of a long line of groaning men who were all waiting for the surgeon's attention. His face, even paler than usual, was contorted with pain, but he smiled at the sight of John.

John felt tears start to his eyes. Kit looked smaller, younger, almost like a little boy.

'I thought . . . Tom said you'd died.'

'No, but Nat did.' Kit's voice was weak and John had to

bend down to hear him. 'He saved my life, John. He was a hero.'

'I know. Mr Barton told me.'

'I feel so sorry that I wasn't nicer to him.'

'You were better than the rest of us.'

Kit shook his head fretfully.

'No. I will always regret—'

'But what about you, Kit?' John interrupted. 'Your wound, is it bad?'

Kit gritted his teeth as a shaft of pain shot through him.

'Not as bad as many here. There is a musket ball in my shoulder. Mr Catskill says he will take it out when he's finished with the amputations. It will hurt.' He tried to put on his Captain Bannerman face. '"You will be tested to the limits of your courage . . ."' he began, but grimaced and stopped. 'I'm scared, John. I'm really scared.'

'But the pain won't last long, Kit. And you're not going to die. You're going to get better.' John tried not to sound as if he was asking a question. 'When I thought you'd died, I . . .'

'You still here?' The surgeon's mate was back. 'If you're going to stay you can make yourself useful. Fetch a bucket, why don't you, and cart off all them amputated limbs. Then you can start scrubbing the blood off the—'

'No, no, I must go,' John said hastily. He wanted to touch Kit's hand in a farewell gesture, but was afraid of hurting him. 'Good luck, Kit, with the operation. I'll see you soon. I'll come back as soon as I can.'

'Not down here, you won't.' The surgeon's mate was still hovering. 'This little messmate of yours'll be shipped up to the sickbay soon as Mr Catskill's done his work. All nice and airy it is up there. All dainty and quiet.'

He went off at last, shaking his head and laughing.

'What's the matter with him?' John said, puzzled. He

looked down at Kit again, but Kit's eyes had closed and his lashes lay dark against his chalk-white cheeks.

John gratefully gulped in the clean fresh air when he came back up on to the open deck. The ship was already being put to rights. Sailors were swabbing away the sand and blood while others scrambled around in the rigging, lowering the torn sails. The French prisoners, guarded by marines, had been herded into their prison quarters below. The guns had been securely lashed, and fresh cannonballs were being brought up to fill the racks.

Nat, thought John. Nat Claypole. Who'd ever have thought it?

He could almost see Nat's weaselly face, his pale, sly eyes and thin down-turned mouth.

I only saw him smile once. Nobody liked him. Maybe that's why he was so mean.

He tried to summon up a feeling of grief for Nat, but instead he felt only gratitude. Kit was alive, that was the main thing. Kit had been saved.

The bosun's whistle sounded, and a joyful command rang round the ship.

'Up spirits! Splice the main brace!'

Casks of rum were already being brought up from below, and the seamen were gathering to get their ration. Someone fetched up a fiddle, another a flute, and as the sun sank down towards the silvery sea, the *Fearless* settled down to lick her wounds and celebrate her victory.

It wasn't until the middle of the next morning that John was able to visit Kit again. Mr Tawse had downed his grog the night before like a man with the thirst of a desert. It had set a kind of rage upon him, and the ship had rung to his curses. Everyone had kept out of his way. John, Tom and Davey had crept off to join their various gun crews, and John, slumped down with his back against the gun, had fallen asleep in the middle of a long rambling story Mr Stannard was telling about a mermaid he was sure he'd once seen off the coast of China. John woke early, stiff and sore.

In the morning, Mr Tawse had been like a wounded bear, growling and snapping at anyone who dared approach him, and setting the boys to start a new task before they'd had a chance to finish the first one.

It was Jabez who sent him off at last to the sickbay.

'Get you off now, John, and find out what that young malingerer Kit is up to,' he said, trying to sound severe, with one wary eye on Mr Tawse.

John shot off at once, darting away as fast as he could before Mr Tawse could call him back.

The sickbay was towards the bows of the ship. Hammocks were slung over the guns which took up most of the space even here, but the gun ports were open, allowing light and fresh air to penetrate round the sick men.

It took John a little while to find Kit, as his hammock was half hidden behind a bulkhead, away from the rest. Kit's eyes were shut and his face deathly pale, but he heard John approach and looked up at him.

'Have they done it yet? Taken the ball out, I mean?' said John.

'Yes.' Kit smiled weakly. 'Last night. It wasn't so bad. They gave me a lot of rum. Drunk as a lord, I must have been. I fainted anyway, so I didn't feel it.'

'Did they say . . . what did they . . .'

John came to an awkward halt.

'Oh, it's good,' Kit said, understanding him. 'No vital organ was touched. I'll be right as right as soon as the weakness passes and the healing goes on.'

John wanted to laugh aloud as a weight seemed to roll off him.

'I thought we'd got rid of you at last,' he said, grinning cheerfully. 'Thought I'd have all your things to call my own.'

Anxiety sparked in Kit's eyes.

'You didn't . . .'

'No, you great looby. I didn't look in your precious bag.'

Kit shifted, trying to raise himself, but winced with the pain and sank back.

'John, there is something I must tell you.'

'Tell me? What?'

Kit took a breath, but then said nothing.

'You can trust me,' John said, affronted. 'I can keep a secret.'

'I know, but . . .' Kit's face was filled with indecision. 'Oh yes, you are right, I know I can trust you. And it cannot be hidden any longer. Listen, John, you may not wish to continue being my friend when you know what—'

'A visitor, I see,' said a disapproving voice. John turned to see Mr Catskill, the red-faced surgeon, ducking his head under a low beam as he approached with Mr Erskine just behind him. John tugged his forelock respectfully.

'Go away, boy,' Mr Catskill said, with a mighty frown. 'I don't permit loafers here. This is a sickbay, not a theatrical spectacle.'

Mr Erskine coughed discreetly.

'Mr Catskill, I would not wish to countermand your medical rules, but in this instance, especially in the light of the matter we have just been discussing, I would prefer John Barr to stay.'

The surgeon's brows snapped even closer together.

'It's damned irregular, Mr Erskine.'

'Quite so,' said Mr Erskine tactfully. 'The responsibility will be mine.'

The surgeon continued to stare at him.

'You have asked me and my orderly to keep this revelation a close secret. Tell the boy what we know and the whole ship will be privy to it before tonight.'

'I believe not,' said Mr Erskine coolly. 'Now, Mr Catskill, if you please.'

The surgeon went off, shaking his head.

John looked down at Kit, whose face had flushed a dull red. He looked back at Mr Erskine and was surprised to see an amused smile lift the good side of Mr Erskine's ravaged face.

'Well now, Kit, how are you faring?' Mr Erskine was saying. 'A nasty wound in the shoulder, I believe.'

'Yes, but there is no danger. I will soon be well,' said Kit, trying again to lift himself.

Mr Erskine put a restraining hand on his good shoulder.

'Lie still. You did well, I hear, in the battle. You put yourself constantly in danger in the line of duty.'

'Not as much as Nat,' said Kit. 'He saved my life, Mr Erskine.'

'I know. It was an act of remarkable courage.' Mr Erskine leaned one blue-sleeved arm comfortably on the barrel of the nearby gun and assumed a conversational tone. 'Now, Kit, there is a problem that has been teasing me, and I'm sure you can help me to solve it.'

Kit seemed to relax a little, but a wary look had returned to his eyes.

'If I can, sir.'

'You told me that your father was the Marquis de Vaumas?'

'Yes, sir.'

'You may remember, Kit, at the time of our last conversation, that your father's name seemed familiar to me?'

'I . . . I didn't notice, sir.'

'I could not at first recall the precise circumstances of

142

how and when I had the pleasure of meeting your father, but it gradually came back to me. Your father was in London shortly before the revolution in Paris. I believe it was at the time of his marriage to your mother. We attended a card party together and conversed for some time.'

'Did you, sir?'

'I was saddened when I heard how he had died, so bravely and so young. His death seemed even more tragic as his wife was expecting a baby. After he died, she gave birth to his first and only child. A daughter. The daughter's name was, I believe, Catherine.'

John was looking from Mr Erskine to Kit and back again, trying to grasp what Mr Erskine was saying.

'You never told me you had a sister, Kit,' he said.

Mr Erskine shook his head.

'There was no question of a brother or a sister, was there, Kit?' he went on. 'Your parents had only one child. A girl. You.'

'No,' began Kit. 'You are mistaken, sir. I . . .'

Mr Erskine frowned.

'No more lies, please. You have deceived all of us for a long time – how, I cannot imagine. But you cannot deceive Mr Catskill, who, while operating on your shoulder, uncovered . . . that is . . .'

He looked disconcerted for once, and Kit blushed scarlet.

John's head seemed to spin.

'But that's impossible, Mr Erskine. Kit isn't a girl. He's a . . .'

But the words died on his lips. He saw in an instant of complete revelation that Mr Erskine was speaking the truth. Kit was a girl! He knew it at once and absolutely.

A hundred small things which had puzzled him in the past crowded through his mind. He had often wondered why it was that Kit had remained so small and slight while the other boys were growing tall, broadening out and developing magnificent new muscles on their arms and shoulders. He had never understood, either, why Kit had always been so modest, turning away from the others when he undressed, creeping to the lavatories only at the quietest moments. He had always hung back, too, when the others had wrestled, slipping quietly away to avoid a challenge, not seeming to care for Tom's taunts and jeers.

He even walks like a girl, John thought, the revelation filling him with disgust. He moves like one.

It was almost worse than losing his friend in battle. This discovery was not only a loss. It was a betrayal too.

'*Why?*' he burst out angrily. 'Why did you do it – pretend to be a boy? Why didn't you *tell* me?'

'I tried to just now,' Kit said pleadingly. 'I've wanted to so many times. I couldn't. This secret, it is like a terrible burden. You would have had to carry it too. You would have treated me differently if you'd known. It would have been even more dangerous – for both of us.' He turned to Mr Erskine. 'Is it . . . a very serious crime, Mr Erskine, to be a girl?' Kit said anxiously. 'Will I be flogged, or just put in irons?'

'Neither,' Mr Erskine said, 'but you will be required to tell the whole truth, and explain yourself to the captain as soon as you are strong enough to leave Mr Catskill's care. For the time being, you will stay here and you will not talk to anyone. And you, John, you will keep this matter to yourself. Do you understand? No word of this must pass your lips. Now, I believe we have trespassed on the patience of our good surgeon for long enough. Get back to your quarters. As for you, mademoiselle, I wish you a speedy recovery.'

PART THREE

JUNE 1808
LANDFALL IN FRANCE

Chapter Nineteen

In the following days, Tom and Davey hardly dared say a word to John, and even Jabez treated him warily. John, was so sore and angry that he snapped like an enraged dog at anyone who came near him. Davey didn't seem to take much notice, but Tom was so provoked that he and John ended by having a fight, punching and wrestling and rolling about on the floor. Luckily Mr Tawse was not there to see them, or punishment would have been swift and severe.

The fight did John good, relieving some of his rawness, and as Tom bore no grudges they were just as good friends afterwards.

John felt Kit's absence keenly. Time after time, when he'd been unhappy, Kit's play-acting had made him laugh himself out of his misery. At other times, Kit's quiet subtle sympathy had braced him through the worst of bad days. They'd shared their food and belongings, lightened each other's work, laughed at, liked and disliked the same people on the ship.

And it was all lies. All deception! he kept telling himself. I'll never trust anyone else, as long as I live.

He didn't attempt to visit Kit again.

''Ow's the invalid, then, John? I'm sure you'll have sent to enquire,' Jabez asked him affably when nearly a week had passed.

John shrugged.

'I don't know, Mr Barton. Mr Catskill doesn't like visitors.'

'John and Kit, they've quarrelled,' remarked Davey suddenly, with a flash of unexpected perception.

'We have not! What do you know about anything anyway?' flared John. Then he stalked away to take refuge with Mr Stannard and his gun crew, who were readying themselves for the next drill.

The *Fearless* had resumed the blockade of the French coast. She was towing the *Courageux* until a British frigate came to take the stricken French ship to England. There she would be refitted, and start a new life under British colours, while the French crew would be sent to languish in British prisons. In the meantime, most of the *Fearless*'s marines were on board the *Courageux*, keeping her sailors under close guard. M. Dupré, the *Courageux*'s captain, though also a prisoner, had been given comfortable quarters on board the *Fearless*, and was being courteously entertained by Captain Bannerman. The two of them, who a few days earlier had been trying to blow each others' ships out of the water, could now be seen walking the quarterdeck each morning, labouring to maintain a polite conversation.

Kit left the sickbay when ten days had passed. Tom and Davey greeted the slight figure with loud whoops of welcome.

'Thought you was going to die, Kit,' Davey said cheerfully. 'Thought old Frenchy had done for you.'

'Show us the scar, then, Kit,' said Tom, reaching out to pull Kit's shirt away from his shoulder.

Kit flinched, blushed and pulled away.

'You will not see anything. There is still a bandage.'

John had turned away and was staring out to sea through an open gun port, his shoulders hunched. Kit looked across at him, started to say something, thought better of it and went to open her chest.

'Eh, Kit lad, 'tis good to zee you back again,' said Jabez, who had approached with an armful of muskets to be cleaned. 'Still a bit peaky, ain't you? Time you growed and filled out a bit, like them other lads. Nice bit o' salt pork there is for dinner today. We'll cut you off a good big hunk. Feeding up, that's what you do need.'

Before he could say more, a seaman poked his head round the canvas screen.

'John Barr and Kit Smith to report to Mr Erskine on the quarterdeck. I don't know what you done, lads, but 'e wants you up there sharpish.'

John's stomach lurched. A summons to the quarterdeck would fill anyone with dread. He hastily tugged his jacket down, then spat on his hands and smoothed his thick unruly hair. He hurried off, his expression set, not wishing to speak to Kit. Kit hurried after him and laid a hand on John's arm. John roughly shook it off.

'John, listen,' Kit said desperately, 'please. You must listen. I'm sorry, I . . .'

'Nothing to be sorry about,' John said curtly. 'You made your decision that you wouldn't trust me. I've made mine that I can't trust you.'

He ran on, taking the next companionway in a couple of leaps. Glancing back, he saw that Kit was struggling to follow, but being still weak from her wound, was pale and sweating with the effort, holding an arm close to the wounded shoulder, which was clearly still painful.

John felt a small stab of sympathy and guilt, but shook it off and hurried on.

It was a fine, fresh morning. The *Fearless* was beating a

tack into the wind, hampered by the drag of the *Courageux* in tow behind her, but still making good headway. The sun was already hot. It sparkled on the black polished guns that lined the open quarterdeck, and whitened to an even paler sheen the bare scrubbed boards underfoot. It was spacious up here, quiet, uncluttered and open, so unlike the cramped, stinking, obstacle-strewn quarters below that John couldn't help squaring his shoulders and breathing in deeply, in spite of his anxiety.

Captain Bannerman, with Mr Erskine beside him, was peering through his telescope at the coast of France, but he heard the boys approach and snapped his telescope shut.

'Come here, you pair of rascals,' he boomed, and John couldn't tell whether his tone was jovial or angry. 'Into the cabin with you!'

It was the second time that John had been in the *Fearless*'s great cabin, but its luxury and elegance still almost overwhelmed him. His eyes flew at once to the figure of the French captain, a tall man wearing a strange uniform, who was staring out of the window with his hands clasped behind his back.

The captain and first lieutenant sat down at the table.

'What's all this I hear?' thundered the captain suddenly, the loudness of his voice making John jump. 'A masquerade on my ship? A deception under our very noses? The truth, if you please. All of it.'

'Wh – what do you wish to know, sir?' stammered Kit, who was ashen-faced and trembling.

Mr Erskine coughed discreetly, caught the captain's eye and nodded towards Captain Dupré.

'Ah, yes.' Captain Bannerman drummed his fingers thoughtfully on the table. 'Captain Dupré will no doubt find this unusual business interesting. However, boys – that is, both of you – there are certain matters which we discussed earlier to which we will not refer. Do I make myself clear?'

'Aye aye, sir,' Kit and John said together.

'Now.' The Captain was glaring at Kit. 'Your story. And you had better convince us that you are telling the truth.'

Kit swallowed, swayed and grasped the back of the chair in front of her for support.

'My father,' she began, 'was, as I believe I told you, sir, the Marquis de Vaumas. When the revolutionaries began to arrest all the aristocrats, he was caught and taken to Paris.' She stopped and glanced fearfully at the rigid back of Captain Dupré, who did not appear to have noticed that anyone else was in the room. 'He was executed there six months before I was born. My mother, being English, felt safer. She managed to hide from the mobs, and she was never caught. She stayed in the country to give birth to me, but a month later she caught a fever. I think my father's death affected her very greatly. She died.'

'So you never knew either of your parents?' said Mr Erskine.

'No, sir.'

'Who cared for you?'

'My mother's English nurse, Betsy. It was dangerous for her. If it had been known that she was looking after the child of an aristo—'

'Yes, yes, we understand all that,' said Captain Bannerman impatiently.

'My father's brother took the title of marquis when my father died,' Kit went on. 'He and my grandmother ran away to Switzerland, where they were safe from the revolutionaries.'

'Why didn't they take you with them?'

A brief smile lit Kit's face, and faded almost at once.

'I think they believed I would not survive. My uncle was

very sorry when I did. The estates, the land, the chateaux, all of it – well, it was inherited by me, sir. He felt it should all belong to him.'

Captain Dupré had turned, and now he spoke for the first time.

'*En effet*, Mlle de Jalignac is from her birth a very great heiress,' he said. 'That is, she would have been, if the honest citizens of revolutionary France had not redistributed her property.'

John couldn't tell from his tone if he approved of the citizens or not.

'I do not think I have any property left to me now,' Kit said. 'The mob invaded our chateau and took everything of value when my father was arrested. My uncle is my guardian. He was supposed to look after my affairs for me, but I believe, that is, I am certain, that he has been . . . well, robbing me all this time.'

'Where is this chateau? Where is your family's property?' asked Mr Erskine.

'Near Bordeaux, sir. Very near to where we are now.'

She swayed slightly as she spoke and briefly shut her eyes. John saw that she was paler than ever, and feared she was about to faint. In spite of his resentment, he couldn't help putting out a hand to steady her.

'Mr Erskine!' trumpeted the captain. 'Why are you keeping this young person on her feet? A chair, if you please!'

Kit slid into the chair Mr Erskine drew out for her. He poured a glass of wine from the carafe on the table and she sipped it gratefully. With each small action, the boy that John had known, the boy that Kit had so brilliantly acted, shrank before his eyes and a new person, a girl, began to take shape and form. There was no real difference in her outward appearance. The girl, Catherine, still wore the old Kit's rough canvas trousers and short blue jacket, but they looked odd now to John, as if all this time she had been wearing a theatrical costume.

John's anger was beginning to subside and he found he was waiting eagerly for the next part of Kit's story.

'So you grew up in France, in the care of this Betsy, your English nurse?' Mr Erskine prompted her. 'That will explain, perhaps, why you speak English so well.'

Kit nodded, and took another sip of wine.

'Only until I was eight years old. By then the revolution was at an end and Napoleon had taken power in France. My grandmother and uncle returned from Switzerland. They visited the family chateau, but it was too ruined for their liking. In any case, they disliked the countryside. They preferred to live in Paris, where my uncle, that is . . .'

She stopped, embarrassed.

'The Marquis de Vaumas,' remarked Captain Dupré, addressing the ceiling as if he was talking to himself, 'is well known in all of Paris to be like a little dog – 'e runs, 'e runs after the men in power. Always 'e is trying to make 'imself rich. And not always by honesty.' He dropped his eyes and looked at Kit. 'It is a great tragedy, mademoiselle, that your esteemed father came so early to such a sad death. France lost a good son, and you a noble father.'

Under John's shocked, embarrassed eyes, Kit burst into tears. She tried to control them, but could not, and dropped her face into her hands while her shoulders shook with sobs.

The effect on the men surrounding her was immediate. Captain Bannerman cleared his throat, gave a loud, embarrassed 'Harrumph', produced a handkerchief from his pocket and blew his nose vigorously. Captain Dupré shook his head sorrowfully, and murmured, '*Pauvre petite, pauvre petite,*' over and over again. Mr Erskine, more practical than the others, pulled his own handkerchief out of his sleeve and pressed it into Kit's hand.

'Your emotion is understandable,' he said firmly, 'but we are busy men, Catherine, and we are waiting. Please compose yourself and proceed.'

This bracing speech had its desired effect. Kit hiccupped, and made a valiant effort to calm herself. John's own feelings struggled inside him as he watched Kit master hers. His resentment had quite gone now. The loneliness and desperation in Kit's small, crumpled figure had touched him in a way his old friend Kit could never have done. He was ashamed now of the way he had rejected her, and wanted to make amends. He bent down and whispered in her ear, hardly knowing what he was saying, 'You'd best stop crying or you'll flood the captain's cabin and spoil his carpet. You'll be on bread and water for a week.'

Kit gave a watery smile and looked up at John gratefully. She swabbed her cheeks with Mr Erskine's handkerchief, wiped her nose and handed it back to him. Mr Erskine took it between his thumb and forefinger and dropped it on the table.

'I'm very sorry,' Kit said. 'I didn't mean to cry. It was what you said, sir, about my father.'

'Yes, well, never mind that,' Captain Bannerman said loudly. 'Don't start the taps flowing again, for God's sake. Your tale, miss, if you please. This ship doesn't run itself.'

Kit sat up straight.

'To be brief, sir, last year, when I was twelve years old, my grandmother told me that I was to be betrothed to my uncle's son.'

The captain's eyebrows rose.

'Betrothed? So young?'

'Yes, sir. In France, it is possible to marry very young. My cousin, she was wed when she was twelve.' Captain Bannerman muttered something inaudible. Kit looked questioningly at him, and he nodded at her to carry on. 'If I'd submitted, and been betrothed to my cousin, my uncle would have had legal control over my inheritance, which up to now he has been enjoying only illegally.'

'Ah –' Mr Erskine nodded – 'I begin to understand.'

'I refused absolutely.' Kit shuddered. 'My cousin Hubert is only seventeen years old, but he is already known for his vile temper and cruelty. Once I saw him kill his own horse when the animal displeased him. He—'

'Yes, yes, the boy's a brute and you refused him. Very understandable,' interrupted Captain Bannerman. 'But that was not, I take it, the end of the matter?'

'No, sir. My grandmother and my uncle tried every means to force me to accept. I was beaten, starved, locked in a dark cupboard and – well, many other things. I tried to write to my mother's family in England, but by that time England and France were at war and the postal service was suspended. While I was looking for a way to send my letter, my grandmother found it. Her anger was so terrible that I decided I had to run away.'

'And why in heaven's name did you choose to run away to sea? To dress as a boy, fight against your own country, submit to the hard life of a sailor and endanger your life in battle?' demanded Captain Bannerman. 'It's a fate which most sensible men will run a hundred miles to avoid.'

'I did not choose it, sir. Betsy, she . . . well, she has a cousin who – I hope I do not betray him, sir, – who deals in contraband wine and brandy. He has friends on the coast near here, at a village called Lacanau. He comes secretly in his little boat, fetches off barrels and transports them to the coast of Kent.'

'In short, the fellow's a damned smuggler,' growled the captain.

'Yes, sir. Betsy asked him to smuggle me to England. To make my escape from the chateau and my journey to the coast easier, she borrowed boys' clothes and dressed me in them. She took me to the beach at Lacanau and I went out to sea with the smugglers. But before we could land in Britain, we were stopped by a British naval vessel, and all of us were pressed into the navy.'

'Why didn't you reveal your true identity to the recruiting officer?' asked Mr Erskine, puzzled.

'I was afraid.' Kit looked down. 'Perhaps it was foolish of me, but I had heard how sailors treat young women. I did not think my story would be believed. On the receiving ship, some of the men were very drunk, sir. To have shown myself to be a girl – I didn't dare. Acting has always come easily to me. I believed I could assume the character of a boy without detection. And then, when I had been assigned to the *Fearless*, and had become servant to Mr Tawse, I saw that I could be safe here. This ship is famous in the fleet for the justice of its captain and the happiness of the crew.'

John glanced at her, wondering if she was merely trying to flatter Captain Bannerman, but she was looking down at her hands, her expression perfectly serious, and speaking no more than the truth.

'Carry on, miss,' Captain Bannerman blustered. 'No need for all that,' but John could see that he was pleased.

'I knew,' Kit went on, 'that no one would think to look for me here. It was the safest place for me to be. After all, even if I had reached England, I did not know if my English relatives would be any kinder to me than my French ones. But here – Mr Tawse and Mr Barton – they truly care for the boys and treat them well. It is only a few months till my fourteenth birthday. By the terms of my father's will, I will be independent then, and able to decide my own fate. If there is anything left of my inheritance, after the years of my uncle's guardianship, it will come to me. I planned to keep myself concealed on the *Fearless* until then. I have done my work as well as I could, sir. Mr Tawse has never complained of me.'

Captain Dupré leaned forward.

'Your story, mademoiselle, is very affecting, but there is one thing that I cannot understand. By joining the Royal Navy, you have taken up arms against your own country. You are a Frenchwoman. 'Ow is it that you permit yourself to fight on the side of France's enemy against your own *patrie*?'

Kit frowned, and the flash in her eyes took John by surprise. He had known Kit to be quiet and pensive, and at other times cheekily comical, but he had never seen aristocratic haughtiness in her face before.

'I am not fighting against France, a country which I love, but against Napoleon Bonaparte, the warmonger that rules her!' she declared. 'In any case, I have no reason to be loyal to my *patrie*, as you call it. My father was murdered. My mother died of grief. My uncle has robbed me and my grandmother wants to marry me to a monster. I wish only for peace between the countries of my parents, but that will never be while Napoleon wages war. I wish for England to defeat him, and then I wish for France to be at peace and to be happy.'

'Well said, miss! Well said!' shouted Captain Bannerman, clapping his hands with delight and shooting a triumphant glance across the polished mahogany table at Captain Dupré, who was frowning down at the backs of his hands as if he had suddenly discovered a blemish on them. 'And now, young lady, what are we going to do with you, eh, eh?'

'Please, sir.' Kit was twisting her hands together. 'I would prefer it if I could be Kit Smith again, and go on as Mr Tawse's servant.'

The captain pondered, puffing out his red cheeks.

'Stay on board you must, for the time being, as there's no means of getting you off, but females on my ship is what I can't abide. Trouble follows the petticoats like night follows day. No, no. Not another word. Sooner or later a frigate will come with our orders, and it will take the *Courageux* in tow to England. We'll pack you off in her, send you home to England and put you in charge of your mother's people. You can learn your music and work at your embroidery like a decent young woman should.'

'But, sir . . .'

'Enough!' roared Captain Bannerman. 'Marquis's daughter you may be, you grubby little powder monkey, but under my discipline you remain, do you hear?'

His face was becoming alarmingly red, but before he could continue, there was a scratching at the door. A marine entered, saluted smartly and said, 'Bosun's mate to see the cap'n. Mr Higgins requests a word.'

The ire in the captain's eyes died instantly. He whistled softly and looked across at Mr Erskine.

'Requests a word, eh? The devil he does. Tell him he can wait.'

Mr Erskine stood up and said smoothly to Captain Dupré, 'Would you oblige us by stepping outside, sir? It's a fine morning, is it not, for a stroll about the quarterdeck?'

Captain Dupré lifted a sardonic eyebrow.

'You are very polite, monsieur, but to a prisoner such as myself a request is of course an order.'

He gave a small bow and went out.

'And you two,' the captain said, pointing in turn to John and Kit. 'Out.'

'Excuse me, sir.' Mr Erskine lifted a hand. 'If Higgins sees them – especially John Barr – here in your cabin, will his suspicions not be aroused? He may suspect that we know of the whole business with the satchel and the code book.'

'Sharp of you, Mr Erskine,' the captain rumbled. 'What's to be done with them, eh?'

'Nothing for it, sir, but to stow them in your sleeping cabin.'

Captain Bannerman's massive eyebrows bristled.

'Powder monkeys in my sleeping cabin? Oh very well, Mr Erskine. Since there's no help for it.' He wagged a meaty forefinger at John and Kit. 'You touch anything, or make a noise, or shuffle about, and I'll have you flogged round the fleet do you hear?'

'Aye aye . . .' began John, but before he could add 'sir' Mr Erskine had already opened the door at the side of the great cabin and pushed them both inside.

Chapter Twenty

It was dark in the sleeping cabin. Even in here, the captain's inner sanctum, half of the space was taken up by a great twelve-pounder gun on its heavy wooden cradle. Only a little light penetrated round the edge of the closed gun port, and by it John could see a box-like bed slung from the rafters. Catherine had already seated herself on the side of the gun carriage. John perched beside her.

'Kit – I mean, Catherine – I'm sorry, I've been so horrible,' he whispered.

He heard her take a deep breath.

'Don't. It doesn't matter. It was a shock for you, I know. And please go on calling me Kit. Are you sure you don't feel angry with me any more?'

He nudged her, as he had so often done in the past, then felt embarrassed at having touched a girl.

'No. Just . . . amazed. And impressed. I don't know how you did it, keeping it secret, pretending all the time. It was so dangerous too.'

'Dangerous? Nothing is dangerous compared to being married to my cousin, believe me. Shh! That's Mr Higgins's voice. Can you hear what they are saying?'

The voices from the great cabin next door were only just audible through the close-fitting door of the sleeping cabin, and John and Kit had to strain to hear.

'Fresh water, eh?' Captain Bannerman was demanding. 'Running short? You surprise me, man. We received fresh water only last week from our supply ship. I would have thought the casks would be all but full.'

'Oh they was, sir, they was indeed. But by an unlucky chance, during the battle, sir, they was dislodged, and leaked, sir. We'll be in a pickle, Captain Bannerman, and Mr Erskine sir, if we don't get no water soon, what with all them thirsty Frenchies drinkin' up our supplies.'

John had never heard the cringing note in Mr Higgins's voice before, and the sound of it made his flesh creep.

'And what do you propose to do about this watery crisis, Mr Higgins?' Mr Erskine sounded amused.

'Well, sir, by a lucky chance, I was talkin' to the bosun of the *Courageux* . . .'

'Speak French, do you, Mr Higgins?' the captain asked drily.

Mr Higgins gave a fulsome laugh.

'French, sir? Oh no, not me, sir. Never 'ad the advantage of no education. The *Courageux*'s bosun, 'e speaks English, of a sort. Was in the wine trade, trading into Rye before the war. 'E was as concerned as I am, sir, about thirst afflictin' the men. Comes from these parts, 'e does, from around Bordeaux. Told me of a spring be'ind the sand dunes, very near 'ere. Quite deserted it is. 'E gave me very precise directions. It occurred to me, sir, that if I was to take a small party of men ashore, under cover of darkness maybe, along with as many casks as we can transport, I could, so to speak, rectify the situation, sir.'

'Now let me understand you correctly, Mr Higgins. You are proposing to land secretly in France, under the noses of the French coastguards, who are undoubtedly patrolling these shores, thereby putting your very life in danger? Heroic, Mr Higgins, I must say. A bold move. Very bold.'

Mr Higgins coughed modestly.

'Ah, but, sir, for the sake of the *Fearless* and all who sail in her . . .'

The captain seemed suddenly tired of the bosun's mate's obsequious manner.

'Very good, very well,' he said impatiently. 'If you wish to play the hero, you shall. Tonight, then, under cover of darkness, we will approach closer in to the French coast on the high tide, put you off with your empty casks and pick you up before dawn. How many men do you wish to take with you?'

'Six should be sufficient.' John could hear ill-concealed triumph in Mr Higgins's voice. 'I've got my eye on the right ones. Good men. Trustworthy. Powerful strong enough to 'eave about full casks all night, they are, sir.'

'Very good. Mr Erskine will supervise the loading of the empty casks into one of the boats.'

'Mr Erskine?' John could hear surprise and dismay in Mr Higgins's voice. 'No need for 'im to trouble 'imself, captain. I can do it easy myself.'

'Not at all, Mr Higgins,' Mr Erskine chimed in breezily. 'If you are to be a hero, the least I can do is to prepare your vessel. Now you no doubt have other duties to attend to?'

'Yes, sir. Thank you, sir.'

There was a scraping sound as Mr Erskine pushed back his chair and the squeak of Mr Higgins's shoes on the floorboards, then a click as the door of the great cabin opened and another as it shut. John expected that at any moment Mr Erskine would let them out, but nothing happened. He could hear the low murmur of Mr Erskine's voice, without being able to follow the words. The captain, easier to hear, said, 'Yes, by Jove, an excellent plan,' once or twice, and, 'Are you sure they are to be trusted with such a delicate mission?' but he could make out nothing more.

At last the door opened and John and Kit stepped back out into the great cabin, blinking in the strong light.

For a moment or two there was silence. Mr Erskine was looking doubtfully at Kit, and Captain Bannerman was frowning under his heavy brows.

'How is your wound? Does it trouble you much?' Mr Erskine asked Kit unexpectedly.

Kit moved her left shoulder experimentally, and successfully hid a wince.

'It's nearly better, sir. I feel quite strong now.'

'Good. Good.'

Silence fell again.

Captain Bannerman cleared his throat.

'You are to listen carefully to what I say,' he began importantly. 'If the slightest hint of this matter crosses your lips to any person whatsoever, I shall have you flogged. Do you understand?'

The severity in his voice and the intensity of his frown made John open his eyes in alarm.

'The copy of the code book found in your satchel,' Captain Bannerman went on, 'was returned to London, as you know, some time ago. It has proved be of quite exceptional value in interpreting the secret messages of the French, which from time to time fall into British hands.'

John couldn't help a proud smile breaking out on his face.

'Yes, yes, very good,' Captain Bannerman said, noticing it, 'but there's to be no resting on laurels. You are now required to do more, much more, in the service of your country.' He puffed out his chest, and John could see that he was preparing to make one of his stirring speeches. 'Times are desperate. Every loyal subject of His Majesty, every man and . . . er, woman . . . must now prove themselves to be true sons – and daughters – of . . .' He caught Mr Erskine's eye, and checked himself in mid flow. 'Mr Erskine, proceed,' he said, shaking his jowls.

Switching his eyes from the captain to the first lieutenant, John caught the tail end of a smile on Mr Erskine's face, but it quickly gave way to an expression of the utmost seriousness.

'The thing is, both of you,' Mr Erskine said, 'that there is something particular, something difficult and dangerous, that we want you to do. We received dispatches from London two weeks ago. They informed us that the men in Edinburgh who had possession of the code book are probably part of a conspiracy of spies working for Napoleon. Mr Higgins, we believe, is a very minor player in this game. He has most probably been tempted to betray his country with the promise of money. But there are others, much more deadly, and much more powerful, of whom our government is extremely anxious to know more.'

'We wish to arrest them, you mean, sir?' asked John.

'Not at all. We wish to use them. If our side can feed the French spies false information about the movement of our armies, the destinations of our ships, the intentions of our commanders . . .'

'It would give us an incredible advantage in the war!' John couldn't help interrupting excitedly.

'Precisely. If we know who they are, but they do not know that we know, we will be in a very strong position.'

Kit cleared her throat nervously.

'What is it that you wish us to do?'

Mr Erskine studied her face.

'You understand that you are at liberty to refuse this mission? I will not disguise from you the fact that it is dangerous.'

'Come to the point, please, Mr Erskine,' the captain said testily. 'Explain the business.'

'Very well, sir. Now, Mr Higgins has had the original code book a long while, and is no doubt increasingly desperate to pass it to his contacts ashore. As you know, he has been signalling to the French for some time. We have been watching him. Every night, until last night, the answering flashes from the French followed the same pattern. We don't know what they signify, but we do know that yesterday the pattern changed and that today Mr Higgins asked to go ashore. We have assumed that Mr Higgins signalled to the French a while ago that he has something important to say and wishes to meet with them. They presumably told him last night that they are ready to receive him. Why didn't they allow him to come straight away? It is most probable that they have been waiting for the arrival of someone more senior in their organization, no doubt from Paris, who will be able to receive the message Mr Higgins is anxious to pass on and give him his new instructions. This is only our guess, but I think it's a good one.'

'I can see that, sir, but what . . .'

'What do we want you to do? Think for a minute, John. You are the only person here who has seen and can recognize the men in Edinburgh who held the code book. There was a lawyer, was there not?'

'Mr Halkett, yes.'

'And another man, the one who pursued you?'

'Mr Creech. And Herriott Nasmyth, I suppose. He could be in it too.'

'Quite so. If any of them have come to France, they will almost certainly be travelling under other names, but we need to know that. We need to know what those names are, what these men's role in the business is, whether they are small fry or ringleaders, who their French counterparts are – in short, every possible detail, however great or small.'

'You want me to go ashore with Mr Higgins, follow him and find out everything I can?' said John, understanding in a rush that made him suddenly breathless.

'Precisely.'

'But there may be no British men there,' Kit put in. 'The contacts for Mr Higgins, they may all be French.'

'It is possible, yes,' nodded Mr Erskine.

'John will not be able to understand them, or be able to catch their names.' Kit was frowning as she thought it out. 'He does not speak French.'

'He does not, mademoiselle. But you do.'

Kit's face was lit up by an impish smile.

'I see,' she said.

'I don't understand, sir.' John's skin was tingling with excitement. 'If we go ashore with Mr Higgins, he'll be suspicious. And even if we didn't go in the same boat, but followed in another, he'd hear it and see it. It would give the game away.'

'That is why Mr Erskine is to supervise the loading of the boats, and row ashore with you,' broke in Captain Bannerman. 'You will be hidden under a tarpaulin behind the empty casks. Mr Erskine will accompany the boat and make sure you can slip ashore while the men are carrying the casks to the spring.'

'But is there really a spring?' objected John. 'Wasn't that just an excuse Mr Higgins gave so that he could go ashore?'

'Oh, the spring is no invention,' said Mr Erskine. 'We are assured by Captain Dupré that there are many of them. He has not enjoyed the brackish taste of our casked water, and frequently expresses a wish that we could replenish our stocks.'

'Do you believe that Mr Higgins will really return to the *Fearless*?' asked Kit. 'Perhaps he will run away. If he does, and we have to follow him far, how will we get back to the *Fearless* ourselves?'

'I don't believe he will desert.' Mr Erskine shook his head. 'The man is much more use to the French as a bosun's mate on board His Majesty's man-o'-war. If, as I believe, he is motivated by greed, he will be anxious to perform further tasks for them and earn more money. He can do that only by continuing in the king's service. As for you, you will do the best you can to find out as much as possible. But if you lose track of him, or you run into danger, you are to give up the attempt and return to the boat. No unnecessary heroics, is that understood? We will wait for you until just before dawn. If by any chance you are delayed, and cannot slip back unnoticed, you are to pass tomorrow hidden in the dunes and we will send the boat back for you when darkness falls tomorrow night.'

John tried to imagine himself skulking about in the dark, following the man he feared most in the world through unknown territory in a hostile land. He couldn't suppress a shudder.

'If anyone sees us, sir,' he said, 'they'll know at once that we are British seamen by our clothes.'

'Very good, damn your eyes!' burst out Captain Bannerman, slapping his thigh. 'The boy thinks ahead like a true conspirator. He was born for the secret service!'

'You must wear plain boys' clothes, not your naval rig, then,' nodded Mr Erskine. 'John, you have your old clothes still, I suppose?'

'Yes, sir,' said John, 'but I've grown so much they wouldn't fit me now.'

'You will be supplied. And you, Catherine . . .'

'I think,' interrupted Kit, 'that perhaps it is better if I am dressed as a girl. No one will think anything of me then. If I am seen, if I am caught even, no one could imagine that I have been a powder monkey in a British ship.'

'Skirts, eh?' said Mr Erskine. 'I had thought this ship was supplied with every kind of necessity, but a girl's clothes . . .'

'There's no difficulty there, sir. I still have my old dress in my chest. It will be a little short now, but not so much. I have not grown like John has.'

'Your bag! That you always keep so secret!' John said. 'They're in there, aren't they – your girl's clothes, I mean?'

'Yes. I was always afraid that Davey would find them, but he never . . .'

'Enough of this chatter,' interrupted the captain. 'John, will you undertake this mission? It's dangerous, and important, and a fine adventure for a boy, and if you succeed, your country – and I – will show you our gratitude.'

John wanted to say, 'And if I fail?' but he didn't dare. Aloud he said, 'Yes, sir. I'll do it.'

'Good lad. And you, miss? You have proved your courage amply up till now, but do you have the stomach for this bold step?'

Kit smiled at him mischievously. John stared at her. Kit the powder monkey would never have dared to look at the captain so boldly. Catherine the young French noblewoman was clearly not prepared to be intimidated.

'Are you sure you can trust me, sir? I am a Frenchwoman, after all.'

'Are you presuming to jest with me, you damned baggage?' The captain's frown was terrible, but John could see that, though she had taken him by surprise, she had amused him.

'No, sir. Of course not, sir,' said Kit demurely.

'Very good.' The captain hid a smile. 'Now return to your duties. Act normally for the rest of the day, and report to

Mr Erskine when the hammocks are piped down this evening. Mr Tawse will be advised not to remark upon your absence. Off with you now, and may Providence smile upon your mission.'

Chapter Twenty-one

The rest of the day passed in a kind of dream for John. Outwardly, everything appeared to be normal. He worked up the foremast, helping to haul in the sails, he ate his dinner (but without much appetite), he played a game of spillikins with Davey (though was soundly beaten as his hands were unaccountably shaky) and went through the motions of the gun drill with Mr Stannard and his gun crew.

By supper time he had almost convinced himself that the morning's extraordinary conversation in the captain's cabin was no more than a weird creation of his own imagination.

Mr Erskine appeared at the canvas screen at half past seven, half an hour before the hammocks were due to be piped down.

'A word, Mr Tawse, if you please,' he said.

Mr Tawse went out with him and came back five minutes later, shaking his head.

'Sendin' boys out on dangerous missions to fetch water is what I don't 'old with,' he muttered disapprovingly, then stopped, aware that he had been surprised into speaking disrespectfully of a senior officer. 'John and Kit, you are to report to Mr Erskine now on the upper gun deck.'

Tom looked up, his eyes sparkling.

'A mission? To fetch water? You mean they're to go ashore, into France? Oh please, Mr Tawse, let me go too. I'll take Kit's place. He's not well enough yet.'

''Old your tongue, Tom,' Mr Tawse growled. 'John and Kit is asked for, and John and Kit is to go.' He held up a silencing hand as Tom seemed about to plead. 'That's enough, or it's bread and water for you, my lad, till you can learn to keep your place.'

Kit had already gone to her chest and pulled out her bag. She nodded at John, who took one last look round the berth as if he was afraid he'd never see it again. Then the two of them, hearts beating fast, skipped out through the canvas screen.

Although it was nearly eight o'clock, the sun had only just set on this balmy August evening, and the sky, still golden, lit up the sea, which shone like polished copper. Mr Erskine was on the upper gun deck, supervising the preparation of one of the cutters that was kept there, resting on its wooden cradle. The covering tarpaulin had been removed, and a couple of sailors were lifting out the cages of chickens that normally lived inside the boat. The birds were protesting with agitated squawkings.

Mr Erskine lounged across to John and Kit, his back to the working sailors.

'What are you boys doing up here?' he called out severely as he approached, but winked at them to show he was acting. He was beside them now.

'You have your clothes?' he said quietly to Kit.

She raised her bundle.

'Good.'

He looked back over his shoulder. The chicken cages were now stowed neatly beside the second small boat.

'You men!' he called out. 'Get below. Mr Higgins is waiting to send up the empty casks. Start bringing them up now.'

'Aye aye, sir,' one of the seaman answered, and they both disappeared down the nearest companionway.

Minute by minute the light was fading. At any moment the ship's bell would sound, the bosun's whistle would blow and hundreds of men would run up to the deck to fetch their hammocks while the lanterns were lit and hung in the rigging and the evening watch took up their stations.

Mr Erskine looked up into the rigging and saw that the man on lookout up there was obscured behind a spar.

'Get into the boat,' he ordered quietly.

'My clothes, sir,' began John.

'Already stowed. Quick. Crawl under the bow seat and make yourselves small.'

A moment later John and Kit had scrambled into the boat and were huddled together in the tiny space under the low boards that covered the bows. They were only just in time. Mr Erskine had barely stuffed a length of canvas in after them, to obscure them from view, when the command 'Down hammocks!' was piped round the ship and the feet of hundreds of men pattered all round them as they ran up on deck to pull their hammocks out of the nets.

With customary speed, they had all quickly gone below, but John could hear the echoing rumble of empty casks being rolled across the deck and the chivvying voice of Mr Higgins, made even more strident than usual by his evident nervousness. Then the timbers of the small boat juddered as the casks were loaded into it.

'Pull out that canvas!' John heard Mr Higgins say irritably. 'Whoever stowed such a mangy bit of old gear under that seat?'

'Leave it, lads,' Mr Erskine contradicted pleasantly.

'There's no time for tidying. Hurry now, the light's gone. It's time we were on our way.'

A startled grunt came from Mr Higgins.

'*We*, Mr Erskine? You surely ain't comin' with us?'

'I most certainly am, Mr Higgins. Oh, never fear. I don't wish, as you clearly do, to risk my life and limb running about in the dunes looking for springs. I shall content myself with staying by the boat on the beach, to guard it.'

'There's men a-plenty can do that, sir.' Mr Higgins was clearly unnerved. 'There's no call for you to put yourself to so much trouble.'

'Come come, Mr Higgins. You can't play the hero alone. You must allow a little glory to rub off on me. Now then, lads, are all the casks in? Very good. Lower the boat!'

With a lurch, the boat rose into the air as the sailors pulled on the ropes to swing it up. It tilted sickeningly as it swung over the side of the *Fearless* and was lowered down to the water. The jerking loosened the barrels and one rolled hard against the canvas, knocking sharply on John's shin. He had to bite his lips to stop himself from crying out.

And then they were down. The boat was floating quietly on the water, and the men were climbing down the cleats on the *Fearless*'s side to board her. The little boat rocked as the men stepped down into her.

Mr Higgins and Mr Erskine, counted John, and the six other seamen. He guessed he knew which ones they would be: the bullying, swaggering familiars of the bosun's mate, who were forever in his company.

The oars were being plied now. The rowlocks had been muffled with cloth to eliminate the sound. All he could hear was the gurgle and rush of water beneath his ear, just below the thin boards. The cutter was moving steadily across the long stretch of water that separated the *Fearless* from the beach. Beside him, Kit shifted.

'My shoulder,' she breathed in his ear. 'If I do not release my arm, the wound will open again.'

He made room for her, moving as carefully as he could, but his foot caught in the canvas, which began to sag. There was a crack now through which he could see. He froze. If he could see out, others could see in.

Straight in front of him was a pair of legs clad in creased white stockings. An officer's stockings. Mr Erskine must be sitting on the bow seat under which he and Kit were hidden. In front of him he could just make out, in the gathering darkness, the back of one of the sailors, whose shoulders were moving rhythmically, backwards and forwards, as he rowed with short, powerful strokes.

He had forgotten that the men would be sitting with their backs to the bows. He breathed in with relief, then wished at once that he hadn't, as a fluffy little feather, no doubt fallen from the chickens' cage, lodged in his nostril.

His hands were trapped down by his sides and he didn't dare move them. He wriggled his nose, gently blew out, screwed up his eyes, and curled his tongue up towards his nose as far as it would go, but the feather was stuck fast. He could feel a sneeze gathering. It was coming. Nothing could prevent it. It would lead to discovery, to disaster, to . . .

He sneezed. At once, Mr Erskine coughed to cover the sound.

'Beggin' your pardon, sir,' came a reproving whisper from Mr Higgins, 'but we can't afford to make no noise.'

'You are right, of course. Carry on, Mr Higgins,' came Mr Erskine's quiet reply.

It seemed like an eternity before the bottom of the cutter grated at last on the soft sand of the beach, and in that time both John and Kit had suffered agonies of cramps. The boat tilted and lurched as the men jumped out and dragged it up on to the beach. John was longing so ardently to climb out and release his tensed muscles that he hardly heard Mr Erskine's quiet commands.

At last there was silence. He could wait no longer and shifted an arm experimentally.

'Not yet,' Mr Erskine's voice hissed. 'Wait.'

Five more minutes dragged by.

'Now,' Mr Erskine said at last. 'Come out now.'

Standing on solid, firm land for the first time in months was the strangest sensation John had ever felt. It took a moment for him to ease the stiffness out of his arms and legs, but then, when he straightened himself, he felt as if the ground was heaving like the sea swell under his feet and he staggered to keep his balance.

Mr Erskine was already thrusting a bundle of clothes into his arms.

'Jump to it, John. Get out of your rig into these.'

John averted his gaze from Kit, who, her back turned, had stripped off her shirt and was already lifting her dress over her head, but once she stood beside him he couldn't help turning curiously to look at her, as she shook her long hair loose from the pigtail into which it had always been tied. All he could see, though, in the darkness, was the blur of some pale material that fell, clipped in at the waist, from her shoulders to her feet and the outline of her face against the dark mass of hair.

'Listen,' said Mr Erskine, 'I've sent four of the men off that way, behind us, to check if all's clear in the dunes, and two of them straight ahead into the woods. Mr Higgins has gone the other way, on his own. Get after him now, you two. Keep as quiet as you can and watch out for yourselves. And don't forget, if you can't get back to me unseen tonight, before Mr Higgins returns, I'll return for you tomorrow. Off with you now, and God speed.'

Chapter Twenty-two

It was now very dark, but it was still possible to make out the white edges of the waves rolling up on to the beach, which stretched long and straight for miles in each direction. Ahead, the sand slanted gently up towards the low ridge of dunes. John had stared across at them from the *Fearless* so often that they had become quite familiar, but close up and in the dark they seemed strange, mysterious and threatening.

The sand was soft and warm under their bare feet. John set off at a run, horribly aware that even in the dark a watcher might be able to make out their shapes against the whiteness of the beach. He looked back, expecting to have to wait for Kit, but she was just behind him, holding her long skirt bunched in her hands.

They reached the dunes and swiftly climbed them.

'We've lost Mr Higgins,' John whispered. 'We'll never find him in the dark.'

'Shh.' She touched his arm. 'Look. Over there.'

He too could see it now. The flicker of a light. It burned still and steadily. Not a lantern, then, swinging from someone's hand out in the open, but a candle, perhaps, shining out through a door or window.

'It might just be a fisherman's cottage,' he said doubtfully.

'No one could live in these dunes. Anyway, fishermen would be asleep at this hour. Come on. Let's see.'

The sharp rough seagrass spiked their feet as they stumbled across the dunes towards the light. It was closer than they had thought. They could see now that it was streaming out through the open door of a hut. Cautiously, they tiptoed up the last short slope towards it.

Voices reached them before they were at the top.

'Stop playing us along, Higgins. You have the book? Hand it over.'

A chill ran through John as he recognized Mr Creech's grating voice.

'I might have it or I might not.' Mr Higgins sounded mulish. 'Depends, don't it, on the colour of your money.'

Someone else snorted impatiently.

'How can we pay you for it if we don't know whether or not you have the thing?' demanded Mr Creech.

'Risks I've taken for this, 'orrible risks,' grumbled Mr Higgins. 'Give me 'alf now, and 'alf when you sees it, or you don't get a look at it at all.'

'Och, pay the fellow, Creech,' said someone else, his Scottish voice sharp with exasperation. 'Let's be done with it and return to Bordeaux. The stench of fish in this hellhole will cling to my clothes for weeks.'

John frowned. He was almost sure that the voice belonged to Mr Halkett, but the afternoon in the lawyer's office in Edinburgh was so long ago, and his memory of it was now so dim that he could not be sure. He edged forwards, circling round the side of the hut so that he could see in through the door. He sensed that Kit had tensed, as nervous as he was of being seen, but she crept after him, keeping close.

There was the rattle of coins from inside the hut, and an exclamation of satisfaction.

'It *is* the code book,' Mr Creech said, not bothering to conceal his triumph. 'Good man, Higgins. Now listen, this is important. Is anyone else on the *Fearless* aware of the existence of this book and what it contains?'

Mr Higgins laughed.

'No, the fools. The boy, John Barr, 'e 'ad no idea. Thought I was just followin' a tip-off to recover stolen goods. Stupid lad 'e is, an' all. I'd beat some sense into 'im if I could get 'im off that scurvy gunner.'

Someone else spoke, this time in French. Kit took the lead now, inching further forward. Directly facing the door of the cabin there was a clump of small, stunted pine trees, bent by the sea wind, on the slope behind the dunes. Exchanging no more than a brief nudge of their elbows, John and Kit understood each other. If they could reach the trees and hide among them, they would see right into the hut and be able to take cover easily.

John gained the trees first. He stood behind one and leaned round the trunk to peer into the little cabin. It was clearly a fisherman's place. A tangle of nets and floats lay about on the floor and in one corner was a pile of wickerwork traps, while a broken oar was propped against the far wall. There were four men inside. Mr Higgins and Mr Creech he recognized at once, and one he'd never seen before, a dandified fellow in a green coat and brilliantly polished riding boots. The fourth man had his back to the door, and it was only when he turned his head to pass the code book back to Mr Creech that John recognized him. It was definitely Mr Halkett. So the Edinburgh lawyer really was a French spy too.

Mr Creech was speaking now. 'You'd beat some sense into the boy, you say? I think, Mr Higgins, we would like you to do more than that.'

'What do you mean, more?' growled Mr Higgins suspiciously.

'Oh, use your imagination! Or has the navy flogged it out of you? John Barr no doubt looked many times through his satchel and puzzled over the meaning of the code book. He is certainly young, and may be stupid, as you say, but I doubt it. At present, with the *Fearless* at sea, there is probably no one with whom he can discuss the book, but if he meets with his father again, they are certain to talk of the matter. Now Mr Barr, though a fool when it comes to business, is a man of education and intelligence. If his suspicions were aroused, and he were to alert the authorities . . .'

'I understand you, Mr Creech. You want me to kill the little gutter rat,' Mr Higgins interrupted brutally.

'In a word, yes.'

John grasped at a low branch of the tree and held it tight, not noticing that pine needles were sticking into his palm.

''Ow?' demanded Mr Higgins. 'Six hundred men there are on board that man-o'-war, and every step a man takes is seen and 'eard. Beatin' a boy, makin' a boy's life a misery, floggin' a boy, starvin' a boy, general persecution, that's easy, but killin' – very risky. Considerable rewards would 'ave to be offered. Very considerable. And even then I don't see 'ow such a thing could be done.'

'But that is absurd! Hundreds of opportunities must present themselves every day!' Mr Creech spoke with horrible eagerness. 'A fall from the rigging, a quiet heave overboard, an accident with a musket! Surely . . .'

'Considerable rewards,' Mr Higgins repeated, shaking his head.

Kit's hand, trembling with indignation, was clutching at John's sleeve.

'Evil. *Evil!*' she whispered. John hardly noticed. He was frozen in horror.

The Frenchman was speaking again. Kit breathed in sharply and leaned forward, craning her neck to see behind the door of the hut which half concealed him. In her eagerness, she nearly overbalanced, and had to take a sideways step to right herself. Under her foot, a twig snapped loudly.

'What was that?' Mr Creech's head had shot round, and he peered out into the night. 'Is someone there?'

Mr Halkett laughed.

'Man, you're as edgy as a cat. This is France we're in, not Britain. Even if there's some peasant passing by, they won't understand a word we say, and if they do, we're on business for the government of France, under the protection of our good friend here, the comte de St Voir.'

John heard Kit's small grunt of surprise.

'But,' Mr Halkett went on, 'to return to the matter of the boy. I have not yet had my say, and I wish to state that murdering children is something I cannot agree to. I will not put my hand to any such resolution, and I strongly urge you, Mr Higgins, to leave the boy alone.'

'And put all our lives in danger,' sneered Mr Creech.

'I'll take Mr Creech's word for it, rather than the lawyer's here,' said Mr Higgins, with what seemed to John a horrible degree of relish. 'Meek and mild I am, as a general rule, but if the reward is considerable, I believe I could bring myself to do the deed. Twenty gold guineas would persuade me. I won't take less.'

'Twenty guineas?' Mr Halkett almost squeaked in horror. 'That's pure extortion.'

The Frenchman spoke softly again.

'Excellent,' said Mr Creech. 'As you so aptly point out, the government of France will pay the money, so we need not concern ourselves unduly. Do it soon, Mr Higgins, as soon as you can.'

'Aye, and I must return to my lads and fetch the water back

to the *Fearless* as soon as I can,' said Mr Higgins. 'As soon as I have ten guineas down, the rest to be paid to me when the deed is done.'

'Five, no more. It is all I have about me,' said Mr Creech, and John heard the clink of money again. 'Now take yourself off, you greedy brute, before that nosy first lieutenant of yours comes after you on the hunt.'

The light was blocked out for a moment as Mr Higgins left the hut. John shrank away from his shadow as he passed.

'What shall we do now?' Kit whispered. 'We can't get back to Mr Erskine before Mr Higgins does.'

'I don't know. I . . . I can't think.'

The knowledge that Mr Higgins was now set to kill him had sent John's mind reeling.

'We'll have to hide and wait for Mr Erskine till tomorrow,' Kit said.

'Yes . . . I suppose so. Listen, they're still talking.'

'I don't like it, Creech. Not at all. I'm not in this business to condone murder,' Mr Halkett was saying.

'No, you're in it for the money, as I am,' said Mr Creech crudely.

'On the contrary.' Mr Halkett's voice had taken on a dry, lawyer-like tone. 'I happen to be an admirer of Napoleon Bonaparte, and I have no love for the corrupt government of Britain and her half-crazed German monarch. Bonaparte is a great man, a man of large, nay, brilliant ideas, a reformer of genius, a—'

'For the Lord's sake, Halkett,' interrupted Mr Creech. 'Stop prating like a minister. You can't turn squeamish now. And don't try to tell me that you're selling your country for your ideals. I haven't noticed you hanging back when it comes to the question of payment from the French secret service.'

'Aye, well, a matter of insurance. That is how I view the

money,' Mr Halkett said primly. 'I have been obliged to act unlawfully, to practise deceit, to connive at an act of gross fraudulence, which, if it was ever discovered, would ruin me and my legal practice forever.'

'Fraud? You mean the business over Luckstone, I presume.'

At the word 'Luckstone' John's fear was forgotten. He leaned forward to hear more clearly.

'The illegal acquisition of Luckstone, aye,' Mr Halkett went on. 'And why you dragged me into that that business, or involved that clumsy, drunken oaf Nasmyth . . .'

'You know very well why Luckstone is important to us,' Mr Creech said crisply. 'Of all the places in Scotland, that little inlet off the Firth of Forth, just across the water from Edinburgh, is the perfect vantage point from which to monitor incoming and outgoing ships, and the fortified house would make a perfect signal tower in the event of a French invasion. When Nasmyth drew it to our attention it was a chance too good to be missed.'

'So you say, so you say.' Mr Halkett was shaking his head. 'But it was a bad business, and I – what was that?'

'*Ce n'est rien*,' the Frenchman said. 'The 'orses, my groom is returning with them.'

'The horses, yes. Our business here is concluded most satisfactorily,' said Mr Creech. 'Higgins may be a rogue, but he has done well for us. Come, Mr Halkett, after you. We shall ride back to Bordeaux for a late supper and a game of cards before bed.'

They were both at the door now. Mr Halkett was the first to step out of the hut, with Mr Creech close behind him. John and Kit turned to slip away through the trees, but before they had taken more than a few steps, the huge shapes of horses, padding silently over the sand, loomed up in front of them. The first horse took fright at Kit's white dress, snickered in alarm and reared back, startling the second, which was following close behind.

John grabbed Kit's hand, pulling her away.

'Quick! Run!' he hissed.

But they were too late. The groom had seen them.

'*Eh, vous! Arrêtez!*' he shouted.

'Who's there? What's going on?'

The three men from the hut came running. Desperate to get away, John and Kit gave up the attempt to remain hidden and bolted through the trees, but the roots of the pines, snaking across the sand, took John unawares and he tripped and fell headlong.

'Go on! Run!' he called to Kit.

'They're English, by God,' he heard Mr Creech's shout behind him. 'Spies! Your pistol, chevalier, quick!'

John had scrambled back to his feet, but before he could run more than a few yards more, he felt a stinging blow as a bullet hit his side. He staggered and would have fallen again if Kit had not caught hold of him.

'A horse!' he called out thickly. 'Take a horse!'

Kit had already had the same idea and had snatched one of the bridles from the groom's astonished grip. She leaped into the saddle, bent down and hauled John up after her.

A moment later they were flying through the trees away from the men, the hut, the beach and the sea, into the forest, which stretched for miles inland from the coast, deep into France.

Chapter Twenty-three

It was merciful that John had felt nothing for the first few moments after the bullet had struck him, or he would not have been able to scramble up on to the horse, even with Kit's helping hand. But the respite didn't last long. With every jolt and lurch, jagged pains, as searing as lightning strikes, shot through his side. It was all he could do to cling to Kit, propping himself up against her back. His whole being was concentrated in the determination not to fall.

Kit was leaning forward over the reins, urging the horse onwards, her feet pummelling its sides. The creature seemed panic-stricken by the strange pair on its back, and Kit's flapping skirts filled it with added terror. It was careering through the trees, plunging recklessly through the darkness. Several times a low-hanging branch almost swept the riders off the saddle and only Kit's quickness saved them from disaster.

John was so focused on staying on the horse's back that he hardly thought of the enemies behind them. He heard confused shouts, and another two shots rang out, which panicked the horse even more, but there was no sound of pursuit. Their own horse's hoofs made only soft thuds on the sandy forest floor. He vaguely supposed, through the waves of pain engulfing him, that the pursuers must be close behind, but he almost didn't care. He simply wanted this jolting agony to stop. He wanted to be set down somewhere quiet, where he could shut his eyes and curl into a ball until the pain went away.

It seemed as if hours had passed when Kit finally pulled the sweating, trembling horse to a halt. She slid off its back, went quickly to its head and soothed it with expert crooning. Then she led it behind a patch of scrubby undergrowth where the darkness was even more impenetrable, hitched the reins round a low branch and looked up at John. He was bent, limp, over the horse's neck.

'John, are you very badly hurt?' she said in a whisper.

'I don't know. It hurts. There's a lot of blood, I think.'

'Where did it hit you?'

'In my side. Help me off. I want to lie down.'

She shook the hair out of her eyes.

'No, we can't stay here. We must get help for you soon.'

'Mr Erskine . . .' John said faintly.

'He'll have rowed back to the *Fearless* by now. You must face it, John, we have left the *Fearless*. We can't hope to get back to her now.'

He barely took in what she was saying.

'What are we going to do?'

His voice was a thread.

'Listen.' She was still distractedly patting the horse's neck as she spoke. 'I don't know exactly where we are, and this forest is so vast it is always easy to get lost, but soon, if we go on, we must come to a road. And then I will know, because my old home, Jalignac, is very close to here. Betsy is there. She is a wonderful nurse. She will know how to look after you.'

'Tomorrow night,' John managed to say. 'We must be at the beach tomorrow night.'

'No, John. Didn't you hear me? We can't go back. You will never recover if you are in the hands of Mr Catskill. You do not know, John, what butchery he . . . Shh! Listen!'

A breeze had blown up from the sea and was ruffling through the pines, making a faint shirring sound, almost like a wave dragging back down a distant beach, but it hardly disturbed the deep silence of the forest. There had never been silence on board the *Fearless*, where the creaking of timbers, the slap of water, the flapping of sails and rigging, the shouts, curses, songs, grunts and quarrels of six hundred men had made an endless background of sound. Here, only the croak of a frog in a distant pond and the hoot of a night owl could be heard.

'There! Did you hear that?' whispered Kit.

John tried to focus his ears, but he was swaying in the saddle and had to concentrate in order to stop himself falling.

'Horses, but far. They are moving away from us now. We've shaken them off.'

Her voice was triumphant. John hardly heard what she was saying.

'Help me off,' he repeated. 'I must lie down.'

'No!' She was already unhitching the horse's reins. 'If you get down you will never be able to mount again. You cannot stay here. There is not even any water. Please, John, just hold on. We must go on. I will ride in front of you like before. You can lean on me.'

By the time the dawn was lightening the sky, turning the forest from a mass of black smudged shapes into a ghostly, endless tract of grey-trunked trees, John was so weak from the loss of blood that he was drifting in and out of consciousness, and only Kit's slender, supple back, to which he clung with the last of his strength, prevented him from crashing to the ground.

It was the creaking of wagon wheels that first told Kit the road was near. She gave a shuddering sigh of relief. For the past hour she had been increasingly certain that they were lost, going around in circles, that she would never find a way out of the maze of trees, and that John would be dead long before she could reach help.

The road, long and straight, was no more than a strip cut through the forest, and the wagon, pulled by a pair of cows and driven by a weather-beaten old woman, threatened to bog down into the soft sand with every turn of the wheels. Kit, who had looked up and down the long straight road carefully before stepping out from the cover of the trees, slid off the horse's back and ran out in front of the wagon.

'*Bonjour, ma mère,*' she called out.

The old woman, who was wearing a blue bonnet with a deep poke which almost hid her face, turned her head and stared suspiciously at Kit.

'*Bonjour,*' she said grudgingly.

'Please,' Kit went on in French, 'Can you help us? My brother is wounded. Bandits. They shot at him. I have to get him home.'

'Bandits? Where?' The old woman was looking round nervously. 'How many? Have they gone?'

'They were in the forest. They ambushed us. Oh please, he's very bad. He's losing blood.'

'Half of it seems to be all over you,' the old woman remarked drily. She hadn't pulled up the wagon, and the cows were still plodding quietly on. Kit walked alongside as she pleaded.

'You could take him on your wagon, somewhere where he can be looked after.' She was feeling increasingly desperate, but was acting the role of helpless young girl to perfection.

'And where would that be? Where do you come from, anyway? You're not from around here. I don't know you.'

'I'm from . . . Jalignac. From *near* Jalignac,' Kit corrected herself. If she gave her name away, the news of Mlle de Jalignac's return would be all over the country by the end of the day. She racked her brains to think of a way of persuading this obstinate old woman. 'Jean-Baptiste, the man who used to work in the chateau, the old groom, he knows me.'

'Jean-Baptiste?' The old woman cackled. 'That old soak? Nice friends you've got, mademoiselle.' She paused, then gave Kit a sideways, crafty look. 'Well, I'd like to help you and your brother, but times are hard. You don't get something for nothing these days.'

Kit looked back. Walking along beside the wagon, she had already come too far from John and the horse. By now he might easily have fainted dead away and fallen to the ground.

'I have no money,' she said helplessly. 'I can't . . .' And then an idea struck her, perfect in its simplicity. 'You can have the horse! Take me and my brother to Jalignac, and I'll give you our horse.'

The woman's eyes opened wide.

'A horse?' she said, unable to disguise her greed. 'Fetch it here. I'm not halting these cows for anything. Once the wagon stops moving, it'll sink right down and get stuck in the sand. I'll never get it moving again. A horse, you said. Broken-down old thing, I suppose.'

But Kit was already flying back down the road to where she had left John among the trees.

The old woman's face softened slightly when she saw John, as she took in the whiteness of his face and the huge stain of red that had spread across his shirt.

'Eh, *le pauvre*,' she said. 'You should have said how bad he was.' But her eyes were already sizing up the horse. 'The saddle,' she said, 'it looks English-made.'

188

'Yes, yes, the saddle is yours too,' Kit said impatiently. 'The bridle, the saddle, everything. Just help me to get him down.'

The old woman had jumped down from the wagon with surprising speed, and, while the cows were still ambling slowly on, was lifting the canvas that covered the back of the wagon. Underneath it were a few baskets full of cabbages, a sack of potatoes and a pair of chickens in a cage. Without ceremony, she tugged at John's leg, caught him in her muscular arms as he fell, with a groan of pain, and a moment later had laid him on the floor of the wagon. Then she hitched the horse's bridle to the wagon's side and climbed back up into her seat.

'Here, mademoiselle, what are you doing?' she called back to Kit, who was untying the girths of the saddle.

Kit finished detaching the saddle, and threw it into the back of the wagon.

'As you saw, it's English-made,' she said, trotting to keep up. 'With all the bandits around, someone might take a fancy to it.'

The old woman looked at her shrewdly.

'Bandits,' she said. 'I don't think I believe in your bandits. But a horse is a horse and a saddle, especially an English one, is a saddle. The bargain's good, and I won't ask any questions. Get in the back there beside your brother, if he is your brother, and mind he doesn't die on us. You'll find a flask of wine and some water in a bottle. Let him drink sips at a time. And here –' she pulled off the coarse linen kerchief she was wearing round her neck. 'It's a sacrifice, but I suppose it's worth it. You'd better take this. Make a pad and hold it against the wound to stop the bleeding. Hop in now before I change my mind. It's six miles to Jalignac, at least, but if these cows don't decide to give us trouble we'll be there in a couple of hours.'

The sun was well up by now, and the heat seemed already to be too much for John, who, though lying on his back, was turning his head from side to side in distress. Kit pulled the canvas covering back across the wagon to shade them both, found the water bottle and the wine flask and gave him sips of each in turn. She made a pad, as the old woman had advised, and steeled herself to lift John's shirt, drawing in her breath at the sight of the ugly, deep wound at the side of his chest, from which blood was still seeping. She pressed the pad gently against it, trying to ignore John's groan of pain.

'All will be well now,' she told him. 'Now you will be fine. I promise you, John. Soon we'll be safe.'

The certainty in her voice comforted John and he shut his eyes, unaware that she felt much less sure than she sounded. She sat silently beside him, biting her lips with worry.

The old woman with her wagon had so far been the only person travelling along the road, but now Kit could hear voices, shouted commands, the jingle of a horse's bit and bridle. She lifted the canvas cover and looked out.

The sight was so horrible she wanted to drop the wagon's cover again, but couldn't tear her eyes away. A long line of men, shackled together with chains, their clothes in rags, their feet bare and bleeding, rough blood-soaked bandages round legs and arms, were shuffling along in the sand, their shoulders drooping with despair. Alongside them rode two gendarmes armed with muskets.

'*Allez! Vite!* Don't lag behind there,' one of them was calling out in French. He lifted his whip and cracked it across the back of the last man in the line, who stumbled and nearly fell.

'What have you got there, monsieur?' the old woman on the wagon called out to one of the gendarmes. 'Cattle for the market?'

'Prisoners of war, madame,' he called back, touching his

hat with mock gallantry. 'Enemies of France. English, half of them. Spaniards the rest.'

'I hope they all rot,' the old woman called out with sudden venom. 'The English killed my boy at Aboukir Bay.'

'Oh, they'll rot, poor devils. They'll rot where we're taking them,' the gendarme said cheerfully.

At last, when the heat in the wagon was becoming unbearable, and the water was finished, and John's voice, cracked and high, was rambling in incoherent, half-finished sentences, Kit felt the wagon lurch as it turned off the long straight road. It halted, and the cover was lifted.

'I hope your young man is still alive, miss,' said the old woman. 'We're here. At Jalignac.'

Chapter Twenty-four

Kit stood outside Jalignac's massive iron gates looking up the long drive to the huge chateau, which crouched on a low rise, its grey roof rising above the surrounding trees. The old woman with the wagon, having discovered that the gates were locked, had pulled John unceremoniously out of the wagon and dumped him on the grass. Then she had gone, switching the backs of her cows with a willow cane to make them go faster and glancing back gleefully every now and then at her new horse.

Kit was used to the emptiness of her family's deserted home, which had usually been shut up since her father's death fourteen years ago, but when she saw how derelict it had now become, how it looked almost ruined, her heart sank even further. She had last stayed here five years ago, when her grandmother had thought about restoring it, but her uncle had refused to spend a single ecu on the place and the old lady had given up and taken Kit back with her to her comfortable mansion in Bordeaux.

It looked now as if nobody had been here for years. Saplings were shooting up out of the once smoothly paved drive. The shutters, sagging and unpainted, were closed over the long rows of windows that ran along the front of the chateau, and the lamp over the front door hung drunkenly from its twisted bracket. Kit vigorously rattled the gates and shouted, 'Is anyone there? Come and open up!'

No one answered. The place seemed quite deserted. Kit shook the gates again. Surely Betsy would still be here? Betsy had always wanted to live at Jalignac, had always loved the chateau, and in his will Kit's father had left her a cottage next to the stables. Betsy had always said she would return here if Kit didn't need her any more.

'She *has* to be here,' Kit said out loud. 'She *is* here, I know she is! I've just got to get in somehow and look round and find her.'

She studied the gates again. They were very tall, made of good strong iron and firmly locked. There were gaps in the wall that surrounded the chateau's vast park, she knew, but the wall was miles long. It might be hours before she could find a way in. By that time John might even be dead.

'Someone!' she shouted as loudly as she could. 'Whoever's there! Open the gates!'

And then she saw it. A thin curl of smoke was rising up out of one of the chimneys in the east wing of the chateau. Someone *was* there!

'Ahoy!' she yelled, unthinkingly becoming a sailor again. 'Betsy! *Il y a quelqu'un? Venez!*'

She thought she could detect the smallest movement of one of the shutters on the far left of the ground floor. At this distance it was hard to be sure, but, encouraged, she screamed 'Betsy! *Betsy!*' with the full force of her lungs.

She hadn't been wrong. The shutter was moving. It was opening now, and so was the window behind it. Someone was leaning out.

'Betsy! It's me! Catherine!'

The window was flung up to its full height and someone,

a woman, was climbing out of it, dropping awkwardly the short distance to the terrace beneath. Now she was running down the long drive as fast as her considerable weight would allow.

'Betsy! Oh thank God, it's Betsy!' croaked Kit, her voice too strained and cracked to shout any more.

Betsy's wispy brown hair was escaping from her mob cap, the apron she wore over her voluminous skirt was awry and the kerchief round her shoulders was coming adrift. She came to a halt inside the big iron gates and stared through them, her blue eyes wide with shock, a plump reddened hand over her mouth.

'Miss Catherine! It *is* you! Oh my dear darling, I thought you was dead. They told me you was dead! What's happened? There's blood all over you. You . . . you're not a ghost, are you? You're really real?'

Kit laughed shakily.

'Yes, of course I'm real. Let me in, Betsy. Open the gates, quickly!'

'I can't do that, my lovey. Jean-Baptiste, he's the one with the key. I hardly recognized you! Where have you been? Why did they tell me . . . not that I believed them. Look how you've grown!'

'Betsy, listen.' Kit turned her head. She could hear a sound from down the road, the jingle of harnesses, bridles and stirrups. Not one, but many. 'There's someone here with me.' She stood back to show Betsy where John was lying, his eyes shut, on the grass. 'He's a British sailor. He's badly hurt. I'll explain everything. He mustn't be found. We've got to hide him, nurse him – oh, be quick, Betsy! I can hear people coming. You've got to let us in!'

'A British sailor! Oh my lor'.' Betsy peered through the gates at John's still body. 'Looks more dead than alive, poor lad.' Then she turned, put her hands round her mouth and shrieked, 'Jean-Baptiste! Where are you? Jean-Baptiste!' Without waiting for an answer, she set off up the drive again at a lumbering trot.

Kit stepped out into the road to see who was coming. She gasped in dismay. A troop of French cavalry, plumed helmets nodding, metal breastplates gleaming, was trotting down the road towards her. They would be level with the gates of Jalignac at any moment. There was no chance of Betsy returning before they passed, and when they did they couldn't fail to see John, lying covered in blood, at the gates of the chateau. She would have to think fast, and make the best of it.

She ran to an overgrown bush beside the gate and managed to twist off a couple of big leafy twigs. Then she sat down on the ground beside John, covered the bloody mess on his shirt with one twig, and began to fan him with the other. She arranged her skirt attractively around her, tucked her wildly flowing hair behind her ears and pressed her arm across her chest to cover the marks of John's blood on her own chest as well as she could.

She waited, shutting her eyes as she thought herself into a new role.

The troop of cavalry was here already, level with the gates, twenty men at least. Their sabres rattled at their sides as they rode. At their head was a young officer. He turned and stared curiously at Kit, then called out, '*Continuez, les garçons!*' to the troopers, wheeled his horse round and cantered up to Kit. He looked admiringly down at her from the immense height of his magnificent black horse.

'*Bonjour, mademoiselle.* A maiden in distress? Do you need a knight to come to your rescue? In which case, I offer you my services.'

She tried to smile charmingly.

'No, no, monsieur. My brother was overcome by the heat.

Well, to be frank with you, he drank too much last night. He fell dead asleep. I'm waiting here until he wakes. We can make our way home quite easily.'

The officer laughed.

'Drunk, eh? I'll soon bring him round.'

He took his feet out of his stirrups, ready to swing himself off his horse.

'Miss Catherine!' Betsy was back at last, fumbling at the gates with the key. Kit leaped to her feet and dashed across to her.

'Say he's my brother,' she hissed. 'Pretend he's drunk.'

Betsy turned the key and the gate swung open on creaking hinges. She marched across to where John lay and stood over him, her hands planted aggressively on her hips.

'Drunk again,' she said, in heavily accented French. 'What your father's going to say about this . . .'

The officer coughed. He had already replaced his feet in his stirrups.

'If you need any help . . .'

'And who are *you*?' demanded Betsy, glaring up at him. 'Making up to my young lady, I suppose. We'll see what her father has to say about that too.'

The officer backed his horse away.

'*Mille pardons, mademoiselle*. I leave you, quite clearly, in capable hands.'

He looked over his shoulder and waved as he rode away. Kit waved back, then wished she hadn't. The officer's brows had twitched together at the sight of the blood staining her dress.

Betsy had already lifted the twigs off John and was staring down at him, clicking her tongue in dismay.

'We'll have to get him up to the house,' she said. 'There's only one habitable room in my cottage since the roof began to leak. One good thing is that there's no fear of hurting him.

The poor lad's fainted clean away. Take his legs, Miss Catherine. Hurry now. There'll be others coming along this road soon enough. He looks mighty young to be a sailor, but I suppose you know best.'

She bent down as she spoke and picked up John's shoulders in her strong arms. Kit took hold of his legs and, lumbering and lurching under the weight of John's hefty bone and muscle, they staggered up the long drive to the chateau.

John knew nothing of what was happening. He had fainted dead away when the old woman had dumped him out of her cart. When he came to, he seemed to be lying on some kind of mattress, covered with a sheet like the ones he had always slept between at home.

'I'm at home. I'm at Luckstone,' he thought, with no particular surprise.

It needed an effort to drag up his eyelids, but when he had managed it, nothing he saw made sense. Light was coming towards him, stripes of light, as if through thick bars.

Not Luckstone. Prison, he thought indifferently.

But that wasn't right either. He narrowed his eyes, trying to see better. Yes, that was it. What he had mistaken for bars were actually the slats of wooden shutters. They were closed on the outside over tall windows, three windows, stretching down one side of a big, empty room.

There was a sound of footsteps on a creaking woodblock floor at the far end of the room. John tried lifting his head to see who was there, but the effort sent a wave of pain crashing through him. He groaned, and dropped his head again.

Kit heard him and came running over.

'John! You've come round! Oh, John, I thought you were . . . Here, take a sip of water. Betsy!' She turned her head as someone else came up behind her. 'Betsy, he made a noise! John, can you hear me? Open your eyes. You must drink, John.'

He tried to open his eyes again, but the effort was too great. Instead he opened his mouth to accept the water that someone was dribbling into it. It felt good. He swallowed, and opened his mouth for more.

'That's enough, my lovely,' a strange woman's voice said. 'A little bit at a time. You don't want to go choking on it.'

There were questions in his mind. Puzzles. Nothing seemed right. Everything was strange. Only Kit's fingers, patting and stroking his hand, seemed real, and only her voice was familiar.

'John,' she was saying, 'you're going to be fine. Betsy's taken out the bullet. All you have to do now is rest and sleep. You're safe here. I promise you, there is no danger now.'

Chapter Twenty-five

Afever took hold of John that night and for many days he knew nothing of what was happening around him. In his wandering mind he sometimes believed that he was at Luckstone, and that the woman leaning over him, changing the dressings on his wound and holding cups of water to his lips, was his barely remembered mother. Sometimes he was on the *Fearless*, struggling to get out of his hammock at the sound of the bosun's whistle, only to feel arms around him holding him down and cold rags laid on his forehead.

When he came to himself at last, and opened his eyes, he was so weak that even the effort of turning his head was considerable, but his mind was clearing rapidly.

Where am I? he thought. What's happened?

He tried to piece together the last things he remembered. There had been the overheard conversation in the fisherman's hut. He'd been shot in the side. There had been a terrible ride through a dark forest. Some vague impression of a horribly jolting journey in a dirty wagon.

Kit! he thought. No, not Kit. Catherine. Where is she? Did she bring me here?

The effort of trying to work it out was too much. He let his gaze wander round the room. A good deal of light penetrated through the slatted shutters. Though this was the grandest room he had ever been in, it seemed half ruined. On the far side was a huge fireplace, with a stone mantelpiece on which was carved what seemed to be a coat of arms. Above it, a vast mirror in an elaborate gold frame stretched all the way up to the ceiling. The glass, though, was broken, cracks and splinters radiating from a hole that had been smashed right through it.

There seemed to be very little furniture, apart from the bed – no, it was not a bed, but only a mattress – that he was lying on. A chair with a broken back was beside it, and in front of the nearest window was a table covered with a white cloth, and another chair.

Parts of the walls were covered with carved and gilded panelling, but most of it seemed to have been ripped out, exposing the bare brick underneath. But the ceiling! The ceiling was magnificent! It was painted all over to look like the sky, and in the middle was a woman who might be a queen or a goddess sitting on a cloud, with naked baby cherubs all around her. As John looked at it, the painting seemed to swim towards and away from him, the cherubs swooping and diving like fat little birds.

Why was it so quiet here? Was he all alone in this vast place? The only sound was the twitter of starlings somewhere outside, and further away the raucous cawing of a crow. He was in the countryside, then, not in a town. There was no mewing of gulls. He must be far from the sea.

And I'm in France! he remembered, with a jab of alarm. The *Fearless*! I must get down to the coast and find a way to get back to her!

He tried to sit up, pushing off the sheet that covered him,

but a dull pain began to throb in his side and his head reeled with the effort. He gave up.

He was trying to pull the sheet back over him when he heard the door squeak open.

'Who's there?' he said weakly.

He heard a gasp, and made out the shape of a woman, young and slim, in a pale dress. She ran over to him and stood beside his mattress with her back to the light.

'John! You spoke! Oh, I can't believe it!'

'Is that you, Kit?'

He stared at her, puzzled, trying to make her out. He still wasn't used to seeing her in girls' clothes. She was no longer in her bloodstained white dress, but in another one – he could see now that it was blue – with a high waist and some kind of pattern round the neck. Her dark hair, which he was used to seeing tied severely back in a sailor's pigtail, was piled up on the crown of her head. A couple of stray locks fell down to her shoulders.

She went across to the table to pick up a cup and he saw her face. It looked oddly familiar, yet completely different. He stared at her, as if seeing the small pointed chin, long nose and dark pools of her eyes for the first time.

'You're beautiful,' he mumbled.

He felt annoyed. Kit had vanished, and this new Catherine seemed strange and remote. Then the horrible thought struck him that he'd spoken out loud, and he shut his eyes, embarrassed.

'Don't go to sleep again!' Her fingers touched his forehead. 'Has the fever really gone?'

'I don't know. Did I have a fever?'

She laughed.

'Did you have a fever? You have been half dead with it for days and days. At least ten. I've lost count. We were sure you were going to die.'

He was afraid, for a bad moment, that she was about to cry.

'Who's "we"?' he asked.

'Betsy and me, and Jean-Baptiste.'

'Betsy?' he said, trying to remember.

'My nurse. I told you about her. She's been looking after you all this time. She took the bullet out of your side. She's as good as any surgeon. She knows about herbs and nursing too. You would have died so many times without her. She sat here beside you, night after night. She's downstairs now, with Jean-Baptiste, making you some broth.'

'With who?'

'Jean-Baptiste. The old groom. He's been the guardian here since the family left. He's quite old, and a little – well, he totters – but he's completely loyal. When the gendarmes came he was magnificent. I would never have believed it.'

He had hardly taken in what she was saying, but the word 'gendarmes' alarmed him.

'What gendarmes?'

'Don't you remember? No, I suppose not. You don't remember anything, do you? Well, it was so frightening. When we arrived here that first morning after you'd been shot, and I was trying to open the gates, a cavalry officer saw us. I told him you were my brother, and tried to make him think that you were drunk. I thought I'd fooled him, but I think he saw the blood on my dress. Anyway, he must have been suspicious, because he went to tell the gendarmes in Bordeaux. They were already looking for a wounded boy and a girl, because the comte de St Voir – he's the Frenchman who was with Mr Higgins and the others that night in the fisherman's hut – he had reported that his horse had been stolen by English spies. The whole countryside was hunting for us! As soon as they heard from the cavalry officer, they came straight here.'

John was following only with difficulty.

'But they didn't find us.'

'No, they didn't find us. Jean-Baptiste was wonderful. "A boy and a girl?" he said, sounding very old and vague. "Where? Who?" And then Betsy came hurrying out. "There's only one girl here," she said, "and that's Mlle de Jalignac, who is the owner of this chateau." "Mlle de Jalignac?" said the gendarme. "Everyone in Bordeaux knows that she's dead." "Dead? How dare you?" says Betsy. "Those ruffianly revolutionaries killed her poor papa, but they never laid their dirty hands on my poor little Miss Catherine. It was a wicked lie put about by her enemies."'

As she spoke, the characters she was acting came alive for him, and he relaxed. This was the old Kit he knew so well, full of mischievous mimicry. If he shut his eyes he could pretend that the strangely beautiful Catherine didn't exist at all.

Kit was in full flow now.

'"And where are you from, then?" says the gendarme, sounding quite annoyed. "You sound English to me. An English spy, I don't doubt. I'll see your papers, if you please." "English? Of course I'm English, and I'm proud of it," says Betsy. "I've lived in this country quiet as you please since I was a girl, and say what you like, my papers are all in order. Now if you'll wait here I'll go and fetch mademoiselle and you can see her for yourself."'

He laughed at the Betsy she had conjured up before his eyes, then winced at the pain in his side.

'So she ran up here and made me quickly change my dress and pin up my hair, all in five minutes. And I went downstairs and pretended to be very formal, like my grandmother. I was very scared! Since the revolution you never know how the authorities will treat the aristocrats. "Are you really Mlle de Jalignac?" the sergeant of the gendarmes asks, staring at me till I feel really uncomfortable. "Yes, of course I am," say I, trying to look haughty, like Grandmama.

'And then he really surprised me. "Your father," he said, "is greatly missed, mademoiselle. Most of the aristos, they were thieving rascals, and I don't regret what happened in the revolution, though I'm not a bloodthirsty man myself, but your father, he was a good one. It's only in respect of his memory that I'll refrain from arresting this Englishwoman, which I've a perfect right to do."'

She had dropped her joking tone, and her voice thickened. Then she cleared her throat and rattled on.

'So I thanked him, and then he said that anyway he still had his duty to do and his men would have to search the chateau. And Betsy, she was ready for that. "Of course you do," she said, all calm and smiling now. She saw that losing her temper had been dangerous. "But it's a hot day and I was just going to fetch up some of my home-brewed ale from the cellar, where it keeps so cool, and if you'd like to refresh yourselves first in the kitchen . . ."

'So they all went into the kitchen, and Jean-Baptiste came up with me and we carried you into a cupboard under the grand staircase. You were so sick you never even moved, or knew anything about it. The gendarmes had no idea how strong Betsy's beer was, and by the time they came to look over the chateau they wouldn't have seen a coach and horses if it was standing right in the middle of the dining room.'

John had stopped following what she was saying. Words had become slippery things that kept sliding out of reach.

'But we're safe now, aren't we?' he murmured.

'Oh, John, I'm sorry. You're not strong enough to talk yet. I'll go and fetch Betsy. No – here she comes now, with the broth, and Jean-Baptiste too.'

She ran across to the door and took the tray from Betsy, who wiped her hands on her apron, crossed the big empty room and bent over John, feeling his forehead as Kit had done.

'The fever's gone,' she said with satisfaction. 'You'll do now.'

Beside her stood an old man. He nodded down at John, gave a wheezy chuckle and said something in French to Kit.

'This is Jean-Baptiste,' said Kit. 'He says he's glad to see you looking better.'

John, looking at the old man through half-closed, weary eyes, thought he was seeing a relic of a former age. Jean-Baptiste wore a patched pea-green coat with a standing collar, a dirty white wig, askew, with rows of curls over his ears, torn breeches, grubby white stockings with holes in them and black buckled shoes from which his toes peeped through the cracks. John shut his eyes, wondering if he really had returned to reality, or if he was still in some feverish dream.

He felt Betsy's firm arm under his shoulders, lifting him up.

'You drink this broth now, young man,' she said, with a firmness that demanded obedience. 'All of it. It'll do you more good than anything. And then we'll leave you to have a nice long healing sleep.'

PART FOUR

PART FOUR

AUGUST 1808
JALIGNAC

Chapter Twenty-six

Now began for John a dreaming, unreal time of summer and healing, warmth and light. At first, he was only able to leave his mattress for a few minutes each day, but the minutes turned into hours, and his faltering steps became longer and firmer. Progress was slow, though. Weeks later his limbs were still horribly feeble, and his head felt confused and muzzy. He was incapable of thinking clearly about his situation, but he was strangely happy.

The chateau of Jalignac, on its small rise within the park walls, seemed to float above the surrounding forest. It was an enclosed, private world, untouched by anything outside. John felt safe, almost superstitiously sure that nothing could break into the chateau's enchanted isolation and harm anyone there.

He was living with women for almost the first time in his life. He and his father had been alone at Luckstone ever since his mother had died. Life on the *Fearless*, of course, had been rigorously and exclusively masculine.

Betsy's tongue could be rough at times, but she treated him as if he was her son, telling him sharply not to spill the pan of peas he was shelling at her command, or to get out from under her feet and take the bowl of corn out to the chickens in the stable yard. But she was affectionate too, touching his shoulder with a fond caress when she passed his chair.

The roof of Betsy's cottage had been so badly damaged in the previous winter's storms that she had been forced to take up residence in the chateau with Jean-Baptiste. They lived mainly in the kitchens, a vast, rambling domain half underground. Betsy had made the old housekeeper's room her sleeping quarters, and Jean-Baptiste kept to his old room above the stables.

The mob which had invaded the chateau after Kit's father had been executed had looted everything they could lay their hands on. They had scoured the mansion from the attics to the cellars, removing every last stick of furniture, ripping the panelling from the walls, the locks from the doors, the curtains from the windows and the carpets from the floors. The great copper pans had gone from the kitchen, the candelabra from the ballroom, the lanterns from the hall. What they had not been able to remove they had smashed, in an orgy of destruction.

Of all the vast numbers of servants who had once lived on this great estate, the maids and footmen, cooks and gardeners, grooms, stable boys, valets and gamekeepers, only Betsy and Jean-Baptiste had remained.

'Why did you stay?' John asked Betsy curiously one golden evening, as they sat on the sun-baked terrace behind the great house, topping and tailing the beans they had picked from Betsy's vegetable patch that afternoon. 'Why didn't you go home to England?'

'Where's home? What's home? This is my home,' she had responded tartly. 'I've lived here more than half my life. I'm used to it. Who'd remember me in England? Any road, I never really believed them when they said Miss Catherine was dead. I knew she'd come back one day.'

'But it's dangerous for you, isn't it, Betsy? You're an Englishwoman here in France. We're at war.'

She took the basket of beans out of his hands.

'You're taking too much off each one,' she said severely. 'Waste not, want not, Master John.'

'No, but be serious,' he insisted. 'Are you safe here?'

'There's English people a-plenty in Bordeaux,' she said, not meeting his eye. 'People who've lived here for years, like me. In the wine trade most of them. They stay quiet, like I do, and mind their own business. Everyone knows me round here. Even that uppity gendarme sergeant, he knew I was no spy. I'm safe here as a bug in an apple.'

John settled back in his old sagging chair, raised his arms cautiously and leaned his head back into his hands. The wound in his side was almost completely healed now. He could stretch with no more than a twinge of pain.

She's right, he thought lazily, wanting to believe her. We are safe here. No one ever comes. No one ever will.

But later, when he followed her into the chateau kitchen, kept cool even on days of fiercest heat by the thick stone walls, and watched her set an old iron pan to boil on the fire for the beans, a feeling of unease crept over him.

No one would take Betsy for a spy, he thought, but I really am one, I suppose. It's why I came ashore, after all. There's information I should be passing back to England. I shouldn't be idling my time away here. I shouldn't be in France at all.

He pushed the thought away.

It was August now. The sun shone from morning till night, ripening the peaches that grew against the soft yellow stone wall of the vast overgrown kitchen garden. Betsy had been at work here, reclaiming a corner from the jungle of weeds and brambles to grow her own stock of vegetables. Kit, watching and helping, would bite her lip in shame. Her grandmother, she knew, had long since ceased to pay Betsy her wages. Betsy's clothes were wearing out and her shoes were holed.

'It won't be long now, Betsy,' John often heard her say. 'I'll be fourteen soon and have money of my own. You'll never have to darn your stockings again, I promise you.'

'We'll see about that,' Betsy would reply. 'No point in building castles in the air. Now you go out and pick the mint, Miss Catherine, so I can hang it up to dry. It'll be winter soon enough, and we'll need everything we can set in store now.' But the winter seemed impossibly far away. John couldn't believe that these blue, calm mornings and hot, sleepy afternoons would ever give way to the blasts and chills of December.

As he grew stronger, he joined Kit in endless explorations of the chateau and its vast grounds. It was almost as new to Kit as it was to him. Though Jalignac was her own domain, she had scarcely ever been there before, and only in the repressive company of her grandmother.

In the golden summer days, alone together, Catherine became the old Kit again, to John's infinite relief. Together they penetrated the overgrown gardens and climbed the once beautiful stone terraces. They raided the trees in the orchard and the raspberry canes by Betsy's abandoned cottage. They scrambled into the hayloft above the stables, and slid down the bank to the stream that fed the ornamental lake. Here, in a ruined boathouse, they found an old dinghy, and with cries of delight they launched it on the water.

'Cast off, Mr Smith!' John shouted. 'Climb aboard at once, or I'll damn you for a landlubber!'

'Aye aye, sir!' cried Kit, jumping nimbly after him. 'Hard to starboard! Take in a reef there, or you'll send us down to Davy Jones's locker!'

They took an oar each and rowed with the efficient short

strokes of seamen to the middle of the lake, where Kit suddenly let out a purely feminine scream.

'John, watch out! We're sinking!'

She was right. The boards of the little boat, quite dried out with lack of use, had shrunk, and water was gurgling up through them. Hardly able to row for laughing, they made it back to the bank and stepped out, soaked, leaving the dinghy half submerged at the water's edge.

There was one part of the estate that they always avoided. The front of the chateau faced the road, and though the avenue which led down to it was long and overgrown, the frontage of the house was still clearly visible through the wrought-iron gates. Looking out from inside, through the slatted shutters, John had seen an increasing volume of traffic passing up and down. Fresh troops, their muskets polished and shining, the blue of their coats still bright from the tailors' hands, were marching south to join Napoleon's armies who were fighting against the British army in Spain. Passing them, travelling north away from the war, came carts and tumbrils carrying the wounded, and, sadder still, chained gangs of British and Spanish prisoners.

But inside Jalignac's enchanted park it was easy to forget the road and its reminders of the world of war outside. The chateau itself took days to explore. John and Kit investigated every corner. They ran from room to room, startling nesting pigeons in the chimneys, climbing grand staircases and small winding ones too, emerging on to the roof with its forest of chimneys and dormer windows, delving into cellars with their broken wine racks.

And then, one morning, when August was nearly at an end and the last ripe plums had been gathered in, they found themselves once more in the ballroom. Kit hummed the tune of a minuet and danced a few steps under the great chandelier which, though dull with dust, still hung from the gilded ceiling on its massive chain. John caught her round the waist and twirled her round and round. He had never danced more than a few Scottish reels and a sailor's jig in his life, and he was clumsy, catching his feet in the hem of her dress. She fell against him, laughing. He looked down into her face.

Something shifted in his chest. His heart began to hammer inside his ribcage. Abruptly he let her go and turned away to hide the scarlet flood that was rising in his face.

Kit had turned away too, but he could see that her cheeks were red as well. He wanted to catch her again, and hold her for longer, to feel her soft hair against his chin and her slim waist between his hands. But she had already darted away from him and had disappeared from the room.

'I'm up here, John,' she called out.

He looked up. She was leaning over the carved balustrade of a small gallery that ran along one end of the ballroom, grinning down at him. 'Did I make you jump? There's a little staircase. Come on up.'

Her smile was doing strange things to his breathing.

'I've had enough,' he said crossly. 'I'm tired of all this.' And he stumped out of the ballroom and took refuge in the library, where he sat down on a window seat and leafed unseeingly through one of the torn, dusty books which the mob, unable to read, had left scattered on the floor.

I must have been mad just now, he told himself, flinging the book down again. I'm not going to think about her like that. She's Kit to me, not a girl at all. I hope she didn't see what I was feeling. If she did, she'd think I was an oaf. A stupid, stupid oaf.

Chapter Twenty-seven

The next day, for the first time in weeks, it rained. Clouds boiled up out of the west, thunder rolled round the chateau's turrets and violent gusts of wind rattled the windows. Betsy sent John off to sift through the mangers in the old stables, where the hens liked to roost. The next heavy squall of rain caught him as he ran back across the stable yard, clutching two precious eggs in his hands. As if the touch of water had broken an enchantment, he stopped in his tracks, letting the sparkling drops dash against his cheeks and soak through his shirt. The last time he'd felt the rain on him he'd been aboard the *Fearless*. He'd been aloft, up the foremast, taking in a reef. The great warship had heaved beneath him on the swell, the men had worked in perfect unison, singing 'Come all you valiant seamen, and each jolly tar', as they struggled to haul in the soaked canvas. Later, there'd been a round of grog. He'd stripped off his wet clothes and fished dry ones out of Kit's chest. That night there'd been fiddle music, and the men had danced jigs on the gun deck.

He felt an unexpected pang of longing for that masculine,

ordered world, with all its hardship and danger. He felt ashamed too.

I shouldn't be here, he told himself disgustedly. What use am I here? It's my duty to get back to sea and report what I know to Mr Erskine.

The shell of the egg in his right hand cracked in his tightened fist, and its slimy raw contents oozed through his fingers. Irritated, he shook the dripping hair back out of his eyes, missing the feeling of his sailor's pigtail, which Betsy had cut off while he'd been ill. He felt as if he'd been sleep-walking and had woken up. He snuffed up into his nostrils the scent of rain on the dry baked earth. It was nothing like the salt tang of the sea, but it was the smell of water, nonetheless.

He took a deep breath and splashed across the yard into the kitchen.

'Kit, Betsy,' he began. 'Listen, I must . . .'

He stopped in surprise. A stranger was sitting by the fire, holding his sodden boots out towards the blaze. In a glance, John took in the man's massive forearms, his unkempt black hair and weather-beaten face. He felt an immediate alarm. Was this another gendarme, come to arrest him? Then he saw that the man was looking anxious too.

'There's nothing to fear, John,' said Kit, running forward to take the remaining whole egg from him. 'This is Jem. He's Betsy's cousin. He's English.'

Something stirred in John's memory. Hadn't Kit talked about Betsy's cousin that morning in the captain's great cabin, when he'd first learned that she was a girl? Something about a smuggler, who'd taken her off in his boat from the French coast.

He strode forward and held out his hand to grasp Jem's, then remembered it was still dripping with raw egg. He bent over the pail of water set by the hearth and quickly washed the mess off.

'Have you come from the coast?' he asked eagerly. 'Do you have news of the *Fearless*?'

Jem smiled.

'You're John, then. The tales these women tell about you! Glad to see you in the pink, as they say. Nasty wound them villains gave you, so I hear.'

John pulled up a chair beside Jem's. In spite of the coolness the rain had brought outside, it was stiflingly hot in the kitchen, where Betsy had built up the fire to dry off Jem's clothes. She was hovering over him now, trying to put a glass of something in his hands.

'Yes, I'm John.' He tried to hide his impatience. 'The *Fearless*, is she still on blockade?'

Jem took the glass from Betsy's hands and sipped, smacking his lips with enthusiasm.

'Not that I know of. We came ashore last night, slipped in to the deserted stretch of coast north of Arcachon on this westerly. We've been waiting out at sea for weeks. Flat calm, it's been. Water still as a farmer's duck pond. First chance we had we came ashore. There's been no sign of a British ship for days. One'll still be out there, though. No saying if she'll be the *Fearless* herself, but it's more than likely, unless they've swapped her for another damned naval busybody. Lurking out of sight of the river mouth, she'll be, hoping to lure out another French ship, like the cunning old sea wolf she is.'

John was barely listening.

'I've got to get back to her,' he burst out. 'Can you help me? Please, can you take me out to sea when you go, and get me back on board her?'

Jem laughed.

'Want to get back to sea, do you? Pining for salt beef and weevily ship's biscuit? Strange lad you must be. Nice snug berth you've got yourself into here, among the petticoats. Wouldn't mind casting anchor myself here, given half the chance.'

'As to that, Jem,' said Betsy gruffly, and John was amazed to see a brick-red flush suffuse her face, 'you know that any time you like . . .'

He stood up, put his arm round her waist and gave it a squeeze.

'I know, my girl. I know. But a man has a living to earn, inside the law or without it. I come as often as I can.'

He planted a smacking kiss on her lips.

John and Kit looked at each other. Kit let out a giggle of embarrassment. John felt an answering one bubble up inside him, and knew that if he gave way to it he'd soon be laughing uncontrollably. He dragged his eyes away from Kit's face.

Jem's the real reason why Betsy stays here, he thought, in a moment of revelation.

Betsy pushed the smuggler away with a reproving frown, and he released her.

'Please, Jem,' John persisted. 'When are you weighing anchor? Couldn't you take me with you?'

A crease split the leathery skin between Jem's heavy brows.

'I could take you off with us,' he said. 'But then again, I don't know as how it would help you. The best I could do would be to take you back to England, and put you off on a quiet little beach I knows of, on the Kent coast, but to go anywhere near a man-o'-war – why, it would be mortal folly, and my men would mutiny at the very idea. Pressed into the navy again we'd all be before we could take in our sails. Our brig would be taken, and all our wine and brandy, that we're paying good money for, would go glugging down the throats of your captain and his thirsty officers.'

'Then never mind the *Fearless*. I'll come with you to Kent,'

John said. He couldn't understand why he was suddenly so desperate to leave Jalignac. 'When do we leave?'

'Listen to him, the fire-eater!' marvelled Jem. 'I thought he was bold enough sitting here as cool as you please in the heart of the enemy's country. Now it turns out he can't wait to get back to the navy so's he can take another pop at them. We'll not leave for a fortnight at least, young John. I've my new cargo to purchase and load, and business to complete in Bordeaux. Takes time when all must be done in secrecy. And now that the wind has turned to the west, it might be long enough before it changes back to give us a favourable course. I'll take you with me, if you're that set on it, but you must bide your time and wait for word that we're ready to slip our moorings.'

'Thank you. Thank you! I'll be ready. I'll be waiting for you every day.'

He was extraordinarily elated at the thought of action, and impatient at the delay. He turned to Kit, expecting her to mirror his own feelings, as she had always done in the past, but she had turned her back and was staring at the rivulets of rain sluicing down the window.

He went up to her and touched her arm.

'Just think! To be at sea again . . . !' he began.

'Oh, leave me alone!' she interrupted and ran out of the kitchen, slamming the door behind her.

The rain had cleared by early afternoon. John had gone off in search of Kit, but though he had hunted in all her usual haunts he hadn't been able to find her. The sun came out, steaming the water off the terrace. Once the storm had passed, his excitement began to die down. What would he do when he was back in Britain? He knew nobody south of the border. Even if Jem kept his word, and landed him on the coast of Kent, the chances were that he'd be caught up quickly by the press gangs that operated everywhere on the south coast and sent to an entirely different ship. How would he get to London? How would he find the right people and tell them about the nest of spies operating out of Edinburgh? He would never make them believe him. And how would he find his father and put right the fraud that had taken Luckstone from them?

I'll talk it through with Kit, he thought. Where is she, anyway?

As he walked up the dusty grand staircase, searching through the chateau for the second time, he remembered how she'd shaken his hand off her arm and refused to speak to him.

Maybe she thought I wanted to get away from *her*, he thought. Perhaps I hurt her feelings. He was on unfamiliar ground and felt uneasy. The memory of that moment in the ballroom came rushing back. He pushed it away.

She probably doesn't care if I'm here or if I go, though she might miss me a little. She just feels restless, I expect, like I do, and wants to go back to sea.

He kicked aside a piece of plaster that had fallen from the decaying ceiling.

She couldn't go back to the *Fearless* now though. Not any more. She's become too much of a girl. Even though she's such a great actress, she couldn't take everyone in again. She's changed too much. Yes, that's what the matter must be. She's jealous at the thought that I can get away, while she has to stay.

This conclusion made him smile with relief. He'd reached the long gallery now, with bare patches along the walls showing where portraits had once hung. He walked along its vast length slowly, thinking hard.

'But then again,' he said out loud, 'I could be wrong, after all. Maybe she could turn back into Kit again. If she could do it before, why couldn't she do it again?'

It would be the best thing of all, if they could just slip back into their old lives, dress in their sailors' rig, sling their hammocks side by side, share all the privations, the triumphs, the camaraderie, the hardships and the glory of life on the man-o'-war – go back, in fact, to how things were before.

I'll persuade her, he told himself. She'll come with me, I know she will. I need her, anyway. I couldn't bear life on the *Fearless* without Kit.

A sound from outside caught his attention. He went to the window at the end of the gallery and looked down on the avenue that led to the main gates. Jean-Baptiste, in his ancient green coat, was slowly dragging shut one of the heavy wrought–iron gates. It must have been the protesting shriek of its rusting hinges as it opened that he had heard.

A man had ridden through the gates on a big chestnut horse. He was now trotting serenely up the avenue as if he had been there a hundred times before.

John caught his breath and moved out of sight behind the ragged curtain.

The stranger was no smuggler, like Jem. His horse was glossy with good grooming, his blue riding coat smartly cut, the cravat at his throat a pure, sharp white. He was French. An official of some kind. He'd been here before.

Jean-Baptiste knows him, John thought, registering the points one by one. This could be dangerous. I must hide. Before he had time to move, a door at the far end of the gallery opened and Kit appeared.

'Where have you been?' John said self-consciously. 'I've been looking for you everywhere.'

He thought, though he couldn't be sure, that her eyes were red, as if she'd been crying.

She shook her head.

'It doesn't matter. Listen, you must hide. The man outside, he's M. Fouchet, my father's agent. The family's man of business. He must have heard from the gendarme that I'd returned. He's a good man. He's looked after all our affairs for years, but he mustn't know you're here. I must go and warn Betsy to get Jem out of the kitchen. Go into the ballroom and up to the gallery. It's out of the way. Even if he wants to go round the house, he'll never look up there. Don't make a sound, and don't worry. I'll get rid of him as soon as I can.'

Chapter Twenty-eight

It was dusty and dull in the ballroom gallery. After five minutes of watching a spider weave a web between two pillars, rebellion stirred in John. Who was Kit, to tell him where to hide? He wasn't her servant. He wouldn't be packed off to skulk in secret like some low criminal.

He crept down the balcony steps and stood in the middle of the ballroom. He listened. No sound echoed through the great empty rooms of the chateau. If the agent was doing an inspection, he was either unnaturally silent or he was in another part of the building entirely.

I can easily keep ahead of them if they come this way. I'll hear them long before they reach me, John told himself. He opened the high double doors at the end of the ballroom that led out to the head of the grand staircase. He stopped, and listened again. Nothing. More boldly, he ran lightly down to the stone-flagged hall below.

Feet crunched cautiously on the gravel outside. A short stocky figure stole past the window. Jem, his bundle in his hand, was on his way from the kitchen to the stables, where he was no doubt planning to hide himself.

The kitchen! That's where the fellow will be, John thought

triumphantly. Betsy will be feeding him one of her pies in the kitchen.

Long corridors, several dusty rooms and a flight of steps separated the hall from the kitchen. John went quietly, ears pricked, slipping from one doorway to the next.

He heard the murmur of a man's voice as he reached the top of the kitchen stairs. He'd been right, then. They were still in the kitchen.

This is folly, he thought. If I'm caught I could find myself in prison, or worse. But he couldn't help going on. He'd been idle, lazy, tied to women's apron strings for long enough. He needed excitement. Risk. Danger.

He reached the bottom of the stairs. From here, he could see in through the half-open kitchen door. M. Fouchet stood facing the table at which Betsy and Kit were sitting. He was haranguing Kit in rapid French, the material of his blue serge coat creasing and uncreasing across his shoulders as he waved his arms in expressive gestures.

Moving cautiously, John edged round the end of the staircase. There was a cavity underneath it, a dark place where Betsy stored old barrels and preserving jars. He could easily dart in there to hide, if he had to.

He wished again, as he'd often wished before, that he'd applied himself more diligently to learning French during these last slow months. He could understand a little, and say a few words and phrases, mimicking Jean-Baptiste's broad accent to make Kit smile. But the French agent's rapid speech was lost on him. He could barely make out a word.

He began to wonder if it was worth standing here, in this dark musty corridor, listening to a tirade he couldn't understand. He was about to start creeping back up the stairs, when Betsy's voice rang out, in sharp, clear English.

'What's the man saying, Miss Catherine? What is all this

about? I can't follow no more than half of it. He speaks all in a rush.'

M. Fouchet coughed politely.

'*Pardon, madame*. I can of course converse in English if it would convenience you. You 'ave lived in France so long you are to me as a Frenchwoman. I thought you spoke so good French.'

'I speak French well enough,' Betsy said crossly, 'but you're getting in too deep, jabbering away too fast for any mortal soul. Have my ears being playing tricks, or was you talking about that woman Josephine just now?'

'He was, Betsy.' Kit's voice was nervous. 'The Empress Josephine is coming to Bordeaux next week.'

'Is she now? And will that monster Bonaparte – will *His Majesty* the *Emperor* be accompanying her royalship?'

'Betsy!' Kit broke in hastily. 'No, the emperor remains in Paris. The empress comes alone.'

'I 'ave been telling your young lady,' M. Fouchet broke in, 'that there presents itself an opportunity too wonderful to ignore. Perhaps you do not understand, madame, 'ow serious are the affairs of mademoiselle. 'Er uncle, I regret to say, 'as for many years been attempting to . . . to . . .'

'Defraud the poor chick,' broke in Betsy. 'Aye, I know it. And that old witch her grandmother too. As wicked a pair of villains as any you might meet in Newgate jail.'

M. Fouchet laughed.

'I see you do not 'ide your opinions, madame. In this matter, at any rate, I agree with you. I was explaining to Mlle de Jalignac that I 'ave, for all these years, done my best to save for 'er what I can. I too, like you, did not believe in 'er demise. She 'as been telling me 'ow she sought refuge with an old school friend in Switzerland, where she 'as been safely 'iding all this time. Mademoiselle is like her admirable papa, for whom I had a great respect and, may I say, affection. There are papers I retained in secrecy, at some risk to myself, from the grasp of the new Marquis de Vaumas. That gentleman 'as done much, while in Paris, to gain the favour of those in power. A little more effort from 'im, a little more time, and everything will be lost. Mlle de Jalignac is young, alone, without friends of influence who can speak for 'er. Soon enough 'er uncle will 'ear that she 'as returned. Such news spreads quickly. 'E will rush 'ere, bad man that 'e is, to get 'er once more in 'is power. What am I? A man of business, no more. I am telling 'er, Mme Betsy, she needs support at court. She needs a strong interest, someone who will take 'er part. She is beautiful, young, *charmante*. She must grasp this one chance, go to the empress, 'erself a woman full of sentiment, and beg for 'er aid.'

'Beg help from that baggage?' Betsy burst out. 'The wife of the most vicious—'

'*Betsy!*' Kit's voice was sharp with warning. 'M. Fouchet is very kind to think of it. He has been working selflessly, you know he has, with nothing but my interests at heart.'

'Yes, well, yes. That's true enough.'

In his hiding place, John smiled. He could imagine how Betsy looked – like a hen with ruffled feathers which were slowly settling smooth again. 'You're right, my lovey. M. Fouchet has been very good, I'm sure. Where are your manners, Miss Catherine? Offer the gentleman another slice of cherry tart. His plate's been empty these last ten minutes.'

John heard the scrape of a knife on a plate and the sound of a chair grating on the kitchen's stone floor as M. Fouchet settled himself down at the table again.

'M. Fouchet is right, Betsy,' Kit was saying in a low voice. 'It's an opportunity too good to miss. To speak to the empress herself, to gain her support – it would be worth everything to us. However much influence my uncle has gained in Paris, what can compare with the voice of Napoleon's own wife?'

'Yes, but think, Miss Catherine. How will you do it? You can't just walk in from the street, all on your own, looking like a milkmaid in those old clothes of yours, and say to everyone, "I'm Mlle de Jalignac, that everyone thought was dead, only I'm not, and now I want to see Her High-and-Mightyship and get my inheritance back." Laugh? They'd choke themselves. And then they'd pop you in prison, as like as not, for impersonating a dead person.'

M. Fouchet had swallowed the last of the cherry tart and now he cleared his throat.

'Madame is taking too bad a view of the matter,' he said. 'For the dress, it is surely of no difficulty to create an ensemble that would enhance the beauty of mademoiselle. And the occasion – that will be of great magnificence. The city of Bordeaux is to give a grand ball at the Château Royal to celebrate the visit of the empress. It will be soon – on Thursday of next week. I myself am one of the committee that is making all the arrangements. It is a matter of ease for me to secure an invitation. Mlle de Jalignac will be presented to Her Majesty by Mme de Montsegard, a client of mine, a noblewoman of the first respectability, who remembers with fondness the Marquis and Marquise de Vaumas. She will undertake to introduce Mlle Catherine to the empress, in person. After that, it will be up to mademoiselle to bring 'er plight to the attention of 'Er Majesty, and touch the imperial 'eart.'

There was a short silence. Kit broke it.

'I . . . I didn't realize. A ball? Dancing, in front of a crowd of people? To go there and not know a single soul? I can't do that. I couldn't do *that*!'

'Oh yes, you can, my girl.' Betsy spoke roughly. 'There's a few old dresses of your mama's that I have laid by, things the rascally revolutionaries never laid their hands on. Make up nicely the blue silk will, into a pretty ball gown. Jewels you don't have, but that don't matter, being young as you are, and jewels unsuitable for an unmarried girl. Slippers now, slippers . . .'

She fell silent.

'But I'd need a coach to take me there!' Kit sounded breathless with panic.

'There's your grandfather's coach mouldering away in the coach house, as well you know. Clean out the hens' nests, polish it up, smarten the paintwork – it will do very well.'

'A coachman! Who would drive it?'

'Jean-Baptiste, of course. The man's a doddering fool, but he was driving coaches before you was born.'

'You will not need your own coach to arrive at the ball,' M. Fouchet broke in. 'You will go accompanied by Mme de Montsegard in her own elegant equipage. All you will need is a footman to accompany you.'

'Betsy! I can't! I won't do it! You know I can't!'

'Can't is a word I never taught you, Miss Catherine,' Betsy said severely. 'I never thought to hear you say it. 'Tis only a part you have to play, and you so good at acting. You'll pull it off easy. Think of your poor papa, going so bravely to his death, and your mama, wanting all that was best for you. You owe this to their memories. You must make a push to help yourself and take your rightful place – or marry your charming cousin Hubert or live a pauper for the rest of your days. The choice is yours.'

'A footman!' Kit said wildly. 'M. Fouchet is right. I need a footman, and I don't have one!'

John, with a flash of inspiration, knew what he had to do. He groped under the stairs, lifted out an old earthenware preserving jar and holding it to his chest marched into the kitchen.

'Here's the jar, miss, what you sent me to look for,' he said, in what he thought was a suitably subservient tone. 'Where did you wish me to set it down?'

The effect of his entrance was dramatic. Kit gasped and took a step backwards, but her eyes were dancing with excitement. Betsy frowned ferociously and glared at him. M. Fouchet turned to stare at him, his thin eyebrows raised suspiciously.

'And who might this person be?' he asked.

John put down the preserving jar and tugged his forelock.

'Mlle de Jalignac's footman, at your service, sir.'

'Another English person?' M. Fouchet was frowning. 'What is this, mademoiselle? Mme Betsy, she is one thing. She 'as lived in France for many a year. She is known in Bordeaux. But this . . . an Englishman . . .'

'English? Oh, I'm not English!' John smiled broadly as if the idea amused him. 'Scottish by birth, but now a citizen of the United States of America. That's what I am. I've no more love for King George and his murdering redcoats than you have yourself, sir.'

'An American!' The agent smiled delightedly. 'You are the first from that country that I 'ave met. Your Boston, it is a big city, no? The 'arbour, I 'ave 'eard, it is better than Le Havre. 'Ow many ships, would you say . . . ?'

'That will do, John,' Betsy said, bustling forwards. 'Get along with you now. Find Jean-Baptiste and tell him to fetch out the coach from the coach house and start to clean it up. Whatever Mr Fouchet says, we'll need to get about somehow. My lor', there'll be so much to do these next few days we won't none of us find the time to blow our own noses!'

Chapter Twenty-nine

John had plenty of time during the next few days to regret his rashness. He barely saw Kit. She was closeted with Betsy talking about dresses. They were measuring lengths of silk and rummaging through the dusty old boxes full of feathers, artificial flowers, beads and ribbons that had once belonged to Kit's mother, and which Betsy had managed to squirrel away.

Mme de Montsegard, who came clattering out from Bordeaux in a smart carriage, looked briefly at Betsy's accumulated treasures and rolled her eyes derisively. The fashion had changed completely, she announced. No one wore such sad stuff any more. Stiff coloured silks had been consigned to history. White muslin and the flimsiest satin, with perhaps a dusting of tiny pearls, were all that could be allowed. She offered to dress Kit in a ball gown in the appropriate style, entirely at her own expense. She added that her son, the Chevalier de Montsegard, would be delighted to squire Mlle de Jalignac to the ball, as he was on leave from his regiment, and that he had already requested the honour of the first dance.

'Oh, I've heard all about *him*. Spendthrift fortune-hunting nobody,' Betsy muttered under her breath when she heard this. 'After my poor duck's fortune, if she ever gets it.'

Mme de Montsegard looked John over with a cold eye as she left. She remarked that footmen were hard to come by nowadays as all young men with a shred of patriotism in them had gone off to join the emperor's glorious army, but informed Kit that she would send over a livery and wig for him to wear at the ball.

'American, you say?' she said to Kit, turning John round to look at his back, as if he was a horse she was planning to buy. 'They're too democratic as a rule to make good servants, but I suppose he'll have to do.'

She lifted her skirts as she stepped fastidiously down the rubble-strewn steps outside the chateau's great front door.

'It will cost a fortune to set this place to rights, my dear. Why don't you simply leave it to fall down and come to me in Bordeaux? I'll find you a charming husband in no time at all.'

John, understanding the gist of her words only too well, punched out at her departing shadow and stalked off to the coach house, where Jean-Baptiste, with infinite slowness, was washing down the panels of the antiquated coach.

'Jem not back?' he asked the old man in his halting French.

Jean-Baptiste didn't bother to answer, and John didn't press him. Jem had vanished days ago, sidling away from Jalignac while M. Fouchet was still eating pies in Betsy's kitchen. John had no real expectation of seeing him return. He berated himself daily for letting his one chance of escape slip away so easily.

He helped Jean-Baptiste for a while, relieving his feelings by scrubbing so hard at the coach's yellow wheels that he was in danger of taking the paint off along with the grime.

'*Trop fort!* Don't rub so hard!' Jean-Baptiste grumbled, coming up behind him.

'Oh, do it all yourself, then,' said John, flinging down the rag he'd been wielding and marching out of the stable yard.

He wandered through the gate in the high brick wall that surrounded the kitchen garden. The peaches and apricots had long since been gathered in, but the apples were ripening now. A few days ago he and Kit would have climbed the trees together. They would have munched through the apples and thrown the cores at each other, hurling insults in sailor's language till they were both weak with laughter.

Kit was slipping away from him. When he looked at her, he could see no sign of the boy who had been a powder monkey. Sometimes he could hardly believe that that Kit had ever existed.

'We were equals. Shipmates,' he said out loud to the wasp that had fastened on to the apple in his hand. 'What am I now? Her stupid, mincing footman.'

He was revolted at the thought of dressing up in a fancy livery, cramming a hot, itchy, powdery wig over his own thick hair and bowing and scraping like a servant to the wife and hangers-on of Bonaparte, his country's deadly enemy, the man that every British sailor was sworn to defeat.

At the same time, he had to admit, the idea of the ball scared him too. What if he was found out? What if anyone guessed that Mlle de Jalignac's footman was in fact a Scot, a seaman in the Royal Navy, who had come ashore in pursuit of French spies? The thought of what they would do to him sent a chill running down his spine.

But they won't guess. Why should they? No one looks at footmen anyway. They just stand about like rows of dummies. It'll be Kit they'll look at. She'll be so pretty there'll be men crawling about all round her, sniffing after her and her fortune, like Mme de Montsegard's revolting son, and I won't be able to do anything about it.

He blew the wasp off his apple and took a savage bite.

'John! *John!*' Kit came flying through the gate. 'I've been looking for you everywhere.'

He turned reluctantly.

'Really? What for?'

He knew he sounded sour, but he couldn't help it.

'That horrid woman, Mme Montsegard, she was so proud and rude. I hated the way she looked at you.'

'Oh. You noticed.'

'Of course I noticed.' She raised her eyebrows and stared down her nose, looking so like Mme de Montsegard that in spite of himself John had to laugh. She grinned back. 'Listen, John, you don't have to do this – be my footman, I mean. I can see that you feel bad about it. Anyway, it's dangerous. All the other servants will be French. They're sure to suspect something when you can't speak to them, even if you say you're American. I can manage this thing on my own. I'm sure I can.'

But he heard the doubt in her voice.

'I don't care if it's dangerous. I'm not scared. You'd like me to come, I know you would. You'd feel better if I was there with you.'

'Oh yes! Just to know that there was someone I could trust, a true friend nearby, who knows, who understands . . .'

Her hand was on his sleeve. He couldn't help putting his own over it. The warmth of her fingers sent a shock right up his arm and he snatched his hand away.

'I've said I'm doing it. I'm not changing my mind.'

'But anyway, John, admit it. Aren't you a bit anxious to see Josephine? In person? I want to. She is so beautiful, everyone says, and lazy, and charming.'

He made a face.

'Why should I care about Napoleon's woman? That's the worst of it. I'll have to show respect to her and all her lackeys when I should be out at sea, on the *Fearless*, trying to blow holes through her husband's ships.'

She stretched up to pick an apple for herself.

'I know. The war and everything. It confuses me. Did you see the troops this morning, marching up the road towards Bordeaux? They must have come back from Spain. They were wounded, half of them, and the others were in rags. It's so stupid – hundreds of thousands of men marching off to kill each other. And all for what? For nothing!'

'All so the husband of your precious Josephine can rule over the whole of Europe! I don't want him marching in triumph down Edinburgh High Street. I'll come to your precious ball. I'll be your footman, but afterwards, don't you see, I *have* to get back to the *Fearless*.'

She nodded.

'I know. And I'm coming with you.'

'What? You can't!'

'I must. There are still five months to go till I'm fourteen. Until then, even if I gain the empress's favour, even if M. Fouchet manages to regain my inheritance for me, I'm still in my uncle's power. He's my guardian. He can do what he likes with me, and my grandmother will help him every way she can.'

'He can't force you to marry your cousin. No one can actually make you.'

She shivered.

'You don't know my uncle.'

'Anyway, you're too young to get married.'

'No, I'm not. My cousin was married last year. She was thirteen. Nothing will change for me, John. Not till January next year. As M. Fouchet said, sooner or later my uncle and grandmother will hear I'm in Bordeaux. It'll be very soon, in fact, now that I'm going to be seen in public. There'll be a scandal, since they let it be known that I was dead. They'll come racing down here as fast as they can, to make everyone believe they're delighted to hear that I'm alive after all. I'll be caught. My only hope is to get away and wait until my birthday.'

His heart had lifted.

'You'll be Kit again,' he said.

'I will if Captain Bannerman will let me.' She stuck out her chest, lowered her chin, frowned mightily and pretended to look through a telescope. '"Females on my ship is what I can't abide,"' she said in a deep gravelly voice.

He laughed.

'He can hardly turn you adrift at sea, though, if you somehow manage to get on board.'

'No, he can't. Not Thundering Sam. Though some captains would.'

They had turned out of the kitchen garden and were walking slowly back towards the chateau.

'How will we do it, Kit? How can we get back out to sea?'

'I don't know. I've been thinking and thinking. But we'll find a way. We have to! As soon as I've met the empress and secured her support, we'll track Jem down again. If he takes us within sight of the *Fearless*, and lets us have his little skiff, we can row the rest of the way ourselves. Just imagine how astonished everyone will be to see us again!'

'They probably think we deserted,' John said gloomily. 'You know what the punishment for that is – hanging from the yardarm.'

'Don't be silly. The captain and Mr Erskine know the truth. We've information to give them, anyway.'

They found Betsy outside the kitchen door, working the rusting pump in the yard. She stopped when she saw them and tucked her brown curls, dampened with sweat, back inside her mob cap.

'Get over here, do,' she said sharply, 'and give me a hand with this pump. If I have work this thing much longer I'll melt like a pat of butter and run all over the cobblestones.'

Chapter Thirty

J ohn glared into the mirror, moving his head to see between the cracks in the glass. He loathed the sight of himself in this silly rig. The white wig, liberally powdered by Betsy, made him look much older, and anonymous. He wasn't himself at all.

He went across to the bed in the corner of the huge room, on which his green livery tailcoat, resplendent with brass buttons, had been laid out. He put it on and did up the buttons, then slipped his stockinged feet into the shiny black buckled shoes which Mme de Montsegard had also provided.

They squeaked as he walked across to the door. He hesitated on the threshold and looked back into the room. It had changed beyond recognition in the last few weeks. Since word had begun to leak out ▓▓▓ the surrounding countryside that Mlle de Jalignac was ▓▓▓▓▓ ▓d at all, but had returned to her chateau and was making moves to take control of her inheritance, the local farmers, one by one, had been calling at the gate. Anxious to make a good impression on one who might soon be their powerful landlady, and sorry for a young girl who had so cruelly lost her parents, they were returning items which they had, so many years ago, gleefully looted from the chateau.

Every day Jean-Baptiste staggered up from the gate with some odd thing or other, a rolled-up tapestry, or a huge framed portrait balanced on his shoulder, or a carved wardrobe door tucked under one arm.

These ill-assorted items were now scattered around the chateau's echoing rooms. John's own chamber, once so bare, now boasted three inlaid chairs, a porcelain candelabra and a small chest of drawers with gilded handles.

He felt odd at the thought of leaving the chateau and going outside into the world beyond the rusting gates again. He hadn't passed through them since that day, so many months before, when the old woman had hauled him, unconscious, out of her cart, and dumped him on the grass verge.

He went downstairs to the hall and let himself out through the front door. Jean-Baptiste was there already, sitting on the coachman's seat of the lumbering old carriage, to which two stolid plain horses, borrowed from a nearby farm, were harnessed. The old man's wig was askew and his coat buttons were done up wrong. When he saw John, he fumblingly hid the bottle he'd been drinking from and fiddled ostentatiously with the reins.

John leaped lightly up to him, fished the bottle out from behind him and flung it away into the bushes on the far side of the drive.

'You're drunk, you disgusting old man!' he said. 'Pull yourself together. You can't ⬛⬛⬛ down – not tonight.'

Jean-Baptiste looked at him ⬛⬛⬛gh wet bleary eyes.

'*J'ai peur*,' he whined. 'It's so long since I drove a coach and pair.'

'I know . . . You're nervous . . . It's been a long time,' John mimicked unsympathetically, pulling the man's wig straight and redoing his buttons. 'Sit up now. She's coming.'

Kit had appeared at the front door. John, who had jumped down from the box, frowned ferociously, trying not to let his heart turn over at the sight of her. She was wearing a simple, perfect high-waisted gown made of a floating white muslin, over which was an overdress of shimmering white satin. Tiny seed pearls were sewn round the puffed sleeves and at the neck, and over her arms was draped a shawl of the flimsiest cream silk. Her dark hair was piled in a mass of curls on the crown of her head. She looked much older, and almost frighteningly beautiful.

'How do I look?' she said, spinning round.

'Lovely,' his voice croaked.

She had spun too far and nearly tripped, sending her little beaded reticule flying.

'Devil take the plaguy thing,' she said, in Jabez Barton's deep voice.

He laughed, feeling better, and went to retrieve her reticule.

'Stop it, Kit. You're supposed to be a lady, for heaven's sake.'

Betsy had opened the door of the coach and was doubtfully prodding the stained cushions of the seat.

'Get in now, Miss Catherine. Mme de Montsegard will be waiting for you. And for heaven's sake don't lean back against them squabs. For all they've been brushed over a hundred times, I don't trust this old contraption not to mark your dress.'

Kit flung her arms round Betsy's neck.

'Thank you, dearest Betsy, for everything. You know I'm doing this for you. If I succeed, you'll never want for anything again.'

'I know, I know. Get on with you now.'

'You'll look after yourself, Betsy, while we're gone?'

'Lord, my lovey, you'll be home again tomorrow morning.

239

Now take care and mind your manners, no more than one glass of champagne, and if there are oysters don't touch 'em. I ate a bad one in Bordeaux last year and it all but carried me off.'

She had bundled Kit inside the coach and shut the door. John leaped up to the footman's stand behind, Jean-Baptiste flicked his whip, the horses shook their manes and the ancient equipage groaned its way down the drive.

Looking back at Jalignac as he closed the gates behind the coach, John had the oddest feeling that the great building itself, along with Betsy, who was waving from the front steps, was bidding them farewell.

Flaming torches had been lit outside the Château Royal in the centre of Bordeaux. Now that darkness had fallen, they sent long shadows flickering across the flagstones as the line of carriages moved slowly up to the magnificent gateway, pausing only to set down their grandly dressed occupants before moving on to make way for the next one.

The old Jalignac coach had been left, along with Jean-Baptiste, at Mme de Montsegard's grand Bordeaux residence. Mme de Montsegard's carriage, though quite small, was new and very smart, and the chestnut ponies that drew it were high-steppers. John had become almost used now to standing on the footman's plate between the carriage's back wheels. At least he wasn't shut up inside, like poor Kit, with Mme de Montsegard, whose oily charm towards her young protégée made John's skin creep.

From this vantage point he could see over the heads of the crowd that had gathered to watch the fine folk arrive for the ball. He looked carefully at the magnificent cream stone building as they approached, on the lookout for a back entrance, an open window – some way out in case he had to make a hasty getaway.

Mme de Montsegard's footman stood beside him. A tall, gloomy-looking fellow, named Robert, he barely addressed a word to John.

'*Américain?*' he'd asked, when they'd first climbed up to the footman's plate together.

'*Oui.*'

'*Tu parles français?*'

'*Non.*'

They'd left each other alone after that.

The carriage pulled up at last outside the grand entrance and John and Robert jumped off. Robert opened the door on Mme de Montsegard's side and let down the steps for her. John did the same for Kit.

She clutched his hand convulsively as he helped her to descend.

'Nervous?' he asked.

'Terrified.'

'Me too. But we'll be fine. Worse things happen at sea.'

'You think I don't know that? But I wish you were coming inside with me.'

'So do I.'

'Mlle de Jalignac!' Mme de Montsegard was staring at them with her eyebrows raised.

'*Pardon, madame.*' Kit quickly let go of John's hand.

Mme de Montsegard gave John a look of venomous dislike.

'*Viens, mon enfant.* The Empress Josephine has already arrived.'

John watched as Kit and Mme de Montsegard disappeared through the great doors and saw them mount the grand staircase. He had never seen anything as dazzling as the two rows of magnificently uniformed lancers that lined the steps, with their tall shakos and drawn swords. He had never seen the like, either, of the huge chandeliers, sparkling with such brilliance, or of the hordes of elegantly dressed young women, flocking together, chattering, as they moved slowly upwards to disappear into the gilded salons above.

Robert tugged his sleeve.

'*Par ici*,' he said.

He followed Robert through a side door into a small room, which was already crowded with footmen in a variety of liveries. They were all elderly, and many seemed to know each other. They were exchanging shouted greetings, handshakes and slaps on the shoulder. He took a deep breath. This was a dangerous moment. He didn't want questions. He didn't want anyone to notice him.

He stood near the door and, when his opportunity came, slipped outside into the cool of the evening. He sat down on a stone mounting block by the wall, settling himself for a long wait. From above, he could hear the sound of a band playing a polka and the murmur of conversation, above which a woman's laugh or a man's shout of greeting occasionally rose.

The minutes passed slowly. He heard the quarter-hours chime on a distant clock. Nine, a quarter past, half past, a quarter to ten, ten.

Napoleon's wife is up there, he thought, and Kit's fate is being decided.

He leaned against the wall, and in spite of himself felt his eyelids droop. He could almost feel himself falling asleep.

He was jerked upright by a hand on his shoulder. Robert was shaking him.

'Your mademoiselle,' Robert was saying. 'She is calling you.'

'Kit's calling me? She wants me?' he said stupidly. 'Where?'

Robert pointed upwards, shrugged and went back inside to join the other footmen.

His heart in his mouth, John approached the great doors. The staircase was empty now. The guard of honour had left their posts on the steps and were standing about in ones and twos, yawning. They glanced at him as he entered, but seeing only another footman in a smart livery, looked away. Similar people had been coming and going all evening, summoned by their employers above.

John ran up the staircase, trying not to go too fast. Why had Kit called him? Was she in trouble of some kind? Did she need him?

He stood in the doorway of the great salon almost blinded by the brilliant light from the two vast chandeliers that winked and shone above. There was a huge crowd in here. How would he ever find her?

And then suddenly she was beside him.

'*Jean! Enfin! Où étais-tu?*' she said loudly and angrily, for the benefit of a turbaned matron nearby, who was nodding and smiling at her. 'Follow me,' she said in English, under her breath.

She moved round a corner. They were out of sight now behind a pillar.

'What's happening? Have you seen her?' he asked urgently.

'Seen who? Oh, the empress. Yes. She was very nice. She said she'd take my part. I don't care what you think, John. I liked her. She'll help me, I know she will.'

'Then what's happened? What's the matter?'

'You won't believe this. In one of the coffee rooms. Off the main salon. I didn't know at first, because that night I hardly saw them, but then I heard them speak. In English. With Scottish accents.'

'Heard who? Who are you talking about? For heaven's sake, Kit . . .'

'Mr Creech and Mr Halkett! They're here!'

'What? It can't be true! Are you sure?'

'No. That's why I sent for you. I thought you could pretend to be a waiter, and take in some wine or something. The waiters are all in powdered wigs, like yours. No one will notice you. You just need to take a quick look, no more. One glance will be enough to tell you if it's them. Just think, John, we might find out more about this whole spying thing. It's what we came ashore to discover, after all.'

John's heart was thudding.

'They'll see me. Mr Creech will recognize me, even if Mr Halkett doesn't.'

'He won't. No one looks at waiters. Anyway, you look completely different in that livery, without your own hair showing. And you're much taller than you were. You must be nearly six feet now, not like the young boy he last saw. They haven't seen you for nearly two years, don't forget. And they won't be expecting to see you here. You'll be miles away from their thoughts.'

He knew she was right.

'A tray. I'll need a tray, with glasses on it. I'll take wine into the room as if I was serving it.'

'I thought of that. I noticed a tray that a waiter had put down on one of the small tables in the salon. I'll show you. The coffee room is the first door on the left. They're in there.'

A man in a dark coat, with a medal sparkling on his chest, passed by and bowed politely. Kit smiled gracefully, then turned back to John.

'That's the comte de St Voir. I was introduced to him just now. Don't you recognize him? He was the man in the fisherman's cabin with Halkett and Creech. He must be their French contact.'

She shivered, and John felt a cold chill pass over him too at the thought of the danger they would be in if their true identity was uncovered.

'I'll go now,' he whispered, 'and look at them myself – see if it's really them. Where are they exactly?'

'Follow me,' said Kit, moving back into the ballroom.

Holding his back stiff and keeping his expression as neutral as possible, John followed her into the crowded salon. No one looked at him. He was just a servant, as unremarkable as any of the dozens of other footmen and waiters. People parted to let him through without giving him a glance.

'*C'est Mlle de Jalignac,*' he heard people murmur. '*Qu'elle est charmante!*'

He had a momentary glimpse, through a side opening, of a woman lounging gracefully on a dais, surrounded by a group of white-clad women. Jewels flashed in her hair as she turned her head. She was smiling with a condescending air at a man in a sumptuously braided military uniform who was bending over to kiss her hand.

Josephine, he thought.

Kit had stopped. She waited for him to catch up with her, indicated, with a flick of her head, a tray with glasses on it on a table by the wall and then looked pointedly at a door on the far side of the room.

'*Ah! Vous voilà, mademoiselle!*' someone cried. A stout young man who was sweating profusely inside the heavy uniform of Napoleon's regiment of guards was forcing his way through the crowd towards them.

'Mme de Montsegard's horrid son,' Kit said through gritted teeth, and then she was borne away on the young man's arm.

John picked up the tray and edged round the side of the salon towards the door of the coffee room. He looked inside. It was darker here. Card tables with seated players were dotted about the room, and the atmosphere was thick with tobacco smoke. Clusters of men stood about talking, and waiters, all in white wigs, passed among them with trays of full glasses in their hands.

John scanned the room. He saw Mr Creech immediately. The sight of that sharp, scrawny face and the hooded eyes set deep in it set his heart thudding and made his hands slippery with the sweat of fear.

Mr Creech was in earnest conversation with two other men. One, he was almost sure, was Mr Halkett. He could see only the back of the other one. He swallowed hard and, gripping the tray so tightly that his knuckles showed white, approached the little group. He could hear Mr Creech's loathsome voice now, though he was too far away to distinguish the words. The second man spoke. There was no mistaking that dry, precise Edinburgh voice. It was Mr Halkett, without a doubt.

And then the third man moved sideways, out of the shadows, turning his head to answer Mr Halkett. John would have known that terrible profile anywhere, that puckered skin, the mouth drawn up towards the eye, the fearsome scars of an old burn that had disfigured the man forever.

It was the first lieutenant of the *Fearless*, the man to whom, above all others, John would have entrusted his life. Mr Erskine.

Chapter Thirty-one

John froze. He stood immobile for a long moment, his mind in turmoil, unable to think. How could Mr Erskine possibly be here, out of naval uniform, in the heart of the enemy camp, under the very nose of the Empress Josephine, miles away from the *Fearless*?

He must be one of them, he thought stupidly. A spy! A traitor! He can't be! Not Mr Erskine! It isn't possible. But if he isn't with them, whatever is he doing here?

Someone bumped into him from behind and swore at him for standing in the way. John murmured an inaudible apology and stepped back. There was a convenient pillar beside an alcove near where Mr Erskine was standing with Mr Creech and Mr Halkett. If he stood beside it, holding his tray, he'd look just like any other waiter, and he'd be half concealed from them. He might be able to overhear something of their conversation.

He took up his position, making his face as impassive as possible. He realized that the glasses on the tray were jingling together. His hands were shaking. He controlled them with an effort and strained his ears to pick out the English conversation. It was hard to hear anything against the hectic waltz music coming from the ballroom next door, and the babble of French all around, but he discovered that, if he stood at a certain angle, the concave wall acted as a sounding chamber. He could hear the men's conversation quite well.

'It's a pleasure to meet fellow countrymen at such a time and in such a place,' Mr Erskine was saying. 'Since I arrived in Bordeaux I have been surprised at how many Scots and English there are here, and that we are still received in the best circles, in spite of the fact that our nations are at war. Have you gentlemen resided long here?'

'We come and go, come and go,' Mr Creech said, and his well-remembered voice sent a shudder down John's spine. 'The wine trade is our business, as it is of everyone else here, I imagine. In spite of the blockade, commerce struggles on. Men must drink, however hard the times, and wine must be found for them. There is, as you have pointed out, a considerable number of British people here. We lie low. We behave peaceably and try not to offend the authorities. They let us alone, for the most part, unless they suspect that we are here on government or military business. Then, of course, a quiet disappearance, a dungeon, a swift execution . . .'

Mr Halkett broke in. 'Ah . . . your name, my good sir. I didn't catch your name.'

'Ferguson. Andrew Ferguson,' Mr Erskine said, 'and, like yourselves, interested in matters of business. Your names also – in all this noise and bustle I failed to catch . . .'

'Simon Wilson, at your service,' said Mr Creech, 'and my friend here is Mr William Kerr.'

'Kerr! I have a good friend, Archie Kerr, who resides at Hawick,' Mr Erskine said. 'Would he be a kinsman of yours, perhaps?'

'No, no,' Mr Halkett said testily. 'There's no one of that name related to me.'

A burst of laughter from a card table nearly drowned out the next exchanges. One of the players looked round, saw John and beckoned him over. Reluctantly, John left his post behind the pillar and went across to him. Without looking at John, or speaking to him, the man took four glasses off the tray and handed them to the other players. John waited politely beside him for a moment, till a wave of the man's hand dismissed him, then he melted back to his listening post.

Mr Erskine doesn't know them. He can't be one of the traitors, he thought. I don't know how he comes to be here, but there's a good reason for it, I'll bet my life on it.

'I'm interested to hear, Mr Ferguson, that it's the trade in brandies that brings you to Bordeaux.' Mr Creech's voice was silky. 'I can't say why, precisely, but I would have put you down for a military man. Possibly even one of our brave naval officers.'

Mr Erskine laughed.

'Ah, my unfortunate face! Would that I could boast of some death-defying deed of valour in defence of my king and country to explain these horrid scars! But I must disappoint you. My face was ruined by no act of war, but an unfortunate and entirely mundane affair in a warehouse, some years ago. Brandy is damnably inflammable. A clumsy spillage, a dropped match – I was fortunate to lose only my appearance. It could have been far worse. Ten barrels of the best cognac might have been lost to the world forever!'

The other two laughed.

'Your glass is empty, Mr Ferguson,' Mr Creech said politely. 'Let me replenish it for you. There was some fellow about just now . . .'

He looked round. John tried to shrink against the wall, but Mr Creech had seen him. He was snapping his fingers at him, calling out imperiously, '*Garçon! Du vin, ici!*'

His heart in his mouth, John stepped forward. Keeping his back to the light, he offered the tray, his eyes cast down. He saw three hands reach out and each take one of the five remaining glasses. Daringly, he looked up and for a fleeting moment Mr Creech met his gaze. No flicker of recognition stirred in the man's cold eyes.

Mr Erskine and Mr Halkett had not looked at him at all. They were talking again. John stepped back and resumed his position behind the pillar.

'This war? You are very right, sir. A sorry business indeed,' Mr Halkett was saying in his precise lawyer's tones. 'The sooner it is brought to a satisfactory conclusion, the better it will be for all of us. Trade is most seriously affected. As you have no doubt observed, Bordeaux is in a sad state. The British naval blockade, though no doubt necessary in the grand scheme of things, has ruined the city. When I first came here the river was a forest of masts, ships jostling for space at the quays, the commercial houses hives of activity. You have seen for yourself the rotting hulks of the few ships that remain and the air of dereliction in the warehouses.'

'We should drink to a speedy victory, then,' Mr Erskine said, dropping his voice to a cautious whisper. 'To our good King George, and his valiant army and navy.'

John dared to look round the pillar, curious to see the effect of this on Mr Creech and Mr Halkett. He watched as they exchanged a swift, conspiratorial glance.

'A dangerous sentiment, sir, to express here, surrounded by such a company,' said Mr Halkett, his voice as dry as parchment. 'Walls have ears.'

'But French walls have French ears,' Mr Creech said with a laugh. 'Look around you, man. There is not a soul in this room could overhear us, in all this hubbub, and even if they did, how many of them could make out our English speech? Tell me, Mr Ferguson, do you have news of home?'

John felt the sweat break out on his palms. Mr Erskine seemed entirely at ease, relaxing in the company of his fellow countrymen.

I'll bet my life he's here for a good reason, John thought. He's trying to do what he sent me and Kit ashore for, to sniff out spies. But he can't know who he's talking to, or how dangerous they are. One slip, one hint, that he isn't who he says he is and they'll uncover him. It'll be all up with him then.

What I can I do? I must do something! Now!

'News of home?' Mr Erskine was saying. 'My dear sir, I wish I had some myself. It's so long since I was in England. My home is in Bordeaux now. I have lived here for years.'

There was a short silence.

'That is a splendid coat you are wearing, Mr Ferguson,' Mr Creech said smoothly. 'The cut is unmistakable. Made by Scott, I believe? An English coat is impossible to copy. That set of the shoulders – it's quite a new style, I believe. Now when did you say you were last in London?'

Mr Erskine laughed, but before he could come up with an answer, John had darted out of his hiding place. A second later he was standing with his back to Mr Creech and Mr Halkett, facing Mr Erskine. He lurched forward, pretending to trip, and the two remaining glasses of wine on his tray shot forwards, spilling their contents down Mr Erskine's handsome cream silk waistcoat.

With an exclamation of annoyance, Mr Erskine grasped John's arm, then looked up. His mouth dropped open as he recognized John's face under the powdered wig.

'What on earth . . .' he began.

The tray had clattered to the floor. John pressed his forefinger to his lips and sent as urgent a warning as he could from his fiercely frowning eyes.

'Clumsy oaf. He should get a whipping for this,' Mr

Creech said furiously, laying a hand on John's shoulder in an attempt to spin him round.

John shook him off and bent down to retrieve the tray and the broken glasses.

'He shall indeed receive a whipping, but from my hands,' Mr Erskine said lightly. 'Gentlemen, you must excuse me. I am obliged to retire for a moment to repair the damage to what is, I fear, a favourite waistcoat. Can I count on you to remain here for a while? It will be most interesting to me to resume our conversation which this young fool has so rudely interrupted.'

Out of the corner of his eye, John saw the two men bow politely. He glanced up and read fury in Mr Creech's face and sour frustration in Mr Halkett's.

'*Pardon, messieurs,*' he murmured in his best French. '*Je regrette beaucoup . . .*'

And then he was gone, leading Mr Erskine as quickly as he dared to the door of the coffee room and out through the ballroom beyond.

They didn't stop until they had skirted right round the dancing couples and were standing at the head of the grand staircase, where, a few moments earlier, John had stood with Kit.

'John Barr! It *is* you!' exclaimed Mr Erskine. 'What the devil are you doing here?'

'It . . . it's a very long story, sir,' John said. 'The *Fearless* – is all well? She hasn't been captured, has she? That's not how you come to be here?'

'No, no. The *Fearless* is doing her duty as she always does, out on blockade off the coast. I must confess, my dear boy, I am delighted to see you. I was very much put out when you failed to return to the *Fearless*. I was afraid that I had sent you and young Catherine to your deaths. Or worse.'

'Nearly, sir. I was shot and wounded. I was out of things

for a while, but Kit – Catherine – took me to her home. I recovered there. She is here. Have you not seen her?'

'The devil she is! Turning heads, I've no doubt. You must point her out to me.' He chuckled. 'Imagine the scandal if it was to come out that the noblest of the young French ladies at this elegant occasion was in fact a rascally little powder monkey in His Majesty's navy!'

In spite of his anxiety, John couldn't help an answering grin. It quickly faded.

'No, but listen, sir. Those men you were with just now, I had to get you away from them. They are the very ones in league with Mr Higgins. They gave you false names. I was listening to you behind the pillar all the while. The man who called himself Wilson, he's Mr Creech, who set Mr Higgins on to get the code book from me. The other one, who says he's Mr Kerr, is really Mr Halkett, the lawyer from Edinburgh, where the code book first fell into my possession.'

Mr Erskine's eyes had widened.

'Are they, by Jove? I wondered why that fellow was so interested in my coat. It was a nasty moment, I must confess. I almost feared that I was about to be caught out. Your intervention was most timely, John. My mission was hanging by a thread.'

'But what is your mission, sir? How do you come to be here?'

'Why, the same as yours was, John, when you came ashore. Captain Bannerman has received an urgent request from London for more information with regard to the spy ring we seem to have uncovered. They queried the names of Creech and Halkett, who, it appears, have friends in high places at home. The authorities are most reluctant to believe that they can be implicated in this matter. The Admiralty is not content, I fear, to accept the evidence of a couple of – pardon me

– mere ship's boys. They wished for more official confirmation.'

'But how did you do it, Mr Erskine? Come ashore, I mean, and get yourself invited to the empress's ball?'

'You're a fine one to ask me that, young John. How did you manage it yourself? In fact, it was a great deal easier than one would suppose. There is a surprisingly large British community living here in Bordeaux, and I have a cousin who has been here for more than twenty years and is well known and respected. I was rowed quietly ashore a few nights ago, and found my way to my cousin's house. A good command of the French language has helped greatly, of course. My cousin received me warmly, and easily procured an invitation to tonight's party. My intention was to make discreet enquiries. I was on the lookout for Messrs Creech and Halkett. As a matter of fact, I was beginning to suspect those fine gentlemen even before they showed such unwelcome interest in this damned coat.'

'But how will you return to the *Fearless*, sir, and when will that be?'

'Why, tonight, I hope, on the falling tide. But I have a little more work to do first. I must return to our good gentlemen to find out more, if I can. I shall lay a few small traps for them and see if I can't get them to damn themselves out of their own mouths.'

'How, sir? Please, you must be careful. They are dangerous, unscrupulous . . .'

Mr Erskine patted John on the shoulder.

'Don't worry, my boy. I know what I am about.'

He moved away towards the ballroom door, but John caught his sleeve.

'Take me with you, sir, when you return to the *Fearless*.'

Mr Erskine raised his eyebrows.

'But of course I will. We don't want you taken up for a deserter, now, do we?'

'A deserter? Me?' John was indignant.

'Shh, you young hothead. Footmen don't raise their voices,' Mr Erskine said reprovingly. 'I'm glad to know, in any case, that you prefer the privations of life at sea to the career of a liveried footman. Now, wait for me below. Watch the door, and join me as I leave.'

'I'll have to tell Kit – Catherine, sir,' said John. 'I know for a certainty that she wishes to escape Bordeaux too.'

Mr Erskine shook his head.

'Does she, indeed? That is another matter. Abducting young ladies is not what I have in mind. Don't tell her of my presence here. The more who know of it, the greater the danger.'

John's brows snapped together and he felt the ready blush rush to his cheeks.

'You can trust Kit with anything, sir. I'd trust her with my life.'

Mr Erskine smiled.

'Lost your heart to her, have you? Sailors must learn to leave their lady loves behind, my lad. I'll see you later. And don't draw any more attention to yourself. No more glasses of wine down waistcoats, if you please.'

He disappeared once more into the ballroom.

It took John a full minute to recover from the confusion that Mr Erskine's remarks had set up in him, and before he could pull himself together, and hurry off to look for Kit, he was distracted by a stir of activity at the great doors below. A party of late arrivals had caused the bored soldiers to leap to attention. Looking down, John saw an elderly woman, dressed in an old-fashioned hooped ball gown of sombre magnificence, who was treading slowly up the stairs leaning on the arm of an impatient man with pale, restless eyes, whose face wore a forbidding frown.

They reached the top of the stairs and murmured their names to the magnificent black-clad master of ceremonies who stood at the ballroom door.

'Mme de Jalignac!' he boomed, 'and the Marquis de Vaumas!'

Chapter Thirty-two

The arrival of Kit's grandmother and uncle sent an audible ripple through the ballroom. John followed the pair inside, desperate to find Kit and warn her. Though he could not understand all the words, he could grasp the gist of the comments flying about as people parted to let them through.

'The old woman fooled us all! Everyone believed that her poor little granddaughter was dead.'

'Do you know where she's been hiding all this time?'

'Switzerland, I believe. With an old school friend.'

'To fake the death of your own grandchild! Disgraceful!'

'That's the uncle. He's after her money, I'm sure of it.'

'I'm surprised they dare show their faces after what they've done.'

No one came forward to greet the newcomers. John saw old Mme de Jalignac's back stiffen in its rigid whalebone corset. He heard the marquis draw in his breath, and say something in a furious undertone to his mother.

John scanned the crowded room, but when he saw Kit it was too late to reach her. A path had already opened up in front of her grandmother. It led straight to Kit herself. She was standing with her back to the wall, her hands spread out on it as if for support.

John was taken aback by the sheer panic on her face. He had seen Kit the ship's boy climb the *Fearless*'s rigging in a raging gale, take his part with a lion's courage in a deadly battle at sea, steal a horse in the dead of night and ride helter-skelter through an unknown forest. He had never seen Catherine, or Kit, for that matter, show a fraction of the terror that now seemed to be paralysing her, turning her face so deadly pale that John was afraid she would fall down in a faint.

Her grandmother reached her. No one in the crowded ballroom seemed unaware now of what was taking place. Everyone was craning their necks to see.

Mme de Jalignac stopped in her tracks when she saw Kit, and from behind John saw the feathers that crowned her high turban quiver. There was a long moment's silence, then she gave a theatrical groan and threw out her arms as if in invitation.

'Catherine! *Ah, ma petite chérie!* My little one! Restored to me from the grave!'

The sound of her voice seemed to galvanize Kit. She darted sideways, burrowing through the crowd. John, dropping his servile manner, pushed aggressively through the press of people towards her. He came face to face with her. She was wild-eyed and frantic.

'Calm down. Pretend you are unwell. I'm going to take you outside. Try to look normal.'

She took a deep breath, and nodded.

'*De l'air!*' she murmured, for the benefit of those around her. 'I need some air!'

The servants' entrance to the ballroom was only a few steps away. John opened it and pushed her through. A moment later they were leaping down the stairs, then running down the long passageway towards the kitchens.

They emerged from the maze of corridors and serving rooms at last to find themselves outside, in a side street behind the Château Royal. Kit seemed about to take to her heels and bolt blindly down the nearest alleyway, but John pulled her back.

'Stop! Where are you going?'

She tried to fight him off.

'I don't care. Anywhere. I've got to get away. You too. They'll find out who you really are, and get you taken off as a prisoner.'

A little of her fear infected him, but he subdued it.

'Stop, Kit. *Listen!* It's all arranged. We're leaving tonight, for the *Fearless*. I've seen Mr Erskine.'

She stopped struggling and stared at him, open-mouthed.

'Mr Erskine? You can't have done. Where?'

'Here. He's at the ball.'

Quickly he told her what had happened. Then, behind them, someone shouted. He turned round. A watchman with a lantern was bearing down on them. He spoke roughly to John, who didn't understand, but Kit answered him with a haughty stare. The man grunted and moved away.

'He thought – you were bothering me,' she said, not looking up. 'I told him you were my cousin, just returned from the war in Spain. We can't stay here. We're too conspicuous. Where are we meeting Mr Erskine? Did you arrange something?'

'He told me to wait at the main entrance and watch for him.'

'I can't go back there!' She sounded panicky again. 'I can't go where anyone – where they might see me!'

'Listen, Kit.' He shook her arm. 'You must be sensible about this. Your grandmother's an old woman. Your uncle's a middle-aged man, and not particularly fit, by the look of him. Why are you so frightened? We could both outrun them easily. Anyway, they can't just kidnap you and carry you off. Even the empress is on your side!'

'You don't know them, John! They're capable of anything! And when I'm with them, it's as if I was a child again. They *destroy* me!'

'I won't let them. Now think. We must find Mr Erskine. For all I know, he may already have left the ball. He may be looking for me. If he doesn't see me, he might give up and leave without us. He has to catch the tide. He can't row all the way back to the *Fearless* against it.'

She nodded reluctantly.

'You're right. I'm sorry. Finding Mr Erskine – that's the main thing. You told him I was with you, that I was coming too?'

'Yes.'

He couldn't tell her that Mr Erskine had refused to take her.

He began to walk back towards the front of the chateau. To his relief, she walked quietly alongside him, and he saw that already she was beginning to stride like a boy.

'I have nothing with me,' she said, sounding worried. 'No money, no clothes, only this stupid ball gown. How can I go on board dressed like this? Everyone would know my secret. I'd never be able to become a boy again.'

'Don't think of that now. The important thing is to get safely away from here.'

They had reached the corner of the road. Ahead were the twin spires of the old cathedral and the open square in front of the chateau. In spite of the lateness of the hour, dozens of people were standing about, staring up at the brilliantly lit windows and listening to the dance music. Soldiers stood on guard, their drawn swords gleaming in the torchlight, waiting for the wife of their emperor to leave.

'Wait here,' John said softly, pushing Kit back into a shadowy doorway.

He walked up to the grand entrance, through which he had passed so easily hours earlier in the wake of Mme de Montsegard. A soldier barred his way.

John struggled to find words, wanting to explain that he was a servant of one of the guests, but his French deserted him. He shrugged and stepped back. He could watch for Mr Erskine just as well from here.

Someone tapped him on the shoulder. He spun round.

'I thought I'd lost you again, young John Barr,' Mr Erskine said. 'You have a great talent for disappearing. I've been dragging my anchor out here for the last quarter of an hour.'

Relief washed over John.

'Oh, sir, I was afraid we'd . . . I'd missed you.'

'And I was afraid we'd be caught here in the doldrums, missing tonight's tide. Come on, now. We must be off.'

'Please, Mr Erskine . . .'

'What is it now?'

John swallowed.

'It's Kit. She's here. With me. Her grandmother and uncle have arrived. She's had to run away. She has to come with us, sir. She's . . .'

Mr Erskine's scarred face puckered irritably.

'I though I'd made it clear to you. No young ladies. Get going now. There's no time to lose.'

John folded his arms.

'I can't come with you, then, sir. I'm sorry. I can't leave Kit in the trouble she's in. She's . . . he's my shipmate, sir.'

Mr Erskine's tone hardened.

'John Barr, you are now under naval discipline. You are to come with me this instant, or I'll have you posted a deserter.'

'Then post me, sir. I'll not leave without her.'

'You young fool . . .'

Kit, flying on slippered feet across the flagstones, suddenly appeared between them.

'Mr Erskine! Oh, I'll never deny that there are miracles again! You have come in time, sir, just in time to save me. My uncle will stop at nothing. He means to murder me. I saw it in his eyes.'

'Mlle . . . Catherine . . . Kit!' For the first and only time since John had known him, Mr Erskine seemed lost for words. Kit had taken hold of his arm, and in the light of the thousand candles streaming from the chateau's windows, John saw the beaming joy in her dark eyes, and he watched as Mr Erskine's expression began to soften and a rueful smile touched his lips.

'Oh, what the devil. In for a penny, in for a pound. You are a baggage, miss. I hope you remember how to row. There's a long pull ahead of us back to the ship.'

'To row? Of course I remember, sir! I'll row the whole way. I'll make the boat fly – you'll see!'

Mr Erskine had already set off, covering the flagstones with his long stride. The others had to trot to keep up with him.

'Excuse me, Mr Erskine, sir,' Kit said breathlessly, 'the quay, it is over there. We are going further into town.'

'I know that. We must pass by my cousin's house to pick up my bundle. He'll give me a change of clothes for you. I'm a fool to take a young woman back to the *Fearless* with me. I'd be a madman to do so with one dressed in what is – if I may say so – an exceedingly elegant ball gown. Now keep up, the pair of you, and no more chattering.'

John felt Kit's hand take hold of his. He looked down at her, and she smiled back at him, her eyes sparkling with triumph and gratitude.

The dark narrow streets of Bordeaux seemed to close around them. Mr Erskine, pausing once or twice to check his way, walked fast ahead. Here and there, through the darkness, a stray gleam of light shone on a mask-like stone face, grinning down from above a doorway, between closely shuttered windows. The only sound was the ring of their feet on the cobbles. Once, a cat yowled as it streaked out from beneath them, making John and Kit jump. They saw and heard no human beings.

Mr Erskine stopped at last at a heavy doorway and knocked quietly. A shutter upstairs creaked open.

'*Qui est là?*' someone called out softly.

'It's me, your cousin,' Mr Erskine answered.

A moment later the door opened, and Mr Erskine's cousin appeared in nightgown and nightcap, a candle in his hand.

'You're a late owl tonight,' he said yawning. 'Enjoy the ball? Why, who's this with you?'

'I'm sorry, Daniel. There's no time for the full tale.' Mr Erskine had bundled John and Kit inside. 'Listen, man, we must away tonight. We must leave at once. My mission's done.'

'With these two?' His cousin, now fully awake, stared in surprise.

'Yes. Can you do me one last favour, my dear cousin? This young lady needs more suitable attire – a boy's clothes. You have something that will do?'

His cousin burst out laughing.

'*Boy's* clothes? Why, what a shame it would be to hide such charming . . .'

'Daniel, please! There's no time to lose. Will you do as I ask?'

'What devils you naval fellows are!' Mr Erskine's cousin said, shaking his head in amusement. 'All these fits and starts and secret goings-on. But I shall play my part, poor dull wine merchant that I am. A costume shall be found. At once. And horses. You'll need horses to take you to my warehouse, where my little boat's concealed. I shall saddle up a pair myself.'

A surprisingly short time produced a transformation in Kit. She had stepped into the nearest room a beautiful young woman in an exquisite ball gown. She emerged a boy, roughly clad in breeches, a loose shirt and a leather waistcoat. Her feet were bare. She had pulled out the pins that held the curls on the top of her head and was matter-of-factly plaiting her long hair into a sailor's pigtail.

John watched the change with bemusement. In front of his eyes, Catherine was disappearing, and Kit was coming back. He was relieved. He could forget the complicated feelings that Catherine had aroused in him and simply enjoy being with Kit again. And yet, as Kit turned and pulled a funny face at him, he felt an unexpected sense of loss. Catherine had disturbed and perplexed him, but she had thrilled and charmed him too.

Catherine's still there, he thought, watching the girlish grace of her movements as she rolled up her ball gown and tied it into a bundle. I suppose she'll never quite be simply Kit for me again.

They were ready to leave. Mr Erskine's cousin, still in his pink flannel nightcap, had brought a pair of horses, ready saddled, from the stable at the rear of his house to the side door. As she stepped out into the yard, Kit turned to shake hands with him.

'I am so grateful to you, sir,' she said, 'but will you do one last thing for me?'

She was a girl still, pleading and flirtatious. He could not help responding.

'What is that, my dear?'

'Could you somehow send a message to Betsy, Betsy

Fletcher, at Jalignac? She's the servant there. Just to let her know that I am well and safe, that I'm with John and that we've returned to the *Fearless*. Tell her that I'll come back when I can. She mustn't worry about me. I won't come home till my birthday's past. She'll understand. The message is for Betsy, and no one else, please, sir.'

Mr Erskine was already in the saddle.

'Daniel, I'm devilish grateful to you. The boat's under the willows at Pauillac? I remember the place. We'll leave the horses in the stable there. Mount, John, and take the reins. Catherine, you'll have to ride behind him. Come quickly! It'll be light in a few hours. There's no time to lose.'

Chapter Thirty-three

It was a hard, fast ride to Pauillac, some miles downstream from Bordeaux and halfway to the sea. Mr Erskine rode ahead, pushing his horse fast, looking over his shoulder from to time to time to make sure that the second horse, with its double burden, was keeping up. The moon had risen, fortunately, turning the long, straight, dusty road into a silver ribbon ahead of them.

It was two hours before they were finally able to slide down from their saddles. They were standing on the banks of the Gironde, at the entrance to the courtyard of a small warehouse that fronted the river.

'Down there, below the willows,' Mr Erskine said quietly. 'My cousin's boat is hidden under the branches. Bring her round to the steps below the warehouse. I'll see to the horses.'

A moment later, they were on board the little rowing boat. The air was cool now, and a chill breeze ruffled the surface of the water. Kit shivered. John took off his footman's coat and draped it round her shoulders.

'It's too tight for me, anyway,' he muttered, embarrassed by his own gallantry. 'I can't row in this thing.'

Mr Erskine had already cast off from the bank. John, who had taken the oars, rowed with short seaman's strokes into the fast-flowing current as the falling tide sucked the great river down towards the sea.

They were silent as the bank receded. John, rowing hard, felt his wound twinge in his side with the unaccustomed exercise.

'A quarter of an hour each,' Mr Erskine said softly. 'We'll take it in turns. We must get past the point at the river mouth and be well out to sea before dawn. There are gun batteries at the point, and the sentries there are always alert. They'll try to blow us out of the water if they see us.'

'The moonlight, sir,' panted John. 'Won't they see us anyway?'

Mr Erskine pointed to a bank of clouds that was billowing up from the horizon. As John looked, he saw a flicker of lightning spark between them, and a moment later, above the gurgle and splash of water, came a faint roll of thunder.

'Storm's blowing up,' Mr Erskine said. 'It may save us if it gets to us in time.'

'Or it'll sink us,' Kit said cheerfully.

'That's right, my girl,' Mr Erskine said severely. 'Keep our spirits up, do.'

'Aye aye, sir. Sorry, sir.'

They rowed in silence for the next hour, changing round each fifteen minutes. Though the river was running fast, the bank seemed to slide by with cruel slowness.

John had fallen into a lethargy, lulled by the steady rhythm of Mr Erskine at the oars, when a shot rang out, making him leap with fright. From the massive hulk of what he had assumed to be a derelict warship, a guttural voice commanded them to heave to, in the name of the emperor.

Without a second's pause, Kit shouted back, thickening her voice to assume the local dialect. The man hesitated, then issued an unmistakable command, but Kit's quick answer brought a shout of laughter from him.

'*Allez-y, mademoiselle,*' he called. 'And trust me. I won't report you to your father!'

'Whatever did you say to him?' John murmured, when they were out of earshot.

'You'd blush if I told you,' she said, 'so I won't.'

'Well done, young woman,' Mr Erskine said approvingly, resting for a moment on the oars. 'Damned if I'm not delighted to have brought you with us after all.'

They conversed in low voices after that. The river was broadening all the time, and they were out now in the centre of the channel, rowing swiftly downstream, safely out of earshot of either bank. At Mr Erskine's prompting, John and Kit went over in as much detail as they could remember the conversation they'd overheard in the fisherman's hut, when Mr Higgins had handed over the code book.

'The comte de St Voir?' Mr Erskine said thoughtfully. 'You're sure it was him?'

'Quite sure, sir. I recognized his voice and then I saw him talking to Mr Creech and Mr Halkett. I couldn't have been mistaken.'

'That is very useful information. Very useful indeed. M. de St Voir is a gentleman to watch. The word will be passed to our contacts in Paris. But I can scarcely credit what you tell me of Mr Higgins. The *Fearless*'s own bosun's mate! Actually taking money to murder one of his ship's boys! I knew the fellow was a rascal, but a hired assassin! This beats everything.'

'He'll have the chance now, won't he, with John back on board?' Kit said anxiously.

'You can leave our Mr Higgins to me,' Mr Erskine said grimly. 'He'll be rendered as a harmless as a newborn babe. What puzzles me, Catherine, is how to deal with you.'

'If I could just return to Mr Tawse, as his servant . . .' Kit began.

'It's out of the question. You passed as a boy before, I grant you, and you were adept at effacing yourself. Even so, it was a miracle that you were not discovered. The captain won't be prepared to countenance such a deception again.'

'It's only till January, sir. Five months away. As soon as I've turned fourteen, I'll be out of my uncle's power. By the terms of my father's will, my estates – everything – will come to me then. The empress herself assured me that she would interest herself in the matter.'

'That's as may be.' Mr Erskine's voice was dry. 'The *Fearless*, however, is not a haven of rescue for persecuted young French ladies. It is, may I remind you, a warship engaged on a serious mission of national importance on whom many lives depend.'

'Sir, that is . . . that's unjust!' John burst out, trying to restrain his anger. 'Kit's not . . . well, she is a young lady, but much more than that! She rescued us both, back at the fishermen's hut, when those men were about to capture us. If they'd caught us, they'd have realized that their plotting was discovered and that the code book was now known to us. It would have been useless to our government. And just now, you saw yourself, we'd never have got past the sentry if Kit hadn't been so quick.'

'Yes, yes.' Mr Erskine sounded a little irritated. 'His Majesty owes a debt to Mlle de Jalignac, I agree. It's what to do for the best now that puzzles me.'

'Well, sir,' Kit said tentatively, 'I have been thinking about it myself. I thought – I wondered – I have learned quite a bit from Betsy, my old nurse, about caring for the wounded. When I was in the sickbay, I saw how very . . . well, how careless and rough the orderlies are, working under Mr Catskill. The sickbay is out of the way of the rest of the ship. I would hardly be noticed there. I could make myself useful, and Mr Catskill knows my secret anyway.'

John was taking the oars from Mr Erskine as she spoke.

'A possible solution to a tricky problem,' Mr Erskine said, easing his stiff shoulders. 'Though all such decisions lie with the captain. Ah! Here it comes!'

They had been rowing for several hours now, and the clouds, gathering pace as they rolled across the sky, were low overhead, though they had not yet engulfed the moon, which was sinking towards the horizon. The first drops of rain, round and heavy as peas, were already spitting down. A moment later, they were pelting out of the sky, flattening the choppy water on each side of the boat and soaking instantly through its occupants' clothes. Then the clouds at last obscured the moon, and they were in darkness.

Mr Erskine had been anxiously looking about, taking advantage of the last of the moonlight.

'Not very much further to the point,' he said, raising his voice above the hissing rain. 'We're almost there. This rain's a godsend if we can keep a straight course. Another half-mile or so, and we should be able to see the light from the light-house. The *Fearless* is lying two degrees north of it. It's a hard pull till we reach her, but the tide's still in our favour, and . . .'

A gust of wind tore the words from his mouth, and the cravat from his neck. A wave, seemingly rising from nowhere, smacked against the side of the little boat, dousing the three of them with a shock of cold salt spray. The smooth waters of the Gironde had met the turbulence of the storm-driven sea.

It was impossible to speak after that. The sudden summer tempest ripped across the mouth of the river with furious intensity. The little boat, which had seemed a sturdy craft on the calm fresh water, now felt horribly frail, bobbing like a cork in this wild, wet, dark world.

'Keep her steady! Keep rowing!' Mr Erskine roared at John.

John, gritting his teeth, worked at the oars till his muscles felt as if they would crack. Sometimes, when the boat rode high on a wave, the oars sawed through nothing but air. A moment later, the little craft would be at the bottom of a deep trough and he was afraid that the next surge would swamp them.

'The light, sir! I can see the lighthouse!' Kit called out.

'Good girl. Hard to larboard, John. And keep her on a straight course.'

'Aye aye, sir!'

He struggled on, shaking the rain from his hair like a dog when it leaps from a pond to the land.

'We're shipping water!' he heard Kit call out. 'I think we've sprung a leak!'

'The devil we have,' muttered Mr Erskine. He ducked down and started to feel along the bottom of the boat. 'It's no good. I can't make out where the water's coming in. It's too dark to see my own hands. There are bailers under the bow seat. Fetch 'em out. John, give me the oars. You two, bail like the Furies.'

The water had already risen up to John's feet and was lapping round his buckled shoes.

It'll be by drowning, then, he thought, quite calmly. Not from a wound, or in battle. I'm to die by drowning.

He felt oddly detached from the idea. It wouldn't be so bad. It wouldn't hurt, anyway.

A sharp bang on his elbow made him jump.

'Here, John! Your bailer!' Kit was shouting. At once his detachment left him. He couldn't die. He couldn't let Kit die either.

He grabbed the bailer out of her hand and began to work, scooping up the water and hurling it over the side.

They bailed in a frenzy of effort, scooping and throwing, scooping and throwing, as the storm raged on around them.

At last, Kit sat back on her heels.

'It's no good,' she panted. 'We're going down.'

'My dear, I do believe we are,' Mr Erskine said. His voice was light, almost amused, but John could hear that his throat was constricted.

John leaned over, exhausted. He was on all fours, the bailer floating on the water that now half filled the boat, covering his legs and above his wrists as he rested his hands flat on the bottom. There was no doubt about it. They were sinking fast.

Father will never know what's happened to me, he thought. No one ever will.

Then he felt it – a movement under his right hand, a sensation of welling, of water pushing upwards.

'Sir! I think I've found the leak!'

At once Mr Erskine was beside him, splashing down to feel about in the bottom of the boat.

'Yes, it's here. Good lad. It's coming in between these two boards. Press down hard with your knee, John, and hold them together. Let me feel. Good. I believe that's stopped it. Now bail, both of you, for your lives!'

Kit was already back at work, scooping and throwing. John, who had thought he'd been working as fast as anyone could, discovered that he could go much faster.

'The water's going down, I think, sir,' gasped Kit at last.

'It is. Most definitely. Take the oars, Catherine, and give me your bailer. Steer a steady course, two degrees north of the lighthouse. We'll make it yet. Keep your knee pressed down, John, and bail.'

They went at it again like machines, feeling the water around them slowly fall. The next time John looked up, he saw with surprise that the storm was over. The last black cloud, fringed with white, was drifting away from the face of the moon. The land was far behind them, a low dark mass on the horizon.

Kit, who had been rowing her hardest for a long time, slumped forward across the oars. Mr Erskine gently moved her aside and took her place. She staggered to the bow seat and sat bent forward, her chest heaving as she gasped for breath. John wanted more than anything to go to her, but his knee, now stiff and numb, was still pressed hard down on the boat's boards. He shifted slightly, trying to ease the pressure, and looking up, saw something he'd feared he'd never see again.

'Look, sir! The *Fearless*! She's over there!' shouted John.

In the distance, no more than a mile or so away, the *Fearless* rode serenely to anchor. She looked magnificent, yet fragile, and terribly alone, as she floated on the moonlit, silver sea. She was the most beautiful thing that John had ever seen.

Chapter Thirty-four

By the time the little craft had bobbed alongside the *Fearless*, her three occupants were so spent they could barely speak.

'Ahoy there!' croaked Mr Erskine, lifting an oar to rap it against the great black side of the warship. 'Is the watch all asleep? Ahoy! Wake up!'

An astonished face peered down from above.

'Mr Erskine? Is that you? How came you . . . ?'

'Never mind that! Get down here, you lubber, and fetch us up. This damned boat's filling again. If you don't stir yourself, we'll be shark's feed before five minutes are up.'

A moment later, sailors were climbing down the ship's side, and John, tossed over a mighty shoulder as easily as if he was a sack of flour, was being carted up the cleats.

He was tumbled down on the deck beside Kit in a dripping, exhausted heap.

'Why, Mr Erskine, it *is* you!' The midshipman in charge of the night watch had run up, a lantern in his hand. 'Are you all well, sir? Who's this?' He swung the lantern high. 'But I know you two! You're the lads who went over the side and drowned, months back. Good God, how came you . . . ?'

'Contain your amazement, if you please,' said Mr Erskine testily. 'Present my compliments to Mr Catskill and stow these two boys in the sickbay. Find them dry clothing, a round of grog and a berth for what remains of tonight. No questions, do you hear, or I shall be obliged to ask in turn why a boat managed to approach up to the very hull of this ship without the watch noticing. Good heavens, man. We could have been a French boarding party. You should be flogged for this.'

The midshipman stepped backwards.

'I'm sorry, sir. I . . . I much regret, sir . . . It won't happen again, sir.'

John, recognizing the fear in the young man's voice, felt his spirits sink. How could he have wished to come back to the *Fearless*? How could he have forgotten the wretchedness of life in the navy, the cruel discipline, the suffocating heat of the decks below in the summer time and the dank chill in the winter, the boredom of the routine, the back-breaking work? The stench from beneath was rising to his nostrils even up here on the open deck. Already he was missing Betsy's tarts and pies, her stews and casseroles. His stomach rose at the thought of the salt pork and stinking water that would be all he could expect from now on.

He picked himself up with an effort, and had to restrain himself from helping Kit to her feet.

She's not a girl any more, he told himself sternly. She's a boy. A boy.

He would have to keep a close guard on himself if he was not to give the game away.

They were stumbling down the nearest companionway, on their way to the sickbay, when they met a shambling, sleepy figure coming up.

'Davey Gow, is that you?' said John.

Davey's mouth, falling open, made a perfect O in his pale, shocked face. He let out a scream of terror.

'Ghosties! It's ghosties! John Barr, who was drownded dead, and Kit Smith, come to haunt me! I never did nothing to hurt you, John, or you, Kit. Don't haunt me. Don't! Go away! Please!'

John laughed and put out his hand. Davey shrank away from him.

'I'm no ghost, Davey. I never drowned. I'm here. Look. Touch my hand. It's warm – well, it would be if I wasn't so wet.'

With great daring, Davey put out a finger and touched the proffered hand.

'Is it really you, John? I'm glad. I liked you when you was alive. I still do. And you, Kit.'

'What is all this?' the midshipman said, clattering down the companionway behind them. 'What are you doing, you boy, out of your hammock?'

Davey drew himself up. He was a foot taller than the young midshipman, but he pulled his forelock respectfully.

'On my way to relieve myself, sir. Trouble in my stomach, sir.'

'Go along with you, then, and keep quiet. Do you wish to wake the entire ship?'

Davey trotted on.

By next morning the entire crew of the *Fearless* was marvelling over the news that the two ships' boys who had disappeared months ago, and were reported missing and drowned, had miraculously returned from the deep. John and Kit, however, knew nothing of it. They had crashed into their berths, under the grumbling eye of the unwillingly roused ship's surgeon, and were so dead asleep that it took Mr Erskine a good few minutes to rouse them.

The first lieutenant, shaved and once more in uniform, looked remarkably fresh.

'A story has been concocted to account for your being missing,' he told them, as they stood to attention beside their hammocks. 'Any who are interested, and that includes the entire ship, will be told that an unlucky fall took Kit over the side. John, who is known to be an excellent swimmer, plunged in to rescue him, but the current, being exceptionally strong here, carried him away from the ship. Your cries went unheard. Fortunately you kept your heads above water and were eventually cast up on the beach. You managed to live in hiding in a derelict chateau, thanks to the offices of a kind English lady (your Betsy, you see, comes into the story). You stumbled by chance upon the nefarious doings of treasonous spies, whom you followed, in the hopes of uncovering their wicked deeds. You both assumed the character of footmen, in order to observe polite society and find out more about their treachery, and by a lucky chance met me in Bordeaux. I brought you back here.'

'Rather far-fetched, sir, isn't it?' said Kit, her brow wrinkled.

'No stranger than the truth, and as near it as possible.'

'I suppose so, sir.'

'I have seen Captain Bannerman,' Mr Erskine went on. 'It is all agreed. Kit – (as I shall now call you) – you will remain here in the sickbay and work under Mr Catskill. You will resume your male identity and will endeavour to remain as inconspicuous as possible.'

'Thank you, sir,' said Kit, beaming with relief.

'As for you, John, the captain wishes to see you in his cabin. You are to report to him at once.'

With each word, the golden time at Jalignac was fading away from John, the weeks rolling themselves up like a carpet and disappearing from sight. The navy was reality now. It held him once more in its iron grip.

'Aye aye, sir,' he said, in a colourless voice.

But the interview that followed, in Captain Bannerman's cabin, was far from colourless. It was so extraordinary, in fact, that as John left the august presence and emerged, blinking with astonishment on to the sunlit quarterdeck, he was half convinced he had been dreaming.

Mr Erskine was leaning on the rail, talking to a tall, narrow-faced midshipman. He beckoned John over.

'Well, Mr Barr, and how did you find the captain this morning?'

'Sir, I hardly know. I'm amazed. That is, I never thought, for one moment . . .' He heard himself babbling and stopped.

'Mr Barr has been promoted from the lower deck to be a midshipman,' Mr Erskine said to the young man beside him. 'He will be joining you in the midshipmen's mess. This, Mr Barr, is Mr Williams, your new colleague.'

The midshipman put out his hand, but his expression was sour.

'Congratulations,' he said, without smiling.

'Thank you, sir!' John was almost light-headed.

'No need to "sir" me,' the other said contemptuously. 'My name will suffice.'

He walked off.

'You will be keeping a different kind of company from now on, Mr Barr,' Mr Erskine said, watching thoughtfully as the stiff-backed young midshipman descended from the quarter-deck. 'I have two words of advice for you. The first concerns your previous companions on the lower deck. You will now be in a position of command over them, and it will be neces-sary to establish new relations. Don't be familiar with them, as you were in the past, but don't be officious, either, or flaunt your new authority. There is a fine line to tread. The second concerns your new messmates.' He paused. Mr Williams had now reached the gun deck below and was talking to two other midshipmen, who turned their heads to stare up at John. 'A period of . . . adjustment . . . is inevitable. They are excellent fellows in the main, but apt to be a little boisterous in welcoming newcomers.'

John kept his face impassive, but his heart sank.

'I see, sir.'

'An account of your exploits in France will stand you in good stead. You may tell a certain amount, but you may not disclose the real names of Messrs Creech and Halkett. You will also, of course, keep the true identity of Mlle de Jalignac a close secret, and you will not visit her in the sickbay. Is that understood?'

'Yes, sir, but won't people think it odd that I have been rewarded with promotion, while Kit is to simply help out in the sick bay?'

'Easily explained, my dear boy. Kit was wounded again during your dramatic escape from the spies and has sadly not fully recovered. He is obliged to stay close and quiet under Mr Catskill's observation. Now report to the purser. He will provide you with the appropriate uniform and other items necessary to support you in your new rank, the cost of which will be deducted from your pay. Then get along to the schoolmaster. There is a navigation class in progress this morning, for which you will be damnably late.'

John took a deep breath.

'Aye aye, sir.'

He turned to go.

'Oh, and, John, there's one more thing. You need not concern yourself about Mr Higgins. I should not say this, but I am happy to tell you that he is no more.'

'He's *dead*, sir? How?'

'He was arrested last night as soon as I returned to the ship and confirmed to Captain Bannerman his involvement with the spies. He was put in irons while the captain considered how to proceed. The crafty fellow bribed one of his low friends to release him during the night watch. He managed to acquire a musket, loaded and primed, and forced two men to hoist out the jolly boat for him. It was the stupidest thing I ever heard of. Of course, he was bound to be discovered. The marines were alerted, and they shot after him as he tried to row himself ashore. One of their bullets pierced his heart. Mr Higgins won't bother you any longer, John. You are quite safe from his attentions now.'

PART FIVE

DECEMBER 1808
CORUNNA

Chapter Thirty-five

It was winter now. The days had grown shorter and the winds colder. Foul weather in the Bay of Biscay buffeted the *Fearless*. Storms and squalls tore at the rigging, turning even hardened sailors green with seasickness as the ship rolled and pitched, standing to northward, then turning south again and again in her endless patrol across the mouth of the Gironde.

By the end of December, the crew of the *Fearless*, tired and dispirited by the crushing boredom of the seemingly endless blockade, had grown restive. Fights broke out with greater frequency. Mutterings of discontent occasionally boiled over into threats of outright mutiny. Captain Bannerman, never a vindictive man, had been forced to resort to frequent floggings to keep the men in order, and the normally pleasant relations between officers and crew had become soured with mutual distrust.

The four months that had passed since John had rejoined the ship had been almost the hardest of his life. He had missed Jabez and Horace, Mr Tawse, Tom and Davey, and he had felt awkward when they'd spoken to him respectfully and called him 'sir'. He had visited his old berth once or twice, but the only boy left with Mr Tawse was Davey. Tom had joined the elite corps of topmen and was learning fast to work at the very summits of the masts, managing the highest sails and spars. Sometimes John caught sight of him way up aloft, trying to outdo the others in daring, earning his new scarlet waistcoat by braving the windiest weather and iciest cold.

John's new companions, the other midshipmen, who ranged from thirteen to thirty years of age, had treated him disdainfully at first, and one or two had set out to humiliate and bully him. He'd held his ground and was accepted now, more or less, in their boisterous, noisy company, but he had made no close friends among them. He knew his reserve made him unpopular, but he could not change himself.

He desperately missed Kit. Twenty times a day he thought of something he wished to tell her, or heard something he knew would make her laugh, or flared with indignation at an injustice he knew she too would have hated. They managed to meet from time to time, slipping up to the fo'c'sle in the evening watch, but these occasions were frustratingly rare. Mr Catskill kept her closely confined to the sickbay, which an outbreak of fever had filled with groaning sailors. John found himself pacing the deck most evenings alone, returning cold and bad-tempered to the midshipman's berth when the hammocks were piped down.

It had seemed to John, and to the rest of the bored and weary crew, that they would be stuck forever churning backwards and forwards through the choppy water along the coast of France, while the great war in Europe raged inland and other ships in His Majesty's navy cruised the high seas, taking prizes, fighting battles and covering themselves with glory.

But everything changed one cold, breezy morning in early January.

'Sail-ho!' the lookout aloft cried out.

John, who was on the lower deck taking a message to Mr Erskine, heard the stir on the main deck above as everyone ran to look. By the time he had gone up himself, the ship was alive with speculation. Not one, not five, but thirty sails out at sea had been counted already, and more were becoming visible all the time. The captain was marching up and down on the poop deck, his telescope to his eye.

'It's an entire fleet, so it is,' a sailor near John was saying, raising a tattooed hand to shade his eyes as he looked out to sea. 'Is it from God and all the saints, now, or from the divil himself? If it's the Frogs, we'll be all be singing with the mer-maids before the day is out.'

John, used to the empty splendour of the sea, watched with amazement as ship after ship, the whole day long, blew towards them out of the horizon. The fleet had quickly been recognized as British, and everyone had waited with longing for the command to set sail to join them, only to watch with mounting disgust and despair as it sailed serenely past.

'I zeen two hundred transports, a deal of frigates and ten or more ships of the line,' John heard Jabez say to Mr Tawse, as the two of them stood looking out to sea, their collars turned up against the bitter north-east wind. 'What do you make of it, Mr Tawse?'

'What I make of it, Jabez my lad, is that something big's afoot, and if this ship's barkers ain't all in perfect working order, heads will roll, yours and mine especial.'

'I reckon that means a general inspection of the guns, don't it, Mr Tawse?' Jabez said slowly, after a moment's rumi-nation.

'It does, Jabez. It does. Stow that plaguy parrot of yours out of harm's way and get those gun crews hoppin'.'

The early dusk of winter was settling over the sea, smudg-ing the horizon to a grey blur, when a frigate, detaching itself from the vast fleet, scudded across the water towards the *Fearless*. An hour later a young lieutenant in a smart uniform fresh from an English outfitter was being piped on deck. He disappeared into Captain Bannerman's cabin, a bundle of papers under his arm, and for the next half-hour rumours ran wild round the ship.

John, who had come up on deck to see what was going on, caught sight of Kit, who, in a rare moment of freedom, had ventured up from the sickbay to breathe some fresh air.

'What's happening?' she said, looking with astonishment at the white sails crowding the sea, which were still just visible in the evening light.

'We'll know soon. Someone's come on board from that frigate over there. He's with the captain now. He must be bringing orders.'

She shivered.

'It looks like an invasion fleet. It must be heading for Spain. There'll be action soon.'

'Do you think so?' He grinned at the thought. 'I hope we're part of it. If we have to stay here much longer, doing nothing, the ship's company will go up like a volcano.'

She shook her head at his obvious excitement, but smiled back at him.

'What are you looking so pleased about?' he said.

'It's my birthday.'

'Your birthday? Today?'

He was taken aback. He had lost count of the days.

'Yes. I'm fourteen. I've done it, John! I've kept myself hidden all this time, and I'm free of them now. I'm out of their power. I don't have to hide any longer.

'What do you mean? What are you going to do?'

'You know what I have to do!' She looked up at him earnestly. 'I must find a way to get back ashore. I must go back to Bordeaux, to Jalignac, and claim my rights. They need me there, John.'

'You can't leave the ship,' he said roughly. 'How would you get ashore?'

'Oh, I don't think there'll be any difficulty with that. Captain Bannerman is longing to see me go. He's tolerated me all this time, but he glowers whenever he catches sight of me. I was planning to try to see him this morning, to ask if he could have me rowed ashore as soon as possible, but now, with all this happening, I can't get near him.'

'You were hoping to go as soon as possible? I suppose you'd planned to say goodbye.'

His voice was stiff with hurt.

She took hold of his hand, then pulled hers away and looked round to check that no one had seen.

'I haven't seen you all this week, John. I've tried and tried to slip away, but Mr Catskill watches me all the time. He's like a cat with a mouse. I *hate* that man. If you knew what he was like . . .'

'What do you mean? He hasn't . . . touched you?'

'He comes too close to me all the time. And he's a bad surgeon. He doesn't care about the sick men at all. You don't know what it's like.' He had never before seen her look so miserable, all her usual liveliness crushed. He didn't know what to say. 'It's been . . . I've been . . . I'd have gone mad if I hadn't been able to see you sometimes.'

He knew he was blushing, and felt embarrassed.

'It's the same for me. If only I could tell you! I know you'll have to go home, sooner or later, but, Kit, when you do . . .'

'Letters for Simon Snelling! Michael Flynn! Pasco Penhaligon! John Barr!'

John had hardly been aware of the lieutenant nearby, waving a bundle of letters and calling out names, but the sound of his own name made him spin round.

'A letter for *me*?'

The lieutenant tossed a small envelope to him, and John, catching it, cried out in astonishment as he recognized his father's spidery, elegant handwriting.

'Franked in Scotland,' he said, his heart leaping for joy. 'He's alive! Safe! No longer at sea! He's gone home!'

The memory of his terrifying last night in Edinburgh, the murder of Mr Sweeney and the hue and cry that had sent him and his father fleeing to Leith came back to him with awful clarity.

But perhaps he's in prison, he thought. Perhaps he's stood trial for murder. He could have been executed already.

He looked up for Kit, but she had already slipped away. With trembling fingers he tore open the envelope.

My beloved son John, (he read)

This message wings its way to you bearing the profoundest love of a parent grown half distracted with anxiety, who scarce dares hope that it will reach its destination. My poor child, I know not whether you be alive or dead, lost at sea, maimed in some frightful battle or stranded on a distant shore. No longing could be greater in any man's breast than mine, to gaze upon you once more and clasp you in my arms.

Since last we met, on that woeful day when we were torn from each other in such horrid circumstances, I have been through many a sad trial and faced discomforts and humiliations too many to enumerate. Suffice it to say that my service on the Splendid, *being not greatly appreciated by her ill-educated captain, ended in my being sent ignominiously ashore two months ago, at Yarmouth, where I was informed that I was no longer required. Insulting remarks about my person, my good sense and my abilities as a clerk were flung at my head in a way which – but on that I shall maintain a dignified silence.*

You will be pleased to hear, my dear boy (if, indeed, you ever receive this letter), that the fortunes of our sadly depleted family have taken a turn for the better. The vile Nasmyth is no more. Inflamed with strong drink, as he so often was, he indulged in one brawl too many. His assailant left him with a broken head in the very wynd where our poor Mr Sweeney was so ignobly slain. Mr Nasmyth never recovered from the attack.

After his death, numerous facts relating to his life, his knavery, foul dealings, trickery and general wickedness came to light. As a result, all charges against me were dropped. His friend Creech, and their dastardly legal accomplice, Mr Halkett, had disappeared from Edinburgh, having not been seen there for many months, and so were unable to throw the wool over the eyes of the righteous. In short, dishonesty has been discovered, villainy has been overcome and Luckstone has been restored to us.

It is, indeed, from our beloved home that I now write to you, sitting in the parlour, with a great fire burning in the hearth.

My joy, however, is set at naught by the loss of you, my dearest boy. Oh, where are you? Do you yet live? Have you forgotten one who loves you above all other?

If this small missive should reach you, send a line – a word! – to relieve the anxiety of he who holds you dearer than life itself,

Your loving,
Father

While John had been reading, the *Fearless* had faded away from his consciousness. Instead of the deck rising and falling on the sea's swell under his feet, he was standing once more on the green grassy bank above Luckstone, smelling the wood smoke that curled from the old tower's chimney, his father's voice in his ear, while a profound joy took hold of him.

He came to with a start at the shrill sound of the bosun's whistle and then a sharp shouted command.

'All hands ahoy! Full sail ahoy!'

Chapter Thirty-six

During the following days John had no further chance to speak to Kit. The *Fearless*, so long on her own, was now part of a vast fleet, which was speeding with all sails crowded to the north-west tip of Spain, and he was fully occupied with his duties.

'The port of Corunna, that's where we're bound for,' Mr Erskine had told the assembled midshipmen. 'We're on the greatest rescue mission ever mounted. Pray God we reach the place in time.'

The British army, he had explained, had been fighting with their Spanish allies to drive the French out of Spain. They had failed, and the British soldiers were now in a pitiful state. Napoleon's troops had pursued them further and further north. In the cold of winter, short of food, their clothes in tatters, beset by injury and sickness, the British army was now retreating through the harsh countryside of northern Spain towards Corunna, with the French hard on their heels.

'If we fail to get them on board the ships in time,' Mr Erskine told the silent midshipmen, 'our poor brave soldiers will be cut to pieces. Get to your duties now, and send those damned mutinous rascals up aloft to let out the topsail reefs, which should have been done half an hour ago.'

The atmosphere on board the *Fearless* had changed. The deadly boredom of blockade duty had given way to the thrill of competition as the great warship strove to outstrip the rest of the fleet and be the first to reach the coast of Spain. Murmurings and discontent were all forgotten, and everyone worked with a will.

John, standing in the bows, felt his heart swell with pride as the *Fearless*, her sails billowing, surged at last into Corunna harbour. She was among the first ten vessels. Her prow cleaved cleanly through the water and her pennants streamed out bravely in the wind.

It was evening, and the light of the short, cold winter day was already fading. John screwed up his eyes as he looked towards the shore. The bay made a perfect curve, the fort of Corunna at one side, with the town rising steeply towards it and more houses stretching round behind the beach.

Even from this distance, a good mile away, John could see that the whole place was seething with movement. There was a turmoil of men and horses covering the beach, while on the ridges of the low hills rising behind the town he could make out what could only be a vast mass of soldiers and clutter of gear. As the *Fearless* closed in towards the town, the last rays of the sun winked on the metal of guns and wagon wheels and lit up the pale faces of the men on the shore, who were looking with anxious longing towards the ships. He could hear their ragged cheers go up as each new sail appeared round the headland.

The *Fearless* had hardly furled her sails and cast her anchor when the first ships' boats were lowered. Before they had even scraped on to the sand, eager soldiers were wading out towards them, carrying wounded men on their backs. They lowered their comrades gently down on the boards and splashed back ashore to fetch others.

A lieutenant hurried up to John.

'I've been looking for you,' he panted, out of breath.

'Am I to take a boat ashore, sir?' John asked, eager to be of use.

'No. Captain wants you now, in his cabin.'

The usual mixture of nervousness and anticipation sent the hairs rising on John's head as he hurried up to the quarter-deck and presented himself at the door of the great cabin.

'Ah, come in, my boy. Come in!' Captain Bannerman said jovially, looking up at him from his chair by the table, at which Mr Erskine was seated too. John's pulses quickened at the sight of Kit, standing beside the table, her bare toes curling into the rug on the floor.

'Excellent, excellent,' began the captain, puffing out his cheeks. 'Now then. Little time to spare. Lengthy explanations unnecessary. Special mission required. Vital to national interest. Volunteers needed. Some risk involved. Do I make myself clear?'

Kit and John exchanged mystified looks.

'Not entirely, sir,' said John.

'Could you be more precise, sir?' said Kit.

'If I may explain, captain?' Mr Erskine interposed smoothly.

'Do so, do so, my dear fellow, but make it short. Devil of a lot to do. We have twenty thousand men to embark, and if the French bring up their guns before they're all aboard, they could blow the whole lot of them – and us – to blazes.'

'Yes, sir. I'll be brief. Now, Kit, and you, John, listen. We are proposing to send you on a special mission. You are not obliged to undertake it, but if you do you will be performing a great and important service for His Majesty's government and the British nation.'

'Yes, yes, Erskine, they know all that. Cut to the point,' blustered Captain Bannerman.

'Of course, sir. The point is that the *Fearless* has received fresh orders. As soon as the evacuation of the army is complete, and we have shipped our quota of men to Portsmouth, we are to undertake the escort of a convoy of British ships. These ships are carrying an exceptionally valuable cargo of gold and other supplies, which they are to transport from Jamaica to Portsmouth. The *Fearless* is to accompany that cargo to protect it from enemy action.'

'I see, sir. May I ask . . . ?' began John.

'What has this to do with you?' interrupted Mr Erskine. 'Be patient. We have reason to believe that the French have received information about this particular convoy and its precious contents, and that those of their ships still operating in the Atlantic are very likely to attack us. Our navy is stretched beyond its capability. The admiral has informed us that he cannot send any other vessel to guard this important convoy and that the *Fearless* will be guarding it alone.'

Kit coughed. Mr Erskine, thinking she was about to speak, held up his hand.

'Our best chance of getting through safely, without being attacked by the French, is to plant false information which will lead them off the trail and send their ships hunting for us in the wrong direction. If our enemies are led to believe that this huge prize is being sent, not from Jamaica to Portsmouth, but from Jamaica to Bombay, around the Cape of Africa, they will sail south to intercept it in the Bay of Biscay, leaving us free to cross the Atlantic unmolested.'

'The code book again,' said John, light dawning. 'If we can write a false message in code, and get it to the French . . .'

Mr Erskine shook his head.

'We have considered that option, John, but ruled it out. Think for a moment. Who would the message be from, and to whom would it be addressed? We don't know. We have no information about the chain of the French command. Only a few of their people are privy to the secret code. If they receive a message in it, from an unknown source, they will suspect at once that it's false, and will also suspect that their code is in our hands. They will change the code, and our great advantage will be lost.'

A loud rumbling sound signalled Captain Bannerman was about to speak.

'I do not give away any vital secrets,' he boomed, 'if I tell you that my latest despatch from London informs me that the knowledge of the French code has already been extremely useful to our people. Several vastly important messages passing between Paris and Madrid . . .'

'Quite so, sir,' broke in Mr Erskine with a warning frown. 'The details may be left to the imagination, I believe.'

'But, sir,' said Kit, wrinkling her forehead, 'if you are not to pass a message in code, how are you to convey it?'

'There is only one possible way, my dear, and that is by special messenger, who can supply the French with false information in person.'

John, watching him, could not read the expression on his scarred face.

'I don't understand,' said Kit. 'Why should the French believe a messenger sent from us?'

'They must not, of course, believe that he does come from us,' said Mr Erskine. 'The messenger, who must be able to speak perfect French himself, must be able to persuade the French that he has genuine information from a credible source. He must be able to make himself heard by the highest commanding officers and make them believe that he knows for a certainty the real destination of the convoy and that the information he brings them is true.'

There was a short silence. Kit was looking steadily back at

him, and John was alarmed to see the familiar daring smile lift the corners of her mouth.

'Why do you say "he", Mr Erskine?' She was speaking much more boldly to the first lieutenant than any normal seaman would have dared. 'Surely you are suggesting that this is a mission for me, that *I* am to be the messenger. You wish me to go ashore, to reach the French army, talk my way into seeing the top generals and convey your message for you.'

Mr Erskine said nothing, but bowed his head.

'But, sir!' burst out John. 'It surely isn't possible! It's too much to ask of Kit! He . . . *she* would be in the greatest danger, even from the men of our own army! Let me go, sir. I could slip through the lines. I could—'

'Never said the thing wasn't dangerous,' growled the captain, ignoring John and frowning at Kit. 'The question is, do you have the stomach for it, miss? By so doing, you must remember, you will greatly reduce the risk to every man on board the *Fearless*.'

Kit was thinking hard, frowning with concentration.

'If I was dressed as a girl – as a lady of quality – and accompanied through the British lines by one of our own, and . . . and . . . if I had the good fortune to meet up with a respectable French officer on the other side, yes, I believe I could do it. It would even be safer for a woman than a boy. A boy would be stopped by all the pickets, and easily disposed of. And it would be much easier for a woman to gain admittance to the generals. I know just how I would play it.' She seemed to be thinking aloud, talking to herself. 'Like Mme de Montsegard. Yes, I would model myself on Mme de Montsegard.' She looked up at Mr Erskine. 'But how would the French be persuaded to take me seriously? How would I account for the fact that I had this important information?'

'We have thought of a convincing reason for your presence on board a British warship,' Mr Erskine said. 'You were last seen cutting a considerable dash in Bordeaux, in the presence of the empress herself, from which city you dramatically disappeared. People must have wondered what became of you and where you have been since then. I would suggest, my dear, that you had the great misfortune, after your flight from the ball, to fall into the hands of a gang of desperate smugglers (who, as we know, are common in Bordeaux). They took you prisoner, hoping at some future date to claim a ransom for you. Their small craft was, luckily for you, taken up by a British man-o'-war, the *Fearless*. You were honourably treated by His Majesty's navy, which has no quarrel with the women of France. While a guest on board the *Fearless*, you overheard a conversation, not meant for your ears, which informed you that the *Fearless* was shortly to sail for India, escorting a convoy of great value. In all the bustle and chaos in the port of Corunna, you seized your opportunity to escape from the *Fearless*, and, desperate to return to France, you made your way through the British lines. You realized that you had accidentally overheard important information, and felt honour bound to pass it immediately to the French authorities.'

'Yes,' Kit said delightedly. 'An excellent story. Yes, I could say all that.'

'You do realize, Catherine,' Mr Erskine went on gently, 'that once you have left us and broken through the British positions to reach the French army, you will not be able to return to the *Fearless*? You will have to follow the thing through, in the character you have assumed, and go back to your home in Bordeaux.'

Catherine glanced quickly at John, then away again.

'It's what I want to do,' she said. 'I want to go home.'

'Excellent. Splendid. Good . . . er . . . lad,' said Captain Bannerman. 'Be off with you now. Dismissed from the service. Delighted to have had you on board. Very irregular circumstances, but we've brushed through the whole thing as well as possible, with no fuss or scandal. Women on ships . . . humph! I will say no more. Now, Mr Erskine, if you please, arrangements for the evacuation of the guns . . .'

'Excuse me, sir,' interrupted Kit.

'Yes, girl? What now?'

'Do I understand that John Barr is to be my escort, sir, through the British lines? Until I'm in sight of the French army.'

The captain raised his massive eyebrows.

'Of course. For what other reason do you suppose he was summoned here with you? Mr Barr will take you through to the far side of the British army before returning to the ship. You will proceed alone.'

'Sir, I must go with her all the way,' John burst out. 'I can't let her go alone into a rabble of soldiers! I'll pretend to be her footman again, her manservant. I'll be able to guard her, if—'

'Think, John. Think,' said Mr Erskine, his injured cheek twitching. 'Mlle de Jalignac will be far safer on her own. Your presence will instantly arouse suspicion. A young man, with the tar-stained hands of a sailor, who speaks only English – why, you would give the game away at once. You are recognizable at a glance as a seaman, and a British one at that.'

John stared at him.

'I suppose you are right,' he said unhappily, after a silence.

'Right? Good God, of course he's right!' boomed Captain Bannerman irritably. 'Damn your impudence! To "suppose" the rightness of a superior officer? I never heard of such a thing. Now be off with the pair of you, and . . . ah . . . may your mission be crowned with success.'

Mr Erskine led them both to the door of the great cabin.

He smiled down at Kit, then, to her great surprise, took her hand in his and kissed it.

'I salute you, mademoiselle. You are a young woman of immense spirit and high courage. I predict a great destiny for you. If I wasn't a penniless sailor, old enough to be your father, with a ruined face, I believe I would . . . but I will send you off in the tender care of Mr Barr. There's no need to glower at me, young John. Catherine, take your leave of Mr Catskill, assume your female dress and be ready to leave within the hour.'

Chapter Thirty-seven

It was quite dark by now. John and Kit, eager to get out of earshot of the marine guards at the door of Captain Bannerman's cabin, took refuge in a quiet corner of the quarterdeck. A chill wind was blowing off the sea, but though they both shivered, they barely noticed it.

'You don't have to do this.' John took Kit's arm and shook it more roughly than he had meant to.

She pulled gently away.

'I do! Don't you see? This is my only chance to get back to Jalignac. Once the *Fearless* is on convoy duty, she may never return to the coast of France. It could be years before I am home again. And just think, John, what if I don't go? What if the French attack the convoy and there's a battle? How many men will the *Fearless* lose? Which of our friends will they be? Jabez? Tom? Mr Erskine? Davey? You?'

'Not Davey,' John said, trying to smile. 'His fortune-teller told him he's going to live forever.'

'You know what I mean. I couldn't bear it if any of them died, knowing there was something I could have done to prevent it.'

They were huddling close together, sheltering from the wind. John could hear her teeth chattering. He wanted to put his arms round her to shield her from the wind, but knew that the eyes of the marines guarding the great cabin door were on them.

'You'd do the same if you were me, wouldn't you, John? It's the *right* thing to do.'

He nodded reluctantly.

'I would. Yes, I suppose I would.'

He wanted to say more, to try to give voice to the turbulent feelings raging inside him, but one of the marines began to cough and shuffle his feet. He was closer than John had thought.

'Anyway –' he could hear the smile in her voice – 'only think what an adventure it will be!'

He took a deep breath. He couldn't let her courage leave his behind.

'You needn't worry,' he said. 'I won't argue any more. I'll help you as much as I can.'

'Thank you.' He heard the relief in her voice. 'I must go back down to the sickbay. I don't know what to do about clothes. All I have is the ball gown I was wearing in Bordeaux. I'll freeze to death in a few minutes if I go out in only that.'

They were descending the companionway now, down to the gun deck, the surface of which had all but disappeared under a jumble of military gear. Exhausted soldiers, some with bloody bandages round their heads or slings holding their arms, their clothes in tatters, their filthy feet bound in rags, had already been brought on board. They were leaning, eyes shut, against the bulkheads or lying prone on the floor.

A cavalry officer, his spurs still attached to his boots, was kneeling on the deck holding a flask of water to the lips of a groaning man who lay on his back on the scrubbed boards.

John's eyes narrowed at the sight of the thick cloak which the officer had thrown back over one shoulder. He waited until the man had stood up again and went across to him.

'Excuse me, sir.'

The officer turned. John was struck by how pale and thin he was, his cheeks so wasted that his eyes seemed to have sunk deep into his head. They blazed, though, with such relief and happiness that John stepped back.

'Yes, yes, my dear fellow,' the officer said, grasping John's hand. 'How may I be of service?'

'I . . . it's an odd request,' began John, taken aback by the man's enthusiasm. 'I need . . . you see, for a very particular reason, I need to purchase a thick cloak, such as the one you are wearing. It's not for myself, but for . . . a person who needs it. If you know who might have such a one to spare . . .'

The officer was already unclasping the chain at the neck of the cloak and tearing it off. He thrust it into John's arms.

'It is yours. Have it. No, no, I protest. If you only knew how all of our sad army have longed for this moment of rescue – when we saw your beautiful ships, our English ships, so serene and strong, sail into the harbour, and knew we were saved . . .' He stopped and, to his great embarrassment, John saw that there were tears in his eyes. 'Safe at last, within these wooden walls, and warm, and fed . . . Thanks to our friends, our brave tars.'

He stopped at last.

'But I must pay you,' John said, mortified.

'Pay me? My dear young man, you have not examined the cloak. At least three bullet holes . . . a sabre rent . . . mud coating the hem . . . scorch marks . . . and the silk lining is sadly tattered. I would not dare show my face in London in such a garment. Why, I would be the laughing stock of Hyde Park. No, no. Such as it is, it is yours.'

The man on the floor groaned again. The officer knelt down and held his flask once more to the thin cracked lips.

'No more groaning, Curzon, my good fellow. You are safe, do you hear? And you are to be fed. *Fed!* I have it on good authority that a supper of – what do these sailors eat? . . . salt beef and pea soup – is to be served to us shortly. So there is no need for you to die after all now. None at all.'

John hesitated for a moment longer, then turned away.

I don't have any money to pay him with anyway, he told himself.

In the darkness and confusion, the shouting and bustle, with boat-load after boat-load of troopers, wounded men, guns, ammunition and supplies being brought aboard the *Fearless*, nobody noticed another midshipman clamber down the cleats into the next empty boat, and no one even glanced at the heavily cloaked and hooded figure nimbly following him. The sailors, bending to the oars, sent the boat scudding through the water towards the shore, where the next group of soldiers was waiting to be taken off.

John and Kit threaded their way across the crowded beach till they were standing under the harbour wall.

'Wait here,' John said. 'No one will see you here. I'm going to find out where we should be going.'

Catherine stepped back into an angle of the wall where the deep shadow hid her.

'Yes, go. I'll stay here.'

He moved along the beach, peering to right and left, not knowing whom to approach. In the small gleams of light coming from the windows of the town some way away he could barely see anything, but the cries and groans of the men all around told him he was among the crowds of sick and wounded soldiers. Hands grasped at his trousers and voices pleaded with him to bring water.

No point in asking anything of these poor souls, he told himself, shuddering. They seem more dead than alive.

A sudden, terrified, whinnying scream brought him to a halt, and a second later something huge and black, something snorting and rearing, surged at him out of the darkness. A horse, maddened with fear, was bolting along the beach. Even in the darkness he could see the white of its rolling eye, the foam flecking its open mouth and the mane erect along its neck. Instinctively he put out his hands to protect himself, and found he had caught the horse's reins. It plunged to a halt, jibbing and bucking, lashing out with its hoofs.

He was trying ineffectually to calm it when a cavalry man came running up.

'You've caught 'im,' panted the trooper. 'Thank you, my friend. I don't want no one but me to do the deed, not after all me and 'im 'ave been through together. Come, Rufus, quiet, Rufus. 'Ere, 'old 'im, will you, while I cock my pistol.'

'Your pistol?' John was needing both hands and all his strength to hold the panic-stricken horse.

'Yes. One clean bullet to the brain. It's the last service I can do for 'im.'

'But why? Why do you want to shoot your horse?'

The man laughed bitterly.

''Tain't me as wants to shoot 'im. Ask the colonel, God rot 'im. "You're off on the boats," 'e says. "Can't take no 'orses with you. Don't want to leave them to the French. A gift they would be to them. Shoot 'em, boys," he says. "Do it quick." But a 'orse to a trooper, well, 'e's closer than a man's own brother. Rufus and me, we've been in that many battles, you wouldn't believe the times 'e's saved me with 'is quickness.'

He caught hold of the horse's mane and Rufus stilled, trembling, as his master murmured, broken-voiced, into his ear.

'I'm sorry, Rufus, me old friend,' John heard him whisper. 'Forgive me for this. I'll make it quick and easy. You wouldn't want no butcher doing a bad job, would you, boy?'

He pulled back, and with a trembling hand lifted the pistol till it was pointing directly at the white diamond star between the horse's ears.

'No, no!' John struck his hand aside. 'I could use a horse.

Give him to me. There's a . . . there's someone I have to transport from here. I hadn't thought of it before, but a horse is just what we need.'

The man gaped at him.

'You'll take 'im? You'll take Rufus? Oh, lad, if you only knew . . .'

'Yes, but listen.' John was thinking fast. 'I need help. I'll take your horse, I'll save him, I promise you, but you must give me information.'

The man squinted at him, his eyes narrowed.

'Wait a minute. I can see you proper now. You're a sailor, ain't you? What's a tar like you doin' wantin' a man's 'orse? What's your game, bully boy? What are you plannin' on doin' with my Rufus?'

'It's not for me.' John stepped back from the man's face, which was now thrust into his own. 'There's a . . . a lady. I'm to escort her. Up there.'

To his relief the trooper laughed and stepped back.

'Oho! A lady, is it? Bit young for all that sort of thing, ain't yer? 'Sright what they say about you sailors, then? A wife in every port! Spanish, is she? Pretty, I'll bet.'

'Yes. Yes, she's Spanish. I've promised – for someone else – to take her back to her village. But I need to know – how close are the French? How far do the British lines extend back from the town?'

The trooper was still patting Rufus's neck, and the horse was calming down.

'Hard to say, sailor. Our boys are up on that ridge, nearest the town. That I do know. In a bad way, too, most of them. Shocking state they're in. Why—'

'Yes, but the French!' John interrupted. 'Where's the French army? How far away?'

'Comin' up behind us fast.' The trooper had eyes only for his horse. 'A day, two days, I dunno. Not more'n five miles at the most, I'd say. They've followed us up the road all the way from the south, 'arrying, 'arrassing, skirmishing. Mad beasts they are. Mad, mad beasts.'

Shots rang out further along the beach, and the unearthly screams of dying horses filled the night air. Rufus reared back and seemed about to bolt again.

'Take 'im, quick. Just take 'im and get 'im away from 'ere, before my sergeant finds out I ain't done it,' the trooper begged. He leaned forward and kissed the horse's nose. 'Go on, my old darlin'! I done what I could for you.' He stepped back. 'Brave as a lion, 'e is. Charge into any guns. Only one thing scares 'im: water. If there's a stream you 'ave to cross, don't try to ride 'im through it. 'E'll do it for me, but not for no one else. Dismount, and lead 'im. Talk 'im through, gentle like. Oh, I can't stand this any longer.'

He turned and stumbled away.

John, left standing with the reins of the huge black charger in his hands, felt a moment's misgiving. Wouldn't it have been easier, after all, to manage on foot, in this unknown country, in the dark? What if the horse was vicious, or nervous? It might shy and throw Kit off.

'Here, Rufus,' he said uncertainly, clicking his tongue. To his relief, the horse stepped forward and began to follow him, stepping neatly between the wounded men on the beach.

'Hey! You!' someone shouted behind him. 'All horses to be shot! You heard the order!'

'Not this one. He's requisitioned for the navy!' John called back, making his voice sound as commanding as he could. 'Come on, Rufus. We've a long way to go tonight.'

Chapter Thirty-eight

The narrow streets of Corunna were hopelessly crowded with men, mules, heavy guns and baggage carts, making their way down towards the shore, and it seemed impossible to John that they would be able to force their way uphill against the tide of traffic. There was no point in trying to ride Rufus. Kit, who had welcomed the old charger with surprise and pleasure, had taken control of him, and Rufus, calm now, accepted her authority with perfect docility.

'It would have been much easier to get through without him,' John said, as Kit tried to back Rufus under an arch out of the way of a huge piece of heavy artillery. 'Perhaps we should just let him go.'

'No!' She had to shout to make herself heard over the deafening rumble of iron-bound wheels on the cobblestones. 'He'd be killed, and anyway I just know he'll be useful later.'

Rufus snorted and dropped his great black head on to her shoulder as if he understood.

They were out of the town at last. They stood on the verge of the road that led up the hill watching the endless lines of weary troops stumble down towards the beach.

'Which way do you think now?' Kit asked.

'I don't know.'

He bit his lip and looked up. A long line of fires flickered above them, and he guessed that the soldiers, waiting for their turn to be sent down to the shore, had lit them on the ridge above to keep themselves warm during the cold night.

'I suppose they're ours, but what if . . . maybe they're the French,' he wondered out loud.

'Those ones are British, I'm sure,' Kit answered. 'Look there. Behind. In the distance.'

He could see now, where she was pointing, much smaller, fainter pinpricks of light as if on a far range of hills.

He shivered.

'Yes. The French army. That's where it must be.'

It was impossible to tell how far away the French fires were, and how long it would take Kit to reach them. John felt his confidence ebbing away and at the same time tiredness threatened to overwhelm him.

'Let's find somewhere to rest till it gets light,' he suggested. 'We can't see where we're going, anyway.'

'Yes!' She sounded grateful. 'It must be very late. It'll be morning soon.'

The shadow of a building loomed up ahead of them. They felt their way round it. It seemed to be some kind of barn. The great wooden doors were locked, but on the far side, away from the wind, there was an open shed full of straw.

Kit led Rufus inside and tied his reins to a corner post. Then she sank down, exhausted, with her back against the bales of straw. John sat down beside her. It was a little warmer in here than outside in the biting wind, but his short midshipman's jacket and canvas trousers were only a poor protection from the cold and he rubbed at his arms, trying to warm them.

'Here,' Kit said shyly, 'this cloak's big enough for both of us.'

She unhooked the clasp and threw it round John's shoulders, then leaned back against the straw. He did too. He could feel the warmth of her against his arm and shoulder and smell the freshness of her skin.

'Kit,' he whispered.

But just as he spoke, Rufus, who had been lipping over a mouthful of straw, snickered noisily down his long nostrils.

'Did you say something?' she yawned.

'No.'

There was a long silence.

'John?'

'Yes?'

'I think I'm a little bit afraid. Not as much as I was before the ball, but still . . . afraid.'

'Don't be. I'm going to make sure you get through. You've got to trust me.'

'I do.' He could hear the smile in her voice. 'Oh, I do.'

A moment later her regular breathing told him that she was asleep. He shut his eyes and tried to sleep too. But sleep wouldn't come. He was intensely aware, through every nerve, of her presence beside him. For the last few months it hadn't been hard to push away the feelings she'd aroused in him at Jalignac. In her sailor's clothes, she'd almost been a boy again, the friend and companion of before.

But not really, he told himself. She's hasn't really been Kit at all. She's Catherine, and I love her, and I always will.

Admitting it to himself at last made him feel tremblingly happy and blunderingly stupid at the same time.

She mustn't know, he thought. I mustn't give myself away. She'll think I'm a clumsy, ignorant fool.

He wanted to turn over and put his arm around her, but he didn't dare move in case he woke her. He let the warmth of her arm, still touching his side, seep into him and comfort him. Before he knew it, he was asleep.

They slept longer than they had intended, and the sun was over the horizon when they finally woke. Kit sat up first. She looked down at John and laughed.

'What's the matter?' he asked sleepily.

'You. You've got straws stuck in your hair. You look like a scarecrow.'

He grinned at her, relieved to hear the friendly jokiness in her voice.

'What do you think you look like?'

She stood up and shook out the skirt of her thin dress. It was hardly recognizable now as the elegant ball gown it had once been.

'I wish we had some breakfast,' she said. 'I never thought of bringing anything to eat.'

'I did.'

He reached inside his jacket and pulled out a small flask and a cloth-wrapped package.

'Ship's biscuit and grog,' he said. 'Not much, but better than nothing.'

They breakfasted quickly.

'We'd better get going,' said John, unhitching Rufus's reins.

He wanted more than anything else to stay in their little haven and blot out the knowledge of the parting that lay ahead, but he knew they could remain there no longer.

The stream of men, with their mules and carts, had slowed to a trickle now, and it was easier to walk up the hill against the flow. The soldiers, limping and weary as they were, seemed in good spirits.

'Whoa there, sailor!' one of the them called out to John. 'Goin' in the wrong direction, ain't yer? There's no need to come up 'ere and fetch us. We're gettin' ourselves down to your bleedin' ships as fast as ever we can, ain't we, boys?'

John, not bothering to answer, grinned at them and walked on. To his relief, none of them showed any interest in Kit or Rufus.

It was well past midday when they reached the top of the ridge. Soldiers stretched in both directions, as far as the eye could see, waiting for the order to start down the road to Corunna and the ships that would carry them home. They sat hunched over or lay on the cold ground, some curled up as if trying to hug themselves warm, others on their backs with their hands under their heads and their hats over their faces. None of them moved much, or spoke. The silence, hanging heavily over the many thousands of them, sent a shiver down John's spine.

And then he looked up, and gasped. The next ridge of hills was nearer than he had thought, and all along the top of it, mustering thickly, were more soldiers. Many more. Thousands more. As he watched, the wind tugged at a flag fluttering from a pole on the highest point, and it slowly unfurled to show the unmistakable red, white and blue stripes of France.

'They're there,' he said to Kit. 'Up there.'

She caught her breath.

'Yes.'

Nearby, stood a couple of officers. One was shading his eyes, looking anxiously up towards the French on the skyline, as if he was trying to count them. The other was staring back wistfully towards the sea, where hundreds of little boats were busily ferrying soldiers from the beach to the safety of the fleet.

'Will they attack?' John called out to them. 'Will there be a battle?'

One of the officers shrugged. The other laughed shortly.

'Heaven help us if there is,' he said.

Another hour brought John and Kit to the furthest edge of the ridge. A valley, swooping down and up again, separated them from the French on the far side. The ground everywhere was broken up with walls and hedges, little fields and farmsteads. John and Kit stood still, looking uncertainly ahead. It would be madness simply to set off into the empty space between the two opposing armies. They would be challenged immediately.

'What'll we do if there's a battle?' Kit said, trying to sound calm.

John didn't answer. He had seen an ominous ripple of activity run down the length of the French lines, and now he could hear shouts and bugle calls echoing through the thin winter air. Then, with deafening, shocking suddenness, the French guns opened fire.

Kit started and stepped back instinctively. John ducked his head and looked round for cover. Rufus snorted, pricked his ears and began to paw the ground, as if expecting a bugle to sound the cavalry charge.

And now all around them the soldiers, who had a moment earlier been lying in exhausted heaps, leaped to their feet, like corpses coming to life. Within minutes their knapsacks had been buckled to their shoulders, their weapons were in their hands and their shakos on their heads. They were laughing and shouting to each other, jostling into position to form tight, disciplined columns, while the air rang to the click-click of bayonets being fixed to musket barrels.

John grabbed Kit's arm.

'Quick! We'll be caught in the middle!'

He looked round wildly.

'There. Down there!' Kit cried. 'That farmhouse!'

He saw at once that she was right. The farmhouse's thick stone walls might give them some kind of shelter if they were caught in the crossfire. He took off, leaping down the rough grass of the hillside, scrambling through hedges and over ditches, with Kit and Rufus close behind.

Chapter Thirty-nine

The farm was no more than a small cluster of stone buildings. Shutters were fixed across the windows and an iron padlock secured the main door. A quick survey showed John and Kit that no one was there. The inhabitants had obviously fled at the approach of the two warring armies, driving their animals with them. The door of what was clearly a cow shed was open, however.

'These walls are solid,' John said, leading Rufus inside. 'At least they're stone. If we're bombarded, there won't be any flying splinters.'

At the far end of the cow shed was a small window. Kit ran across to it, the hem of her gown trailing in the thick dirt on the floor, and pushed open the shutter, which creaked on its long-disused hinge.

'John! Look!' she gasped.

He stood at her shoulder and, as he looked out, he felt the blood drain from his face.

The far hillside, facing them, was a moving mass of men. Thousands upon thousands of French soldiers, tightly assembled in square, solid columns, were streaming down from the heights above, coming closer by the second. From behind them roared out Napoleon's great guns, sending forth hails of murderous shot that must be tearing brutally into the British troops massed on the slopes above the farm.

'We're right in their path,' Kit said, and John could tell that she was trying hard to keep panic out of her voice. 'We can't stay here. We don't even have a cutlass between us.'

John felt the hair rise on his scalp. He ran back to the door of the cow shed and looked up the hillside behind them. A wall and a line of trees obscured his view, but he could see flashes coming from further along the ridge as the British guns sent answering fire slicing into the French columns. Then, suddenly, the hillside all around the farm was swarming with red coats as British soldiers came scrambling down over the walls and bursting through the lines of trees to meet the French.

From all around came the shrieks and groans of wounded men, the shouts of officers' commands and the rattle and crash of musket fire. John looked to the left and right, in an agony of indecision, then raced back to where Kit was still watching through the window as the French advanced. Should they stay, clinging to the shelter of the farm, such as it was? Or should they take a chance and try to get out from between the two armies?

Rufus, whose reins Kit had thrown over a post in the cow shed, was excited by the noise, whinnying and tossing his magnificent black head, his hoofs pawing the ground.

There was turmoil now all around the farmhouse. The massed ranks of the French lines had broken as the British troops had poured in among them. Knots of men stabbed and shot and lunged at each other, bellowing like wild animals as they did so.

Kit had left the window at last and now she ran back to the door of the cow shed.

'What shall we do? Stay here? Or go?'

'Stay,' he said, sounding more confident than he felt. 'Yes, for now, best to stay.'

A yell close behind him made him jump and turn round. A pair of soldiers in ragged kilts had run into the farmyard. The first one stopped in astonishment when he saw John and Kit. The second burst out laughing.

'What for did you leave your ship, to come a-roving around in the middle of a battle, sailor boy? And who's your bonny wee friend?'

The man lunged forwards and grabbed Kit round the waist. She struggled, but he tightened his grip and bent his head to kiss her. John, his eyes seeing nothing but red, launched himself at the soldier, biting, pummelling with his fists and lashing out with his feet. The violence of his assault took the man by surprise and he let go of Kit and turned to John with a snarl, his bayonet threateningly close.

The rattle of musket fire just over the farmyard wall made them all start back.

'Come on, Jimmy!' the other one called. 'Leave the lassie be. There's Frenchies here for the takin'.'

The next moment, several French soldiers had leaped up and over the wall. They dashed towards the Scots, their swords outstretched. John put out his arm to push Kit back into the shelter of the cow shed, but she had seen a new danger. Wisps of smoke were curling into the cow shed from under the eaves and an ominous crackling could be heard overhead.

'The roof, John! The roof's on fire!' she cried.

Rufus had smelt the smoke. Before, he had been merely excited. Now, he was frightened. His ears were laid back and he was trampling the ground nervously, straining at his reins.

'Here, boy. Quiet, boy.' Kit was unhitching the reins from the post. 'Off with you now. Get away while you can, and good luck to you.'

She lifted her hand, ready to slap him on the rump and send him running away.

'Wait!' John called out. 'We'll ride him! It's our best chance to get away!'

He cupped his hands and held them low for her. She put one foot in them and launched herself on to Rufus's bare back, then leaned down to give a hand to John. He scrambled up behind her.

'Which way?' she said, turning to him.

He tried to think.

'Up the hill. On to higher ground. So we can see what's happening.'

She was already digging her heels into Rufus's flanks.

The horse leaped out of the burning cow shed and dashed for the farm gate. Looking back, John saw that a desperate fight was in progress between the two Scots and the French attackers. He saw one of the Scots lift his musket and, with a blood-curdling shriek, plunge the bayonet into the breast of the Frenchman facing him, whose sword arm was raised to cut at his adversary's head.

But there was no chance to see more. Rufus was out of the farm gate already and was taking off at a gallop along the lane. John, looking over Kit's shoulder, could see more Highlanders running down towards them and, as he watched, several of them jumped into the air and fell, hit by bullets from the French below.

'We're running into more trouble!' he shouted in Kit's ear. 'Pull across into that field to the right. There's a gap in the hedge beyond the tree.'

Kit swerved into the field, and Rufus took off over the rough grass. The ground dipped down at the far end, and John suddenly saw the flash of sunlight on the water of a stream.

'Hold on,' Kit called out. 'We'll jump it.'

'No!' shouted John. 'He won't . . .'

But he spoke too late. Rufus had seen the water too. Instead of sailing over it in an easy bound, he came to a skidding halt and locked his fore hoofs into the ground, so suddenly that Kit tumbled off over his neck and John slid down to the ground on the other side.

'I forgot to tell you,' John said, picking himself up and giving a hand to the shaken Kit. 'He doesn't like water.'

'But he saved us. Look,' she said, pointing ahead.

There was a row of trees on the far side of the stream, and through it John could now see a line of French soldiers. They were running silently forwards, their bayonets bristling in front of them.

'We'd have run straight into them,' she whispered. 'Well done, Rufus.'

A little further up the stream, a small copse of trees stood in the angle between two walls at the corner of the field. John and Kit saw it at the same time, and without exchanging a word began running towards it. Rufus trotted after them.

'We'll be safer here,' panted John.

He could see that they would be almost invisible among the trees, while the stone walls would provide shelter from stray bullets from the skirmish now taking place in the field beyond.

'Rufus!' Kit was calming the horse with trembling strokes down his nose. 'Thank you for my bruises. They were worth it.'

Now that they were, for the time being at least, out of danger, John suddenly discovered that he wanted to be sick. He was seeing again, in his mind's eye, the blood spurt out of the French soldier's chest as the Scots soldier's bayonet had gone in.

I'm glad I'm not a soldier, he thought. I couldn't do that. I couldn't look into a man's face and then kill him. Fighting's different at sea. You don't see them when you fire a broadside from a ship, and if you have to board the enemy it's all over much faster.

'What's the matter?' Kit said. 'You look a bit green.'

He looked down at her.

'I've discovered that I don't like war, that's all. I'm no hero. I wouldn't dare say it to anyone else. They'd think I was a coward.'

'A coward? *You?*' She smiled incredulously. 'I'm the coward. I hate war. I *hate* it. I just want it all to stop.'

Rufus, his reins tied to a tree, was contentedly browsing on a tuft of grass, oblivious to the battle in the next field, which seemed to be receding now into the distance. For some reason, out of the blue, the words of Captain Bannerman's speech, which had so inspired John when he had heard it, on his very first day on board the *Fearless*, sounded in his ears.

You are here, lads, for a noble cause, Captain Bannerman had said, *to serve your country as her true and faithful sons.*

It's not that easy, thought John. I want to serve my country, but I don't hate her enemies. I *like* the French. Kit's French, after all.

Kit had moved further into the copse and was leaning against the wall.

'We might as well stay here as long as we can,' she said. 'It's as safe as anywhere else, probably.'

The winter sun was already lowering to the horizon, touching the bare branches of the trees and the stones of the old walls with deep pink light. It was impossible to tell what was happening beyond their small haven. From the far side of the valley they could still hear the boom of the great French guns. Closer to them, all around, but still at some distance, rang out the rattle of musketry, the yells of men attacking and the screams of the wounded.

Suddenly, everything beyond the little thicket seemed miles away to John.

She's going away, he kept thinking. I'm not going to see her any more. I'll probably never see her again. These are the last few minutes we'll ever spend together.

'We must wait till it's dark,' Kit was saying. 'The fighting's sure to stop then. I'll ride back to the farm and take the path down from there. It leads through the valley and up the other side into the French camp. I saw it from the cow shed window.'

John, standing at the edge of the copse, squinted up at the sky. The sun would be down in half an hour, no more. There would be a short interval of twilight, then Kit would be gone.

He went back to her. He opened his mouth, but didn't know what to say. She spoke before he could find any words.

'John.'

Her voice was so quiet he had to bend down to hear.

'Yes?'

'I just wanted to ask you – I wanted to know if – whether you mind that I'm going. Because I really, really mind leaving you.'

The trembling that had seized him had nothing to do with the chill evening breeze that was rattling the few dead leaves still clinging to the twigs overhead.

'You want to know if I *mind*?' He thought he would choke and grabbed her hands, squeezing them tightly. 'Kit, are you mad? I'm dying from it. From losing you, I mean. It's killing me.'

A brilliant smile lit up her face, taking his breath away.

'I didn't know. I never knew you felt that too.'

He let go her hands and put his arms round her. She felt small and delicate, and he was afraid of crushing her. He realized he was standing on her foot and stepped back hastily, but she moved forwards, back into his arms. Their kiss was clumsy, but it sent fire and joy raging through him. He had had no idea he could ever feel like this.

'You'll come back to Jalignac, to find me, won't you,' she said at last, 'when the war's over?'

'That mightn't be for years and years.' He could barely speak for the thudding in his heart. 'You're going back into your old life. You're an heiress, Kit. You're rich. I'm nothing – just a sailor. You can't tie yourself to me.'

He was taken aback by the ferocity of her frown.

'Don't ever, *ever* say that, John. Don't *ever* think like that. I'll wait for you, no matter how long it takes. You know I will. You're the only person in the world that I'll ever really trust.'

He bent his head to kiss her again, but Rufus, who had been grazing nearby, butted him sharply in the back with his long black nose. Recalled to the real world of war, they stepped cautiously out of the copse and looked round. The light had faded and it was almost dark. They realized that the sounds of battle had died away. The guns were still. On the hill behind them they could see great bonfires and the shadows of British soldiers passing in front of the flames. On the far hillside were the fires of the French, who seemed to have withdrawn to their positions of the night before.

'Our fellows have beaten them back!' John said exultantly. 'All our soldiers – we'll be able to get them off into the ships now.'

Kit pulled her cloak tightly round her shoulders.

'John,' she said. 'It's time.'

'I know. You have to go.'

They held each other for one last, long moment, and then he joined his hands for her and she stepped lightly into them and leaped up on to Rufus's back.

'Don't,' she said, looking down at him.

'Don't what?'

'Don't get yourself killed.'

'I promise,' he said. 'And you must promise me. But I feel . . . oh, I don't know . . . that nothing can hurt either of us now.'

He ran beside Rufus, holding the stallion's bridle, until they had crossed the field and were back at the farm. The buildings were still on fire, the flames casting a lurid glow across the hillside. In its light they could see the scattered bodies of dead men. From the far hillside, an occasional gun boomed out sonorously into the night. Behind, from the closer, British lines, he could hear the groans and cries of the wounded.

When they reached the far side of the farm, where the lane set off down into the valley, she hesitated for a long moment, and he reached up and gripped her hand.

'I'll come to Jalignac, as soon as I can,' he said. 'As soon as the war's over. I swear it.'

'And I'll be there, waiting for you,' she answered.

Before he could say another word, she drove her heels hard into Rufus's side, and he saw the cavalry officer's cloak billow out behind her as she galloped off down the lane.

He knew she wouldn't look back. He ran after her, determined to see her safe for as long as he could.

A few moments later he had lost sight of her in the dark, but he could still hear the sound of Rufus's hoofs on the hard packed surface of the lane. Then a sharp voice came out of the night.

'*Arrêtez! Qui va là?*'

'A citizeness of France!' he heard her answer in a high, commanding voice. 'Inform your colonel that I wish to speak with him!'

He waited for a long time, until all sounds from ahead had died away, then he turned and went slowly back, up towards the British lines.

Nobody challenged him. He passed straight through the

sentries and went on, down the long road, overtaking the lumbering carts of bleeding, wounded men retreating towards the sea. He barely saw them. His heart was full only of Kit. Ahead of him lay the beach, and the boats, and his duty on the *Fearless*, which was riding serenely at anchor, out in the bay.

PART SIX

1809–1817
ENDINGS

Chapter Forty

Letter from Captain Samuel Bannerman to the Secretary of the Admiralty, Whitehall, London:

21 June 1809

Sir,

You will please acquaint their Lordships of the Admiralty with the news of the safe arrival into Portsmouth of the convoy of sixteen merchant ships under the protection of HMS Fearless. *The passage from Jamaica was concluded without incident.*

Sightings however of a force of two French sail of the line and three French frigates were reported to me by Captain Spellen of HMS Firebird. *Before these ships came within sight of us, Captain Spellen observed them being in communication with one of their own frigates, after which they bore away to the south.*

It is my belief that false information regarding the destination of our convoy, which was laid with the French at Corunna, was the cause of this fortunate alteration to the French fleet's course. If they had met with us, their guns would have grossly outnumbered ours and our convoy would in all probability been captured.

I would like to put forward for their Lordships' attention the courageous actions of Kit Smith (ship's boy, no longer serving with the Fearless) and Mr John Barr, midshipman.

I remain, sir, your obedient servant,
Samuel Bannerman

Letter from Catherine de Jalignac to John Barr:

12 July 1810

My dearest John,

It is so long since we parted, and I have never heard news from you. I am very afraid to know what has happened. In my bad moments I fear something terrible – that you are hurt, or even lost forever, but even in those times I believe in my heart that you are alive and that we will be together one day.

If you did not receive my previous letters you will not even know that I came safely home from Spain, though the journey was filled with dangers. It was the biggest adventure of my life! Now that I am settled here at home I can hardly believe all the exciting times I have lived through. No one who knows me here, as a proper young lady, would ever believe it if they knew the truth.

News almost never comes to us. I have seen Mr E's cousin once or twice, but he knows no more of your whereabouts than I do. He begged me not to visit him for fear of creating trouble, as he keeps very quiet and stays unnoticed. I am giving this letter to Jem, who has managed to visit us again, in the hopes that somehow it will find its way to you, as I fear the others did not.

You will be happy to know that all is going on in a good way for us. M. F. has done miracles for me. He has worked day and night. He even went to Paris (a dangerous journey now, with brigands everywhere on the roads) and received an audience from Her Majesty. Whatever you think of Josephine, you cannot deny that she has been a kind, true and generous friend to me. The chateau, and everything that my uncle did not steal, is safely now in my name. The money is not important to me – except that with it I can make all safe and comfortable for B. and J-B., and for the old tenants of my father, who have suffered so much in the past years.

Oh, John, I wish you could see us now! We have a new coach (the smell in the old one made me sick!) and the rooms are being cleaned and repaired. The hay field behind the house is a lawn again. It's beautiful! And B. has two maids to help her in the kitchen, besides other servants for the house, gardens and stables. As for Rufus, he is king of all the horses, and I ride him every day.

My grandmother was so angry with me that she became ill when she found I had disappeared after the ball. I feel a little guilty that it was my fault, but I cannot feel very sorry, for now she is so weak and her mind confused, she has become quite kind to me. She doesn't frighten me any more. She stays quiet in her house in Bordeaux and I visit her very often. My uncle thought that he would be arrested when his dishonesty was discovered, so he ran away to Switzerland, like the coward he is. I have heard he is only able to live by gambling. I am sure he cheats. He has no power over me now. I am safe here, with my dear B.

There is little to amuse us in Bordeaux, and life is very quiet. All the young men are away at the war, and everyone complains of hardship, with the port still unusable. Sometimes Mme de M. takes me to the theatre, but she talks all the time only about her horrible son. She is determined that I will marry him. I will not. Never. You know why.

Dear John, how can I know if this letter will ever reach

you? I cannot. I send it out into the unknown, with all my
hopes attached to it. It holds inside it the heart of
   Your Kit

Letter from John Barr, on board the *Fearless*, to Catherine de
Jalignac at Jalignac:

3 August 1811

My dearest, dearest Kit,
Your letter was written a whole year ago, but it reached me
only yesterday. The paper is all blotched and smudged, with
dirty finger marks and heaven knows what other stains
besides. I can hardly imagine what travels it has made to
reach me here, and whether this letter of mine will ever get
to you.

   I wish you had heard my shout of joy when yours was put
into my hands. I startled everyone around me! I have read it
already so often that I can recite every word by heart. It is my
most precious possession. Only to know that you got through
safely, and arrived home, and that all your business there has
gone well – it was the most wonderful news I ever received in
my life.

   I am not at liberty to tell you much about myself in case I
reveal too much, for who knows whose eyes may fall on this
letter? But you will happy to hear that our old friends are
well. Tom has a splendid new scarlet waistcoat, which he likes
to show off on all occasions. Davey is still concerned with his
chickens and piglets (his brains are just as confused as before).
Mr E. is the same, and still the best man I ever knew. Your
old master is busier than ever, though he must miss you, for I
don't think the boy he has now as his servant knows how to
sew at all.

   I have new companions now. There are some good fellows
among them, but I miss my best and dearest friend every day,

more than I can ever say. I have roved about here and there since we parted (now two whole years ago!) and will go on, no doubt, to destinations new until this terrible war ends. We have been in one or two small scrapes, but the outcome, thank God, has always been in our favour.

Dearest Kit, I think of you every minute of the day and try to imagine how everything at your old home must now look. Is the lantern over the front door hanging straight now? Are B.'s tarts and pies as good as ever they were? I would give anything to eat one again! Is Rufus still afraid of water?

The only thing that makes me unhappy is the thought of Mme de M.'s hideous son. Is he the only one? Are there not many more trying to make up to you? When I think about it, I feel mad with rage and I want to take my fists to someone.

I would like to write much, much more, but the fellow who brought me yours is waiting, and he has promised to try to get a letter back from me to you.

I love you, Kit. I always will. All I can do is to hope, with all my heart, that this terrible war will soon be over, and you will once more be with

Your loving
John

Letter from John Barr, on board the *Fearless*, to Patrick Barr, Luckstone, Fife:

26 November 1812

Dear Father,
I received your letter last month, off the frigate Firebird, *and was very happy to hear your news and that all goes on well at Luckstone. I am happy to tell you that since I last wrote I too have been in the best of health.*

Today is my eighteenth birthday, and I reckoned up this morning that I have now been at sea for more than five whole

years! When I remember the miserable little boy who couldn't tell a halyard from a sheet, and was too scared to go aloft, I feel amazed at the good fortune which has been my lot on board this ship, which is so well and justly captained, when others I know of have suffered extremely under harsh and unreasonable discipline.

You asked me in your letter if I would not now leave the service and come home to you at Luckstone. Of course I would dearly love to see you, and tramp about the old place, which I remember so fondly, but I cannot. The Fearless is now constantly engaged at sea and there is no opportunity to leave her at present. Do not pity me, however. To be a midshipman of a man-o'-war, such as the Fearless, is not a bad thing, after all. I am likely to bring home eventually some amount of prize money, as a result of the many ships we have taken. This will be needed at home for the repairs you tell me are becoming urgent, and there is no money to carry them out.

But there is another reason, dear Father, which would keep me from home even if I were able to leave the ship. I have written to you about Mlle de Jalignac, and told you everything about her situation, and our feelings for each other. As long as I am here at sea, I am sometimes within sight of the coast of France and know she is not far away. If ever the occasion arose – if ever I had the chance – I would go to Jalignac before anywhere else, in the hope of seeing her.

Please forgive me, Father, if this reply disappoints you. I do long to see you, and am confident that soon these troubled times will give way to a proper peace and the Fearless will return to Britain. In the meantime, please believe that I am

your most loving and obedient son,
John

The Times, 22 June 1815

The official dispatch from the Duke of Wellington, dated Waterloo, 18 June 1815, states that on the preceding day Bonaparte attacked, with his whole force, the British line. The attack, after a long and bloody conflict, ended in a complete defeat of the French army.

Glory to Wellington! To our gallant soldiers! Bonaparte's reputation has been wrecked, and his last great battle has been lost in this tremendous conflict.

Fellow countrymen – the war is at an end!

The Times, 27 June 1815

Shipping News

Yesterday the men-of-war lying off Portsmouth fired a salute from their guns to celebrate the great victory won by our brave army.

In consequence of orders received, the Channel fleet is to be reduced greatly. The ships will either be paid off or remain in harbour with a small complement of men.

Arrived yesterday His Majesty's Ship *Fearless* into Portsmouth harbour, to return her guns, stores, etc. She will not return to sea.

Chapter Forty-one

It was a brilliant, sunny morning in late July. The road running past the gates of the chateau of Jalignac that had once been crowded with troops, horses, guns and prisoners, on their way to and from Spain, was now deserted. Blackberries were ripening on the hedgerows, and crickets chirred in the long grass.

A young man, around twenty years old, appeared in the distance, riding slowly on a sluggish hired horse. He was tall, and he sat his horse uncomfortably, like a man unused to riding. His thick fair hair was tied at the neck, and he had clearly taken trouble with his clothes. His blue coat was well brushed, its brass buttons gleaming, his cravat was neatly tied and his boots highly polished. Anyone looking closely at him might have noticed the magnificent muscles in his arms and shoulders, the deeply tanned skin of his face and the small wrinkles round eyes that had often been screwed up to scan great distances. They might have guessed that he had spent many years at sea.

The horse arrived at the chateau gates and John Barr dismounted. The journey from Scotland had taken longer than he had expected. He had stayed at Luckstone for no more than a few days, just long enough to see his father and assure him that he was well, and then he had been off at once, first on the Leith smack to London, and then the packet to Bordeaux. The closer he had come to France, however, the more his courage had failed him. When at last he had stepped ashore, and seen how changed everything was, how busy and bustling Bordeaux had become, and how well people were now dressed, he had become horribly aware of his own rough appearance. Instead of rushing straight to Jalignac, as he had planned to do, he had spent several days in Bordeaux, visiting a tailor and having a smart new coat made, getting his hair cut and buying these uncomfortable new boots. And all the time, the longer he had delayed, the more his courage had failed.

It's been six years since I saw her, he kept telling himself. She'll have changed completely. We were hardly more than children. I've had only one letter from her in all that time. She'll be married, almost certainly, with a couple of babies too. And even if she isn't, why should she remember me? There's nothing sadder than a sailor without a ship, and only a bit of prize money tucked away in my pocket – hardly enough to buy her a ring. What do I know about high society, and chateaux, and life on shore? I can't even speak French.

He was almost at the gates and had slowed right down. I'm being ridiculous, he told himself. Kit and I are old shipmates, that's all. I've simply come to call on her. If she wants to see me, that's fine. We can talk about old times together. If she doesn't, I'll go home to Luckstone. There's no reason why she should still feel about me as she once did. She won't have been thinking of me every day for the last six years, as I have of her. I'll be friendly, but formal. I'll keep my distance. I'll try not to make a fool of myself.

He was at the gates now, looking up the long drive towards

the house. The shock of what he saw made him gasp out loud. He had expected to see the new Jalignac, which Kit had described in the one letter he had received from her, four years ago. He had thought that the lawns would be mown, the shutters painted, the house cared for, and that Jalignac would once more be a noble chateau, nobly maintained.

Instead, he was looking at a blackened ruin. The facade still stood, but the roof behind it had clearly fallen in. The soot-blackened shutters hung drunkenly in the empty windows, through which he could see nothing but sky. Weeds sprouted from the gravel drive, and the lawns were hay fields once more.

Dread clutched at John's heart. What could have happened here? What terrible disaster? Had the fire, which had clearly destroyed the house, carried Kit away too? Could she possibly still be alive? Surely no one could be living here now, in all this devastation!

He pushed at the gate. It swung open to his touch on rusty hinges. The squeaking sent a flock of crows cawing and flapping out of the old walnut tree nearby. John started to walk up the drive, but the fear that was gripping him made him break into a run.

Kit! he thought. Kit!

He was saying her name out loud. By the time he reached the chateau, he was shouting it. He looked in through the gap where the front door had once been. Behind, there was nothing now but a pile of rubble, blocks of masonry, charred beams, a twist of metal from a fallen lantern, dust and destruction.

'Kit!' he yelled uselessly into the ruin. 'Are you there? Kit!'

He ran along the front of the house and looked down the side to where the pump had stood in the yard outside the steps that had once led down into the kitchen. The pump was still there. A bucket of water stood beneath it and the space around it was clear, as if it had been swept.

Someone's been here, thought John. Betsy, perhaps, or Jean-Baptiste.

The thought of Betsy reminded him of her cottage. It was no more than a few hundred metres from the pump, between the kitchen garden and the orchard. He raced off towards it, noticing as he did so that the path was well trodden and in frequent use.

The cottage, unlike the chateau, was clearly lived in. A battered chair stood outside the front door. Beside it was a bowl half full of unshelled peas. The small front garden was overgrown with weeds, but flowers had been planted here not long since, and some of them were still in bloom.

John ran up to the door and shouted, 'Betsy! *Betsy!*'

No one answered. Half mad with frustration, he ran further along the little path towards the orchard. Just before he reached the well-remembered gate in the old brick wall, a sound stopped him. A sharp exclamation of annoyance.

He pushed open the orchard gate. Kit was standing on a ladder which was propped up against an apricot tree. She had caught her sleeve on a twig and was trying to release it. The basket dangling from her arm was tilting, and already some of the apricots she had picked were falling out of it.

'Kit!' cried John.

Kit jerked her head round, saw John and gave a little scream. The ladder swayed underneath her. She dropped the basket, lunged for a branch of the tree and grasped it just in time as the ladder fell to the ground, leaving her swinging in the air.

'Wait!' called John. 'Don't fall! I'll catch you!' He was underneath the tree already, holding up his arms. 'You can let go. Don't worry. I'm here.'

She let herself drop. He tried to catch her but missed, and

they both tumbled down, unhurt, into the grass. They sat, stunned, surrounded by squashed apricots, staring at each other.

'John!' whispered Kit. 'It can't be true. You're a . . . a phantom.'

'No, I'm not. I'm real. Touch me.'

She put out a hand and touched his arm, then drew a deep breath and burst into tears.

'What's the matter, Kit?' he said, puzzled. 'Aren't you pleased to see me?'

The dinner they ate that night, sitting outside Betsy's cottage in the warm evening, as the light slowly faded and the stars came out, was quite, quite different from anything John had imagined when he had set out from Bordeaux that morning. He had helped Kit to her feet after her fall from the tree, noticing as he did so that her gown was a plain country-woman's and was much patched around the hem. Together they had gathered up the bruised and battered apricots and taken them back to the cottage. He had taken off his fancy coat and cravat, helped her dig up a few potatoes from the overgrown kitchen garden and collected some eggs from the manger in the stable. Only one horse was in there now. He recognized the old black charger at once.

'Rufus!' he said with a laugh, rubbing the horse's black nose.

He felt strangely awkward with Kit. She had quickly dried her tears in the orchard, and for the rest of the afternoon treated him to terse little smiles and short answers.

It wasn't until they had finished their supper, and were sitting over the few remains on the table, that he dared to say, 'What happened here, Kit? What happened to the chateau? And where's Betsy? Did she go off and marry Jem at last?'

Kit swallowed hard and stared at him fiercely.

'Betsy's dead. She died in the fire. Jean-Baptiste too. It was my fault. All of it.'

She was struggling to control her tears. He sat and waited, giving her time.

'Start at the beginning,' he said at last. 'When I last heard from you, it was four years ago, in the summer of 1811. Look, I have your letter here.'

He pulled the dog-eared, worn sheet from the pocket of his shirt. She smiled for the first time.

'You kept it.'

'Of course I did.'

'I wrote to you so many times, but only this one reached you, I think.'

'Yes, only this one.'

She hesitated.

'It was good then, in 1811. I came home, and M. Fouchet sorted out my affairs. My grandmother was alive, but different towards me. Much gentler. She had quarrelled with my uncle. I became almost fond of her in the months before she died. There was some money, enough to repair the chateau and restore some of the rooms. We lived here quietly, Betsy and I.' She squeezed her eyes tight shut for a moment, then went on, 'It wasn't bad, but I didn't at all like being the mistress of this great place. It was a relief, quite honestly, when I didn't have to worry about it any more.

'I was invited everywhere at first, in Bordeaux, but I didn't choose to go. It was difficult, being on my own, without a female relative to chaperone me, and Mme de Montsegard dropped me completely when she realized that I would never marry her son.

'And then, in May, it was so hot here – everything as dry as tinder. A man came to the chateau. He said he'd been sent by my uncle. He gave me a letter my uncle had written. In it, my uncle said that he was sorry for all that had passed between us, that he had heard I was living here on my own, and to make amends he was recommending this excellent man to help me in any way that he could. He said I'd find him capable in many different ways. I was so . . . lonely, John. I wanted to be reconciled with my family. I accepted the fellow and wrote to thank my uncle.'

She was holding a walnut between her fingers, squeezing it so tightly that the shell cracked open.

'If only I had had more sense! If only I'd sent him away! Betsy warned me. She knew. But I wouldn't listen.'

'So there was a fire?' John said into the silence that followed. 'Did you suspect this man of starting it?'

'Suspect? I *know* he did! It was the evening of the fair in the village, and all the servants I had taken on had gone. I had been in Bordeaux with Betsy. We came home to find the house ablaze. My uncle's man was nowhere to be found, of course.

'"That old fool, Jean-Baptiste!" Betsy cried out. "He was half drunk in the kitchen when we went out. I'll wager he's in there still."

'Before I could stop her, she had dashed inside. A second later, the roof collapsed, and . . . and . . . oh, if only I'd listened to her! If only I'd sent that villain away!'

She covered her face with her hands.

'Kit,' John said. 'Listen to me. Kit.'

She didn't answer.

'It wasn't your fault. Do you hear me? You did nothing wrong.'

'I know.' She sniffed violently, searched her pocket, pulled out a crumpled handkerchief and blew her nose. 'I know.'

'Do you mean to say,' said John, looking at her in amazement, 'that you've been living here, on your own, next to this terrible ruin, since May? That's . . . let me see . . . three whole months!'

She nodded.

'I think you're the first person I've seen in two weeks,' she said, 'since M. Fouchet last came to call.'

'He's still your man of business, then?'

She laughed, but without humour.

'Hardly. There's no business any more. When Napoleon fell, my uncle ran straight back to Paris. He has cleverly insinuated himself with the new government, and by telling anyone who would listen that I was an intimate friend of Josephine's he has reversed everything. All my property is now in his hands. Only the chateau was still mine. I think that's why he wanted to destroy it, to punish me for standing up to him. I spent my last sou a month ago, John. I've been living on the vegetables Betsy and I planted in the spring. I've been waiting . . .'

She bit her lip, and stopped.

'Waiting for what?'

'For you, of course,' she said defiantly. 'What else? Just as I've been waiting ever since we said goodbye at Corunna. As soon as the war was over, I hoped . . . I *knew* you'd come.'

He stood up and stretched, feeling lighter, as if a weight had fallen off his shoulders. Then he started laughing.

'What's so funny? What did I say?' she said, suddenly anxious.

'Oh, Kit! Kit! You can't know the relief! I bought that hideous coat and those horrible boots in Bordeaux, thinking I'd be paying court to a rich, noble lady. I hardly dared show my face here at all. I was sure you'd be married to some rich lord by now, and would have forgotten me altogether. What did I have to offer Mlle de Jalignac? A sailor in peacetime! No future prospects in the navy, not much money, just a simple tower house and a farm in Scotland, that isn't yet my own. But now, Kit, I can dare everything. Will you come home with me, to Luckstone? Stop grinning like that, can't you? Don't you see that I'm serious? Don't you realize that I'm asking you to marry me?'

Chapter Forty-two

It was a wild night, raw, with rain in the air. The bitter wind picked up a seagull's feather from its nest on the topmost turret of the tower of Luckstone and whirled it down to the cobbled courtyard beneath. Rufus, his breath billowing in white clouds from his nostrils, stood close in under the eaves of the byre while John unsaddled him and rubbed him down. Then he took the other man's horse and led both animals into the stable.

The tower's heavy, studded door opened, and Kit appeared, a lantern held high in her hand.

'John!' she called out. 'Is that you? How were things in Edinburgh? Oh, is that someone with you?'

'Yes, Mlle Catherine, someone is with him,' came a well-remembered voice, and Kit started with astonishment to see Mr Erskine emerge from the shadows.

'Mr Erskine!' she exclaimed. 'How wonderful! How came you . . . ?'

'Let us in, Kit, for heaven's sake,' John said, gently pushing her aside. 'We're wet through. The rain in Edinburgh – I never saw anything to match it today.'

She led the way quickly up the worn stone steps and into

the square sitting room which filled one entire floor of the tower. A fire was blazing in the hearth and Patrick Barr was snoring in front of it, his long legs stretched out towards the flames.

'You are very welcome, sir,' Kit said, relieving Mr Erskine of his dripping cloak. 'We had no idea you were in Scotland. How . . . ?'

'All in good time, my dear Catherine,' said Mr Erskine, stretching his hands out towards the fire. 'Take that man of yours away and put him into something dry. He's soaked through.'

'But you must also need to change your clothes,' protested Kit.

'No, no. The rain penetrated no further than my cloak. I am quite dry beneath. I shall stay here and converse with . . .' He raised his eyebrows towards Patrick, who had woken with a snort and was rising unsteadily to his feet.

'Oh, I'm sorry,' John said hastily. 'This is my father, Patrick Barr. Father, this is Mr Erskine, the first lieutenant from the *Fearless*. But you are now a captain, are you not, sir? Captain of HMS *Jupiter*?'

'Captain? Congratulations!' said Kit. 'Your own ship, at last. When did you receive your promotion?'

'Later, later,' said Mr Erskine, waving them away. He turned to Patrick. 'I am delighted to meet you, my dear sir. You are a naval man yourself, I believe?'

'Indeed I am!' Patrick said eagerly. 'Sit down, Captain Erskine, do. Whisky shall be forthcoming, or would grog be more to your taste? I well remember, on board the *Splendid*, how our good captain . . .'

John and Kit were already outside the room, hurrying up the narrow spiral stair to their bedchamber.

'Tell me!' begged Kit. 'How did you meet him? Why is he here?'

John stripped off his sodden shirt. Kit handed him a dry one and waited impatiently until he had put it on.

'I saw the *Jupiter* lying at anchor off Leith,' John said. 'I was chatting away to some fellows on the quayside, about that consignment of slates we have been waiting for, for the new stables, when one of them mentioned that Mr Erskine was now her captain. At once, of course, I wondered if there was any chance of seeing him, and they told me he had been observed, just a few minutes previously, walking into the King's Wark tavern. It gave me quite a turn to go in there, I can tell you. I hadn't set foot in the place since the night Father and I were taken up by the press gang.'

He shuddered.

'Go on, John. What happened next?'

'He was there. I saw him at once, talking to the landlord. When I came up to him he looked round at me, amazed, and said, "Why, here's a coincidence! I was this very moment asking this good fellow if he knew of a John Barr of Luckstone in the neighbourhood of Edinburgh." So I asked why he was looking for me, and he clapped me on the shoulder and said, "My boy, I have a very particular proposition I wish to put to you."'

'Oh.' Kit was standing very still. 'And what proposition was that?'

'He would not say. He wanted to see you first and speak to us together.'

She was slowly picking his wet clothes up from the floor. She turned her back on him, deposited them on a chair and stared out of the window into the darkness.

'What's the matter, Kit? I thought you'd be pleased to see Mr Erskine.'

'I am, John, but . . .'

'But what?'

'What is this proposal of his? I suppose he wants to offer

you a place on board his ship, to make you a lieutenant and take you off with him on the *Jupiter*. Is that what you want, John? Is that why you're looking so pleased?'

He stared at her.

'Kit, are you mad? You cannot seriously believe that I want to return to sea? Think what it was like! Can't you remember? Would I ever again want to sleep squashed up in a hammock, eat nothing but weevily biscuit, be permanently cold, soaked and at risk of my life, live as close as hogs in a sty with a set of fellows I don't care about, and be without you, apart from you, for months and years at a time?'

She smiled with relief.

'I'm sorry. For a moment I was afraid that I would lose you again. But you've said only the bad things about the life at sea. There were good things too. Just now and then, when I look out from the turret upstairs and see a fine ship well manned surging up the Forth on the incoming tide, her sails set, her pennants flying, beating into a fair wind, something tugs at me. Don't you feel it too? The adventure of it – oh, I don't know . . .'

Her voice tailed away.

He went up to her and put his arms round her.

'Aren't you happy here at Luckstone, sweetheart?'

'Yes. Most of the time. It's only . . .'

'Only what?'

'I'm not very good at being a farmer's wife, John. I'm not like Betsy. I miss her so much. Every day. She would know how to stop the cow from kicking over the bucket when I milk her, and how to cure the bacon, and make the raspberries into jam. I can't get the trick of it all, somehow.'

'You're doing fine.' He planted a kiss on the top of her head. 'That butter you churned yesterday, it was the best yet. But I know what you mean. I'm not sure if I'm much good at this life either. You should see the furrow I ploughed in the top field yesterday. It's as wavy as the wake of ship with a drunkard at the helm.'

They smiled ruefully at each other.

'I'll fetch the supper into the sitting room,' she said at last. 'It's all ready. It'll be warm and pleasant to eat in there.'

When John pushed open the sitting-room door he found his father in full flow, waving his long fingers in the air, absorbed in the telling of his story.

'"Quickly, Mr Barr," the captain said to me. "Consign these dispatches to the deep. We are about to be taken by a French privateer. It will be a disaster if these communications fall into enemy hands." And so, Mr Erskine, I threw the papers overboard, duly weighted with lead, as I had been instructed, so that they would sink at once and be out of reach. The gesture, however, was unnecessary, for in the engagement that followed we triumphed over our enemy. And when the dust had settled, imagine my chagrin to discover that instead of destroying the admiralty's dispatches, I had thrown overboard the captain's private correspondence – the letters he had received not only from his wife, but from his mistress!'

Mr Erskine gave a shout of laughter.

'I hope you do not mind me saying, Mr Barr, that I am glad you are not my clerk.'

'So am I, my dear sir. So am I. The life of a gentleman lubber on land is much more to my taste.'

When supper had been eaten, the fire banked up and everyone was sitting in the warm with a toddy in their hands, an expectant silence fell. Mr Erskine looked round at the three fire-lit faces and smiled.

'I said I had a proposition for you, and you'll be wondering what it is.'

'I confess we have been speculating, sir,' said John.

'And you, Catherine, will no doubt be afraid that I am about to spirit your husband off to sea again with the temptation of a lieutenancy.'

'It had crossed my mind, Mr Erskine.'

'Put yourself at ease, my dear. There is no chance of that. In peacetime there are precious few new appointments to be made and far too many officers scrambling for good berths. I count myself fortunate indeed that I have been given command of the *Jupiter*. I had not expected to be made a captain so soon after the end of the war.'

He paused, and looked from John to Kit and back again.

'I have a task in mind for both of you. It is a delicate matter, requiring skills that few people possess.'

'What skills, sir?' asked John, puzzled. 'I have none, as far as I know, apart from a rudimentary knowledge of seamanship.'

Mr Erskine raised his eyebrows.

'You are selling yourself short, my dear boy. I shall never forget my amazement at finding you masquerading as a footman, as bold as brass, at the Empress Josephine's ball, or the extraordinary deftness with which you ruined my favourite waistcoat. And as for you, Mistress Catherine, the astonishing courage of your ride through opposing armies on the night of the battle of Corunna, your successful laying of false information, to which action the *Fearless* undoubtedly owed her very survival – these are skills possessed by no other mortals I have ever met.'

The blood was beginning to pulse through John's veins. Looking at Kit, he could see excitement in her face too.

'What is it you want us to do, sir?' Kit said breathlessly.

Mr Erskine took a pull at his whisky.

'You know, of course, that I have been given the command of the *Jupiter*. But what you cannot know is that I have also been assigned special duties by the government. Secret duties, with the secret service.'

'You were already working for them when you were on the *Fearless*, were you not, sir?' interrupted John. 'When you went ashore to Bordeaux.'

Mr Erskine nodded.

'Let me explain. Since the end of the war with France last year, His Majesty's government has not had a great deal of time to rest on the laurels of victory. There are stirrings in the east. Russia, the great bear, is growling at the borders of the Turkish empire, and the sultan is faced with rebellion at home. No one in London has a clear idea of the sultan's character, his strengths and weaknesses, his inner self. They don't know how best to approach him. But approach him they must, for Britain's interests in the east depend on us making an ally of Turkey. To find out more about the man, get to know him, understand him – this is the task I have been asked to perform.'

'The Sultan of Turkey?' said John. 'But how could Kit or I . . . ?'

Mr Erskine held up his hand.

'Very few people know that the Turkish sultan, who rules his vast empire from his capital at Constantinople, has an unusual background. His mother is French. She was captured by pirates as a girl and sold as a slave, ending up in the harem of the present sultan's father. She quickly became his favourite wife, and it is her son, Mahmoud II, who now rules.'

'But . . .' began Kit.

Mr Erskine ignored her.

'Perhaps you do not know that this lady, Aimée Dubucq, who is known in Turkish as Naksh, the Beautiful One, is the cousin of Josephine, the former wife of Napoleon and

Empress of France, a lady who, if I recall, once used her influence on behalf of Mlle Catherine de Jalignac.'

Kit was staring at Mr Erskine with wide-open eyes. He smiled at her.

'I believe you have guessed it already, my dear, with your usual quickness.' He paused again, and took another sip of whisky. 'I have been cudgelling my brains to think how I might achieve this impossible task, and I came to the conclusion that it can only be done with the help of two people, both loyal subjects of His Majesty, both resourceful, intelligent, unafraid of danger and good at playing different roles. It would not be impossible for you, my dear Kit, with your perfect French, and your past contact with the empress, to gain admittance to the harem and win the confidence of the Beautiful One, who is said to be very close to the sultan, her son. Who knows a man better than his own mother? And what mother does not love to talk about her son? With a little cleverness and patience, you would be able to find out more about the sultan than any number of envoys sitting with him in formal conversation.'

'It's Kit you want, then,' said John gruffly, unable to keep the disappointment out of his voice.

'I want you both,' Mr Erskine said crisply. 'Catherine cannot possibly do this thing alone. I need hardly say that there are . . . risks. Strategies will be needed, schemes hatched, different roles played. You, John, will lay the groundwork, and organize the rescue if – which I am sure will not be the case – Catherine is suspected of being an agent of the British government.'

Silence fell.

'I see, sir,' said Patrick, staring mournfully into his whisky glass, 'that you intend to snatch my children away from me once more, though we have been reunited for barely six months.'

'I fear that I am, sir. I am sorry for it, for your sake.'

Patrick heaved a sigh.

'But I am not sorry for theirs. If I am to be honest, I know that life at Luckstone is not for them. Not yet, in any case. One day, perhaps, when they are older, and the fidgets have all been knocked out of them, then the settled life, the call of the ancestral home, a clutch of children perhaps . . .' His voice died away.

'You would not mind, then, Father,' said John, his eyes blazing, 'if we were to leave you for a further spell?'

'I would, my boy, I would. But this time you will have my blessing.'

'So, John and Kit, what do you say?' said Mr Erskine. 'Will you undertake this mission for king and country? Because if you will, I must tell you that there is no time to be lost. The *Jupiter* is ready to sail for the Golden Horn. Her supplies are on board, her crew is mustered. I wish to sail in three days' time, if the wind is in our favour. Can you be ready by then?'

John and Kit looked at each other, and exchanged the briefest of nods.

'Aye aye, sir!' they said together.

Now you have read the book, take part in your own seafaring adventure!

FREE COMPASS

To claim your compass: fill in your details, cut out this page, and send to:
Free Compass Offer, Marketing Department, Macmillan Children's Books,
20 New Wharf Road, London, N1 9RR.

My name: .... My age: ....

My parent/guardian's signature ....

(You must get your parent/guardian's signature if you are under twelve years old.)

Send my compass to: ....

....

Postcode:

....

For more on *Secrets of the Fearless*, Elizabeth Laird, and all of Elizabeth's other books, log on to: www.elizabethlaird.co.uk